# SWORDFISH

# What Reviewers Say
# About Andrea Bramhall's Work

"[*Ladyfish*] is Andrea Bramhall's first novel and what a great yarn it is… fast and fabulous and great fun."—*Lesbian Reading Room*

"[*Nightingale*] is a tale of courage and determination, a 'don't miss' work from an author that promises a stellar career thrilling us with her skillful storytelling."—*Lambda Literary*

"[*Nightingale*] will move you to tears of despair and fill you with the joy of true love. There aren't enough stars to recommend it highly enough."—*Curve Magazine*

"[I] recommend *Nightingale* to anyone, lesbian or feminist, who would like to read a thought-provoking, well-written novel about the clash of cultures."—*C-Spot Reviews*

"[*Clean Slate*] is a great story. I was spellbound. I literally couldn't put it down."—*Lesbian Reading Room*

Visit us at www.boldstrokesbooks.com

# By the Author

Ladyfish

Clean Slate

Nightingale

Swordfish

# SWORDFISH

*by*

## Andrea Bramhall

2015

# SWORDFISH

ISBN 13: 978-1-62639-233-5

This Trade Paperback Original Is Published By
Bold Strokes Books, Inc.
P.O. Box 249
Valley Falls, NY 12185

First Edition: January 2015

---

CREDITS
EDITORS: VICTORIA OLDHAM AND CINDY CRESAP
PRODUCTION DESIGN: SUSAN RAMUNDO
COVER DESIGN BY SHERI (GRAPHICARTIST2020@HOTMAIL.COM)

# Acknowledgments

To everyone at BSB, thanks for all your help and support. Sheri, for yet another fantastic book cover; Vic, Cindy, and the amazing team working behind the scenes, you make this look easy, when I know it's anything but. Thank you.

To my team of willing beta readers, Louise, Kim, and Dawn, your help is invaluable, both in terms of support, and your eagle-eyes spotting some of those early…glaring…plot holes! Lol!

But mostly I'd like to thank everyone who reads this book. Because of you, my partner doesn't have to suffer my ramblings alone any longer. She thinks of you as her support network, and she's thinking of setting up regular meetings. Anyone interested should e-mail me, and I'll pass your details on. Apparently, she's already got a secret password, a funny handshake, and everything. (What's the keyboard shortcut for a winking smiley again?)

P.S.
I have to acknowledge Jazz Bramhall-Smith. Without her inspiration for "Jazz," I could not have written one word of this book. Thank you, Jazz.

P.P.S.
Merlin Bramhall-Smith De First, Queen of all She Surveys, would like it noted that she didn't want to be in "no stupid book" and that she isn't sulking. She's just watching cats…in a sulky way.

## Dedication

Just like stories, life has a beginning, an ending,
and a series of pivotal moments between the two.

Louise, thank you for being my beginning, my ending,
and every moment in between.

# PROLOGUE

Concrete dust and rubble showered down on him, a sign that another bomb had gone off nearby. His ears were still ringing from the first explosion that had destroyed his home. He cradled the body of the six-year-old boy to him and continued walking, stepping over lumps of concrete and avoiding the twisted, red-hot steel bars that had previously been buried deep inside that concrete. Concrete that had been a home only a few minutes ago. His home.

He shifted his brother's weight in his arms—his dead weight—as he stared at a pile of rubble he couldn't climb over. He felt the sticky, wet heat of Risil's blood seeping through his shirt. The iron scent of it was so thick he could taste it on his tongue, but he had to keep walking.

He stumbled and fell to one knee as he tried to skirt the pile of debris, but he quickly found his feet again. The jeers and sniggers of the ever nearing line of soldiers was more than enough to spur him on. And in that instant he remembered the story he had been reading to his brother before the detonation had ripped the house apart. The story of Ataba and Zarief E-ttool. It had been Risil's favorite. It helped him sleep, he'd said, hearing the story of how the handsome young Palestinian, Zarief E-ttool, had made his dreams come true and achieved great wealth, power, and esteem along the way to winning the hand of the woman he loved, Ataba.

Risil had said it was good to know that you could do anything, be anything, if you worked hard and never, ever gave up. When he had asked his young brother what he wanted most, his answer had been simple. He wanted to feel safe. He wanted to go to sleep at night and not worry that tomorrow, or the next day, he would have to fight and say good-bye to more people he loved. He had thought it the foolish wish of a child, and attributed it to the eight-year difference between them. At fourteen, he felt far older and wiser. *Sleep peacefully now, my brother.*

The line of soldiers pointed their guns at him, but he didn't flinch. It was the first time he had stared down the barrel of a gun. He doubted it would be the last.

The bombing was retribution for his older sister's martyrdom. Her sacrifice had claimed six Israeli lives in a coffee shop in Tel Aviv, and the Israelis' policy was to destroy the homes of martyrs within forty-eight hours to prevent them from becoming shrines. They had timed their attack to coincide with her memorial service. It had been a lucky occurrence that he had been upstairs with Risil trying to calm him at the time. He looked at the battered and bleeding body in his arms. *If you can call this luck.* Blood dripped onto Risil's face, and he realized he was bleeding. He knelt down, resting Risil on his bent knee and felt his own face. A ragged tear down his left cheek felt like a piece of mutton beneath his fingertips—pulpy, sticky, and barely holding together. It didn't matter. He was still alive.

He had left the bodies of his parents, his older brothers, his uncles, and his grandmother burning and broken in the home that had never been safe. But it had been home and as safe as any Palestinian home in the Gaza Strip could ever be.

He stopped six feet from one of the soldiers, determined not to cry. He would never let them see weakness. "They are all dead. You can stop now."

The soldier in front of him didn't move, but orders came from behind him to search the wreckage for incendiary devices, weapons, and anything else of interest.

They really meant anything of value they could steal, and he was glad he had pulled the rings from his mother and grandmother's fingers before he carried Risil from the building. He hated that his family was defiled in such a way, but it was better he did it than the bastards who converged on the rubble like locusts.

He took in every detail of the soldier still staring down at him and filed it away. There would be a time when they would all pay, them and everyone who helped them. The British had crawled away on their bellies in 1948, leaving them unarmed and at the mercy of an enemy who wanted nothing more than to pound them into the dust. The Americans had continued to support them, financially and with arms, and in their unwavering support for their claims on the land the Israelis stole.

He swore on the body of his brother, on the lives of his dead family, that one day he would make them all pay. He wouldn't give up until it was done or his body was cold in the ground.

Every one of them would pay.

# CHAPTER ONE

B ailey Davenport breathed in the hustle and bustle of Quincy Market, only a few yards from Boston Harbor and a mere two-minute walk from her apartment. She scanned the menus above each of the food stalls, just as she had done most nights for the past five years. The mouthwatering aromas of Thai food, pasta, pizza, and sandwiches of every variety warred with freshly baked cupcakes, bread, pretzels, and freshly brewed coffee. A feast for the eyes and the stomach, yet she couldn't find anything that appealed to her tonight, so she chose an old favorite. She ordered a hoagie from the Philly Steak and Cheese counter and winced inwardly when the server greeted her by name. *Maybe it's time for a change of routine.* She took her sandwich and bottle of water and bypassed the busy dining area. No matter how busy it was, she never had a problem finding a place to eat. There was always one seat available somewhere, but the idea of eating alone in the crowded market hall made her feel awkward tonight.

She crossed the cobbled and uneven pedestrian street under the shadow of the historic Faneuil Hall. During tourist season, people filled the streets for the fine shopping, good food, and the pilgrimage to "the cradle of Liberty" as the hall was better known. But it was December, and only the locals and a few hardy souls braved the snow and the bitter wind coming off the water. She pulled her scarf tighter around her neck and watched where she was walking, careful not to lose her balance on the icy, snow-covered stones. She juggled her items as she keyed the lock and pushed open the door to her apartment. She tossed her keys onto the small table in the hallway and hung up her coat, knocking the few flakes of snow from the shoulders. She clicked on the light and riffled through her mail.

"Junk, junk, junk, and a credit card application for a Jesus Hernandez. Return to sender," she said as she tossed it all into the trash can.

The small one-bedroom apartment was clean and fit what fashionistas described as "the minimal look." There was one recliner facing a TV that wasn't plugged in, and a two-seater sofa sat under the window. There was a single photograph on the bookshelves lined with crime novels and her graduation picture from the Boston Police Academy.

She hated silence.

A quiet so profound that she could hear her own heartbeat seemed to fill the small apartment, and she couldn't bear it. She'd never been able to. Sitting in a car, on the street, in an empty building, she had no problem with the silence. She loved the peace she could find in the early morning when the streets were practically deserted. But in her home she couldn't stand it. No, it was her apartment, not her home. Silence meant thoughts took on a life of their own and the memories wouldn't stop.

The dining table was covered with papers, notepads, and photographs. She unpacked the thin briefcase she carried with her and wrote a note on a small index card. She highlighted the title of the card carefully and pinned it to the corkboard over her dining room table. A photograph at the center of the board had strings leading to a wide variety of different cards in a kind of spider web formation. Some were addresses; others were misdemeanor codes, felony codes, and sentences. All of them were tiny tidbits in the life of the woman in the picture: an occasional prostitute and a full-time junkie with a string of convictions for theft, fencing stolen property, possession, and the one that had changed the life of Bailey when she was only ten years old—child neglect.

The card she pinned up today was highlighted in blue with the address of yet another halfway house. Another dead end in a search she had never officially been a part of, but had been working for almost twenty-five years. She was just one more missing person in an ever-increasing number of faces that would be forever missed by those who loved them and would never know why, or where, or when. The most important case in her life, and it was one she worried she'd never solve. She ran her fingertip over the picture, the only one she possessed of the mother she hadn't seen in thirty-nine years.

She turned on the stereo to drive the silence back into the shadows and rolled her shoulders as she let the expressive jazz sound of Nina Simone's "Don't Explain" soothe the tension of the day from her body. She rubbed absently at the scar on the left side of her abdomen. It felt like an itch she could never reach.

She grabbed a beer from the fridge, sat at the table, and unwrapped her sandwich. She quickly popped the top off her beer and held it up toward the picture.

"To the next address, Mom. I'll get you next time." She winked and took a long swig before taking a huge bite of her hoagie.

# CHAPTER TWO

Cassie turned off the ignition and rubbed her eyes. They felt gritty and tired. The drive from Boston to Glens Falls, New York, should have taken her around three and a half hours. Instead, an accident on the highway had added an hour to her journey. The trees were bare, and the winter sun was so weak it barely warmed the chilly December morning. She shivered as the warm air from the heater dissipated now that the engine was off; she grabbed her coat, purse, and keys as she climbed out of the car, trying to ignore the trembling in her hands.

It was the first time she had visited the cemetery, and she had no idea where to start looking. The pain and guilt of that was something she had learned to live with—it was just one more issue she'd picked up along the way.

She approached the counter in the cemetery office and smiled at the elderly woman behind the desk.

"Welcome to Glens Falls Cemetery. How can I help you today?"

"I'm looking for the grave of Karen Riley." Her voice caught in her throat as she spoke Karen's name. She coughed gently to try to clear it, offering a solemn smile as she did.

"Of course, what year did she die?"

"Two thousand and one."

The woman smiled sweetly and tapped at her keyboard. "Here we are, dear. The grave is a little way from the building so I'll mark it on a map for you." She drew a red square around one of the fields with a small x a little way in from the right-hand boundary. "It should be fairly easy to find, but I can get one of the ground's staff to come and show you if you like?"

Cassie shook her head as she studied the simple map. "No, thanks. I should be fine with this." She looked up and smiled. "Thank you for your help."

"You're welcome."

Cassie opened the door and wrapped her coat around herself as the cold wind stung her cheeks. The grounds were immaculately tended, and as she walked slowly toward her destination, she couldn't help but think how Karen would have liked that. She had spent hours in the small gardens of the various places they had called home over the years. Herb gardens mostly, because she had so loved to pick the fresh herbs to use in her cooking. Cassie's eyes watered, and she tried to convince herself it was from the bitter wind.

She found the small gray stone easily despite the moss growing across the rough surface and obscuring half of Karen's last name. She knelt on the grass, ignoring the growing damp seeping into her jeans as she set about cleaning away the moss.

"I won't let it get so bad again, sweetheart. I won't leave it so long." She wiped her nose with the back of her glove. "I don't have to anymore. He's in prison." She stifled the slightly hysterical laugh that had kept threatening to erupt ever since she had read the newspaper article the day before. "Daniela's safe from him now." She plucked a tuft of grass from the bottom of the stone and tossed it away. "I'm so sorry, Karen. I'm so sorry it ended up like this. That he found you." She swallowed thickly. "That I couldn't do anything to save you." She dabbed her eyes with the sleeve of her coat. "I'm sorry you won't get to see her again. We gave up so much for her. But she's safe now. My little girl's safe now."

She continued to pluck grass away from the edge of the grave. "I have so much to tell you, I just don't know where to start." She laughed. "I guess I could start with the newspaper article. It says that William has been captured and charged with murder, money laundering, terrorism, kidnapping, and a boatload of other stuff, too. It doesn't give a great deal of detail about the charges, especially the terrorism charge, but given what he wanted from me, I think I can take a wild guess that it involves some kind of biological weapon." She pushed her hair behind her ears. "It also says that Daniela has testified against him." Tears spilled down her cheeks. "She's so brave." She wiped the tears away. "I know exactly how hard it is to stand up to that man, and I had you to support me every step of the way. I wasn't there for her, Karen."

She buried her face in the crook of her elbow and leaned heavily on the gravestone. The tears fell hot and fast from her eyes, and her shoulders shook with heaving sobs. In the distance, a truck rumbled down the road, birds tweeted in the trees over her head, and slowly, her crying eased.

"I won't let that happen again, sweetheart. I won't let her be alone again." She reached into her pocket for a handkerchief. "I'm going to find her." She wiped her eyes and smiled sadly at the deep carving on the stone. "I'm going to find her, and when I do, I'm never going to let anything come between us again."

## CHAPTER THREE

Daniela Finsbury-Sterling, Finn to anyone who expected her to answer, aimed the camera at the spoked cable spool of the Cayman Salvage Master, adjusting the focus so that it was sharpest on the soft coral formation growing on the outermost edge. She tweaked the lights to pick up the purple tones. Twenty-three meters below the surface of the water, enhancing color was no easy task, but it was a challenge she enjoyed, and for the time being it allowed her to relax and focus on anything but the other challenge facing her.

In the week since Andrew Whittaker had come to her, begging for her help in his own demanding way, she had done nothing but think, talk, and plan how to do what was being asked of her. Could she pretend to be the cold-hearted bitch her father had tried, and failed, to create? She captured the coral image and swam around to the other side. She needed to capture as many angles as possible for the website shots.

Six weeks ago, she had discovered that her father had coerced a colleague of Finn's into corrupting her scientific work to create a biological weapon from a technique she had developed to treat cancer patients. He'd intended to sell the toxin that scientist Ethan Lyell had prepared and named Balor to a terrorist for more money than any one man should have. He was going to let half the world's population die before "suddenly" developing the cure and cashing in. Again. Now her father was languishing in prison, his companies were at the mercy of shareholders, and terrorist Masood Mehalik was trying to find someone else to re-create Balor.

Agent Andrew Whittaker had interrupted their Thanksgiving dinner to ask her to go undercover and help get this madman out of circulation. It had to be done. He had to be stopped before he created a global disaster. It was only a matter of time before Mehalik came after her, as she was the next person in line who understood the chemistry behind the weapon. Everyone from Whittaker to Interpol, the CIA, and Oz's family agreed on that, if little else. Now, tomorrow, next week, it didn't matter. He knew she could do exactly what he wanted. And he wanted it very, very badly.

She kicked back to line up the long shot down the length on the wreck and waved Oz out of the picture.

She knew Oz didn't want her to take the risk. She wanted to try to keep her safe at home and let the authorities tackle it without her.

She knew her lover was speaking from the heart and not from her head or her own highly developed sense of patriotism. Oz was scared that something would happen to Finn, and she respected that. But if it weren't for Finn, Balor wouldn't exist in the first place. She had to do everything she could to stop it from being a threat. If going undercover and trying to get Masood Mehalik to come to her was what it took to make up for the mistake she made in trusting her father with her breakthrough, then so be it. It was the right thing to do. Even if she was terrified.

She took her last shot and signaled that she was done. Oz clasped her hand and led her back toward the mooring line to begin their ascent. She still had to pack before the flight to New York tomorrow, and she knew leaving Oz at the airport was going to be difficult. Even after only three months together, imagining a day without her was pretty much impossible, but saying good-bye and then getting on a plane, and not knowing if she would see her again…Finn felt her heart start to race. No. It wouldn't come to that. It couldn't.

"Did you get all the shots you wanted, baby?" Oz asked as soon as they broke the surface.

"Yes. Thanks for bringing me out today." She didn't want to leave the website updates unfinished. These were the last pictures she needed to leave something of herself behind for Oz. Something tangible. Maybe even something to remember her by. As much as the agents involved assured her this was a simple mission and nothing could go wrong, she didn't believe them. She found it increasingly difficult to trust anyone but Oz and her extended family.

Oz helped her out of the water and her gear and then stripped off her own wetsuit while Finn submerged the camera housing in a bucket of fresh water to rinse it off.

"Let me get your zip for you." At six feet tall, Oz towered over her own five-foot-three-inch frame, and the feeling of being enveloped by Oz made Finn feel safe and protected and horny. Oz gathered Finn's long hair into a ponytail and slid it over her shoulder and pulled on the tab to Finn's wetsuit. She followed it with a string of kisses down her spine that made Finn shudder as she pulled the clinging neoprene down her arms. She needed to feel Oz's skin on hers.

"Thank God you insisted on us coming out here alone." She turned around in Oz's arms and pushed her fingers into Oz's short, golden hair and pulled her in for an intoxicating kiss. They kissed until the need for oxygen forced them apart momentarily. Oz dropped to her knees and helped her out of the rest of her suit before scooping her up in strong arms and carrying her inside the salon.

Space was a precious commodity on the commercial dive boat Oz owned, and every inch was taken up by useable fittings. As a result, Finn found her bottom perched on the edge of the dining table while Oz removed her bikini top and wrapped her lips around Finn's diamond hard nipple. Finn braced herself as Oz removed her bikini bottoms. She reached to take off Oz's suit, but Oz was faster, and before she could reach the flimsy black material, it was already heading for the ground.

"I love you," Finn whispered as Oz kissed her neck and settled her hips between her thighs. She loved the first moment of full skin on skin contact. For her it was when she felt the most loved, cherished, wanted, and desired. It was the instant she was reminded exactly where she belonged and that home was in the arms and the heart of the only woman she had ever loved.

Oz's fingers found her soaked center with unerring accuracy and claimed her without hesitation. "I love you too, baby." She used her body weight to add depth to each stroke and clamped her left arm around Finn's hips, holding her in place. "I love you so much."

Finn stared into Oz's eyes with the intention of memorizing every second. The light filtered through the portholes and made the stunning blue she saw every day change color slightly. Instead of the usual cornflower blue, they took on the cobalt shade that reminded her more of the Atlantic—dark blue and stormy. Her wide forehead and cheekbones were covered in droplets of seawater and a fine sheen of sweat as she worked hard for Finn's pleasure. Thickly muscled shoulders bunched with each thrust, and her breasts bounced tantalizingly out of reach of Finn's lips. She licked her lips, and a knowing smile pulled at the corners of Oz's coral pink lips.

"Do you want something, baby?"

Finn caught her lower lip between her teeth and nodded.

"Remember, all you have to do is ask, and it's yours." Oz twisted her hand so that her thumb hit Finn's clit with each thrust. Finn whimpered. She wouldn't last much longer and they both knew it. "I'm all yours, baby. Just ask."

She knew why Oz wanted her to vocalize her desires. She'd told her several times. Finn's decidedly British accent was a huge turn-on for Oz. The way her voice dropped an octave in the throes of passion, combined with her accent, made Oz nearly come on the spot. "I want to suck your nipple."

Oz groaned, but Finn didn't have time to embrace the jolt of victory at eliciting the response from her. Oz's stone hard nipple was quickly presented for her to wrap her lips around and feast upon. She wrapped her arm around Oz's back and firmly squeezed her arse.

"Come with me, love." She refused to look away from Oz's eyes and she knew they were both close. She wrapped her legs around Oz's thighs and pumped her hips. Oz trembled in her arms, and she realized that each thrust was pushing the back of Oz's wrist into her own clit and it would be seconds before they climaxed together.

She bit down gently on Oz's flesh. The strangled groan alone would have been enough to trigger her own release, but the final thrust of Oz's hand pressed upon the tender area inside her turned her to liquid. She felt hot and cold at the same time and every muscle in her body contracted.

She could feel herself clamped around Oz's fingers, and in them she could feel Oz's heart beat. She had never felt so connected to her as she did in that moment.

They clung together, waiting for their breathing to return to normal, just holding each other, stroking soft, random patterns over each other's skin.

"I wish I didn't have to go," Finn whispered against Oz's neck.

"Then don't."

"Oz, we've talked about this. You know I have to do this."

"Why?"

Finn sighed and pulled away. "I've explained that to you."

"Explain it to me again, Finn. Why?"

"I don't want anything to do with this." Why did Oz have to do this now? Why couldn't they just enjoy their last few moments in each other's arms? The feeling of peace vanished in the wake of the second most familiar emotion she felt lately. Anger. "I don't want to go near that lab again, or my research. I don't want to create this…this…goddamned apocalyptic bacteria. I don't want you to be in danger. I don't want to be in danger. But I don't have any other choice. If I don't make it, I can't create the vaccine, and I can't control it. The knowledge of this is out there now, Oz, and at some point this madman will find someone to engineer it for him, someone who doesn't give a flying fuck about killing innocent people." Anger morphed quickly into fear.

"So why don't you wait and see if someone else does create it? Maybe you're worrying over nothing?"

"No. Trying to retro engineer a vaccine after an outbreak will be damn near impossible in the time frame we'll be looking at, and I can't even think about the people who will be dead and suffering by that time. Plus, if another scientist were to try, it would be different. There's no telling the ways it could be made worse."

"This thing would kill damn near everyone it comes into contact with. How can it be worse?"

"A faster incubation period. Then we'd have no chance against it at all. I have to create an effective vaccine to this thing or I'll never be able to rest."

"You didn't create this."

"No. But I made it possible for my dad to do so. If I hadn't developed the protocol to merge the DNA of the E.coli bacteria with another substance this just wouldn't be possible. I have to fix this. It's a ticking bomb if I don't."

"But you'll be putting yourself in so much danger."

"I know."

"No, Finn, you really don't. You think surviving your dad means that you can come through this too," Oz said.

Finn disagreed. She knew that the chances of her coming through this ordeal were so much slimmer than the ordeal with her father.

"Mehalik makes your dad look like a pussycat. He will eat you up and spit you out. I can't let you do—"

"Do you know what I see after I fall asleep every night?" She held her tears back by sheer force of will. "Every night I hold you in my arms and watch Balor steal you from me." She blinked and swiped angrily at the moisture running down her cheeks. "Even if I die trying, I need to do this. I can't let you stop me, Oz. I love you, but I can't let you stop me."

"Fucking Whittaker. Why the hell did he have to drop into our lives?"

"It isn't his fault. He isn't the one murdering microbiologists and trying to re-create a bug that could kill everyone on the planet."

Oz sighed. "I know. That doesn't mean I have to like him for walking in on Thanksgiving and turning our world upside down." She pulled away, grabbed a shirt, and pulled a pair of shorts up her long legs. "Again." She walked out of the salon and untied the rope that had secured them to the mooring buoy.

"What're you doing?"

"Taking us home, babe. We've got packing to do."

"What?"

"I told you before. I'm not going to leave your side. Wherever you go, I go. And what I was trying to tell you a few minutes ago is that I can't let you do this—alone."

Finn was reeling. Oz had made it clear she didn't want Finn to risk her life, but she hadn't expected her to come with her. She wasn't expecting this. She had responsibilities. "What about the shop?"

"What about it? Rudy can take care of it, and I'm only at the end of the phone if he needs anything." She turned on the engine and started them back toward shore. She glanced at Finn and grinned. "You might want to grab some clothes before we get to shore. I mean, I don't mind the natural look, but I don't think you want to share that much of yourself with whoever is on shore."

"Funny." Finn quickly got dressed and rejoined Oz in the cockpit. "I'm not sure Whittaker will allow it, sweetheart."

"Well, if you tell him that you won't go without me, he'll let you do whatever the hell you want."

"Do you think so?"

"I know so. Where are we going anyway?" Oz asked. "You never told me where your dad's US bio lab was based."

"New York."

"New York? Seriously?"

"Yup." Finn waited. She knew how much Oz hated the cold, since she'd proposed the idea of a ski trip for Christmas. The look on Oz's face had been priceless as she declared there was no way Finn was getting her to put stupid sticks on her feet and throw herself down a mountainside covered in ice. She'd been supremely confident in her ability to break her neck under those circumstances.

"It's December."

"And?"

"It's snowing in New York."

"I know."

"I live in Florida."

"Get to the point."

"I only have a little denim jacket."

Finn laughed. "Guess I'm gonna have to take you shopping then."

Oz scowled and pulled out her cell phone. "Billy, it's Oz."

"I'm your father, Olivia, and we've discussed this before."

Oz grinned. "Yeah, but you're gonna have to get used to it if this plan's gonna work." She laughed and even Finn could hear him growl. "Billy, I have a situation."

"So help me, you're enjoying this far too much."

"Yeah, yeah."

He sighed. "What's the situation? You need me to come and pack your bag for ya?"

"Nope. But I think we're gonna need some resources based on our new location."

"I'm guessing we don't have a huge amount of time. What do you need me to scare up?"

"Probably arctic gear."

"Huh? Where the hell are we going? Alaska?"

"Might as well be. The lab's in New York." Finn heard the theatrical shiver down the phone line.

"That little runt."

"What?"

"Junior. He's been there before. It was his bloody team that went in to retrieve the intel before Thanksgiving. Little runt must be laughing his ass off right now."

"Pops, there ain't nothing little about my cousin. Even if he wasn't a SEAL, he's still got four inches on you."

"Not when I get finished pounding on him." Oz laughed at her father's familiar empty threats and the banter that made difficult situations a little easier for them all to deal with. "Full sets of arctic gear coming up." He hung up.

"You can't be serious." Finn stared at her. "Arctic gear? It's only New York."

"I live in Florida. I don't do cold."

Finn laughed at the shudder that ran through Oz. "Wuss."

Part of her was irritated that Oz had obviously made a plan with her family without speaking to her about it. But it wasn't like she'd given Oz any real option to stop her, and Oz was far better qualified to do the mission side of this than Finn could ever hope to be. Years of training and working as a highly skilled Navy diver had made Oz a formidable woman, and Finn had to admit it made sense for her to be with her. But it scared the hell out of her too. Just as it was Oz's instinct to protect her, Finn felt exactly the same. She knew that physically she was no match for her lover. Nor was she likely to be a match for any of the adversaries she was likely to come up against. The only protection she could afford anyone was to keep them as far from her and Balor as she could. "You don't need to come with me, my little hot house flower." She smiled to take any sting out of her words, but she knew that her eyes would hold the truth of what she was offering. Even as she knew Oz would refuse.

"Yeah, I do. If I didn't and left Dad and Junior up in the cold with you, they'd never let me live it down." Oz kissed her softly, murmuring her pleasure at the soft lips, and warm mouth—until it disappeared with an audible pop.

"What? Your dad and Junior are coming too?"

"Yup."

"Why?"

"'Cause you're family and we keep our family safe." Oz kissed her gently on the forehead. "I know you need to do this. You're right. You're the only one who can do this the right way. But I need to keep you out of harm's way as much as possible. I can't think of any other way to do that than be by your side every step of the way."

"Thank you." She reached up and kissed her again.

"Doesn't mean I have to like it."

Finn chuckled. "I would expect nothing less." She patted Oz's belly as she pulled away. "So what's your plan?"

"My plan?"

"Don't try playing dumb with me, Zuckerman. You, your dad, and your cousin must have a plan in mind or your dad wouldn't be on red alert. Spill."

"So demanding."

Finn crossed her arms and waited.

"Fine. We don't have anything specific, other than we're going to be your security team. I think I like Valkyrie Security as the name of your new personal security agency. Uncle Charlie's squared it all away with Junior's commander, and his team is on standby in case we need more backup. Andrew Whittaker is our Interpol liaison for this operation, and we'll be meeting with the CIA guy too. The one who interviewed you, Stephen Knight."

Finn nodded. He'd been nice enough when he interviewed her. She'd actually thought it was him at her door on Thanksgiving when Whittaker turned up; the two looked so alike they could easily pass for brothers. "And your dad?"

"What? Oh, yeah. He's got clearance from Mom to come play."

"Funny. I mean he's been retired for how long now?"

"Almost ten years."

"Is he…I mean he's not exactly…can he…"

Oz laughed. "He's more than capable of doing what we need to do here, baby. Besides, he's probably going to be running comms, cameras, and intel gathering. He knows what all our strengths and weaknesses are, and he was a damn fine operational commander before he retired. We're in safe hands, baby."

Finn blushed. "Okay. Sorry."

"No need to be sorry with me. You might want to start running when I tell him you questioned his physical prowess."

"You wouldn't!"

Oz smiled. "That sounded like a challenge."

"Oh God." Finn closed her eyes and tipped her head back, offering a silent prayer. "You could try the patience of a saint."

"I've been told that before." She wiggled her eyebrows comically.

"So let me get this straight. Your uncle, Rear Admiral Charles Zuckerman, base commander at Key West, has managed to get authorization to use two retired naval officers and a serving SEAL on a mission that's supposed to be run by the CIA and Interpol."

"Yup."

"How?"

"I didn't ask that, and even if I had, Uncle Charlie never would have told me the favors he's pulled in to make this work. All I know is that he has friends in very high places, and when he brought this to them, they gave him authority to do whatever needs to be done to eliminate the threat to national security."

"But—"

"No buts, we're all in this with you. So tell me about the lab. How big is it? How many staff work there? Where is it situated exactly? Other than the frozen Northern Wastelands."

Finn laughed. "It's New York City, hardly frozen, barren wastelands. Is this your research?"

"Yup. And I didn't say barren. But since you mention it, I plan on being ready for anything."

She stretched up to kiss her, wrapping her arms around her neck. "I love you."

"I love you, too. And you're never alone."

# CHAPTER FOUR

Bailey sipped her double espresso and waited for the caffeine to hit her system. She didn't drink the scalding liquid anymore for flavor alone. She needed it to function. She only hoped her mark would stay at the café long enough for her to finish her intake before he took off again. She slumped back against the aluminum mesh chair digging uncomfortably against the backs of her thighs and hoped no one questioned her sanity for sitting outside. But despite the fact that it was December and she was in the middle of Boston, the day was fine and the sun shone brightly, if not warmly, and it would be all too soon before they were chased inside again by the weather. She was determined to enjoy whatever outside time she could get, even if it did make her arthritic knees ache.

She paid close attention to the door of the café, making sure that her target hadn't left, while taking a few photographs of the surrounding area. It was good cover—playing tourist—taking a few shots of the parks to her right. Blackstone Square was beside her, just across the road, and Franklin Square was diagonally across the intersection. She pretended to be taking pictures of the trees, maybe a bird or two, chirping away. She didn't know. Hell, she didn't care. It was good cover and that was all that mattered. If need be there was always the Salvation Army building across the street with its memorial stone at the top. Whatever it took, just like always.

She turned her chair so she was facing Blackstone Square. Out of the corner of her eye, she could see the man she was following inside, with his arm draped over a young female student. She knew the girl was a student because she was one of *his* students. Bailey had followed them from the high school where he taught, and she was sickened by the implications of what she was seeing. So far he hadn't behaved in a way that would seem out of the ordinary for a father toward his daughter. But that sure as hell wasn't his daughter. So much for his wife's suspicion that he was cheating on her.

Mrs. Marsden had called Bailey two days prior, crying, and convinced that her husband was seeing someone else. She was worried he was going to leave her for his mystery woman while she was heavily pregnant.

*You're better off without him.* She swallowed another mouthful of her rapidly cooling coffee and shot another couple of pictures. *There's not much I haven't seen, Mr. Marsden, but you and your ilk really make me sick.* She pulled a notepad out of the pocket of her overcoat and scribbled down a few notes. She knew she wouldn't need to refer to the pad again; the simple act of actually writing the information down committed it to her memory. But if she didn't write it down, she could guarantee she'd forget something important somewhere down the line. It was a habit that had been ingrained over many years of training, first as a cop, then as an FBI field agent working sex crimes.

She had a good view of what was happening inside the café, and she could see the bastard's hand touch the girl's knee under the table. Bailey clenched her teeth and stayed in her seat, barely. If she was going to make it concrete and stop this guy from trying this again, she needed more than him touching a kid's knee.

The girl jumped up from the table, spilling her drink across the surface and covering Mr. Marsden with it as she dashed for the door. Bailey stood quickly, her knees complaining, and moved in front of the scared girl who bolted from the café. "I'm not gonna hurt you. I saw what happened in there," she said, pointing into the café, "and I want to make sure you get home safe and sound."

"Yeah, right. How am I supposed to believe a total stranger? He's been my teacher all semester and he's just turned out to be a disgusting prick."

"You're right. You have absolutely no reason to trust me, and he is a disgusting prick. I'll offer you another option then. One that doesn't involve you telling me any information, or moving away from here with me." She fished her cell phone out of her pocket and held it out to the girl. "Call home and have someone come pick you up. I'll wait with you until someone comes to get you. Someone called Mom, Dad, or a legal guardian, though. Not your BFF, or your boyfriend, or anything like that."

The girl stared reluctantly at the phone. "My mom'll go ape shit at me being here."

"Well." Bailey shrugged. "I can see her point, and after what happened in there, I'm pretty sure you can understand why."

The girl sighed. "I guess."

"Cheryl, there was no need to run out." Mr. Marsden stepped outside and smiled at Bailey. "It was just an accident. Why don't you come back inside and I'll get you another drink?"

"No, thanks." Cheryl took the phone from Bailey's hand and quickly dialed the number. "Mom, can you come get me please?" She paused and turned her back on Mr. Marsden, clearly dismissing him. "No, I'm not in trouble, but something's happened and I need you to come get me."

"Cheryl, what are you doing?" Marsden said.

Bailey stepped closer to him, towering over him. "I'd keep very quiet if I were you."

Marsden bristled. "Do I know you?"

"No. But you're going to." She took a step forward and he inched back, trying to shrink away from her.

"I don't know what you're talking about."

Bailey laughed. "Sure you do. I can see the fear in your eyes. Sweat on your forehead, upper lip." His legs met the edge of the chair she'd been sitting on and it skittered across the pavement as she got closer to him and poked one finger into his chest. He flinched and raised his hand to protect himself, clearly fearing what punishment she was going to dole out. She smiled. Years of interrogations had led her to perfect a feral grin that seemed to scare even the hardest of men she'd come across, and she let it loose on Mr. Marsden with pride. "Shallow breathing and there's a vein at your temple that's throbbing at about a hundred and sixty a minute. I'm guessing you feel a little dizzy right about now. Like the whole world is closing in on you." She inched closer so they were nose to nose. "And you know what, buddy? It is. Now sit down and don't move." She pushed him easily and suppressed a laugh as he dropped heavily into the chair like a pin had been pulled from his knees. *Pathetic little weasel.*

"My mom said she'd come right away. We live pretty far from here though so it's gonna take her a while." She handed the phone back to Bailey.

"Not a problem." She ushered the girl a little away from the shaking man and spoke quietly. "Want to tell me why you came here with him?"

"He said he was gonna help me with an extra credit assignment. That it would give me a better chance at getting into college if I got a good grade, and he said he thought I was worth the effort. He said he didn't want other students to think he was playing favorites though, so we needed to go away from school. He said he'd give me a lift close to home afterward, so that I wouldn't get into trouble with anyone."

"I have to call the police."

"No way."

"Please, listen a second." Cheryl opened her mouth to argue, but Bailey stared at her and had to stifle a laugh when the girl's mouth closed, her teeth clicking together loudly. "Thank you. Now, the reason I have to call them is this. He's a predator. A predator after young girls, and he works in a school filled with them. The story he told you was practiced. He's done this before, and if I don't report it, he'll do it again. Next time, the girl might not be as lucky as you've been today."

"I hear ya, but I don't want everyone at school to know."

"They don't have to know anything you don't want to tell them. The school will be happy to keep this quiet, believe me. You can control that. All you're going to have to do is tell the police what you've told me, and answer their questions."

"They're gonna think I'm stupid."

"Why?"

"For believing him."

"No, they won't. He's the adult here, and he's earned your trust and respect in a position of authority. He's abused that."

Marsden clambered to his feet and took off. He ran awkwardly, and Bailey caught up to him in half a dozen long strides, twisted one arm up his back, and spun him into the wall.

"I told you not to move."

"Let me go. You don't know what you're talking about. The kid's lying if she said I touched her." He tried to shrug her off, but Bailey wasn't going anywhere.

"She hasn't said that. I saw it."

He stopped struggling. "Fuck."

"Cheryl, my cell phone's in my coat pocket. Can you get it and call nine one one?"

"What do I say?" She pulled the phone out and dialed.

"Just tell them what happened."

Cheryl was pale and shaky as she explained what had happened and the reality of what could have happened seemed to sink in. She dropped heavily into a chair and waited. A waitress came out of the café and asked if she could help.

"Thanks, but the police are already on their way. Cheryl here called for me. Maybe you can get her some sweet tea, and if you have any cable ties in there that would be great." Bailey smiled at the young woman.

"I'll see what we can find."

"Thanks. Cheryl?" Bailey looked over at the girl and noted the shivering body, slumped shoulders, and the glassy-eyed look. "Cheryl? Hey, kid, come on, listen to me."

Cheryl blinked and made an obvious effort to focus on Bailey. "Don't call me kid."

Bailey smiled. *That's better.* "You got it."

"What did you want?"

"I need you to pull that chair around for me." She indicated a toppled chair. "If the waitress can find some cable ties, I'm gonna secure him to it until the police get here. How long did they say they'd be?" Bailey knew they'd have uniformed officers there in about ten minutes, but she needed to keep Cheryl focused and not thinking about what could have happened. She wanted to stop her from going into shock.

"They didn't say how long, just that someone would be here soon." She picked up the chair Bailey had pointed to. "You really gonna tie him up?"

"Hell yes, I am."

"You can't do that, bitch. I've got rights." Marsden struggled again.

"So you do." Bailey twisted his arm a little further up his back and used her body weight to press him harder against the wall forcing the wind from him. *That ought to shut you up, you sorry son of a bitch.* "And so does Cheryl. She has the right to tell the police and the school exactly what you tried to do here today. And I'm exercising my right as a concerned citizen to give her the opportunity to do that."

The waitress came out balancing a tray expertly on one hand. "Here you go, ladies. One cup of tea, and I'm afraid I couldn't find any cable ties, but I found some duct tape in the back. Will that do?" She grinned at Bailey.

Bailey laughed and pushed Marsden into the chair. "Oh yeah. That'll do." She gripped his wrists against the metal arms. "Cheryl, would you like to do the honors?"

Cheryl nodded and reached for the tape, wrapping it securely around the mid forearm and the metal. Bailey was glad to see her hands had almost stopped shaking completely by the time she was wrapping his second arm.

"Legs too, Cheryl. Then he can't try to run with this big ol' chair stuck to his butt."

Cheryl giggled as she started to bind his calves.

"I'm gonna sue you pair of bitches."

"Yeah, yeah." Bailey leaned closer to his ear. "Better men than you have come up with worse threats than that, and you know what?"

He didn't answer, but he met her eyes and waited.

"I'm still here. Still takin' out the trash."

His lip curled and she could see him working the saliva in his mouth.

"Don't even think about spitting at me. If you do, I'll have Cheryl put a nice big chunk of that tape over your mouth. And let me tell you, it hurts like a son of a bitch pulling this stuff off skin."

He paused, obviously weighing how serious her threat was, then swallowed visibly.

"Good boy."

"Can I help you ladies with anything else?" the waitress asked.

"We're good, thanks."

"Well, if you need anything I'll be just inside. I'm Rachel, by the way." She held her hand out.

Bailey glanced at her and slowly stood to her full height. She gripped Rachel's hand. "Bailey. And thanks for your help."

"Sure, sure. Anytime. I never liked the look of that guy. He's creepy." She dipped her head and smiled before heading back inside. Bailey dropped into the chair next to Cheryl and watched as she sipped her tea.

"Was she hitting on you?"

Bailey chuckled. "I think she was just being friendly."

"Uh huh." She put the cup back on the table. "I think she was hitting on you."

"I don't think so."

"Not your type?"

Bailey was glad that Cheryl was distracted. She just wished she'd found a different source of distraction. "A little young for me, I think."

"Well, she didn't seem to think so. Didn't you think she was cute?"

"Well, I guess."

"So, go get her number."

"Maybe later."

"That's old people talk for 'no, now shut up.'" Cheryl shrugged. "Whatever."

Bailey laughed again. "Thanks, kid."

"Hey, I told you not to call me that." Cheryl scowled at her and Bailey smirked.

"Then don't call people old."

"Excuse me, but you called yourself old."

They chatted for a couple more minutes before the police officers arrived. When they did, she gave her statement while they waited for Cheryl's mother to arrive. There wasn't anything left for Bailey to do except inform her client of the result of her investigation. She wasn't looking forward to it.

She pulled open the door to the silver Ford Explorer and climbed inside. She ran her fingers through her hair and decided to get a trim. She fished through the papers in her briefcase for Mrs. Marsden's number. She glanced at her rearview mirror and turned on the engine to get the heater going while she waited for her call to be answered. The phone clicked into voicemail and instructed her to leave her message after the beep as she watched a dog emerge suddenly from the park across the street.

"Mrs. Marsden, this is Bailey Davenport. I have a report to give you on your husband's activities. I feel it would be best if we talked sooner rather than later."

The voicemail clicked off and Mrs. Marsden answered. "Ms. Davenport, thank you for calling."

"No problem. Would it be okay for me to come to your home? I really think we should talk."

"No. I don't want you to be here when Alec comes home."

"That really isn't necessary."

"I'll meet you at your office in twenty minutes."

"Mrs. Marsden, you really—" The line went dead. "Don't have to worry about your husband coming home right now." Bailey sighed and glanced in her mirror again. The dog ran across the street, barely avoiding traffic. Bailey couldn't see a leash, or anyone running after it. It weaved in and out of cars, causing mayhem, and seemingly terrifying the poor dog even more. Bailey rolled her eyes. She didn't have time for this, but she got out of the car anyway.

"Here, pup. C'mere." She clapped her hands to try to get its attention without startling it further. The dog slowed as it approached her and stopped a few feet away, tail tucked firmly between its legs, hackles raised, and head ducked. There was no aggression evident, just fear. "It's okay, pup. C'mere so I can see your collar." She held her hand out, held the dog's gaze, and waited. It approached slowly, cautiously, nose working the air furiously for her scent. The dog kept eye contact, and Bailey could see the intelligence as it sniffed her hand carefully. A car honked behind them, startling the dog again. But this time it moved close to Bailey and turned to face the noise, clearly putting itself between Bailey and danger. Bailey smiled. "Sweet girl. Good girl." The dog wagged her tail slightly under the praise, and Bailey decided to push her luck a little. "Come on, girl. This way."

She stood and started for the sidewalk. The dog tipped her head in Bailey's direction, then trotted behind her to the safety of the sidewalk. "Good girl." She ruffled the top of the dog's head. "Now, let me get a look at your collar and see who you belong to." She trailed her hand down and around the dog's neck, but couldn't find any collar, no ID tag, no harness, nothing.

"Well, it looks like you're not gonna make it easy to find your owner, and I don't have a great deal of time to waste here, girl. Let's see if you'll get in the car and I can solve your problems after I talk to Mrs. Marsden." She opened the back passenger door to the Explorer. "What do you say?" The black and white border collie looked up at Bailey, then into the car. Bailey tipped her head in the direction of the backseat and the dog jumped in. "Good girl." Bailey stroked her head again and closed the door. By the time she rounded the car and climbed in the driver's side, the dog was sitting on the passenger seat, leaning against the backrest, and staring out the window. Bailey laughed. "Well, someone's clearly been spoiled. Fine, but only because I don't have time to argue with you."

Bailey turned the engine on again and buckled her seat belt. The dog whined and looked at the belt on the passenger side. Bailey put the car in drive, and the dog whined louder, looked at Bailey, then at the passenger seat belt. "Please don't tell me you get car sick or something. That really would make my day. I'll roll the window down a little bit when we get moving. Okay?" Bailey started to ease off the brake, when the dog barked and pawed at the seat belt. "You've got to be kidding me."

She put the car back into park, pulled the seat belt around the dog, and clicked it into the holder. "Happy now?" The dog panted. "Well, good. I'm working here, you know." Bailey sighed. *I'm talking to a dog. A dog I just met. A dog who likes to be seat-belted in.* She flicked the switch to turn the radio on and smiled as the sultry, gravelly tones of Nina Simone's "Please Don't Let Me Be Misunderstood" filtered out of the speakers. The dog let out a rumbled sort of howl and Bailey turned to look at her. "You like jazz?" Another singsong rumble and Bailey laughed. "Nina Simone stays then. But no singing. You're out of tune." She pulled out, turned east on Washington, and headed toward the waterfront, her office, and a difficult conversation.

The conversation with Mrs. Marsden was even more difficult than Bailey had expected. The poor woman was distraught, confused, and

Bailey felt nothing but sorry for her. Throughout the meeting, the dog had curled up beside Bailey, watching her intently, never moving more than three feet from her side.

After more than an hour of trying to comfort the poor woman, and eventually calling a friend to come pick her up, Bailey was on her own again. Which was exactly how she liked it. She needed her space, time away from the lowlifes and scumbags she followed and dealt with on a day-to-day basis. People she'd dealt with for as long as she could remember.

She dropped heavily into her chair and closed her eyes. A weight landed on her knee, and she opened one eye to look into the compassionate eyes of the dog at her side, paw resting gently in her lap. "Was that a bit heavy for you too, girl?" She reached down and stroked the top of the dog's head. "Okay, time to solve your problems."

She opened up her laptop and searched for a local vet. Within a couple of minutes, she'd set up an appointment, grabbed her keys, and headed for the door. The dog trotted beside her every step of the way. It only took five minutes to reach the vet's office and the dog walked at her heel from the car without any prompting. "Seems you like me, hey, girl?" The dog wagged her tail as Bailey checked in at reception and they sat to wait their turn. She kept her hand on the dog's back, stroking her fur and noting that she needed a bath. She wondered if the dog had been reported missing yet, and what could have happened to her leash and collar. She was too well trained not to have been loved and well cared for, but her matted, dirty fur, and the ribs she could feel too close to the surface, told her the dog had probably been on the streets for a while.

Bailey was called through and she quickly explained what had happened.

The vet smiled. "Well, this little girl certainly seems to have taken a shine to you. Do you think you can get her on the scales?"

"I'll give it a go." She stepped closer to the scales and pointed to the machine. "On here, girl." She trotted over and sat down, her eyes flicking from one to the other as he made a note of the figure.

"You're right. She is underweight. She's a good fifteen pounds under what she should be for a dog of her breed and height."

"Neglected?"

He shrugged. "Or a runaway."

"I have difficulty believing this dog would run away from her master. She's not ventured more than three feet from me since I found her."

"Let's get her on the table and see what else I can find. Maybe she has a microchip and we can find her family." Bailey lifted the dog onto the table and stroked her head as he ran the scanner over her back. "Nope. Nothing. You're not making this easy for us are you, girl?" She ruffled her ears. "Okay, I'm gonna give her an exam and write up a report for the police to notify them in case anyone reports her missing, then I guess we'll have to take her to the animal shelter."

"What? Why?"

"Well, if we can't find her family, we can't just let her wander the streets."

"I know that. I'll take care of her." *What the fuck?* Bailey wanted to look around and see who had spoken, but she recognized her own voice—even if she didn't recognize the words.

He looked at her skeptically. "Why?"

"Why what?"

"Why do you want to look after her until her family is found?" He ran his hands over the dog's body and frowned.

"Because she doesn't belong in the pound."

"No dog does." He parted her fur and examined a scab, his brow furrowing. "Damn it. Bite marks."

"She's been attacked?"

"Looks like it." He cleaned the wound efficiently and applied some ointment. The dog didn't move though she visibly flinched at one point. "She is a good girl, and you didn't answer my question." He continued his examination.

She looked into the soulful eyes that were begging her for...help? A chance? Love? Bailey didn't know. But she knew she wouldn't be able to let this little girl go to the pound. Not in a million years. "Well, everybody needs a second chance now and then. I guess I want to give her one."

He began cleaning another bite wound. "She's been attacked. Possibly more than once. These wounds appear to have happened at different times."

"How could that happen?"

"Dog fights."

"Excuse me?"

"People training fighting dogs will buy or steal dogs this sort of size to throw in training rings as bait dogs."

"Oh my God. That's..."

"Disgusting? Awful? Evil?"

"All of the above." She looked into those copper eyes again and drew the dog's head toward her, dropping a kiss on top between her ears. "How can people do things like that?"

"Money." He cleaned a third bite wound.

"There's not enough in the world to hurt animals like this." Bailey could feel tears welling in her eyes and she thanked God that this guy didn't know her well enough to know just how out of character it was for her.

"Okay, I'll let her stay with you."

"Thanks."

"But there's some things I'm going to have to do to make sure she's safe. And some things you're going to have to do too, because of what I suspect her background is."

"Like what?"

"She's going to need a series of shots before you can apply for a license. I want to get her micro-chipped, check if she's been spayed, and if not, she needs to be. Then you have to keep her on a lead and watch her around other dogs at all times."

Bailey had seen more than a few dog attack victims when she walked the beat, but she found it really hard to picture this girl capable of savagery. "But she's been really good."

"Not negotiable. She's been attacked by another dog. She may be unpredictable around them in the future. I'd hate to have to put her down because she attacked out of fear after everything else she's been through."

Bailey stared as the words sank in, then cleared her throat. "Well, you certainly know how to get your point across. Okay, fine. I'll get her a collar and leash." She rubbed the dog's head again. "I was going to anyway."

He quickly drew the blood sample and gave her a shot to prevent infection in any of her wounds before he loaded the microchip gun. "I'm going to need a name for her to put on the registration form."

"I don't know her name."

"Pick one." He positioned the gun and injected the microchip. "I can't send this off until you do."

"What if she doesn't recognize the name I give her?"

"She seems like a pretty smart dog. I'm sure she'll learn whatever you choose. Haven't you had a dog before?"

"When I was a kid, sure. But we got him as a puppy."

"Well, you've got a couple of minutes while I fill this out to think of one. Where did you find her? Maybe that would work."

"Blackstone Square doesn't strike me as a great name for this girl."

He chuckled. "True enough." He filled out the details on the form and Bailey laughed.

"Jazz."

"Jazz?"

"Yup. We were listening to it on the radio when she first got in the car." The dog shuffled along the table closer to Bailey and leaned into her.

"I think she likes it." He handed her the pen and pointed to the bottom of the form for her signature. "Looks like you've got yourself a dog."

"Just like that?"

"It's unusual to reunite dogs with families, especially if it's been a while. And if she was a bait dog, they're not looking for her. So yeah, just like that."

Bailey smiled down at Jazz and stroked her head. Would it work? Could she adjust to having a pet? How would the dog be if she left her? Would she arrive home to find her apartment trashed? She looked into Jazz's soft eyes as she licked Bailey's hand and knew it didn't matter if she did. It was a done deal. "Just like that."

# CHAPTER FIVE

Sweat beaded on the man's forehead, formed a tiny river down his cheek, and ran into the cut on the left side of his face. Masood Mehalik always took pleasure in giving his guests a scar that matched his own. A little something to remember him by. The salty sweat must have stung because the seated man winced as the bare light bulb flickered to life, illuminating the dingy cell. The sandstone walls, dirt floor, and barred window only reinforced the situation created by the shackles securing his wrists behind the back of the rickety wooden chair, his feet bound to the legs.

"Dr. Jensen." Masood placed a sturdy chair opposite him, sat down, and crossed one leg over the other as he straightened the cuffs of his shirt. "Thank you for coming to visit me. I trust your journey was comfortable." He didn't expect an answer, knowing full well that the doctor's kidnapping from London and his subsequent journey had been far from comfortable. "I have a request, a project I wish you to complete for me."

"Why are you holding me prisoner? I'm a research scientist. I have no money. I have no trade value. I don't work with nuclear material. I research genetics to help with disease treatment. Why have you brought me here?"

"Doctor, as I said, I have a project for you."

"Then untie me and discuss this like a civilized human being!"

Masood glanced quickly up at Hakim, giving him a silent signal. The blow to the back of Jensen's head was brutal and the crack of Hakim's gun against his skull was drowned out only by the cry of fear and pain from Dr. Jensen.

"Now, the project I want you to work on is a little creation called Balor." He pulled a handkerchief out of the inside pocket of his charcoal gray suit jacket and slowly mopped his brow. "Balor is a beautiful child I had created for me. But before I could set my child free, he was stolen." He pulled a piece of paper from his breast pocket, unfolded it, and held it before Jensen. The diagram showed the molecular makeup of Balor, the combination of the relatively harmless E. coli bacterium and the deadly botulinum toxin. "This is my child, Doctor. I want you to re-create him."

Jensen stared at the page for a long moment and shook his head. "It can't be done."

Masood laughed. "I beg to differ, my friend. It has already been created, so I know that it can be done. I have a plethora of information on how it was created and what is required to do so again. What I do not have is someone with the expertise required. So you see, Doctor, the question is not if you can create it for me, but will you create it for me?"

Jensen looked at the page again, then back to Masood. "It's a biological weapon. I won't have any part in creating this."

Always the same response. So noble they were, these scientists, these inventors, these creative geniuses, in the pursuit of their advancement, and yet so blind to the problem they were truly facing. Masood clicked his fingers and Hakim quickly stepped around the man and held up an electronic tablet.

"No!" Jensen thrashed in his chair. His face turned red as his anger surfaced again. "You bastard."

On screen, a woman huddled with two children next to her, her arms wrapped around them as they cried.

"I will ask you again, Doctor. Will you create Balor for me?"

"No."

Masood nodded to Hakim who pulled a cell phone from his pocket. He continued to hold the tablet up for Jensen to see.

"The way I see it, you have four chances to say yes. And you've already said no to me once."

A quiet pop came from the speakers of the tablet. Like a cork exploding from a bottle of champagne. But the blossoming rose of scarlet spreading across his wife's chest and the screaming of his children left no room for doubt.

"Bridget!" Jensen's voice was little more than a whisper as her lifeless eyes stared toward the cameraman. The children shook her until her face was out of his sight.

"Do not be a hero, Doctor. Your family will not thank you for it."

"You'll kill us all anyway."

He was right, but Masood shook his head. "Ye of little faith, Doctor."

"I have faith enough to know a liar when I see one."

"Come, come, Doctor, your answer?"

Tears ran down his ruddy cheeks. "For the love of my children I won't create your vile disease."

The second pop had the man crying as his son fell haphazardly across his mother's body. The little girl backed away from them both, screaming. Tears ran down Jensen's cheeks and his chest heaved as he sobbed, under his breath he recited a prayer; words to accompany his family on their journey, words of comfort his daughter would never hear.

"Number three, Doctor? Is your daughter's life not worth a little effort on your part?"

"I trained as a medical doctor. I believe in the oath I took. I will do no harm."

"But you are harming your family."

"No. You're doing that."

Masood smiled. Over the years, he'd discovered just how much pleasure taking a life gave him. He had come a long way from scrabbling in the dust trying to survive. And he would go further still. "I believe that was your third no, Doctor."

He screamed as the barrel of a gun became visible on the small screen. The little girl cowered in the corner, crying and begging the unknown gunman not to hurt her. The pop was louder than all the others, and Masood watched as it seemed to take Jensen several seconds to realize that a gun had also gone off in the cell. The iron rich tang of blood filled his nostrils as he watched the girl slump to the ground while life flowed from Jensen's body. Red-flecked spittle gathered at the corner of his mouth as he pulled what Masood knew would be his last breaths into his lungs.

"I hope you never find anyone to create that for you. And I die knowing there's one less person on this earth capable of creating that... abomination."

"I will find someone, Doctor. It is but a matter of time."

Jensen's breath rattled in his chest and gurgled past his lips.

Masood stepped over him as he left the basement, making sure not to get any blood on his Italian loafers. He'd accept no other outcome. They would all pay.

# CHAPTER SIX

Cassie looked up at the red brick building on the corner of Broadway and Melrose, then checked the address she'd written down. It had taken Google precisely three seconds to find a plethora of private detectives working in the Boston area. It had taken Cassie three days to look through websites and testimonials to find one she was happy with. She noticed the Irish pub next door and the Karaoke bar just up the street.

"Hello." The low alto voice was cut off at the end as the static over the intercom grew.

Cassie pressed the button. "Hello, my name is Cassandra Finsbury. I'm looking for Bailey Davenport."

The door swung open when the intercom went dead. "Sorry, I couldn't hear over the static on that damn thing. I'm Bailey Davenport. How can I help you, Ms…?" Bailey held her hand out and smiled.

"Cassandra Finsbury." Cassie shook her hand. "I don't have an appointment. I'm sorry."

Bailey waved away the statement. "No problem. I've got some time right now. I just finished up a case last night. Why don't you come in?"

"Thank you." Cassie stepped toward the doorway but stopped as Bailey looked thoughtful.

"Are you allergic to dogs?"

"No, not at all."

Bailey sighed. "Excellent. Come on in."

She followed Bailey down a short hallway that had been made narrow by a row of filing cabinets along one wall, books and directories of all kinds lined up on top of them in alphabetical order, and on the other wall a giant map of the USA covered the white paint. Cassie decided she liked this organized approach and the use of space left the main office open, light, and airy as Bailey took her seat behind the desk. She pointed to the chair opposite. "Please take a seat. Can I get you a drink? Coffee, tea?"

"A glass of water would be good."

"Sure." Bailey left the room and Cassie allowed herself a moment to gather her thoughts. She noted the diplomas and licenses on the wall behind the desk. There was a huge white board on the wall opposite the desk, and Cassie could imagine Bailey covering it with pictures and images of cases she was working so she could see it all from her desk. There didn't appear to be anything personal in the room though. No family photographs, children's drawings, nothing. She felt something press on her knee and looked down to see a white paw resting on her jeans, a panting dog looked up at her. She smiled as she stroked her head.

"Jazz, back in your bed." The dog turned sorrowful eyes at Bailey but moved away. She threw Bailey one last pitiful look before she dropped onto a large bean cushion bed behind Bailey's desk. "Sorry about her, we're still working on some stuff." Bailey shot the dog a look, who yawned in response.

"No need to apologize. She's lovely."

Bailey handed Cassie her water and took her seat. "So how can I help you, Mrs. Finsbury?"

"Ms. And I'd like you to help me find my daughter."

Bailey picked up a pen and held it poised over her paper. "And your daughter's name is?"

"Daniela Finsbury-Sterling." She pulled some papers from her bag and slid them across the desk to Bailey. "This was what I could find on the Internet. There's information about her, but no address. Not even a state." She shrugged. "I didn't know where to start looking."

Bailey scribbled across her paper. "And you haven't seen her for how long?"

"Almost twenty-five years."

Bailey whistled and looked up. "That's a long time. Why?"

"It's complicated."

"I'm all ears."

"I'm sure, but it's not something I like to talk about." Cassie expected the questions, but she also hoped that cash would override the need to have them all answered.

Bailey frowned. "Okay, but if it's relevant to me finding her now, I need to know."

"It isn't."

Bailey watched her from across the desk and Cassie squirmed under her gaze. She felt those brown eyes examining, studying, dissecting, and then, piece by piece, putting her back together.

"I'm sorry. I don't think I can help you."

"What? Why not? I have money."

Bailey stood and started toward the door as Cassie picked up her papers and stuffed them back in her bag. "It isn't about money. I don't take a job when I don't trust the client. It means I don't know what I'm getting into. If someone won't give me at the very least basic information, then I'm left to assume that they're hiding far more from me than I want to deal with at this point in my life."

"It really isn't relevant anymore."

Bailey held open the door. "You haven't seen your daughter for twenty-five years, but now you want to find her, and you don't think the reason for not seeing her is relevant. Well, in my experience, it's very relevant, and I can't work if I'm being kept in the dark." Bailey sighed. "I'm sorry."

Cassie opened her mouth, but the words wouldn't come out. A chill ran down her spine, and she could feel Daniela slipping through her fingers again. She could see her, feel her, even smell the skin of her small hands reaching for hers, tears running down her face. *Please don't leave me, Mama. I'll be a good girl. Please.* Eyes that had been the image of her own stared at her, begged her, and haunted her every day. She wanted nothing more than to look at her daughter, to tell her she was sorry that she left her. That she wished she could have changed both their lives, but she just couldn't. She hadn't been strong enough. She wanted to explain why she'd stayed away. But there had never, ever been a day she hadn't thought of Daniela. She wanted to tell her there never would be.

But old habits die hard when you've lived on instinct for survival, and fear is a comforting blanket when you've lain beneath it for so long. She closed her eyes and willed the memories and daydreams away.

She gazed up at Bailey as she picked up her purse and felt a pang of regret that she wouldn't get to work with her, but dismissed the thought as soon as it entered her head. She didn't need more empty wishes to waste her time on. "I'm sorry you feel that way." She reached into her purse and pulled out a business card, scribbled Daniela's name on the back, and handed it to Bailey. "In case you change your mind, that's who I'm looking for."

"It's unlikely. I'm sorry." She turned the card over. "Professor Burns." Her frown deepened. "I thought you said your name was Cassandra Finsbury?"

"It is."

"So who is MIT Professor Sandra Burns? Why are you giving me her card?"

"That would also be me." Cassie sighed. "I told you, it's complicated." She walked down the hallway. "Thanks for your time."

The door closed heavily behind her, catching with a resounding thud.

❖

Bailey pushed open the door to her apartment and let Jazz walk in before her. She kicked the door closed and walked down the short corridor. She dropped her bag on the table, shucked her coat, flipped the coffee maker on, and then hit the light switch. The energy saving light bulb flickered into life and slowly built up the level of illumination as Jazz curled herself into the comfy groove on the two-seater sofa.

She glanced at the vast information on her corkboard. It was the reason she spent her life trying to find people who were lost—to reunite families, loved ones, friends. Everyone deserved someone who cared enough to look for them. It was also why she couldn't shake Cassandra Finsbury from her head. Or Sandra Burns, whatever her damn name was. She'd watched the woman battle whatever memories drove her to Bailey's door, and she could see that she wanted to take that final step. But for whatever reason, the strength to do so eluded her. Bailey had seen so many people pull back from the edge and knew there were more reasons for remaining silent than she could ever contemplate. And there were plenty of reasons for changing your name, and Bailey had faced a number of those too.

But the woman she'd sat opposite this morning didn't look like a criminal on the run from the law. She didn't look like a woman who was truly in hiding. She wouldn't be looking for her daughter if she was. Regardless, her past was something she didn't want known, and there were only a limited number of reasons a woman would do that, especially when she was trying to find a part of that past again.

She booted up her laptop and put fresh food out for Jazz before she turned the stereo on. The soul aching sound of Billie Holiday filled the air, and she closed her eyes, letting the music roll over her along with Jazz's less than tuneful appreciation. She laughed out loud and wondered just how long it had been since the walls of her apartment had heard that sound. Longer than she could remember, anyway. Jazz wagged her tail as Bailey continued to chuckle. Such a difference. Less than twenty-four hours, and her cold, lonely apartment had started to feel like a real home. All it took was one stray collie. She selected a frozen dinner without looking at it, stabbed at the plastic film, and tossed it in the microwave.

She opened up various programs and rubbed her chin while she stared at the screen. "I said I wasn't gonna do this, Jazz, yet here I am, staring at the beginning of a missing person search." She looked at the dog, who lifted her head and appeared to be listening intently. "So, why am I?" Jazz whined. "Yeah, yeah, I know you liked her. I liked *her* well enough. That's not the problem." Jazz cocked her head to the side. "Well, see, the problem is that I don't just trust anyone, and I doubly don't when it's so damn obvious they're keeping secrets." Jazz barked. "Sorry, didn't mean to swear." Jazz snuffled a response. "It can't hurt just to take a peek can it? I mean, she did seem really upset when I said I wouldn't help." Jazz wagged her tail. "And it's not like I've got anything better to do right now." She sighed and entered the search terms before leaving to grab her food from the microwave.

When she returned and looked at the screen, she was shocked at the results staring back at her. A newspaper article reported the apparent death of Cassandra Finsbury-Sterling, as the mangled wreck of her car was shown being pulled from the sea. A second newspaper article reported how Daniela Finsbury-Sterling had testified against her father, who was now imprisoned on charges of terrorism.

Bailey let out a long whistle and Jazz barked. "Wow. She said it was complicated, but damn. I should have taken a closer look at those pages she had, hey, girl?" She ruffled the dog's fur and read the articles again. She checked the computer results on Sandra Burns and frowned when the dates didn't make sense. Cassandra had "died" almost twenty-five years ago, but Sandra didn't seem to exist until 2001. "What happened during those missing years? Is that why you're so scared?"

Her mind was running at a hundred miles an hour, trying to filter out the most likely scenarios. Did she fake her own death? If so, why? What made her leave her daughter in the UK and come to the States? She didn't speak like a Brit, so was she from the US originally? If she didn't fake her own death, who did? If they did, was she held captive during those missing years?

She ran a check on Sandra Burns's identity. Everything looked solid. Driver's license, passport, credit cards, everything was in place. But how did a woman who hadn't published anything before 2001, and didn't have experience in teaching, land a plum job at MIT?

Bailey tapped her fingers on the desk. There were more questions than answers, and Bailey knew she wouldn't be able to rest without at least a few of those answers. "I'm not even working the damn case. This is crazy." Jazz put a paw on her thigh. "I know, I should have thought of that before I started the first damn search, but you saw how sad she looked." Bailey laughed. "I'm talking to you like you're gonna answer me. Maybe the problem is that I need a little company." Jazz growled and Bailey laughed again. "Oh, are you the jealous sort, little miss?" She stroked her head again. "Don't worry. It's been a long time, and that's not likely to change. I'm forty-nine years old and too long in the tooth for changing, too prickly for keeping. So I guess it's just you and me, girl."

She picked up the phone. "It can't hurt to make a phone call, can it?" She punched in the number and sighed when it went to voicemail. She left a message after the beep and looked at some more of the details on Daniela. She scanned the article for a location. *Looks like Cassie was right, no address.* It was missing on every document she could find about the court case. *Oh, that smells more than a little bit suspicious to me.* The phone rang. She smiled when she checked caller ID.

"That was quick, Sean."

"Well, it's been six months since you last called. I figured your place must be burning down or some shit."

Bailey laughed. "Yeah, yeah, bite me. My phone hasn't exactly been ringing off the hook either."

"Life gets busy, darlin'. You know how it is."

"I do. Everything okay, buddy?"

"Same shit, different set of bad guys."

"Ain't that the truth."

"You just wanna shoot the shit, or you got somethin' I can help ya with?"

"You never change, Sean. Straight to the point."

"It's why ya love me, baby."

Bailey laughed. They'd been partners for four years in the FBI, and it was indeed one of the reasons they had worked so well together. Sean didn't take bullshit, and he didn't hand it out. He was a good cop, a good man, and a good friend. "I'm looking for someone, but everything I find is too clean."

"A perp?"

"No. I've got someone looking for a family member. Long lost kinda shit. You know?"

"And?"

"Well, I can find info, but there're no locations. Anywhere."

"You tried DMV?"

"I'd be shooting in the dark right now. I don't even have a state."

"Got ya. So what do you think I can do?"

"I'm wondering if this has been cleaned professionally."

"I'll check in house for ya, but it could be a different company."

"I know."

"Do you have a contact over there?"

"No."

"I'll see what I can do."

"Thanks, Sean. I appreciate it." She gave him Daniela's name. "There's something else I'd like you to run while you're at it."

"What's that?"

"Cassandra Finsbury and Sandra Burns."

"What about them?"

"Can you just run the names and see what pops up for me?"

"You getting mysterious in your old age, Bailey?"

"Not trying to be, trying to figure one out. I don't want to lead you in a direction if I'm wrong."

"No sweat. I'll call you."

"Thanks."

She took a seat on the sofa and smiled when Jazz rolled over and offered her belly. She slowly stroked the dog's tummy and tried to focus on Daniela and the problem of locating her, but her mind continued to drift back to Cassandra. She thought about the heartbreaking decision she had made to leave her daughter behind—and more and more she felt that it had been Cassandra's decision but one she was forced to make. She could see clearly in her eyes that she had loved her daughter. She wondered at the strength it had taken her to walk away and stay away for so long. She kept thinking of Cassandra's face, time and again. Those dark green eyes, the long auburn hair, dashed with shots of gray at the temples, and the diminutive frame cried out to be protected, not hunted. She picked up the business card.

"To be fair, Professor, you've done a damn good job of protecting yourself recently, so maybe I don't know what the hell I'm talking about."

The dog whined.

"Thanks, but you really didn't need to agree quite so quickly." Jazz rested her head on Bailey's thigh. She turned the picture toward her. "What do you think?" Jazz lifted her head and panted as Bailey stroked her head. "Yeah, you're right. She's pretty." Bailey laughed. "Actually, she's beautiful." She sighed. "And a puzzle." She stared at her corkboard. "And I'm a sucker for a puzzle."

# CHAPTER SEVEN

Oz pulled her gun from her waistband and checked the peephole. Andrew Whittaker stood outside; a second man had his back to the door, apparently watching the hallway. "Show me your ID, gentlemen."

Whittaker grumbled as he fished in his pocket. "You know me."

"I know a blond-haired Andrew Whittaker." She checked his credentials carefully, more to yank his chain than from any real concern. "What's with the dye job?"

"Blond makes me stand out like a sore thumb. I thought I'd blend in better for this job with the darker hair."

"You two could pass for brothers now." Oz opened the door and pointed to the second man. He was average height, average build, medium brown hair, nondescript features, and fairly small brown eyes. He had no outstanding features, no distinguishing marks or scars. He was someone you'd have a hard time remembering or describing if you ever saw him anywhere. He could be anyone and anywhere from twenty-five to forty-five. Hell, put some fake tan on him and he could look Arabic or Mexican. *Perfect spook.* His ID read Stephen Knight. She liked the name. There was something powerful about it—noble, even. *Let's see if you're as noble as your name.*

He was one of the many, many faces who had interviewed, or rather interrogated, Finn after their ordeal six weeks ago. If not for his name she probably wouldn't have remembered him at all. He was immensely forgettable in every way.

"Ms. Zuckerman, it's a pleasure to meet you again." He held his hand out.

Oz shook his hand. "Mr. Knight."

"We weren't expecting to see you here today. I was under the impression that Daniela would be here alone," Knight said.

"Never gonna happen. We're here to stay."

"I don't think that's the best course of action for this mission. It would be better if you and your family went back to Florida and left this to us."

Oz laughed. "I say again. Never gonna happen."

"Look, Ms. Zuckerman, all I've got to do is make a phone call and you'll be out of here anyway. Make it easy on all of us and save yourself a trip to the cells, book a flight and go home."

"Go ahead. Call whoever you want. This has been cleared way above your pay grade."

He smirked at her. "We'll just see about that." He pulled his cell out of his pocket and turned his back on her. After only seconds of conversation, the relaxed set of his shoulders vanished and he turned back to her, offering an insincere smile as he hung up. "Please call me Stephen. It seems we'll be working together on this project. No need to be formal."

Not fooled for an instant but willing to take the olive branch when offered, Oz nodded. "Then I'm Oz." She pointed to Junior. "This is Lieutenant Commander Charles Zuckerman Junior."

He held out his hand. "Just call me Junior." Knight shook his hand and nodded.

"This is my father, Captain William Zuckerman."

"Billy."

"And, Daniela, a pleasure to see you again."

"Like I told you last time we met, call me Finn." She held out her hand and smiled.

He returned the smile and looked around the room. "There's certainly a lotta stripes around here." Knight glanced at Oz. "And your rank is?"

"Was. I was a commander." Oz smiled as Finn stepped beside her and wrapped her arm around her waist.

"Like I said, a lotta stripes in this room."

"What can we do for you today, Mr. Knight?" Finn asked, determined to remain professional and not give in to the games that he seemed more than willing to play. She had a job to focus on, and she didn't need playground antics to distract her.

"There's been another death in the scientific community, and our source indicates that Mehalik has turned his sights on you, Finn."

"Shit," Oz said.

"Who?" Finn asked.

"I'm sorry?" Knight frowned.

"Who did he kill?"

"A Swedish scientist living and working in London, a Dr. Siegfried Jensen."

Finn sank onto the couch and let her head fall to her chest. "I knew him."

"How?" Oz rested her hand on Finn's back.

"He was a teacher of mine at university. I even met his wife at a fund-raising function once. She must be heartbroken. Can I get a message to her?"

"I'm sorry, no. She's also dead."

"What?"

Finn's voice was quiet, and Oz tightened her arm around her waist when she felt her sag against her. She knew Finn felt the news like a body blow and wished she could ease the pain she must be feeling. Fear crept up her spine as she considered how stupid it was to take on this mission. They were going up against a madman who thought nothing of killing innocent people. She didn't want to think about what he would do to them if he caught them, but she couldn't stop herself. The scenarios played over and over in her mind.

"As are their children. We believe Mehalik was attempting to persuade Jensen to create Balor and used the family as leverage. His refusal cost them all their lives."

"One of the classes he taught was ethics. He was a good man."

"I'm sorry."

"So I'm his next target. Does he know where I am?"

"Not currently. He has his people watching your home in Florida and the shop. You left just in time to evade them."

"How do you know so much about what he's up to?" Junior asked.

Knight smiled. "We have an informant close to Mehalik. He approached MI6 a few weeks ago, and in exchange for his family's safety, he's giving us information."

"How close is he to Mehalik, and how good has his information been so far? Do we have a picture of Mehalik yet? Lord knows that would be a damn useful bit of intel."

"He was Mehalik's bodyguard, but there's been a shift in structure in the last couple of weeks, and now he's one of Mehalik's commanders. And no. We still don't have a current picture of the man. He's wary of technology. Paranoid, really."

Billy scoffed. "Well, you tell him that's the first piece of intel we want."

"You said commanders, right? You make it sound like some sort of paramilitary organization." Junior folded his arms.

"It is. Mehalik is a general in the Hamas organization."

"Wait a minute. Pritchard said my dad had links to al-Qaeda. Now you're telling me it's Hamas. Make your minds up. What the hell are we involved with here?"

"Mehalik is a Palestinian Arab. He's a General in Hamas. And he's had arms dealings with al-Qaeda. It was a logical conclusion at that time to assume he was brokering a deal between Sterling and the al-Qaeda. He isn't."

"And this comes from your source?" Oz asked.

"Yes."

"And how do you know you can trust this source?" Junior asked.

"It was corroborated independently by an intelligence officer we have undercover in an al-Qaeda stronghold."

"Where?" Billy ran a hand over the scraggy stubble covering his jaw then up through his shaggy blond hair. Oz found the difference in her retired and now slightly scruffy looking dad so different from the regimented and impeccable dad she had grown up with during his military career. She'd asked him about it once, and his enigmatic smile and instructions to ask her mother about it were more than enough for her to leave it alone and enjoy the softer, more relaxed side to her father.

"I can't give you that information."

"Then how are we supposed to—"

"The information we've been given by our informant has been sound and verified every step of the way. He's earned my trust."

"Do we get to meet him?" Billy asked.

"Probably. If things progress as we plan, you'll meet with Mehalik, and our informant will be at the meeting." He reached into his pocket. "This flash drive has intel on Mehalik and the PLO so you can bring yourselves up to speed on the situation. There's also the research we retrieved from Dr. Lyell's servers about Balor." He held it out for Finn to take. "Do you think you can re-create it?"

"Yes. That isn't what I'm worried about."

"What is?"

"Creating the vaccine."

"There's also research in the files about that."

"I know. But from what I saw last time, the vaccine that Lyell created wasn't stable, and transmission was limited to intravenous injection. To eradicate the threat of Balor, that just isn't enough. You may as well call it Gamble for how effective it is."

"We don't plan on Balor getting out there, so a widespread vaccine won't be necessary, Finn."

"Mr. Knight, I never thought that the protocol I devised could be used in the way it has been, so please forgive me if I'm now more than a little cautious in just what it could do. I studied to help people, not kill them. I was trying to cure cancer, for Christ's sake. Why can't we pretend that I've created what he wants and use a placebo to get him to come to me? Then we know Balor can't fall into his hands."

"No," Knight and Whittaker said at the same time.

"Mehalik has a scientist with him who will verify all the samples you give him at the proper time." Whittaker continued. "He made your father prove this thing every step of the way. He might not make you jump through some of the same hoops because he knows that you're the one creating it, but he will verify that this is real before he does the deal."

"Without the deal, we can't prosecute him and make it stick," Knight said.

"And with a placebo you won't make it out of the meeting alive," Whittaker added.

"Can you create something that will pass his tests but then die off, or something?" Oz asked.

Finn ran her fingers through her hair, her frown deepening. "I don't see how. The beauty of this bacterium is that E. coli is so resistant and so easily communicable that it's impossible to kill prior to replication. Once it replicates, it's already spreading."

"Finn, I can see how uncomfortable you are with this." Knight looked her in the eye. "I promise you, this will not get out there."

"You can't make me that kind of guarantee, Mr. Knight."

"Yes, I can." He smiled charmingly. "I'm a well trained U.S. operative with the nation's security at stake. There is nothing I won't do to make sure this is contained."

"Those are nice words, Mr. Knight, but I say again. You can't make that kind of guarantee. No one can. You're telling me that the only way to stop this man is to create a bacterium capable of destroying life as we know it on this planet."

"I know that."

"Do you?"

He nodded.

"Really? Because I don't think you do. So before we go any further let's make damn sure we all know exactly what we're talking about, shall we?" She waited for him to respond, relieved to see that he was intensely focused on her. "This bacteria will spread across the globe within a month of being released anywhere, and right now there is nothing to stand in its way. There is no vaccine, no antidote, and no treatment. Once you contract it you've got about four days before you show symptoms. Muscle weakness, fatigue, paralysis, and severe, increasing pain. All of them progressively getting worse, until you drown in your own saliva because you can no longer make yourself swallow or your heart becomes paralyzed in your chest. Of the two options, I'd probably choose that death. At least it's quicker. If you are one of the unlucky one percent who don't die from this, each symptom you develop is yours for the rest of your life."

"It can't be that bad," Whittaker said.

"Yes, it is, Agent Whittaker. It is every bit that bad. And you want me to make this, to capture a bad guy."

"Are you sure we can't fake it?" Junior asked.

"I'm sure I can't create a fake good enough to pass a test and be harmless afterward."

"It will be tested," Knight said. "Have no doubt about it."

"And he is coming for you," Whittaker reminded her.

"I don't really care about that, Agent Whittaker. I'd rather die than see this fall into his hands."

"He'd take pleasure in arranging that." Whittaker stood at the edge of the room glaring at her.

"What the hell kind of crap are you trying to pull?" Billy confronted him as the rest of the Zuckermans in the room bristled.

Finn shuddered. "It's okay. I'm well aware of that, but that still wouldn't end the threat would it? If you don't get him, he will just move on to the next scientist, then the next until he finally finds someone to create Balor. He knows it can be done now. It's only a matter of time. If I let him come for me and refuse him, knowing full well that he'll kill me for it, then I can't control anything that happens beyond that. If I create Balor, I control it."

"And thereby we control him." Knight nodded.

"Isn't that what Frankenstein thought when he created his monster?" Billy asked.

"Frankenstein made the mistake of giving his monster a brain, Billy. Balor won't be so well endowed."

"It doesn't need to be."

"Do you have another option for me?" She'd wracked her brain, but she couldn't think of any other way, though if any of the military minds around her could come up with any other option, she'd gladly take it.

"I say we just shoot the fucker." Junior leaned against the wall.

"Not an option," Whittaker said.

"Why not?"

"We don't know where he is, for one thing—"

"Get your inside man to give you a location."

"And he is a high-ranking Hamas terrorist. He has information that could be vital to bringing terrorists to justice, thwarting other terrorism plans, and maybe even bringing a lasting peace to the area." Whittaker finished with his arms folded over his chest.

Junior shook his head. "That's an awful lot of ifs, buts, and fucking maybes to be pinning on one psycho, buddy."

"We have reliable information—"

"Yeah, yeah, we know. Save it for someone who doesn't know how the game's played."

"Well, gentlemen, if there are no other options for me, I guess I'm left with nothing but bad choices," She looked at Knight again. "If you want me to create this vile thing to flush him out, then so be it. But I won't do it without creating a failsafe to make it harmless."

Whittaker frowned. "Meaning?"

"I want to make the vaccine much more reliable."

Knight smiled. "I wish there were more people like you out there. But then I'd be out of a job." He chuckled. "I just hope we have the time."

"I'm starting work in the morning. I'll make time."

"Which brings me to my next point. We need to make sure that you're seen as taking over Sterling Enterprises. We need Mehalik to think he has a chance of doing business with you, or he'll attempt to kidnap you and coerce you. And that makes our plan a lot harder to pull off."

Finn clasped Oz's hand and squeezed. "I know."

Oz tried to focus on Finn's thumb rubbing soothing circles over the back of her hand. It was the only way she could ignore the rising fear inside her. She wanted to take Finn away from every kind of danger. She wanted to protect her. Just so that she could love her for the rest of their lives. Instead, they were heading into a situation more dangerous than Oz had ever faced, with an untrained civilian she loved with all her heart, and she wasn't certain she could protect. It went against every instinct she had.

"So when's the big unveiling?" Finn asked.

"I was thinking Friday night. There's a fundraising gala at Rockefeller Center. Black tie. And the CEO of Sterling Enterprises has tickets."

"What's the charity?"

"The Children's Cancer Charity. Huge event, and it fits perfectly with the research you were doing."

Oz had to admit it was the perfect event for Finn to make her first appearance as the new CEO of Sterling Enterprises. The multi-billion dollar company incorporated everything from property development and BioTech laboratories, to software development, oil, gas, and alternative energy. The business was huge, and Finn was now at the head of it. It was true that auditors were still combing the books looking for the monies laundered from his illegal practices, and share prices had taken a massive hit since William Sterling had been imprisoned, but the company was big enough to weather the storm. If Finn wanted it, it was all hers. *If* she wanted it. Oz suspected that when this was all over, she would be more than happy to sell it all.

Finn looked at Oz. "Looks like we're going to the ball, Cinders."

"Cinders?"

"Cinderella. Don't tell me you didn't go to a pantomime as a kid?"

"Pantomime? I may have been forced to watch the Disney movie." She pointed at Billy. "He let Mom try to turn me into a girl until I was at least six. What the hell's a pantomime?"

Finn kissed the tip of her nose. "I'll tell you later."

Oz shuddered. *What the hell is it about her and that accent that turns my knees to Jell-O?*

## CHAPTER EIGHT

Bailey tossed and turned. She'd thrown the covers off and woken up shivering, although her feet were the only thing not frozen, as Jazz was using them for a pillow. It'd been four days since Cassandra Finsbury had walked into her office, and she hadn't been able to think of anything else. She was still waiting for Sean to get back to her, and the waiting was driving her crazy. She got up, pulled on a pair of sweats and sneakers, and clipped Jazz's leash to her collar.

"Come on, girl. Let's see if I can walk off some of this excess energy." At five in the morning, the streets were deserted but for the newspaper van delivering to the kiosk at the corner and the bakery tantalizing her with delicious aromas. She stopped in for coffee and picked up a croissant. She loved the early morning, when the day was still so fresh with possibilities and unblemished with the events yet to unfold. She breathed in the air of a city just beginning to waken and let her feet lead the way. There was no direction in mind, no deadline to make, just the peace and solitude to enjoy.

"See, Jazz? This is the life." She picked off a bit of her croissant and held it out for the dog. "Good girl." She smiled, thinking how strange it was that Jazz had become such a big part of her life so quickly. She'd never thought about having a dog before, because she didn't have the time, or the lifestyle, that would accommodate a pet. Besides, she'd had enough to worry about without adding the responsibility of another life to care for.

She crossed the Charles River as she wandered farther and farther from home while the sun chased the night from the sky. The blackness gave way to gentle pastel shades. Before she realized it, they were crossing in front of MIT, with its imposing column frontage and domed roof. She shook her head.

"The brain's a damn tricky thing, Jazz. You know that, right?"

Jazz whined and gave a little bark.

"Oh, so you knew already? Well, I guess that makes you the brains of this outfit." She checked her watch. Seven forty-five. She wondered what time Cassandra would get here. "Might as well wait around and find her since I've obviously changed my mind."

She made her way slowly to the student services desk and asked where she might find Professor Burns. The receptionist gave her directions to her office.

"But she doesn't hold office hours until three today. She's scheduled to give lectures all morning."

"What time's the first one?"

"At eight."

"Can you tell me where? I only need to see her for a moment."

"Why are you looking for her again?"

Bailey waved a pen drive that she always had attached to her key ring. "My daughter's in her class and she has to hand in this assignment. She's sick and doesn't want it to be late. I'm on my way back to take care of her as soon as I give this to the professor."

The woman held out her hand. "I can make sure she gets it."

*Shit.* "I know, but the professor has done so much for my daughter, I wanted to thank her too." She offered what she hoped was a sincere smile. "In person, you know?"

"We don't normally—"

"I know, but I'd be ever so grateful. Jazz has just gone on and on about her since they met. I'd really like to hand this in to her personally. I know Jazz will rest easier knowing that I can say I gave it to her." Bailey wanted to laugh. It was the first thing that came to mind, and it certainly amused her. "Please."

"Okay. But only because your daughter's sick." She gave her the directions. "I hope she feels better soon. I think I know Jazz. She's a lovely girl."

"She is. I'll pass on your regards." Bailey sniggered to herself as she made her way down the hall.

# CHAPTER NINE

"Professor Burns, do you have a moment?"

Cassie turned and smiled at the young woman. "Sure, what can I do for you, Cara?"

"I've been applying for internships over the summer and I have to send a letter of recommendation in with the application. I was wondering—"

"When do you need the letter?"

"Tomorrow."

"Tomorrow? Why didn't you come to me earlier?"

"I only got the application form yesterday. Sterling BioTech was really late in putting out the positions."

Cassie's heart beat a little faster, as it always did at the mention of her ex-husband's company. It wasn't the first time she'd written a student recommendation for Sterling BioTech, because it was one of the closest research facilities to MIT and many students applied for internships there with a hope of securing a position after their graduation. Previously, she had had nightmares that William would see the name Sandra Burns and somehow know it was her. She knew it was a ludicrous fear. He would have nothing to do with the day-to-day running of the laboratories, and there would be no way for him to know who she was. There was no reason for him to even look for Sandra Burns. This time her heart beat faster for a different reason. With William behind bars, who was heading Sterling Enterprises?

"I know it's a lot to ask, Professor, but I'd really appreciate it if you could."

Cassie checked her watch. "I have an hour free at three. Come see me at four and I'll have it for you."

"Thanks, Professor Burns. You're the best."

She liked Cara, the girl showed promise, and she was happy to help, but she didn't want to be inundated with requests she wouldn't be able to fulfill. "Don't go telling your friends. I don't have the time to be doing this for a whole class full today."

"My lips are sealed. Thank you."

Cassie walked down the long corridor to the lecture hall, unable to stop thinking about Sterling Enterprises. More than thirty years ago, she had been instrumental in the business's inauspicious beginnings.

Without the funding from her father, William would never have been able to buy the properties that had begun the avalanche. Property, computers, telecommunications, a bank, the laboratories, it had all come so easily to him. He had coveted the money and the power, and he had reveled in his success, leaving nothing behind of the young man who had charmed her before she had even had the chance to question what she wanted from life. She had thought she loved him when she agreed to marry him. She had berated herself so many times over the years for her foolishness, her naivety, and her desperate desire for love. She was in love with the idea of love, not the man. It wasn't until she'd met Karen that she had realized why she was so unhappy, so unfulfilled, and so lonely. Loving Karen was the irresistible force her romantic heart had yearned for.

She'd asked herself more than once if it had been her actions that had turned William into the greedy, power-driven man he had become, but she knew the signs had already been there. The need to be greater, better, richer, than anyone around him. The aggressive competitor who was ready to rip out the throat of his adversary was a part of the man he had hidden from her when they met, but it hadn't stayed hidden very long. And by the time she left, she knew that it wasn't only in the boardroom where he'd tear out throats. Nothing and no one would stand in the way of William Sterling.

"Professor?"

Cassie turned and her heart felt like it would pummel its way out of her chest. "Ms. Davenport. What are you doing here?"

"Well, it's not a burning desire to learn neurothingymawhatsits."

Cassie smiled. "I can point you to a class about ethics that's about to start in the other auditorium. You should be fine there."

"Thanks." Bailey smiled. "But I think I'll still pass."

"So what are you doing here?"

"I came to say that I think I've changed my mind."

"You think?"

Bailey shrugged. "Yeah. Any chance we can meet later and have a chat?"

"We can, but I can't tell you any more today than I could on Friday. I thought you said you couldn't work like that? That you didn't trust me." She looked over her shoulder quickly, checking that the hallway was empty.

"Maybe you can't tell me anymore, but perhaps I know a little bit more than I did then."

"And what is it that you think you know, Ms. Davenport?"

"That a mother, who loves her child enough to try to find her after twenty-five years, doesn't leave that child without a damn good reason. Especially not like this." She pulled the printout of the newspaper article from her pocket and handed it to her.

Cassie felt the blood drain from her face and her vision faded until all she could see was the mangled wreck of her old car. The twisted metal and rubber still dripped seawater, and the windscreen was cracked. She shivered and Bailey held her hand out like she was getting ready to catch her.

"Hey, I'm sorry. Are you okay?"

Cassie handed her back the page. "I'm fine." Her legs felt rubbery and she feared they'd give way beneath her.

"You sure? You don't look fine."

Cassie waved her off. "It was a shock." She pointed to the page. "Seeing that. That's all."

"I'm sorry. But I understand you have a class to go to, and you don't have time for long explanations." She shrugged. "This seemed like the best way."

"It's fine."

"So will you meet me?"

"When?"

"This afternoon. Wherever you want."

"I have office hours till five. I can meet you at a coffee shop after that."

"Perfect."

Cassie gave her the name and address of the coffee shop and watched her walk away, her gut twisting into knots. *I wanted her to find Daniela. I'm not stupid. I knew if she started she'd find stuff about me. So why the hell does this feel like a huge mistake?*

She pulled open the door and walked into the auditorium. "Good morning, class." She placed her bag on the desk and smiled up at the rows of filled seats. "Today we are looking at the synaptic pathways of the brain and central nervous system. I trust you have all completed the recommended reading. So I will begin."

# CHAPTER TEN

Finn stared at the computer screen. The three-dimensional molecular model rotated slowly as she examined the structure, looking for the weak point, the instability. The protein base for the modified toxin was already in production, and Lyell's original vaccine— or Gamble as Finn had continued to refer to it—was sitting in the fridge. But she wasn't happy with it. His test results showed a less than fifty percent success rate. As far as she was concerned, that wasn't a vaccine— it was a game of Russian roulette. She switched screens and stared at the swirling molecules of the toxin.

Mehalik was expecting a toxin that was built inside a stomach bug, so that's what he'd get. He'd also get the vials of the vaccine that Lyell had created, again as he expected. What she was planning to do, though, was create her own vaccine. Her vaccine would effectively immunize those who hadn't come into contact with Balor, and help those who were infected to fight it off. Just in case the worst should happen. She needed a fast, efficient transportation system that was capable of spreading faster than Balor, but was harmless on its own. And preferably one that was overlooked and resistant to medications. The common cold was the perfect host. Vaccine and antidote all rolled into one, beautiful set of sneezes, and one she would release as soon as it was ready. Once her cold virus had spread, Balor would never be a threat again.

That was the theory, anyway.

The door opened and Billy walked in. He put a sandwich and a cup of coffee on her desk and sat opposite her.

"Thanks." She sipped the coffee and frowned at him. "You okay?"

"I would be if I was getting enough sleep."

"Why aren't you sleeping? Something bothering you?"

"Yeah. Sleeping in a damn chair." He laughed. "I'm too old for that shit, Finn. When are we going back to the apartment to get a decent night's sleep? It's been three days, and you haven't left this office for more than four hours." He sipped his own coffee. "Junior can keep going like this, but my old butt's draggin' on the floor right about now."

Finn laughed at the image, but she also knew he would keep going until he dropped dead if he had to. He wouldn't let down his team, especially when that team was his family, but she was happy enough to play along. "I'm sorry, Billy. Why don't you go on home? We'll be fine."

Billy stared at her from under grizzled eyebrows.

Finn sighed. "Okay, fine. I'll finish up here and we can go. About an hour. Think you can last that long?"

"I'll manage." He started to get up.

"Billy?"

"Yeah."

"Can I ask you something?"

"Anything, darlin'."

"Before this happened, I don't know if Oz told you, but I was trying to find my mum."

"She told me. Said that you got some stuff off your daddy's computer that might have given you a place to start."

"It did. A few years ago, he actually traced my mum and her girlfriend to a place called Glens Falls in upstate New York. He found out that they had adopted different names and he found Karen's grave. She'd been dead since two thousand and one. But there was no sign of my mum there under either name, and no sign of her since. I've tried everywhere I can think of to look. I even tried a couple of tricks that Pete showed me a few years ago to check both names through DMV records and stuff."

"You went hacking, young lady?"

Finn shrugged. "Little bit."

Billy chuckled. "And you still couldn't find her."

"No."

"She may have changed her name again."

"I thought of that, but I don't think there's any way I could find that out. So I was trying everything I could." She laughed derisively. "I even checked the death registry."

"Nothing there either?"

"No. I've got to say I'm glad about that. Until I started thinking that maybe she didn't have ID on her and she is dead, but she's a Jane Doe." Finn let the tears roll down her cheeks. "If that's the case I want to find her so that I can bury her. Give her a gravestone." She reached into her drawer and pulled out a DNA profile. "It's mine." She handed it to him. "Maybe you can…"

He took the profile and came around the desk. He wrapped his arms around her shoulders. "If she's anywhere like that, I'll find her. You leave it with me, darlin'. If she has changed her name though, this won't help."

"I know. But I'll know I did everything I could." Finn pulled away from him and wiped her eyes. "Sorry, Billy, all I seem to do lately is cry."

"Don't you worry about that. There's a ton of reasons for crying, and you've got a whole bunch of 'em right now. I happen to think you're pretty amazing, doing what you're doing with all this mumbo jumbo." He waved his hand at the screen.

"I wish I didn't know anything about this mumbo jumbo, Billy. If I'd never started this then we wouldn't have Balor to worry about and the world would be a safer place."

"You think?"

Finn nodded.

"Want to know what I think?"

Finn didn't say anything. She just waited for him to continue. She knew he was going to tell her that it wasn't her fault, and that she'd had nothing but good intentions when she started her work. She'd heard it before from all of them. She'd tried to convince herself of that fact when she first found out about Balor. It didn't work then, and she doubted that it would work now.

"You're probably right."

Her jaw dropped and she felt herself sag in her chair.

"If you hadn't worked on your idea, this fella, Lyell, he wouldn't have been able to make this bloody thing. He wasn't smart enough to do it on his own. But he wasn't stupid either. He could have come up with something else when your daddy pushed him. Something that could be just as dangerous—I don't know, maybe even more dangerous—than this little tummy bug. And that something wouldn't be as easy for you to fix, now would it? You wouldn't have all these pictures already here to help you make the vaccine, and stop this from being so dangerous." He crossed his arms over his chest. "Hell, you wouldn't even know enough of this mumbo jumbo to do anything about it at all. We'd all be stuck in the hands of someone we didn't know, didn't trust, and who might not know as much mumbo-jumbo as you do. So maybe it's time to stop fretting about what's done and get on with fixing it."

He was right. What's done was done and there was no way to undo any of it now. All she could do now was make the best out of the situation and finish this off once and for all.

"You know, Billy, I wish you'd been my dad."

Billy laughed. "No, you don't. That would make Oz your sister."

"Oh God, that's just sick."

"Everything okay in here?" Oz stood in the doorway of the office.

"Surely is, Ladyfish. Finn here was just telling me that we'll be heading home for a good meal and a decent night's sleep in an hour or so."

"Great. Anyone have any preference for takeout?"

"Pizza," Finn said.

"Sounds good to me. Let me know when you're almost done and we can place the order." She smiled and crossed the room to drop a kiss on Finn's head. Finn grabbed her hand and pulled her in for another, their lips meeting in a quick kiss, just to connect.

"I love you." Finn smiled into Oz's big blue eyes.

"I love you too, baby." Oz frowned. "You sure you're okay?"

"I am. I just have a lot of work to do, and I don't know how much time I have to do it in."

"How long did it take you to create the protocol originally?"

"Three years. I pretty much started on it as soon as I finished my studies."

Oz's eyes widened. "Well, I'm pretty sure we don't have that much time."

"I know. But at least this time I have a blueprint."

"Baby, I know these guys are putting a lot of pressure on you, but if you can't do this—"

"I can. And they aren't putting nearly as much pressure on me as I am."

"Damn stubborn woman."

Finn snorted. "Look who's talking." She kissed her again quickly. "Now shoo, let me finish up today so that we can get pizza before midnight."

Finn turned back to her notes. She punched a series of numbers into the simulation model in the computer and waited for it to generate the data.

## CHAPTER ELEVEN

M asood slid the door closed behind him as he stepped out onto the aft deck of the *Ataba and Zarief E-ttool*. The breeze blew off the Red Sea and cooled his sun-warmed skin. He breathed in deeply, loving the smell of the sea. It felt clean, fresh, and full of life, unlike the dusty, barren, and often acrid stench that had been constant companions throughout his childhood growing up in Gaza where the rubble of martyrs' homes were his playground and color of concrete dust was only broken by the claret of spilled blood.

"General Mehalik, telephone." The young Arab boy held the cell phone out to him. Masood picked up the handset using his sleeve and disconnected the call. He put one hand on the back of the boy's neck and pulled him close.

"Hasan, we have spoken of this before. What are you supposed to do when a call comes for me?" He spoke quietly and flipped the back off the phone letting it fall into the water, the battery followed with a small splash.

"I am sorry, General. I forgot." The boy shivered beside him, and Masood smiled. He let go of him, pulled the SIM card from the phone, and dropped them both into the Red Sea.

"Next time you will not forget to take a number and bring me a clean, untraceable phone. Will you, Hasan?" He slapped the boy hard across the face and watched him stumble and fall to the dark mahogany deck.

"No, General. I will remember in the future. I swear it."

"Good. Who was on the phone?"

The boy climbed back to his feet. "It was Hakim, sir."

He nodded. "Go fetch me a phone."

The boy's bare feet slapped on the deck of the fifty-foot yacht as he ran to do Masood's bidding, returning quickly with a burner phone.

"Go and tell the captain that we will be moving position in five minutes."

"Yes, General."

Masood turned his back on the boy and dialed the number for Hakim Qandri. His onetime bodyguard was his most trusted ally in the fight against the Zionists and all those who supported them in their land theft, and the war they had waged on the Arabs of Palestine for more than sixty blood-drenched years.

"Hakim, my friend, tell me you have good news."

"I wish I could, General. There is no movement at the address you gave me. It appears empty."

"For how long?" Not the news Masood wanted to hear. He rubbed a hand down his face, fingertips brushing the edges of the ragged scar on his left cheek.

"Unknown at this point. I have been watching the house for three days now and there has been nothing. I have even been to her work address."

"No sign there either?"

"Nothing."

"I will check my sources and get back to you."

"Understood."

Masood disconnected and called another number. He left a message before destroying the phone and dumping it overboard.

"Where to, General?" the boat's captain asked.

"To the marina in Eilat. I have business to attend to."

"Very good, sir."

He hated the Israelis, but he loved living under their very noses while he planned the attack that would avenge the millions who had died in the conflict. He would avenge his brother, as he'd promised. He went over every fact he knew about his target. Every detail of her life had been documented by her own father for so many years that all he had to do was follow the trail. But it seemed she'd detoured from the path. And that was not acceptable. She was crucial to his plan and had been from the very beginning, but he was patient. Soon Daniela Finsbury-Sterling would be working on his project for him. One way or another.

## CHAPTER TWELVE

Bailey checked her watch again and realized she still had almost an hour before Cassandra was due to arrive. She parked around the back of the café and retrieved the vest she'd bought for Jazz. She knew she was pushing her luck, but she couldn't stand the thought of leaving Jazz tied up outside and her ending up as a bait dog again. The idea of it upset her so much that she was willing to set aside her discomfort at the fib she was going to portray as she slipped the vest on Jazz and proclaimed her to the world as a service dog. She hadn't quite decided what service Jazz was going to offer her, but she'd cross that bridge if she came to it.

Leash in hand, she pushed open the door to the café where she was due to meet Cassie and walked confidently to the counter. *Act like it's normal, and everyone will assume it is.* She ordered a coffee, sat down, and looked through the notes she'd brought as Jazz settled herself under the table, head resting on Bailey's foot. Her phone rang as the waitress put her coffee down.

"Took you long enough. What'd you have to do, hack the databases yourself?"

"Very funny. I had to call in all kinds of favors to get this info for you. You owe me for this."

"We'll take it off the tab, Sean."

"I'm serious, Bailey. This is some heavy shit. How the fuck are you involved in it?"

"A client came to me trying to find a long lost family member. Daniela Finsbury-Sterling. That's it."

"There ain't no way I can get you a location on her. She's zipped up tighter than a nun's wahoo, and asking about her has got red flags popping all over the goddamned place. The only thing I got, and I do mean the only thing, is that she's being watched."

"By who?"

"You name it, and they got letters."

"Why?"

"I can't tell you that."

"Come on, Sean. I'm not asking for state secrets here."

"I can't tell you, because I don't know. She testified against her old man. That was huge shit. He was brokering weapons deals with terrorists, biological weapons. Now, she's taken over the company, and everyone and their dog wants to know what the hell she's up to. That's all I know."

"She's taken over Sterling Enterprises?" The hairs on the back of her neck stood on end. Bailey found the thought disconcerting. She'd looked into William Sterling extensively when she started looking into Cassandra's case. The company was huge, and at the center of a biological weapons scandal. It didn't sit easily with her.

"Hell yeah."

"Shit." Bailey turned over what the possibilities of that could mean. Did it mean Daniela was taking over from her father in every way, or was this a legitimate business takeover? Did she shop Daddy to the authorities to take over the empire, or was there more going on? "She's being watched? Like not trusted watched, or like she's working for the company watched?"

"Don't know. I got told to back my butt out of the situation and not look around."

Bailey rubbed her hand over her face. That didn't help either way. "Okay, if you do hear anything else, let me know."

"I told you. I'm not involved."

"I know. Just in case."

"Right. Those other names you gave me were a dead end."

"What do you mean?"

"Cassandra Finsbury-Sterling died 'bout twenty-five years ago. And Professor Sandra Burns works at MIT. There's some whispers about a research project she's working on for the CIA, but that's all. Can't get access to her file. It's way above my pay grade."

"She's a neuroscientist. What could she be working on for the CIA?"

"How the fuck am I supposed to know? Do I look like some kind of fucking genius to you?"

"No." Bailey laughed.

"That was a rhetorical question, bitch." Sean laughed with her.

"Thanks for looking, bud."

"No sweat. Be careful. Later."

Bailey hung up, made some notes, and sipped her coffee. She was still scribbling when she heard someone clear their throat beside her.

"I'm sorry I'm a little late." Cassandra sat and stroked Jazz's head as she greeted her from under the table. "How did you get her in here?"

"No problem. And she's my service dog?"

Cassie eyed the vest Jazz sported suspiciously and spoke quietly. "And what service does she offer you?"

Bailey leaned forward and grinned sheepishly. "I was thinking I could say PTSD or something like that. What do you think?"

"Should work. It's believable."

Bailey tidied her papers and smiled. "I think I've just been insulted." She laughed as she signaled the waitress and waited while Cassandra ordered a cappuccino. "I don't know if I'm supposed to call you Professor Burns or Ms. Finsbury."

"For the past twelve years, I've been Professor Burns, Sandra, Sandy—none of it ever felt like it was me. How about Cassie?"

Bailey let the name play in her mind, imagined it rolling over her tongue. She liked the way it felt, the way it sounded in her head. "I think I can manage that. Does anyone in your life know about your past?"

"No. The former head of the department knew. He was the one who authorized my position. He left several years ago."

"There are rumors that you're working on a project for the CIA. Is that why you're at MIT?"

"I can't answer that."

Bailey nodded. Her non-answer told Bailey everything she needed to know. "Fair enough." She sipped her coffee. "You officially died in nineteen eighty-eight. Sandra Burns doesn't appear until two thousand and one. Where were you in between?"

"I stayed in the UK for a number of years, then we went to Glens Falls, New York."

"We?"

"Yes, me and my partner, Karen Riley. I was a teacher there, high school. She worked in a diner, she loved to cook, and she loved it there. It was a beautiful city just south of Lake George."

Bailey felt like she'd been punched in the gut. She didn't know why it should surprise her that Cassie had a lover. She was beautiful, intelligent, and based on everything she was learning, an incredibly strong woman. It didn't make sense for her to not have a partner. *So why do I feel like I've lost the fight before the bell even started the round?* She shook her head.

"So what changed? Why aren't you both still there? You sound like you were happy there."

"We were. Until Karen died."

"I'm so sorry."

Cassie sighed. "Thanks, but it was a long time ago now."

Pieces of the jigsaw puzzle that was Cassie Finsbury slid into place. "Let me guess, two thousand and one?"

"Yes." Cassie stirred sugar cubes into her coffee. She seemed mesmerized by the swirls of cocoa she created in the white foam.

"So that was when you decided that Cassandra Finsbury had to die too?"

"No. She was already dead then. But since he'd found me as Vivian Fenton, she had to go too."

Bailey frowned. *Jesus, this is even more complicated than I thought.* "Vivian Fenton? Another fake name you adopted?"

"Yes. That was the one I used in Glens Falls."

"You said he found you. Who do you mean?"

"William Sterling."

"I'm sorry. I don't follow. You faked your own death—forgive me, I assume you did fake your own death?"

"I did."

"To get away from him?"

"Yes."

"Why do you think he found you and came after you?"

"Because he'd found us before." Cassie sipped her coffee.

"He knew you weren't dead?"

"Not at first, but later he did, yes."

"Jeez, and this is the stuff you can talk about?"

Cassie laughed. "Only because you found out I'm supposed to be dead."

Bailey rubbed her hand over her face. "Okay, so how did he find out you weren't dead?"

"Through Karen."

"She told him?" Bailey couldn't tear her eyes away as Cassie licked the froth off her spoon. The action was sultry and sexy and totally unconscious, and it hit Bailey right in the gut.

"No, she would have never done that. She got a job working for him as a cook."

"Is this before you and she knew each other?"

"No. She and I had been in a relationship for three years when I died." She used her fingers to create quotes when she said the word died and offered a lopsided grin.

"Then why the hell would she go anywhere near him? That's just asking for trouble."

"Daniela." Cassie smiled and fished a photograph out of her purse. She smiled at the picture before she handed it to Bailey. A blond woman smiled at the camera with a child, maybe eight or nine years old, standing before her. She held a trophy in her small hands and beamed at the camera.

"This is Karen?"

"Yes. William hired her as a cook, but she was almost nanny to Daniela in the end. She watched over her while I couldn't." Cassie's voice cracked. "William made a pass at Karen in front of Daniela. Karen refused him, and he fired her. Daniela got sick later in the week, and William wasn't there. She called Karen, crying, in pain, she had a fever, and there was only the chauffeur there to babysit her that night. We were both furious. The only way Karen could stop me from going was to promise to go and take care of her."

Bailey felt her heart go out to the woman who had so desperately wanted to be there for her little girl, but instead had to trust her to the care of another.

"She had someone with her who loved her, Cassie."

Cassie smiled a small, sad smile. "I know. And she loved Karen." She pointed to the photograph. "That was very clear to see. When William found out that Karen had visited Daniela while he was away, he decided he needed to make his point to stay away. He turned up at Karen's house. He was…" She wiped at the tears as they fell down her cheek.

"You were there?"

She nodded. "He was shocked to find me there." She laughed bitterly. "Obviously. But it didn't stop him from doing what he'd planned to do." She picked a napkin off the table and wiped her nose. "He promised that if either of us went near Daniela again, he'd do to her what he'd done to us."

"He beat you?" Cassie looked into her eyes and Bailey knew that he'd done far more than beat her. She'd worked enough cases to guess at some of the possibilities, and her forearms quivered as she balled her fists. She also knew that Cassie wouldn't tell her the details of what happened that night, but she could see it in her eyes, the scars of the horror she had survived. She wondered if she'd ever spoken about it. And as horrible as it must have been for them both, she was glad that Cassie had someone with her then who not only understood what she'd gone through, but was there with her.

Cassie looked down at the table and nodded. The fact that she refused to meet Bailey's eyes confirmed her fear. "Yeah. That was when I became Vivian Fenton, high school teacher in Glens Falls."

She covered Cassie's hand with her own but let go quickly when Cassie flinched under the unexpected touch. "I get it." She hoped she managed to convey that she really did understand the things that Cassie wouldn't—couldn't—say. That she'd seen that look in the eyes of women her whole life, and she understood the shame, guilt, and fear Cassie felt, even though she knew how misplaced it was. "You stayed as far away as you could to protect her."

"I had no other choice at that point. I'd played every card I had, and I lost." Cassie took a deep breath. "He promised he'd kill us if he ever found us again. To this day I don't know how he found us there, but he must have, or Karen would still be here."

"I don't understand. How did Karen die?"

"She was hit by a car as she was leaving work."

"Okay." Bailey sipped her coffee. "And that has what to do with your husband?"

"Ex-husband. It was a hit and run, the police couldn't find a suspect or even the car. It must have been him."

"Why would he send someone after her and not you at the same time?"

"I'm assuming that he couldn't find my new name."

"Then how would he have found hers?"

"The only person who knew our identities at that point was my father."

"And you think he sold out Karen, but not you?"

"Yes."

"Why?"

"Long story."

Bailey couldn't help but think that there was more than a little paranoia affecting Cassie's judgment on this, but she also couldn't disprove her theory. "Say all that's true. William wanted you, Karen was collateral damage, if you'll forgive the term. Why would he want her dead before he could use her to find you?"

"I don't know. Maybe something went wrong. Maybe William's lackey was inexperienced or something and went too far too soon."

The reasoning didn't make sense to Bailey, and she was surprised at Cassie. She was a logical, intelligent woman, and this seemed out of character for her, but there seemed little point in pursuing it further right now. "What did you do after Karen died?"

"I became Professor Sandra Burns."

"I know that. How?"

Cassie sighed. "I'm sorry. I can't tell you that."

"You can trust me, you know?" Bailey took a deep breath. "I was a beat cop for ten years before I joined the FBI. I worked there for twelve years before I retired. I do this job to earn some cash and stop my brain from rotting. I've seen and heard stories that have made me cry, made me angry, and made me fight the urge to beat the living crap out of someone. Your story is complicated, and there's a hell of a lot more to it, I know. But I'm pretty sure I'll have heard some version of it somewhere down the line." She smiled sadly. "The BPD trusted me. The FBI trusted me. And more recently, Jazz trusted me."

Cassie laughed. "That is an important one." She reached down and stroked Jazz's head as she winked at Bailey. "It isn't about me trusting you, Ms. Davenport."

"Bailey. If you want me to call you Cassie, then I expect you to call me Bailey."

"Very well. It isn't about me trusting you, Bailey. If I didn't I wouldn't have told you as much as I have. But like I told you the other day, there are things I can't tell you."

Bailey let out a frustrated breath. It was clear that Cassie was being as open with her as she could be, and considering everything she had been through—the life she had lived hiding in shadows—that alone was pretty amazing. She considered the possibility that Cassie wasn't a person who was naturally guarded, but rather, she'd had to become cautious, secretive, and suspicious of everyone in order to survive. And they were habits that she had learned at a price. Bailey sighed. "Okay, I'm sorry. I'm trying to help, and I'm trying to be patient and work within these boundaries, but it's going to take me time to get used to being kept in the dark."

"Then why did you change your mind about helping me find my daughter?"

It was the same question Bailey had been asking herself all day, and the truth was that she still didn't have a good answer. All she knew was that it felt like the right thing to do. She wondered if her mother had ever tried to look for her. Had she sat in front of someone and begged for their help only to be turned away because she had a turbulent past? Had someone refused to trust her and cost them both a chance to find one another? Bailey didn't know, and she would most likely never know. But if she could help it, another mother wouldn't have to live with the unanswered questions that plagued her. Another daughter didn't have to wonder if her mother had loved her.

"I know what it's like to feel like there's a piece missing."

Bailey stared into Cassie's eyes and she couldn't pull away. Flecks of gold shot through the dark emerald green. She could see that Cassie's lips were moving, but she couldn't focus on the words. She felt as though she were listening from underwater and nothing made sense.

"I'm sorry, what did you say?"

Cassie smiled gently. "I said, I'm sorry."

"What for?"

"Your pain."

"It's fine." Bailey managed to blink and waved her hand. "It was a long time ago."

"Doesn't stop it from hurting, and it doesn't always dim the memories either."

"Do you mind if I ask some more questions?"

"You can ask. Don't be offended if I can't answer."

"Fair enough." Bailey flipped a page in her notebook. "What do you know about your daughter?"

"Very little." She sighed softly and clasped her hands on the table in front of her. "She'll be twenty-nine years old in January. From what I understand, she's been working for her father's company since she finished her education. She's been a researcher at Sterling BioTech. I haven't found any publications of her work yet, so I don't know what she's been working on. As a child, she was quite brilliant." Cassie smiled proudly. "And no, that isn't just parental pride. She was very advanced for her age when I left, and while Karen was with her she was even further ahead of her peers. William had excellent tutelage in place for her. He did well by her in that regard."

"Was he a good father? Is that why you left her with him?"

"He wasn't a bad father." She shrugged. "At least he wasn't then, more an indifferent one. And I didn't choose to leave her there. I had planned for her to come with me. It just didn't work out that way."

"What went wrong?"

"I can't tell you that."

"Fine."

"I'm sorry."

"It's okay. Can you tell me why you faked your own death?"

"William wanted to expand Sterling Enterprises in a way that I wasn't comfortable with, and he needed me to do it. I refused. When I did, I was left with little choice but to die, for everyone's own good."

"I don't understand."

"I'm sorry. I can't say any more than that."

Bailey scribbled a few more notes. "What else do you know about your daughter?"

"I read an article that said she had testified against her father and he's now in prison."

"Yes. Anything else?"

"No."

"Okay."

"This might be totally unrelated, but a student of mine came to see me today, and asked for a recommendation letter for an internship."

Bailey frowned. "Okay, and what does that have to do with this?"

"She wanted a letter for Sterling BioTech. They hadn't put out applications for the summer internship till this weekend. Probably waiting to see what was going on after William's incarceration, I guess."

"So you think something's changed in the company?" The hairs on the back of Bailey's neck stood on end again. Sean's comments about the string of letters watching both the girl and the company made her question whether pursuing this was a good idea. But this woman, Cassie, was a good woman, and if her daughter was even a fraction like her then maybe her help was all aboveboard. Surely they deserved the benefit of the doubt. Right?

"Seems a very likely explanation, wouldn't you say?"

"And what do you think that change would be?"

"Someone's taken over."

"You think your daughter has taken over the company?"

"I have no idea. Maybe she's sold it. But someone is at the helm again."

"Why do you think your daughter testified against her father?"

"Because he's a bastard. As for her reasons, I don't know. I have a suspicion or two, but that's all."

"Can you share those suspicions?"

"The article mentioned terror charges and arms deals. I'd guess that he was brokering biological weapons." She sighed.

"That it?"

"I told you it was just a suspicion."

Bailey scribbled another note. "Somehow I think your suspicions are based on way more than gut instinct and guesswork."

"So does this mean you'll take my case?" Cassie asked.

Bailey nodded as she looked at the pages of notes spread over the table. "Looks like it." She pushed a pad and pen toward her. "Can you write your home details on there for me?" Cassie did and passed the pad back. "You're less than a block from me."

Cassie chuckled. "Small world."

"Yup."

Cassie checked her watch. "I'm going to have to get moving soon. It'll be seven before I get home and I still need to cook dinner."

"I can give you a lift if you like?" She pointed to the Explorer outside. "I really am just down the block from you. Seems silly for you to get the T when I'm passing."

Cassie glanced out at the dark sky and the wet sidewalk. "You sure you don't mind?"

"Not at all."

"And what do I owe you as a retainer?" Cassie pulled her wallet out of her purse.

"We can sort it out later."

"Don't be silly. You've already done a considerable amount of work by the look of your pad. What's your fee?"

"You pay for the coffees and we can discuss it in the car."

"Bailey."

"I've got a pamphlet in there with everything written down."

Cassie sighed. "Fine." She paid the bill and followed Bailey to the car, Jazz trotting quietly beside them. "How long have you been a private investigator?"

"Coming up on five years." They climbed into the car, and Cassie looked on curiously as Bailey wrapped the seat belt around the dog sitting in the backseat. Bailey caught the look. "She barks if I don't put the seat belt on her."

Cassie smiled indulgently. "Okay. Do you enjoy it?"

"PI work?" She shrugged. "Some cases. But mostly it's following guys who are cheating on their wives, or people who are trying to commit insurance fraud. It pays the bills and it keeps me busy." She pulled away from the curb.

"But you're really a cop at heart and being anything other than that is hard for you."

"Yeah. I miss being part of something bigger, something that really made a difference." She snorted a short laugh. "At least in theory, anyway."

"You said you were in the FBI. A field agent?"

"Yeah. I worked with a team trying to make some headway into the number of girls being smuggled into the country for sex slaves. For every one we caught, five more were—are—smuggled in. It's a never ending battle."

"It must have been so hard."

Bailey shrugged. "Some days more so than others."

"Is that why you retired?"

"No. It probably should have been, but I took early retirement for health reasons."

"I'm sorry to hear that. Everything okay now?"

"Yup." She smiled. "Seems when they told God I might be on my way he decided he wasn't ready for me."

Cassie laughed. "I'm very glad to hear that. What is it they say, you can't keep a good woman down?"

"I thought it was you can't put a good woman down."

"That too." They laughed together easily, and Bailey found herself surprised at how much she enjoyed Cassie's company, and found herself wanting to share. She wasn't sure what was going on with her lately, taking in a stray dog, taking chances on people, having fun, laughing.

"I was diagnosed with renal cancer. Had a kidney removed and now I'm all good."

"Full remission?"

"Yup. And if I didn't know I only had one kidney, I would never know the difference. I don't pee less or anything." She laughed. "I wish I did."

Cassie laughed. "Tell me about it. I'm getting up three times a night on a good day. This getting older stuff sucks."

"Yup, laughing doesn't help my cause either. That's why I try to maintain that gruff exterior." Bailey knew from her research that Cassie was fifty-five years old, but if she hadn't seen her birth certificate, she'd never have believed it. Sure, there were a few fine lines around her eyes, a few gray hairs softened the vibrant auburn she had seen in earlier pictures, and the years had softened the lines of her jaw, but Cassie was a beautiful woman. Age twenty or eighty, she always would be, and the more time Bailey spent getting to know her wit, her intelligence, and her humor, the more attractive she became.

"Oh, is that what that is? Your incontinence cure?"

"Yup. It was working up till now."

Cassie grinned. "Sorry."

"Yeah, you look it."

"Everyone needs to laugh sometimes."

"Then I'm glad to be of service." Bailey pulled up outside Cassie's apartment building.

"Do you have that pamphlet for me?"

"What pamphlet?"

"With your fees on it?"

"Oh, right. Hang on." She reached over and opened the glove box. A packet of mints, a plastic ball, and a single glove tumbled onto Cassie's lap while Bailey managed to keep the rest of the contents from escaping. "Sorry, it's in here somewhere."

Cassie giggled as she held up the ball. "No worries. Take your time." She squeezed on the ball, and chuckled harder when it blew a raspberry at her. Bailey looked up, still stretched across the center console, hand still wedged in the glove box. The streetlight illuminated Cassie's smiling face, and her moist lips glistened in the orange glow. Her long hair fell over her shoulders, and her eyes seemed to twinkle in the low light. Bailey's breath caught in her chest and she quickly moved away, pulling the contents of the glove box out and scattering them everywhere.

She hoped the low light covered the blush she knew covered her cheeks as she scrambled to make her brain work. "Sorry, cramp," she said, gripping her thigh, hoping the ruse would cover her idiocy.

"Oh gosh. Are you okay?" Cassie started gathering the dropped items. "Can you get the door open to put your leg out?" She quickly piled the papers and odd items together and climbed out of the car, running to the driver's side.

*Oh shit. I didn't think this one through.*

Cassie pulled open the door. "Here. Stick your leg out and I'll massage it for you."

*Forget that, I wasn't thinking at all.* Mortified, she could think of nothing else to do than swing her leg out and mumble under her breath. "It feels a lot better already. You don't need to do that, but thanks."

"It's no problem." She gripped Bailey's thigh and started to knead the muscle. "This doesn't feel too bad."

"No, like I said, it feels a lot better." *She flinched when I touched her in the coffee shop, but now she's got her hands all over my thigh. What gives?*

"More salt."

"I'm sorry—"

"You need a little more salt in your diet to keep the cramps at bay. I'm guessing you have to watch your salt intake with the kidney, right?"

"Yeah."

"You might need to increase it slightly. Try electrolyte drinks. Sports mix, something like that. It'll help stop the cramps."

"Thanks." Bailey was mumbling, but she couldn't help it. She was embarrassed and remembered exactly why she avoided people. She was awkward in social situations. She could talk to anyone when she had a goal, information to find out, situations to resolve, no problem. But just talking, being friendly, and being comfortable with someone was rare and the people who made her feel that way she could count on one hand. "I'll be fine now. Why don't you go on up and I'll call you when I have some more information."

"You sure you're going to be okay?"

"Positive."

"I have my checkbook in my apartment. You can wait here while I get it, or you can both come up if you like."

Bailey didn't want to wait, and she didn't want to go into Cassie's apartment. She wanted to go home, lie on the sofa with her dog, and forget she'd been an idiot. "I'll tell you what, why don't I pick it up in the morning while I'm out walking Jazz? That way you don't have to come back down and I don't have to climb the stairs." She pointed at her thigh. "What with the cramp and all."

"Of course, but I don't mind coming back down."

"Really, it's fine. I'll be out walking Jazz early anyway, so it's really no problem."

Cassie frowned. "You're sure."

"I am." She smiled, inordinately pleased that she could escape. "I'll see you tomorrow."

"Okay, I have to leave by seven thirty."

"I'll be here before then."

Cassie held out her hand. "Thank you for changing your mind."

Bailey shook her hand and hoped her palms didn't feel as damp as she thought they were, and tried to ignore the tingling skin where Cassie's fingers wrapped around her own. "You're welcome."

"Good night, Bailey."

Cassie closed the car door and trotted up the steps to her front door. She waved before disappearing inside. Bailey thumped her head against the headrest. "And don't you say anything either," she said, looking over her shoulder to the dog sitting on the backseat. "We're just gonna pretend she isn't pretty, and act all professional. She's hired us to do a job, so that's what we're gonna do." Jazz barked, seemingly in agreement. "No drooling, no fawning over her, and no leg humping." Jazz whined. "Okay, you're right, you wouldn't do that." Bailey started the engine. "Professional, girl, we can do that, right?"

Jazz barked.

"I'm glad you have faith in us."

## CHAPTER THIRTEEN

Cassie closed the door behind her and leaned heavily against it. Her head and shoulders slumped under the barrage of memories and emotions she could no longer hold back. She wrapped her arms around herself and slid to the floor, imagining her baby girl cradled in her arms. The sweet scent of her skin as she slept filled Cassie's nostrils, the tiny noises she made echoed in her ears, little feet kicked against the blanket she was swaddled in as she dreamed those first baby dreams, and Cassie cried. Her whole body shook as she let one memory after the other crash over her. She saw herself lifting Daniela onto a swing, pushing her higher with each excited shout from her lips. She remembered Karen on a seesaw with her, laughing as Daniela giggled and tried to kick herself up against Karen's counterweight. Determination was the only thing powering her legs against the impossible task.

"Oh, Karen." She buried her face in her hands. "I'm so sorry."

Her sobs seemed to echo in the empty apartment. It was comfortable, it was functional, but it wasn't home. It never had been. There was too much missing for her to ever call it that. Shelves and coffee tables that had once been bare were now scattered with framed pictures. If anyone found her now, the pictures of her old life wouldn't matter anymore. Daniela smiled out of so many of them. As a young child, with pigtails and a missing tooth, looking up from the pages of a picture book, and concentrating on eating an ice-cream cone without missing any of the drips that ran over her fingers. In every picture, she looked happy. Then as she got older, there were pictures with Karen. Pictures where she smiled, but her eyes looked sad. Pictures taken with her father, where Daniela looked alone. There were pictures from school open events Cassie had snuck into and captured as best she could. A picture of a twelve-year-old Daniela on stage playing piano, her head bent over the huge instrument as she performed. Cassie had been so proud to hear her play. Even now, she teared up whenever she heard the piece, Beethoven's *Moonlight Sonata*. She played it with such melancholia, so much heartbreaking loss, and Cassie couldn't help but wonder at the loneliness her beloved child must have felt to capture the emotion of the piece so completely. That had been the last time she'd seen her. The last time she had watched her child in the flesh, seen her move, and smile, and giggle as she was praised for her performance. The last time she had thought herself and her daughter were safe.

So many times she had wished she could turn back the clock and make a different choice. She could have said yes to William's despicable desires. She could have created some sort of weapon for him. She possessed the knowledge; she had the skill. But what then? Then she would have been dangerous to him as well as no longer useful, and her life would have been forfeit anyway. Of that, she had no doubt. But what of Daniela? Would it have been better for her if she had done as William wanted?

"If wishes were horses." She wiped her face and pushed herself up from the floor. "I'd have ridden over you, you old bastard." She hung up her coat and grabbed a carton of soup from the refrigerator. She washed her face while she waited for the microwave and stared at the image the glass showed. She looked as tired as she felt, and her eyes stung from her earlier tears. She pushed her fingers through her hair and sighed. The additional gray at the temples made her consider just how much time had passed.

The microwave pinged and she flipped the light off and headed to the kitchen. She stopped and put a hand to her chest, nearly fainting at the sight in front of her.

"This tastes funny." A dark haired man stood in front of the microwave and slurped at her soup.

"You nearly gave me a heart attack. What the hell are you doing in my apartment?" She took the bowl of soup away from him and dumped it in the sink.

"Hey, I was eating that."

"Yeah? Well, it's contaminated." She tried to keep control of her temper, but she hated the way he seemed to think he could invade her life whenever he felt like it. "What do you want, Mr. Knight?"

Knight smiled. "Someone has been asking questions about you. Flags have been raised. I came by to make sure you're okay."

"Really? Well, as you can see, I'm just fine."

"Hmmm. And who was that outside earlier? You looked quite friendly, Professor." He placed the emphasis on the title, making sure she understood that it was part of the deal that she abide by the boundaries he had laid out twelve years ago.

"Just someone I had coffee with."

"A date?"

Cassie felt the hairs on the back of her neck tingle, but she didn't know why. "Just coffee." She'd known Stephen Knight for a long time. She'd built up trust with him—of sorts. She didn't like him, but he had always provided what he had said he would, and she'd had little cause over the years to regret her involvement with him. He'd provided her with her alternate identity and career. He'd also given her a chance to try to bring William Sterling to justice. It was just a shame that the plan had taken too long. "Actually, I'm glad you're here."

He smiled. "And why would that be?"

"You caught William."

"Well, not me personally, but yes."

"I wanted to talk to someone about seeing my daughter again." Cassie knew what he would say. It was the reason she hadn't bothered asking before and sought Bailey's help instead.

"I'm sorry. You know the deal. That isn't possible."

"But the situation's different now."

"No, it isn't. Just because Sterling is in prison, doesn't mean he can't get to you. He has a long reach and many people still on his payroll."

"I just want to see my daughter."

"You agreed to the deal to protect her."

"I'm very well aware of why I made the deal, Mr. Knight. I also know that she doesn't seem to need my protection anymore. Where is she?"

"How should I know?"

"She testified against him. I assume the CIA is involved with the case against him. As a witness, your agency must have an address, a telephone number—some way of getting in touch with her."

"Even if we do, I don't. And it's in contradiction to our deal, Professor." Stephen's face darkened. "Contacting your daughter would violate the terms of our agreement, and you would no longer be under our protection." He towered over her. "Am I making myself clear?"

It didn't matter what he threatened her with. She would see her daughter again. She would explain why she'd left her, and that she had never stopped loving her. Cassie refused to cower. She looked him in the eye and hardened her heart.

"Perfectly clear, Mr. Knight. I trust you can see yourself out."

She turned her back on him and listened for the door closing. She didn't hear it, but she hadn't heard him enter her apartment either. She checked that the apartment was empty before slamming the dead bolt in place and checking that all the windows were locked. She lay on the couch and pulled the blanket over her body. The picture of Daniela and Karen was directly in view.

"I don't care what he says, or what it costs me. I will find you, darling."

# CHAPTER FOURTEEN

O z yawned and stretched her legs out in front of her, propping them on the desk. The sounds of machines whirring softly filled the laboratory, and the occasional sound of a pencil scratching paper and fingers clacking away on a keyboard were all she could hear. She supposed that should be a good thing. No distractions or interruptions for Finn while she was working. But in truth it was driving her stir crazy. She did nothing but sit around and wait, feeling useless while Finn did all the hard work.

She looked over at her dad who was tapping away at a computer. She leaned back. "You need any help over there, Pops?"

"I'm good."

"You sure? I can probably type faster than you can."

"I'm sure, thanks."

"What're you working on?"

Billy looked up. "Love letters to your mom."

Junior sniggered and flipped the page in the magazine he was reading. "You had to ask."

"Wish I hadn't."

"Here." Junior closed the magazine with a snap and tossed it to her. "Take a gander at that and chill. You know what it's like. It's a waiting game. Two days ain't that bad."

"I know." She slapped the magazine onto the seat beside her. "I just wish I could do something to help."

"You will. And you are."

Oz frowned.

"By shutting up and keeping out of her way. I tried to get her to explain it to me. That shit she's working on?" Junior whistled. "Man, I couldn't understand one word in twenty that came out of her mouth."

"I know."

"There ain't nothing anyone can do to help her right now."

"I know that. Do you have any idea how that makes me feel?"

Junior shook his head.

"I got a clue there, baby girl. But you picked yourself a helluva girl to fall in love with. Sometimes you're gonna have to learn to take a backseat."

"I didn't pick her, Dad." Oz smiled. "Don't really think I had a choice. Is it wrong of me to want to protect her and keep her away from this crap?"

"Nope," Billy said. "It's not wrong to want to. But belly-aching about it all the time isn't going to help her get done any quicker."

Oz closed her eyes. "I'm scared, Dad. I only just found her and I almost lost her once already." When she closed her eyes she could still see the man's hands around Finn's neck. It had taken a week for his finger marks to fade from the tender skin of Finn's throat.

Billy sat beside her. "I know."

Oz opened her eyes. She hadn't heard Junior leave, but she was grateful for the privacy. "What if I can't protect her this time?"

"Olivia, look at me. I'm your father, but I was a captain a long time, and you don't make commander without being a damn fine sailor. You did everything you could on that damn barge and without you Rudy would be dead now."

"Dad, you don't—"

"Yes, I do know that. I read every report, and I spoke to that boy myself. He's got nothing but praise for you and what you did that day. I would say you had some bad luck, but I'm not even sure of that. They were pirates, baby girl, intent on killing you, and armed to the teeth. You saved a butt load of people, got your partner out of harm's way, and did it while you were injured. You made me a damn proud captain and an exceptionally proud father that day."

"Rudy lost his leg, Dad." An aid mission to help a stricken cargo barge had turned deadly when she and her dive partner, Rudy, had discovered the vessel they were trying to help had been hijacked by pirates. The ensuing gunfight had left her with a gunshot wound to the gut, several people dead, and Rudy fighting for his life. She'd retired from the Navy after that. She knew she'd never be the same again, and she couldn't face the prospect of putting someone else in danger if she failed to carry out her duty.

"Yup. He did. But he's certain that he'd have lost his life if you hadn't done exactly what you did that day. And he loves you for it."

"I feel like I let him down. I'm worried I'll let you guys down, that it'll cost Finn her life. She saved me that day. Not the other way round."

"You're wrong." Finn stood in the doorway. "We worked together and saved each other. That's how I like to think of it, anyhow."

"Finn, if I'd done everything right you never would have had to shoot Jack."

Finn laughed. "That's a bunch of crap, Oz. You knocked him out. Hell, I thought he was dead then. If I hadn't distracted you who knows what might have happened. It's all ifs, buts, and maybes, baby." She crossed the room and sat next to Oz. "And that doesn't help anyone. What I do know is that we both survived it, we came out the other side stronger than we went in, and we still have each other." She took Oz's face in her hands and kissed her. "And that's not going to change."

"I can't lose you." Oz hated the weakness in herself. She'd never felt fear like this before.

"You won't. I already told you, you're stuck with me forever."

Oz wrapped her arms around Finn, pulled her tight to her body, and whispered in her ear. "Forever wouldn't be long enough."

Junior cleared his throat. "Sorry to interrupt this little love fest, but I'm starting to waste away here. When do we get released for rations?"

"Well, I was going to suggest we order in. I've got a test running at the moment, and I really want to be here for the result. If the simulation proves correct, I think I've got the basis of my vaccine."

"Seriously?" Billy clapped her on the shoulder. "I thought this was going to take weeks, not a couple of days."

"It still might. But this really could be a huge breakthrough."

"I'd ask you how, but I wouldn't understand what you were telling me. Are you sure?"

"Ninety percent, until I get this test result back."

"That's great. Really great." Billy stroked his chin. "Listen, I've been thinking about a few things, and I'm not sure how far I trust our friends. They were both far too quick to insist this stuff gets made, for my liking."

"I've never liked Whittaker," Oz said.

"That's just because he interrupted Thanksgiving." Finn pinched her side and made her jump.

"Not just that," she mumbled. "He's got an answer for everything too."

"That CIA dude makes the hairs on the back of my neck stand up." Junior returned and ran his hand over the back of his neck for emphasis.

"Me too," Billy said. "I think we should keep this breakthrough and any development in the antidote between us, until we know for certain what kind of game they're playing."

"They're going to expect some sort of report. I already mentioned that I was going to work on Lyell's research." Finn frowned.

"You're right." Billy frowned. "Do you think you can do something with that, but leave your own work out of the loop?"

"Sure. It's not like anyone's looking over my shoulder or anything."

"Fuck." Junior ran out of the room. "Stay here. Give me two minutes."

"What's that all about?" Finn asked.

"I should have thought about it before. Fuck, I'm an idiot." Oz slapped her forehead.

"What?" Finn stared at her.

Oz pulled her in close and whispered, "He's doing a surveillance sweep. There could be microphones, cameras, anything in the room."

Finn looked around. "What about in here?"

"Possibly, but it's more likely in your work space."

Junior came back in the room and leaned close to them. "There's a camera in the light fitting." He whispered, "I've left it in situ, I can't see a microphone but they'd be idiots not to have one in there somewhere.

I want to run a full security check on your computer systems too. I'm gonna need outside help for that, Uncle Billy."

Billy nodded and kept his voice quiet. "I'll call Charlie and see how soon we can get someone from our team on that."

"Why don't we take ten minutes and grab some subs, stretch your legs and get a bit of air, Finn? That test won't complete before then will it?"

"No. It's got about half an hour to go."

Oz and Finn followed Junior outside. "I want to leave them in place so they don't get suspicious, but that's going to mean you being very careful what you say in your office and how you react, Finn, can you do that?"

"Yes. As long as I know what I'm supposed to react to and what I'm not."

"No worries. Since we don't know who's watching us, let's assume it's everyone. I mean, they could have been there for a long time. Maybe your dad spying on someone, or it could be from when we were watching things at the lab because of your dad. We just don't know, so we're going to be ultra-cautious. We don't care if they know you make Balor. That's what everyone wants. We also don't care if they know you make Lyell's vaccine, improved or not. They'd be stupid if they didn't want that, no matter who is planning to use the damn bug. But no one but us is going to know about the flu-bug angle you're working on."

"Agreed," Finn said.

"I think we need some sort of code name for that. Then we can at least mention it without rousing suspicion," Oz said.

"Good plan." Junior smiled at Finn. "What do you want to call it?"

"Me? Why me?"

"You're the creator. They always get to name cool shit like this."

Finn laughed. "Do you guys know the legend of Balor?" They shook their heads. "In Celtic mythology Balor is the God of Death. He had only one eye and a single look from him would kill anything and anyone instantly. He learned of a prophecy that foretold his death and it was said he was to be killed by his grandson. So to prevent this from happening he locked his daughter in a crystal tower."

"Sounds like something off Jerry Springer," Junior said and laughed.

"Pretty much. Anyway, a druidess helped this guy called Cain get into the tower and Balor's daughter bore triplets. Balor tossed them into the sea, but the druidess managed to save one. A boy named Lugh. Many years later, the boy grew up and faced Balor in battle. As the giant opened his eye to kill him, Lugh managed to rip the evil eye out with a slingshot and killed the Cyclops."

"Wait a minute. That sounds like David and Goliath," Oz said.

"A lot of ancient mythology is seen repeated throughout the bible. It's pretty much an anthology of the best of pagan mythology with the cast of characters changed."

"So how does this get us a code name?"

"Lugh killed Balor." Finn smiled.

"Perfect." Oz smiled. She loved the way Finn's mind worked. Crazily logical and disciplined creativity seemed to spark off her.

"How the hell do you know all that?" Junior asked.

"Google."

Oz laughed. "Gotta love the Internet."

"Just so I can clarify this in plain English," Junior said. "Balor is—"

"The bad shit," Oz said.

Junior rolled his eyes. "Thanks, I got that one. Gamble is Lyell's crappy vaccine that you're gonna pass off to Mehalik, while Lugh is the good shit you've put in a cold, created by Finn."

"You passed, Junior. Now can we go back inside? I'm freezing my ass off."

They walked back into the lab. "Oh, if you two are bored, there's a gym down the hall from my office."

"You're kidding me." Junior grinned at her.

"It's not exactly state-of-the-art or anything, but it's got a treadmill, and an exercise bike, a few weight machines. Enough to keep you occupied for a little while, anyway."

Junior and Oz high-fived each other and pulled Finn behind them back into the building. A brief flash of light out of the corner of her eye made Finn turn around, but all she could see were cars in all directions with their headlights beaming, streetlights, shop windows, and apartment buildings lighting up the evening sky. She disregarded the momentary flash and allowed herself to be tugged along by the two tall, blond cousins. Despite the hard work ahead of her, the potential for danger, and all the unanswered questions that hung over her, she'd never felt happier. She had a family now. People she loved, and loved her. And she didn't doubt that for even a second.

# CHAPTER FIFTEEN

Bailey knocked on Cassie's door, Jazz's leash around her wrist, while she juggled takeout cups and a bag of pastries. She heard movement on the other side.

"It's Bailey."

"Are you alone?"

Bailey frowned. "Jazz's with me." She heard a heavy deadbolt slide back, and the door opened as far as the safety chain would allow. Cassie peered through the crack and as far down the hallway as she could, before releasing the chain and letting her in. She watched Cassie fit the chain and slide the deadbolt back in place. She noted that she was still wearing the same green sweater and gray slacks she'd had on when Bailey dropped her off the night before, and her hair was disheveled. "I'm sorry I woke you. I thought you'd need to leave for work pretty soon."

"I do. I fell asleep on the couch last night. How did you get into the building?"

"The front door was propped open with a note for a delivery guy taped to it. Not very secure."

"Damn it." Cassie ran her hands through her hair. "I've told the building manager about that so many times. He runs and leaves the door open when he does. I've told him it's a security risk, but he doesn't get it."

"I'll go and close it for you." While some people might have considered it an overreaction, Bailey knew where Cassie was coming from.

"No, it's fine. Thank you. I'll be leaving as soon as I get ready for work. What difference does a few more minutes make when it's probably been open for hours?"

"You sure? I don't mind."

"No, thanks." She pointed to the breakfast bar. "Why don't you sit down while I write that check for you."

Bailey held up the cups. "I brought coffee and a Danish each. Maple and pecan, hope that's okay." She spread the contents out on the counter.

"I'm sorry. I'm running so late. I don't have time."

"I was running a little late myself this morning. I have my car downstairs. I'll drive you in when you're ready. That should give you time, and you can always eat in the car while I drive."

Cassie stared at her. "Why?"

"Why what?" Bailey knew what she meant, but she didn't have an answer, so she did the only other thing she could think of. She stalled.

"Why are you doing this?"

"Offering you a lift?"

"And breakfast?"

"Well, I'm working on your case, and I see no reason not to offer a lift to help you out since I'm heading that direction anyway. As for breakfast, if you don't want it, Jazz will eat it." The dog licked her chops and panted as they both looked at her. Bailey looked up at Cassie and said softly, "Did something happen last night?"

Cassie stilled. Her hands seemed frozen, and even her breathing seemed to stop. Bailey couldn't help thinking of a deer caught in headlights. "What makes you ask that?"

Bailey shrugged and tried to downplay it. "You just seem a lot more tense than you were when I left you last night. You seem on edge now."

Cassie started breathing again and looked at her hands as she picked at the hem of her sweater. "I just had a bad night's sleep, and I don't like being late for anything. It's probably just that."

*Yeah, and I can tell when someone isn't being honest with me.* "Well, you go and get ready, and I'll finish my pastry, then I can drive you to work."

"You don't have to. Really."

"I know I don't. But I'm going that way so I might as well. I'd feel bad if I didn't. It's raining."

Cassie smiled, and her face seemed peaceful for the first time since Bailey had walked through the door. "Thank you."

"No need." Bailey stared after her as she disappeared down the hallway. "Damn it, Jazz, I said professional. What the hell was that?" Jazz stared at her. "You're right. That was all me. You were professional. You didn't sniff her butt or anything." She sipped her coffee. "She did seem upset though, right? You at least agree with me on that?" Jazz sighed and lay down, resting her head on her paws. "Gee, thanks a lot, girl."

"Do you always talk to your dog like you expect her to answer?"

Bailey jumped and turned around in her chair. "Yeah," she said. "I usually do. I mean look at that face." She pointed to Jazz. "Don't you think she understands every word I say?"

"I think she understands you. But that isn't all about language. She reads far more into your body language, tone of voice, and routine, than from the actual words you use."

"We don't have a routine. She's only been with me a week."

"Really? I sense a story there. You can tell me while you drive."

Ten minutes later, Bailey threw her trash away, followed Cassie to the door, and did indeed tell her the whole story about Jazz's rescue and subsequent adoption while she drove her to work. She pulled up on Massachusetts Avenue.

"You don't have to tell me what scared you last night, but I know something did." Cassie started to reply, but Bailey held out her hand and offered her a piece of paper. "If you want to talk about it you can get me on that number any time. That's my personal number. It never goes to voicemail."

"Nothing happened."

"You don't have to tell me, but I know something is wrong, so please don't lie to me. Secrets are one thing, but not lies. Okay?"

Cassie held up the piece of paper. "Why?"

"Everyone needs someone to look out for them once in a while."

Cassie smiled sadly. "So you're my knight in a shining Explorer."

"Something like that."

"Thank you." She tucked the paper into her pocket. "I better go. You'll call me when you have some news?"

"You have my word. And I mean it. Call me any time."

Bailey waited until she was inside the building before driving away. "Jazz, I have a sneaky feeling that the good professor may require a little more help than she's willing to admit."

Cassie turned in the doorway and watched Bailey's car drive off. The rain was still falling, but that wasn't the reason she was grateful for the ride. She hadn't been able to shake the unease that Stephen Knight's visit had left her with, but being in the car with Bailey had made her feel safe. She'd even been able to relax a little with her in the apartment. She realized that was the first time she'd had someone in the apartment who didn't make her uncomfortable. She hadn't once looked at the clock and wished Bailey would leave. In fact, she'd regretted the fact that she was in such a rush.

She'd expected to feel awkward with her after everything she had shared with Bailey the day before. Not just the information she'd shared, but something much more profound, and she hadn't even realized it until late into her sleepless night. She'd touched Bailey without even thinking about it. She could still feel Bailey's tight leg muscle beneath her hands. She'd lived in England the last time she'd touched anyone with so little thought. The time before William had changed her in such a fundamental way. She shook her head. She wasn't going there. Not today.

Yesterday, she'd assured Bailey that she trusted her. She'd said the words knowing that Bailey needed to hear them, but Cassie was shocked to find herself actually believing them. Why now? Why this woman? Was she letting her guard down because William was in prison? Was it safe to do that? Stephen obviously didn't think so, or he wouldn't have visited her last night. She snorted a laugh. *Visited? Breaking and entering from CIA agents is the sum total of my social encounters recently. No wonder I trust Bailey—she knocked.* Cassie smiled. *And she brought me breakfast. When's the last time that happened?*

The hairs on the back of her neck prickled as she walked toward the lecture hall. She looked over her shoulder, but she couldn't see anything but a hall full of students and the usual security guards manning their stations. She rubbed the back of her neck and pulled a few strands of hair out from under her collar. *Must have been tickling me or something.*

## CHAPTER SIXTEEN

Masood sat under the umbrella glancing idly at the newspaper as he sipped his morning coffee. The turquoise blue waters of Eilat's marina glistened in the early morning sun, and the boat bobbed on the gentle waves as his crew scurried about, readying the fifty-foot yacht for its next voyage on the Red Sea. He had to admit he enjoyed the opulence and the decadence that surrounded him. He loved the comfort and the ease with which everything came in the highly Westernized resort town. There were no struggles to find food, water, or medical care. Money flooded the resort from tourists who came from all over the world, as well as all over Israel.

He had trained himself not to spit on the ground at the mention of the hated state, but it was still difficult. He battled the urge to disrespect the ground he walked on even as he thought about how it had been stolen from his ancestors, his family—from him.

Before the war, his family had farmed the land. They had good fertile ground and their wealth had been plentiful. Now their land sat in the ruins that were the Gaza Strip. Masood could not legally cross the border to see what remained of his extended family and their lands. The newborn Israeli State had claimed it all and forced them from the homes they had lived in for generations. No compromise. No question. No remorse. Fear had driven them to defend themselves. This Masood understood. All-encompassing fear had driven them to a level of violence his ancestors could not withstand. His grandfather had stood armed with a garden fork against an army of automatic weapons, grenades, shells, and hatred. The British army crawled away, defeated by propaganda, treachery from within its own ranks, and a stomach full of war. There was no hope for Palestine.

*Not then there wasn't.* Masood smiled as his latest disposable phone rang.

"My friend, tell me good news."

"She's working on the toxin."

"Excellent. Do you have a time frame?"

"Not exactly. She said it wouldn't take long. But nothing more specific."

"Anything else?"

"She said she's trying to make the antidote more stable. As you know, Lyell only had it about fifty percent effective."

"Excellent. You have done well, my friend."

"Thank you, General."

"What is the next stage of the plan?" Masood listened. "I will make arrangements and see you there." He hung up, checked his watch, and dialed a different number.

"Yes, good morning, Hakim. I need you to arrange travel for me."

"Of course, General. Where to?"

"New York."

"When?"

"I need to be there on Friday. I am attending a charity function."

## CHAPTER SEVENTEEN

Cassie paused outside her apartment door, key poised in hand, but something was wrong. *I didn't leave it open.* Her heart pounded in her chest and her breath came in short, sharp pants.

She pushed gently on the door and let it swing open. She peered inside before she thought about moving, and the mess inside brought tears to her eyes. Photograph frames were toppled, the glass broken and trodden into the carpet in some places. The TV was by the window, smashed, and she wondered briefly if a thief had dropped it in a hurry to escape and decided to leave it. There was little else of material value in her apartment. She kept her laptop and cell phone with her whenever she went to work and she owned very little in the way of jewelry. She kept a small amount of cash in the apartment for emergencies—just a couple hundred dollars—and wasn't at all surprised to find it missing. She didn't care about the money, or the broken TV, or the broken picture frames. As she riffled through the shards of broken glass, she realized that some of her pictures were missing. One was of Daniela as a child that had been in a silver frame. She found it hard to believe that someone was so desperate for money that they would steal a picture frame, even if it looked slightly valuable. The loss of it cut her to the core. It was a picture she could never replace, and her pictures were all she had.

She let the tears slide down her cheeks and didn't realize she had picked up the phone until she was listening to the low alto greet her at the other end.

"Hello."

"I'm sorry to disturb you."

"Cassie? Is that you?"

"Yes, I'm sorry…"

"Why are you crying?"

"I don't know why I called you, but my apartment's been broken into."

"Get out of there and wait in one of your neighbors' apartments. I'm on my way. I'll find you when I get there."

"Bailey, what are you talking about?"

"I need to make sure that they've gone. Please leave the apartment. I'm on my way." Cassie heard a door close and knew Bailey was only a few minutes away. "Please."

"Bailey, you don't need to do this. I'm sorry. I shouldn't have called."

"I'm glad you did. I need to drive now. Please get out of there and call the cops, okay?"

"There's no one here."

"You're probably right, but please humor me, okay?"

Cassie sighed heavily but her unease was actually growing as she stood in the middle of the mess that used to be her orderly living room. "Okay." She hung up and walked slowly toward the door, trying not to step on any more of the glass. She saw a rapid movement out of the corner of her eye and turned just in time to see an object careening toward her head. She managed to raise her arm enough to deflect it a little, but the blow was solid enough to drop her to the floor.

"Cassie, can you open your eyes for me?"

Cassie moaned in response to the question. Her first inclination to tell the questioner where to go was beyond her right that second. She began to catalogue the various aches and pains in her body. She was on her back, and besides the aching head, her shoulder and knees hurt, there was something sticky on her face, and something warm by her side.

"Cassie, can you hear me?"

Her questioner was persistent, so she gritted her teeth and tried again to make herself understood. "Yes." She didn't recognize her own voice as it passed her lips. It was thick and croaky. *I sound like a damn frog.*

"What happened?"

"There was someone in the apartment." Cassie kept her eyes closed and followed her body's advice on staying still. Bailey was here now. She wouldn't let anything happen to her.

"I told you to leave."

"I was leaving. That's when he hit me." Her thought just before she'd been hit finally registered, and she tried to blame the slight feeling of nausea and dizziness on the blow to the head, but she knew better. Bailey radiated an aura that made Cassie feel safe, protected, something she couldn't remember feeling in a long time. And something she knew she was in no condition to question at the moment. Instead, she allowed herself to enjoy the sensation of being looked after.

"So it was a man?"

Cassie tried to recall. "I think so, but I didn't see clearly enough to say for sure. It may just be that I assumed he was a man."

"Okay. I called the police and the paramedics. They should be here soon, and we can get this all taken care of. Did he take much?"

Cassie shook her head. "Some cash and a couple of pictures."

"Pictures? What of?"

"Daniela. One was in a silver frame."

"Ah. You think he took it for the frame?"

"I don't exactly have a lot of valuable items here."

"Okay, but he didn't take your phone or your briefcase after he knocked you out. I'd have expected a thief to take them too."

"Maybe he panicked."

Bailey frowned. "Maybe. Anything else you noticed missing?"

"No."

"Did you check everywhere?"

"No, I didn't look in my bedroom. That's where he must have been when I called you. The window was open, so I thought the apartment was empty."

"Rookie mistake, Ms. Finsbury." Bailey smiled. "That's why we tell people not to go in and to call the cops."

"You know you talk like you're still a cop, don't you?"

Bailey shrugged. "Once a cop, always a cop."

Cassie held out her hand. "Can you help me up?"

Bailey took hold of her hand. "I think we should wait for the paramedics to give you the once-over first."

"I'm fine."

"Jeez, you're stubborn. You didn't listen to me about getting out of here. Will you please listen to me this time?" Bailey laughed to take the sting out of it, but Cassie knew she was right, and frustrated.

"Fine. But don't think you'll get away with this again."

Bailey smiled. "Trust me, I'm under no illusions."

Cassie finally opened her eyes and looked at Bailey. A small worry line formed a deep valley between her brows, but she was smiling. She was cradled in Bailey's arms, her torso stretched across Bailey's lap, and the embrace was far more intimate than Cassie was prepared for. One of Bailey's arms was wrapped securely around her shoulders and the other was holding her hand and resting on Cassie's belly. Her hand tingled as Bailey's thumb ran back and forth over her skin, so softly she hadn't noticed it before, but now she could feel little else. But it was the change in Bailey's gaze she found the most disconcerting. The concern was obviously still there, but there was a heat, an intensity, that hadn't been there when she first opened her eyes.

It was too much. She hadn't had a chance to prepare herself for the contact. She wasn't expecting it. The nausea she had felt before rushed back, and it was all she could do not to vomit. Her breath was coming in short rasps. She couldn't get enough oxygen into her body and the spots she saw in front of her eyes confirmed her fear. It had been quite some time since she'd had a panic attack, since she'd felt so out of control that she had succumbed to the fear.

"Cassie, what's wrong?"

She couldn't look at Bailey as she tried to roll off her lap and grabbed a paper sack from the coffee table drawer. Her fingers were stiff and quickly becoming the rigid claws that oxygen deprivation made of her hands. She tried to form a tight closure for her to breathe into to help slow her breathing down. The hyperventilation would make her pass out if she didn't.

Bailey took the bag from her immovable hands and squeezed the opening closed, holding it to her mouth without touching her. "Just breathe, Cassie. Long and slow."

She already knew that Bailey was the type to rescue anyone who needed help. That's just who she was, and it didn't mean anything more than that. Cassie closed her eyes and tried to block out the fact that Bailey was not only witness to her weakness, but helping her through it.

Her breathing began to slow while Bailey talked to her, words Cassie couldn't remember later, but Bailey's voice made her relax. Just hearing her voice while still giving her the physical distance she needed helped Cassie get her heart rate back to normal, and slowly, the muscles in her hands began to relax, but she still felt exposed. She felt vulnerable in a way she couldn't handle. She needed a little distance to find her equilibrium, and she knew she wouldn't be able to do it while Bailey was so close to her. She needed a distraction. "Where's Jazz?"

"I left her in the car for a few minutes while I checked out what was going on."

"Go get her."

"She'll be fine."

"So will I, while you run and get her. I don't like dogs being left in cars."

"No, she wasn't keen on it either. You sure you'll be okay?"

"I'll be fine." Cassie was grateful for the emotional space when she left, but she missed her too. The security she felt when Bailey was near her vanished with her footsteps down the hallway.

It was less than two minutes before a distressed Jazz launched herself into the apartment alone and was licking at the blood on her face gently, but with persistence, obviously intent on caring for her wounded flock. Cassie smiled, not in the least bit concerned that Jazz had decided she was hers to take care of. She heard footsteps coming up the stairs and whispered to Jazz, "Either your mama's become a herd of elephants in the last couple of minutes or she's brought the cavalry with her." She scratched at the dog's thick ruff and leaned back against the sofa.

It took twenty minutes for the police to take her statement and the paramedics decided that they wanted her to go for an x-ray, which she politely declined.

"Ma'am, you could have a serious head injury, and a concussion isn't something to take chances with." The young paramedic frowned as he stared at his watch and checked her pulse again. His shaved head reflected the light, and she squinted.

"I'll be fine. I just have a little headache."

"The symptoms can get worse over the next twenty-four to forty-eight hours. You really shouldn't be on your own during that time. I would be much more comfortable if you let me take you in and get the doctor to check you over."

"I'll be fine." She could hear Bailey's exasperated sigh in the background and smiled.

"Look, do you have someone who can stay with you? At least then if your symptoms do get worse overnight they can get you to the emergency room or call us out." He looked at her pointedly. "Again."

Cassie started to tell him she didn't.

"Yes, she does."

The paramedic glanced over his shoulder. "And you are?"

"A friend. But I can stay with her tonight."

"Bailey, you don't need to do that."

"Do you have someone else in mind?"

Cassie shook her head. "You know I don't."

"Well, if you don't have someone with you, I really must insist on taking you to the emergency room."

Bailey leaned close to her ear and whispered, "Don't make me tell him about the panic attack too." Cassie glared at her, but she smiled sweetly and raised an eyebrow. Cassie sighed. Bailey nodded and turned back to the paramedic. "What do I need to look out for?"

He briefed her quickly on things to be wary of, and how often she would need to check on her, and Cassie began to rethink the idea of going to the hospital until Bailey smiled and assured him that she would make sure that Cassie was fine. One of the detectives called Bailey over and spoke to her quietly. She frowned, but nodded as she walked away from him.

She squatted next to Cassie. "Maybe you should have gone to the hospital after all. It's going to be tomorrow before a locksmith will be able to come out and fix that door."

"Damn."

"Yeah. Which leaves us with the option of staying here with no locks."

Cassie felt a shudder run through her. She wasn't convinced she was that much safer with the locks in place, because it certainly hadn't stopped Stephen Knight from paying her a silent, uninvited visit on more than one occasion, and they hadn't kept out tonight's intruder either, but they gave her the illusion, at least.

"Yeah, I'm not keen on that idea either. Which leads me to option two." Bailey paused.

"Which is?"

"My apartment."

"Bailey, I can't put you out like that."

"How is that putting me out? I'm staying with you anyway, and at least at my place I'm pretty sure Jazz isn't going to cut her paws on any broken glass. I have a futon, and I have locks that work."

Cassie had to admit she was curious to see where Bailey lived. She wanted to know more about the woman who was quickly learning what felt like all her secrets. She wanted to see the place Bailey called home. She dismissed it as her naturally curious nature—something that was an absolute must for any scientist—but she was quickly becoming aware that there was more to her curiosity about Bailey. She was attracted to her, and that almost scared her more than the intruder in her apartment had earlier.

"I'll even update you with the investigation."

Cassie looked over at Jazz. "Well, I wouldn't want Jazz to hurt herself for me."

Bailey held out her hand to help Cassie up. She looked at it for a moment and then ignored the butterflies in her stomach when their hands first connected. *Now is not the time to be developing some sort of teenage crush, just because Bailey was chivalrous, and strong, and being nice to me. It does not mean anything. Nothing at all.*

# CHAPTER EIGHTEEN

Bailey's hand trembled as she slotted the key into the door, which she attributed to lack of food, having run over to Cassie's apartment before she'd had a chance to eat her dinner. *Low blood sugar runs in the family.* She shook her head. *Who am I kidding?* She had no idea about the blood sugar, but she knew that her hands were trembling because she was nervous. Since the movers had dropped off the last box six years ago, the only visitor she'd had in her apartment was Jazz. She glanced down at the dog waiting patiently at her heel. She hitched the strap of Cassie's bag higher up her shoulder and pushed the door open.

"It's not much," she said, "but it's home." She ushered Cassie in ahead of her.

"It's nice." Cassie looked around, smiling. Bailey watched her eyes fall on every item in the sparsely furnished place, her attention lingering on her corkboard and the various pictures and information cards that almost covered it. Cassie pointed. "Your missing piece?"

"Yeah. My mom." Bailey led her to the sofa and watched her sit down. "Can I get you a drink?"

"A glass of water would be great, thanks."

"Coming right up." Bailey returned a few moments later, glass of water in one hand and a fistful of takeout menus in the other. "Are you hungry?" Cassie shook her head. "You sure? 'Cause I haven't eaten yet, and I need to get some food pretty quick."

"I'm fine, thanks. But don't let me stop you."

"You're not one of those women who are gonna want to try mine when it gets here, are you?"

Cassie laughed. "And if I am?"

Bailey let out a playfully aggrieved sigh. "Then you better tell me what you don't like on a pizza. Can't have you grumbling about having to pick anchovies or mushrooms off *my* pizza."

"Yuck. As long as you don't have either of those disgusting things on it, we're good. But seriously, I really don't feel like eating right now."

"Your headache?"

"Yeah. I feel like my heart is beating in my head and might make my brain ooze out of my ears."

Bailey looked down at the takeout menus. "I've lost my appetite."

Cassie laughed. "No, you didn't. Go ahead and order. I'll be fine."

"You sure?"

"Positive, and thank you."

"For what? You haven't even stolen my pizza yet."

"For your help, for making me come here, for staying with me." She shrugged. "Thank you."

Bailey ordered quickly and got herself a beer out of the fridge. She got back to the sofa to find Jazz curled up by Cassie's side. She laughed and dropped herself heavily into the recliner.

"How old were you?" Cassie asked.

"What?"

"When you last saw your mom."

"Oh. Ten."

"And you've never found her?"

Bailey shook her head and sipped her beer. She'd never spoken to anyone about her mother. She'd never wanted to. It was too personal, and it hurt too much. Now she found herself wanting Cassie to know. To know that she understood the pain Cassie was feeling. But also because she understood how vulnerable and exposed Cassie must have felt, given how much Bailey knew about her, and how hard it would be to have a panic attack in front of a virtual stranger. One of the girls in her group home had suffered from them, and she'd always had a hard time afterward. It wasn't a surprise that she was looking for information about Bailey to put their relationship on even footing. She'd often seen that with victims while she was a cop. What did surprise her, however, was her own willingness to accommodate the need. "I came close once." She picked at the edge of the label on her bottle, slowly easing the gummed paper away from the brown glass. "I found out she was in prison, but I didn't find out until she'd been paroled." The label tore and the damp paper stuck to her fingers. "When I tracked down the halfway house she was supposed to be staying at, she was already gone." She rolled the paper into a ball and balanced it on the arm of the recliner before trying again, only to repeat the process. "That was eight years ago."

"What was she in prison for?"

"Prostitution."

"Bailey, I'm so sorry."

Bailey shrugged. "It wasn't a surprise. I knew she was a hooker before I ended up in the system. That's life for a junkie."

"Couldn't you have gone and stayed with your dad?"

"Probably not. Even if she knew who he was, customers don't often admit to having kids with their hookers."

"I'm sorry."

"No need to be. It's been a long time since I've even wondered about him, never mind stressed about it."

"I meant about your mom."

"Oh." Bailey sipped again. "Thanks."

"No sign of her since?"

Bailey peeled off the last of the label and screwed it into a ball. "I've found a few possible leads, but when I go there I'm usually told she left years ago. I don't have anything definite for the last five years."

"How old would she be now?"

"Sixty-four." Bailey smiled sadly as Cassie's eyebrows rose. "Yeah, she was only fifteen when I was born and she'd already lived through hell, if you ask me."

"Wow. She must have been very brave to have kept you."

"I like to think so."

"Do you think you'll find her?"

Bailey pursed her lips. "The sixty-four thousand dollar question, and I honestly don't have an answer for it. Some days I think I will. I believe that I'll find where she's living and I'll go and say 'hi, Mom' and she'll tell me she tried to find me but it just never worked out for her." She finished her beer and pushed the wadded up label into the neck. "Other days I think she's dead, and I'll never know if she ever even looked for me. That I'll never find her grave—never get the chance to say good-bye. To thank her for everything she did for me." Bailey wasn't sure where all the words were coming from, but she couldn't stop them. "She's my mom. So, you see, I really do know what it's like to know there's something missing. Something that you really need answers to."

"I hope you find her."

Bailey tilted her empty bottle in salute. "I know the statistics, Cassie. A sixty-four-year-old junkie is a rare find."

"But you still have hope."

Bailey laughed. "That was—is—my mom's name. Hope. So yeah, in my heart I always have Hope." The doorbell rang and Bailey went to retrieve the pizza, grabbing herself another beer as she passed the fridge.

She dropped the open pizza box on a low table between them and found she couldn't look at Cassie as she reached for a slice. She didn't want to see pity in Cassie's eyes. It was the reason she never spoke of her mother or her upbringing. She knew it changed the way people looked at her, the way they saw her. She leaned forward, her elbows resting heavily on her knees, her hair slipping forward to cover her face, and her shoulders slumped. It had seemed like the right thing to do only moments ago, but now she couldn't understand why she had told Cassie about her mother.

"I think you're amazing."

Bailey quickly lifted her head to stare at Cassie. Too quickly. A shooting pain ripped through her neck and she rubbed at it to make it relax. "Say what?"

"Police officer, FBI agent, private investigator, cancer survivor, and still looking for your mother after thirty-nine years. I think you're amazing."

"You missed some stuff off that list." *Like lonely, recluse, antisocial, and unlovable.*

"I'm sure I did," Cassie said, "You're also a good friend, good with animals, and a really wonderful human being."

Bailey could feel her cheeks burning, but tried to laugh off the compliment. "You're just saying that 'cause you want my pizza." She waved her hand over the box. "Help yourself. There's plenty."

Cassie cocked her head to the side, clearly analyzing every action and word that Bailey said—and just as clearly realizing what was behind Bailey's reaction. She reached for a slice of pizza and smiled, seemingly willing to let Bailey off the hook. "You said you'd update me on the case. Is there news on Daniela?"

"That's right, I did," Bailey said around a mouthful of cheese, pepperoni, and Italian sausage. "Well, I tracked her from her London address to the Florida Keys."

"What was she doing there?"

"It seems she was looking into a career change. She passed various scuba diving qualifications, including an instructor qualification. I found her registered with the IRS as working for the dive school as an instructor just a few weeks ago. Once I had the state, a DMV check brought me her home address in seconds. Finsbury-Sterling isn't a very common name."

"Is she still there? Why did she change fields? Why Florida? Do you have an address?"

Bailey held up her hands. "One question at a time. Why the change and why there, I have no idea. I do have an address, and I'm going to fly down and check it out tomorrow. After that, I'll be able to tell you if she's still there. Okay?"

"I'll come with you."

Bailey shook her head. "That's not the way I work."

"Please. If she's there I need to see her. What's the point of you going there, finding her, and then flying back to report it to me, for me to then fly down there. We might as well go together."

"Two problems with that little theory. No, make that three."

Cassie grabbed a slice of pizza. "And what are your problems?"

"One, you have to work—"

"I can get cover. My apartment was broken into and I received a head injury. No problem in getting a few days off, at least."

Bailey had to concede that was definitely workable. "Okay, problem two. Jazz. I was going to ask if you could watch her while I fly down there. If you're with me then there's no one to watch Jazz."

"We could drive instead of fly. Jazz could come with us, and we'll take turns driving while the other gets some sleep. It shouldn't take that long."

"Do you have any idea how many miles it is from here?" Bailey was incredulous.

"Rough guess, about fifteen hundred. If we drove in shifts and didn't stop overnight we could do it in twenty-four hours."

"You're serious?"

"Deadly."

Bailey dropped her head in her hands. "Oh my God. You're crazy."

"What was your third objection?"

"I work alone."

"Why? Surely it's safer to work with a partner. Isn't that what you did when you were a cop and an FBI agent?"

"Yes, but I'm not a cop or a federal agent anymore."

"I know. Even more reason to work with a partner."

"Cassie, I don't want a partner."

"It's just a temporary thing." She ruffled the fur on Jazz's head. "Are you looking forward to a road trip?" Jazz let out a short bark, a doggie smile breaking out on her face. "See, Jazz wants to go too."

She stared at Cassie. Her eyes burned bright with excitement, her cheeks looked flushed, and her chest rose quickly with excitement. She reminded herself that it had been years since this woman had laid eyes on her child, and that she was doing everything she could to find her again. Who was she to deny her any chance of that happening? She felt her own excitement rising at the thought of reuniting mother and child. Seeing Cassie hold Daniela in her arms, the two of them crying, telling each other how much they missed each other.

Bailey flopped back in her seat and closed her eyes. "Fine. But we'll need to set off early. I don't want to hit rush hour traffic near any major cities, so I want to be out of here by five. And see if you can get the rest of the week off. I'm not up to driving for twenty-four hours straight or more. We'll find somewhere to stop on the way."

"You're the boss."

"Yeah." Bailey snorted. "Like I'm gonna believe that line of crap."

"What?" Cassie grinned, both of them well aware that she had gotten her own way.

"Don't play the innocent with me, Professor. I know when I've been played."

Cassie reached for Bailey's hand and squeezed her fingers. "Thank you."

She was beginning to get a handle on Cassie's contact issue. Or at least, she thought she was. If Cassie initiated it, or saw it coming, she was okay. It was when she got caught by surprise that she reacted badly. "Don't thank me. I'm picking all the music."

"I can live with that."

"Great." *Now all I've got to do is figure out what the hell two virtual strangers can talk about for a couple days stuck together in a car. Alone. Each way.* Bailey swallowed hard and swigged down the last of her beer.

## CHAPTER NINETEEN

Finn schooled her face into a serious expression as she looked away from her computer screen. She could barely believe the progress she was making. Lugh was almost ready. The first set of test results on live specimens were due any second. Under the microscope, it was performing perfectly, and all indicators in the lab animals were positive too. She was excited. She only hoped she was doing a good job at keeping that from showing on her face. She knew Billy still hadn't been able to track who the surveillance equipment belonged to, and they didn't want the wrong people knowing about her discovery. She was more than happy with that. The last time she had shared news of a breakthrough with anyone, it had ended up as Balor. It wasn't a mistake she wanted to repeat.

She had made a significant improvement in Lyell's Gamble too. So much so that she was almost ready to let Knight and Whittaker know that she was ready to implement their plan and approach Mehalik about selling Balor to him. Just as her father had planned. Only this time they were expecting to catch all the bad guys. She could only hope the plan went as well as everyone continually assured her it would.

Well, everyone included exactly two people. Stephen Knight and Andrew Whittaker. Oz, Billy, and Junior seemed adamant that neither of them were to be trusted and were intent on putting their own plan into action as soon as she was ready. Well, she was damn near ready, and she was proud of herself, whatever plan they moved ahead with.

The research on Balor was out there and there was nothing she could do to drag that back now, but creating Lugh meant that it didn't matter. For the first time in months, she thought of her research without feeling as though a steel band were wrapped around her chest, slowly getting tighter and tighter.

The computer beeped and drew her attention to the numbers that began scrolling across her screen. She rested her chin in her hand as she watched, in the hope that it kept the grin from spreading across her face. It worked. She'd done it.

She got up from her desk and stretched out stiff and achy muscles before finding Oz. She was in the changing room after working out with Junior in the small gym where they were whiling away many of the hours Finn spent working in the lab. Finn licked her lips as she approached a slightly sweaty and out of breath Oz. Her tank top and shorts clung to her damp skin as she sucked on a bottle of sports drink. She wrapped her arms around Oz's neck, waited for her to stop drinking, and then kissed her soundly.

She felt Oz's arms wrap around her and she whispered against her lips, "It works." Finn pressed her lips hard against Oz's to hide any reaction she might have. They had no idea where other cameras may have been placed. Oz tightened her arms and spun her in a circle.

Oz placed kisses along her cheek to her ear and whispered, "I'm so proud of you, I knew you could do it."

Finn tucked her head against Oz's neck. "I love you." She said it loud enough that any listening device would be able to pick it up and explain easily the long embrace.

"I love you too, baby. I wish we were home right now." She peppered Finn's cheeks, eyes, and nose with tiny kisses.

Finn giggled. "Me too, sweetheart. We'll leave early tonight. I promise."

Oz slowly lowered her feet back to the floor. "I'm going to hold you to that." She patted her on the bottom as Finn turned toward the door. "I have plans for you later."

Finn smiled, knowing there would be a lot of planning to do when they got home. She'd need help coordinating the effort to produce enough of the antidote to make release viable over the next few days, and the only people she trusted were much more adept at depressing the trigger on a gun than the plunger on a syringe. But they were short on time and skilled help. Whittaker and Knight were adamant that everything would move quickly after they announced her presence at the helm of Sterling Enterprises at the function on Friday. So she intended to be ready.

She smiled, thinking how cute Oz would look in a white lab coat, with a stethoscope around her neck and safety goggles covering those baby blues. She licked her lips again as her mouth suddenly went dry. *Later.*

# CHAPTER TWENTY

Cassie hummed along to the radio. Bailey's seat was as far back as it could go, she had a baseball cap pulled over her eyes, and her coat was tucked around her like a blanket. Cassie reached for the volume button, hoping that if she turned it down a little she'd be able to get a few hours of sleep.

"Touch it and I may have to kill you."

Cassie giggled at the meaningless threat. "I was only going to turn it down so you could sleep."

"Then the sound of the engine and the tires will keep me awake instead. At least Billie Holiday sounds good."

"That's a matter of opinion." Cassie checked her rearview mirror and shifted lanes.

"Oh, you did not just say that."

Cassie raised an eyebrow and glanced at Bailey as she twisted in her seat and tried to sit up gracefully. She giggled as Bailey failed miserably.

"You might as well just get out now and walk to Florida. I can't share a car with someone who clearly has no musical taste whatsoever."

Cassie laughed. Six hours into the trip and they were having…fun? She thought about it more and more, and yes, they were having fun. She felt more than a little sad at the fact that it was such an alien concept to her that she almost hadn't recognized it. "And who would you tease then?"

"Jazz." Bailey laughed. "Just kidding. I do think we should stop pretty soon though."

"Coffee or bathroom?"

"Yes."

Cassie laughed. "I saw a sign for a service station a little way back that said ten miles to the next rest area."

"Good. I think I can wait ten miles."

"I'm very glad to hear that."

Bailey smiled. "How is it we seem to end up discussing my bladder with alarming regularity?"

"Just lucky, I guess." Cassie smirked and checked the fuel gauge. "We should fill up while we're there."

Bailey nodded. "Good plan." She looked outside. "Where are we anyway?"

"On I-95 coming up on Maryland."

Bailey looked impressed. "We're making good time. You drive race cars?"

"One or two getaway cars." She winked at Bailey and enjoyed the lazy smile that tugged at the corners of her lips.

"I thought I recognized you from *America's Most Wanted*."

"You got me."

They traveled in easy silence for a couple more miles before Bailey turned in her seat and looked at her. "What will you do if she doesn't want to see you?"

Cassie kept her eyes glued to the road. It was the question she didn't want to face, but she knew that it was a very real possibility. As far as she knew, Daniela believed she was dead, that she'd killed herself. Faced with the reality of a mother who had instead abandoned her—Cassie was terrified that Daniela wouldn't even give her the chance to explain. And if she did, there was no guarantee that she would understand or want anything more to do with her beyond that.

"I don't know. All I know is that I have to try everything I can to let her know that what I did was to protect her. And that I love her. I always have, and that won't change if she says she doesn't want anything to do with me. At least then I'll know. No more questions, you know?"

Bailey sat back in her seat. "Yeah, I know." She was quiet for a few minutes, and Cassie was sure she was thinking about her mother rather than Daniela. "Any answer's better than no answer. Even if it isn't the one you'd hoped for."

Cassie let her slip back into her thoughts and concentrated on the road, unwilling to pry where she wasn't wanted, and the pensive look on Bailey's face was enough to convince her of that. A few minutes later, she turned into the service station.

"I'll take Jazz for a little walk if you want to head in first."

"Thanks." Bailey took off as Cassie opened the rear door and unclipped Jazz's seat belt.

"I still can't believe you need to have your seat belt on. You're a dog." She grabbed her leash and headed for a small grassy area a few feet away. It wasn't lunchtime yet, but her stomach was complaining after such an early start, and all she could think about was getting some food from the restaurant. She sat on one of the benches and let the extendable leash out full-length to give Jazz some space. She remembered the last time she had been in Florida. It was a time of terror and pleading, and loss. She shivered at the memories and tried to concentrate on the here and now.

"I heard your stomach rumbling before we pulled up." Bailey held out a coffee and a sandwich.

"What is it?"

"BLT on rye. Hope that's okay. If not I suppose you can have the roast beef and mustard on wheat."

Cassie took the sandwich and smiled. "BLT's great, thanks." She patted the bench beside her and sipped at the coffee. *Cappuccino, just the way I like it too.* "That's perfect, thank you."

"You're welcome."

*Oh my God, is she blushing?* "You're very sweet."

Bailey's eyes went round and she choked on her coffee. "I…you… that's…" She started between hacking coughs.

"It's a compliment, Bailey. You're meant to say thank you."

She wiped her mouth with her napkin and mumbled her thanks. Cassie bit into her sandwich. She wasn't naïve, she knew she was attracted to Bailey, and unless she was reading the signs all wrong, she was pretty sure that Bailey was attracted to her too, but she also recognized that Bailey was a professional and she was a client. End of story. Period. It didn't mean she couldn't enjoy making Bailey blush now and again, did it? After all, the effect was captivating. Bailey's eyes sparkled, and the way she tried to hide behind those long bangs and shaggy haircut…cute. It was the only word that described it.

"I'm sorry. What did you say?"

"I said I'll take over driving for a while." Bailey cocked her head to the side and frowned. "You okay?"

"Yeah, I'm fine. I was just daydreaming." She felt her cheeks heating and knew she was sporting a blush of her own.

"Hope you were somewhere better than the I-95 then."

"Oh, I don't know. There's worse places to be right now."

Bailey smiled at her. "Yeah, I guess you're right." They slowly finished their lunch before Bailey nodded at the car. "Shall we?" She offered her hand to help Cassie up.

"We shall." Cassie didn't hesitate to wrap her fingers around Bailey's but the quick flash of electricity that surged down her arm caused them to stare at each other.

## CHAPTER TWENTY-ONE

O z opened the door. "On your own, Agent?"
"I'm sorry?"

"I'm surprised Mr. Whittaker isn't with you."

Knight smiled, but it didn't reach his eyes. "He called earlier. He can't make it tonight."

Oz didn't like it. Whittaker and Knight were supposed to be their team coordinators. They were supposed to be leading them, advising them, and ensuring Finn's safety at all times. Tonight's meeting was to organize the way they approached the charity event on Friday. Whittaker was an essential part of that discussion. Something stank. "Problem?"

"Nothing that affects our plan here."

"You sure about that?" Oz felt increasingly confident in their decision to take Whittaker and Knight out of the loop.

"Positive, Ms. Zuckerman."

Oz saw the tiny twitch at the corner of his eye and knew he wasn't as confident as he sounded. What she couldn't decide was whether he *suspected* there was a problem that affected their mission, or he *knew* there was because he was the problem. Until she was sure, they'd continue the charade that they were disclosing everything to the "team" and wait for Finn to succeed. She offered him a small, tight smile and hoped it looked more sincere than it felt. "I'd rather you called me Oz. There's too many Zuckermans here otherwise."

"Then you should call me Stephen." He held up a roll of paper. "Shall we get started?" She waved him in and followed him to the large dining table where he unrolled the plans. Junior and Billy took up positions so they could easily view the diagrams. "This is the observatory at the top of the rock. The charity function is ticket only, and all service people have been fully vetted because the mayor of New York plans on being in attendance tomorrow night." He pointed to the map. "We have one escalator up and one down. The service elevator will be guarded at all times by the mayor's security."

"What about the lower floor?" Junior asked. "Where everyone gets on the escalator."

"Two high speed elevators from the ground floor to the sixty-ninth floor. No one gets in either of them without a ticket. X-ray machines and metal detectors are in place as each guest's tickets are checked against the guest list."

"I have a question." Finn sat next to Oz and ran her hand over her back.

"Shoot," Stephen said.

"Why do we need a plan for me to show up at a party that no one knows I'm going to attend anyway?"

"This is just to make sure that we're prepared for any eventuality, Finn, and to help establish you as someone to be taken seriously."

"Just being there isn't making enough of a statement?"

Stephen shook his head. "No. Your father never went anywhere without his guards, and you never did either. To start doing that now would just be an invitation for trouble when Mehalik finds out."

"What are you talking about? I didn't have guards."

"Yes, you did."

"No, I didn't."

"Finn, I have photographic proof that every function you ever attended, every place you were ever seen in public, you had guards. Whether you knew it or not, they were there, making their presence felt and keeping men like Mehalik, and the others your father did business with, off your back. One of your father's favorite tactics of coercion was to kidnap loved ones and threaten them, torture them, even kill them, to get what he wanted. It's how he got Dr. Lyell to cooperate."

"I know." Finn's voice was quiet and her face paled. Oz knew her well enough to know she was probably close to throwing up at the thought of what her father had done over the years. Every detail added to her burden of guilt and made her more determined to try to atone. Not only for the wrongs she perceived as her own, but his as well. It was a burden that was tearing Finn apart, just a little more every day. And that was killing Oz to watch.

"And it was a tactic he intended to make sure was never used against him. You had your own security so no one could use you to get to him."

"So going without a show of force wouldn't be believable." Finn reluctantly agreed. Oz was overjoyed that she wouldn't have to fight her on it. Finn hated the thought of anyone else being put in danger because of her. They'd talked about it many times over the past few weeks, and she'd expected Finn to fight them tooth and nail, but it had been a fight Oz knew she couldn't afford to lose. She wouldn't risk Finn's safety for the sake of her comfort. That wasn't a compromise Oz could ever make. Fortunately, appealing to the logical scientist in Finn worked better than trying to negotiate with her emotional side.

Knight nodded. "Exactly. These men expect things to be done a certain way. The world they operate in behaves a certain way, and if we want them to trust us, we have to follow those rules. We don't *want* him to trust us, we *need* him to trust *you* if we're to stand a chance of pulling this off. It's a long-range plan, Finn." He pointed to the plans. "This is the first stage in creating a cover for you that will put you in the right place at the right time to make a deal that will change the face of the terrorist community for years to come." He shrugged. "Hopefully, anyway."

"What do you mean by that? Do you have doubts about this plan?" Oz asked, the mere thought of the risk Finn was taking made her stomach knot. For it to all be for nothing—

"No. The only thing I doubt is that it will take years to replace Mehalik. There is probably already someone ready and waiting to take his place. Another reason why we can't just shoot him. If we can get him to talk, he'll know who the next likely candidate will be." He looked from one to the other. "I know you don't know me, and you don't have any reason to trust me, but this plan really does have a good chance of succeeding. All we have to do is play our roles and we can get a very dangerous man out of circulation."

"You don't have to convince me that this is the right thing to do, Stephen. I don't doubt that," Finn said sadly. "I just wish it was over with already."

"Then let's finish up here and we'll be one step closer to it being finished." He pointed back to the plans. "Junior, you'll be with Finn on the observation deck. Stay with her at all times." Oz looked up at Junior and started to object. She should be the one to protect Finn. It was her responsibility. Finn was her partner. She had to do her best to protect her. In that instant the realization hit her that in this situation she *wasn't* the best one to protect her lover. Junior was still on active service and he was a highly trained operative. He was a SEAL for God's sake. His reactions were faster than Oz's. He was stronger, his instincts sharper, and he had just enough emotional distance not to panic with Finn in his custody, should the worst happen. Oz knew she was too close. She'd do what was right to prevent Finn from any danger, mission be damned. Junior would be able to see everything far more clearly than she could. She swallowed her pride and knew her emotions were playing out across her face by the look of comprehension and the softening of Junior's gaze.

"Stuck like glue." He winked at her.

"Oz, you'll be with me on the sixty-ninth floor. Billy, I want you in the lobby with Whittaker."

"I have a problem with that plan," Billy said, scratching his jaw.

"And that is?" Stephen looked him in the eye. His eyes narrowed and Oz watched him study her father like a bug under a microscope. The curl of his lip and the twitch of his nose told her exactly what he thought of the interference he was getting on this mission.

"Who's going to run ops?"

"I have access to people who can keep an eye on the feeds for us—"

"Like hell." Billy's jaw clenched visibly as he worked to control his temper. "I am not working at the say-so of some faceless son of a bitch on the other end of a comm line that I've never met. Not a snowball's chance in hell, boy."

"My people are experts in running operations all over the world from a central command point."

"I don't give a rat's ass what your people are experts in. I ain't working with them."

"Then what do you suggest, Captain?" Knight's accommodating response looked painful for him. He seemed to be working hard to control his own temper, and Oz began to wonder exactly what he had been told by his superiors. And just who those superiors were.

"Junior, get on that there phone and call the admiral. I want AJ here, and I want him here tonight." Junior picked up the phone and followed his command. "I'll be running ops. Get me a surveillance van and a street permit."

"Wait a minute—"

"Junior, hang on a second. Agent, do I need to tell the admiral to make a call and get me a fully equipped van, street permits, and two extra bodies for this mission?"

Stephen stood toe-to-toe with him, and Oz smiled as she watched her father stare him down. She'd been on the receiving end of that intense, do-not-fuck-with-me-or-you-will-be-fucking-sorry stare. She squirmed. Being on the periphery of that look still made her twitch.

"No, sir, I'll make sure you have what you need," Stephen said through gritted teeth.

Oz had to work hard not to snigger. It had the same effect on CIA agents as it did on teenage girls. Sweet.

"I'll just be needing that extra body, Junior."

"Yes, sir."

"Excellent. In that case, I'll be in the van outside running ops." Billy pointed at the plan. "AJ will be on the ground floor with Mr. Whittaker. Agent, you and Oz will take sixty-nine, Junior with Finn. Any questions?" Everyone shook their heads. "Good. Junior, before you hang up I want a word with your dad. There's a couple of things I need him to send down with the boy." He winked at Finn. "Just in case of emergency." Junior handed the phone over, a wide grin covered his face.

Stephen turned to Finn. "Who is AJ?"

Oz smiled and watched the interplay between the two of them, knowing he thought Finn was the easy mark in the room. A few months ago, he would have been right. Her naivety made her trust—it still did, to a certain extent—but she'd been burned now, and her trust was reserved for those who had earned it. He wasn't one of them.

"Junior's younger brother."

"Is he a SEAL too?"

Oz wondered at the questions but realized that maybe the agent wasn't as stupid as it might seem. He'd been a CIA agent for fifteen years. She'd done her homework, and she was sure he'd done his too. He would know the background to her entire family. He'd have to. He wouldn't have lasted fifteen years otherwise. So why ask questions you already know the answer to? Simple. He was testing her, and by extension, all of them. Her opinion of the agent rose. Slightly.

"No." Finn crossed her legs and folded her arms on the table. "AJ's a lieutenant in the Coast Guard."

"Great." Stephen didn't try to hide the sarcasm in his tone.

Finn offered him a sweet, insincere smile. "If you didn't want them to take over, you shouldn't have done a half-arsed job, Mr. Knight."

"I thought I told you to call me Stephen."

"I'd rather not. It implies that I might actually like you."

Stephen threw his head back and laughed. "Oh, my dear Finn, you might actually be able to pull this off after all. You need to let your inner bitch out more often."

"I'll take that under advisement."

"I'm serious. If you want Mehalik to believe that you're prepared to sell him this weapon, knowing exactly what it can do, you need to be able to pull off the callous bitch routine. Your father was a greedy bastard. Mehalik doesn't respect that, but he understands it. You have to give him another reason to understand you."

"Why wouldn't greed work like it did for my dad?"

"Because you've created this, from the root up, as they say. You know this beast too well to be able to let it go for money alone. You need some other reason behind it or he won't trust you. He'll smell the trap a mile away."

"Then what do you suggest?"

"Anger."

Finn frowned. "I don't understand."

"Channel the anger you feel at your father, and play being angry at the world for his failings. Mehalik thinks Westerners are spoiled brats, so he'd believe that. If you can make him think that you're willing to deal with him to prove to your father that you're better than he was, that he should have given you more credit or whatever, he'll believe that. If you can convince him that you're angry at the world for some reason then he'll buy into your willingness to destroy it."

"What possible reason could I have to be prepared to destroy the world, other than anger at my dear old dad?"

"Your mother died when you were a young child. Killed herself, right?"

Finn nodded and Oz could see the tears well in her eyes. She gritted her teeth, knowing how the mention of Finn's mother affected her. She followed Finn's lead though, and gave no indication that anyone in the room thought differently in regards to the fate of Cassandra Finsbury-Sterling. Stephen Knight simply wasn't trusted enough.

"That's enough to screw up a lot of kids. Add to that a father who was trying to steal your work out from under you." He shrugged. "You don't have to actually feel that way, but you need to act like you do. Channel your inner actress."

"She's on holiday right now." Finn smiled and Oz knew she was trying to alleviate some of the pressure she was feeling.

"Then get her back." Stephen looked her in the eye. "You really need him to believe you, or everyone in this room is likely to end up dead."

"You stupid son of a bitch." Oz grabbed his lapels. "Don't you think she's under enough pressure? Do you really think it helps telling her shit like that?"

He wrapped his hands around her fists and tried to break the grip she had on him. "She has a right to know the truth."

"Do you think she's stupid? She knows what's at stake here. Probably more than you do. Like you said, she knows exactly what this toxin can do. She's the one trying to create the damn antidote for it." Oz tugged him closer to her and watched his face pale as she towered over him. "So back the fuck off and help." She pushed him away from her and watched him stumble backward. "Don't put any more roadblocks in the way."

"What are you talking about? What roadblocks?"

"Putting together a piece of shit plan like this one." She pointed to the plans of the Rockefeller Center. "No on site ops? Are you fucking kidding me? And where the hell's Whittaker? He should be here while we plan this." She watched his jaw clench at Whittaker's name and the twitch at the corner of his eye fired again, and she knew without a doubt that he knew more about Whittaker than he was telling them. Fucker. "We're supposed to be working together on this, and it's you putting us all in jeopardy right now. Not Finn. So back off, buddy, and act like the professional you're supposed to be."

"Oz." Billy put a hand on her shoulder. "He's got the message."

"He better remember it then." Oz balled her hands into fists and tried to concentrate on her breathing. She felt soft fingers caress her knuckles and looked down. Finn slowly uncurled one of her hands and entwined their fingers.

"I love you." Finn smiled up at her and Oz felt her anger dissipate.

"I love you too."

"Pops says we'll have everything we need by midnight," Junior said.

Billy grinned. "Excellent."

"Want to fill me in?" Stephen Knight glowered at Oz but took his place next to Billy.

"Just a contingency plan, should we need one."

"We really aren't expecting anything to happen at this party." Stephen frowned.

"I know." Billy pushed his fingers through his shaggy, dirty blond hair. "But I was taught the five P's when I was at boot camp."

"The five P's?"

"Proper planning prevents poor performance." He looked the CIA agent in the eye. "I don't take any chances when it comes to my family."

The room was silent while Billy and Stephen stared at each other. No one moved. The tension in the room went up another notch as the seconds ticked by. Slowly, Stephen dropped his gaze. She'd expected more of a fight. And from the surprised glance from Junior, so had he. Stephen's capitulation had effectively handed control of the operation to Billy.

"Understood."

Oz's distrust of the agent grew. Why would a CIA agent cede control of the operation with so little fight? She'd seen agents cling to a case with their last professional breath and never concede control. She'd also seen the flicker of something in Knight's eyes when she'd stood toe-to-toe with him. He was hiding something. She didn't know what, but she was damn sure she was going to get to the bottom of it. If it had anything to do with Mehalik, it put them all in danger. She glanced at Finn. And that was a chance she simply wasn't willing to take.

## CHAPTER TWENTY-TWO

Bailey pulled into the parking lot at the small motel. It was just after eight thirty, the sun had long since set, and her eyes felt full of sand. Fifteen hours on the road had brought them as far as the outskirts of Savannah, and they still had a long way to go, but she was happy enough to call it a night. Cassie was curled up in the passenger seat, and Bailey smiled at the soft snores that filtered out from under her long auburn hair every now and then. She decided to let her continue sleeping while she arranged them both rooms for the night. Her stomach rumbled loudly as she opened the car door, and she quickly looked over at Cassie to see if the noise had woken her. She smiled as another gentle snore greeted her ears. *Guess not.*

"Jazz, watch the car, then we can worry about dinner." The dog let out a tiny bark, as though she was trying not to wake Cassie either. "I swear you're just too smart for your own good, pooch."

The motel reception was small but clean, with a small office behind the desk. She could hear cries for one player or another to "put the damn ball in the net" or "pass, you greedy son of a gun." She rang the bell on the counter and smiled when a guy poked his head out.

"Hi there." He smiled.

"Sorry to interrupt the game."

He waved his hand. "They couldn't hit the side of a barn with that ball, never mind the damn net. I'm Doug. How can I help you tonight?" Doug was easily seventy if he was a day. The stooped shoulders and thin hair was a dead giveaway even without the lined, weather-beaten face that smiled broadly at her.

"Nice to meet you, Doug, I'm Bailey, and I hope you have two rooms? I have a dog with me too."

"No problem with the dog, just don't leave it in the room alone. But I've only got one room available tonight. It has twin beds though." He smiled. "That okay?"

Bailey shrugged. It would have to be. "Sure." She hoped Cassie would be okay with it, but she wasn't up to driving anymore tonight.

"It'll save you some money, anyway."

"Good point." It was a business trip, after all. She quickly paid for the room and took the key on its oversized key ring. Cassie was still snoring when she got back to the car and let Jazz out. Bailey opened the passenger side door and shook Cassie's shoulder, only to have her hand brushed off, like a fly being shooed away. Bailey grinned and tried again.

"Wakey, wakey, sleeping beauty."

"G'way."

"Come on. Time to get out of the car." Bailey shook her leg this time, and received a slap for her trouble. "Ow."

"I'm not driving anymore."

Bailey laughed. "You were the one who said we should just drive straight through and not stop."

"You should have told me how foolish that idea was."

"I did. And that's why I've got us beds for the night at this fine establishment."

Cassie finally cracked open one eye.

"I could kiss you right now." Cassie paled slightly. "I-I, I didn't—shit—I meant that metaphorically."

Bailey had to work saliva back into her mouth before she could speak. "I figured." Her voice sounded thick and lower than normal even to her own ears. "I'll grab the bags and then we can check out our palace for the evening."

"You already checked in?" Cassie stretched her arms over her head as she climbed out of the car and Bailey couldn't keep from staring as Cassie's sweater pulled tight across her breasts and rode up her tummy just enough for her to catch a glimpse of creamy white flesh. Bailey swallowed hard and slammed the trunk closed.

"Yeah. They only had one room left though."

Cassie raised an eyebrow as she tugged on the hem of her sweater and swung her coat around her shoulders.

"Doug at reception assured me it has two beds though. I haven't seen it. I just checked in. I'm sure we could find another motel somewhere, I just—I mean, I'm really tired and I couldn't face driving around for God knows how long trying to find somewhere else when it's got two beds anyway—"

"Bailey?"

"Yeah?"

"You're rambling."

"Sorry."

Cassie took her bag from Bailey's hand and slipped the strap over her shoulder. "It's okay. Are you going to show me the way?"

Bailey locked up and led them up a small flight of concrete steps. Room twenty was at the end of the row, and the heavy beige curtains danced in the air when she pushed open the door. Neutral colors, a small pine dresser between the two beds, a reading lamp, alarm clock, and telephone on top of it. Not luxury, but functional. The scent of disinfectant in the air attested to the recent cleaning the room had undergone, as did the overlying odor of lavender-scented air freshener.

"Do you mind if I open the window and let some of the hideous smell vent?" Cassie wafted her hand in front of her nose.

"I'll get it." Bailey dropped her bag on the first bed she came to and wrestled with the window catch as Cassie moved to the other side of the room.

"Otherwise it's not a bad room at all." She smiled, and Bailey let out a relieved breath.

"Yeah, I think we can make do with this, don't you, Jazz?" The dog jumped on Cassie's bed and turned in circles a couple of times before dropping down and promptly falling asleep. "I think that answers that question." Bailey's stomach growled again and Cassie giggled.

"Can I interest you in dinner?"

"Afraid I'll eat you if you don't feed me?" As soon as the words were out of her mouth, Bailey wanted to pull them back. She could feel her cheeks burning again, and she hoped Cassie didn't think about what she'd said. The raised eyebrow told her she wasn't that lucky, but Cassie was gracious enough to let it pass.

"I'm a little hungry myself. Did you see anything nearby?"

"Yeah, there's a diner across the street, or I can go to reception and see what Doug recommends."

"Across the street sounds good. I don't feel like getting back in the car again tonight. I'd forgotten how long this drive feels when you're stuck in the car all day." Cassie unpacked her toiletries and tucked her sleepwear under her pillow.

"You've made this trip before?" Bailey was grateful for the change of subject, and it seemed the farther from Boston they got the more talkative Cassie became. She seemed to feel safer with greater distance. Or maybe it was the excitement of getting closer to her daughter. Whatever it was, Bailey didn't care. The more Cassie talked, the less she had to—and that meant she made less of a fool of herself, which seemed to happen with alarming regularity.

"When Karen and I left England. My family lived in Sarasota Springs. We had no one else to turn to for help. We used everything we had leaving England." Cassie quietly finished unpacking her bag, placed her things into one of the drawers in the dresser, and tucked her bag under her bed.

"This was after your death?" Bailey curled her fingers in the air, making air quotes as she commented on Cassie's supposed death.

"Yes. To say they were shocked to see me is a bit of an understatement." She smiled sadly and sat on her bed, slowly dragging her brush through her hair. "I honestly thought my dad was going to have a heart attack right there on the lawn."

"I take it they helped though?"

"Eventually. At first he told me to get out of there and never come back."

"Why?"

"Because of Karen." Bailey was pretty sure the look on her face told Cassie exactly what she thought of that response, and Cassie smiled at her. "She looked at him like that too."

"Sorry."

"No need. It was a long time ago, and as you said, he did help us. He gave us money, a car, and falsified documents. Everything we needed to start a new life. The only catch was that we do it far away from him and my mother."

"Homophobic?"

"It was more than that. By the time he helped us, he was certain that William was watching them. While he didn't like that I was involved with Karen, they would have gotten used to it and been fine, eventually. But none of us could take the chance that William would find us through my parents. It wasn't safe for them, for us, or for Daniela." She put her brush into her drawer as Bailey's stomach rumbled again. She nodded toward the door. "I think we should get going before you start chewing on the furniture."

Jazz beat them both to the door, holding her leash in her mouth and looking up at her "service" vest hanging from a coat peg, which made Cassie giggle. "She has you very well trained, Bailey."

"You're not kidding." The diner was quiet, and they chose a booth in the corner by the window. Jazz slid under the table silently, settling her head on Bailey's foot. They ordered burgers, fries, and a pot of coffee and Bailey watched Cassie fidget with the salt shaker, spinning it around on the Formica table top. "Tell me about Karen."

The salt shaker toppled over, and Cassie hurriedly righted it and swept the spilled salt off the smooth surface. "What do you want to know?"

"How did you meet?"

Cassie smiled, and Bailey was sure she didn't even realize she'd done it. "I went back to work pretty soon after Daniela was born. I'd been working on a project before I went on maternity leave, and I was itching to get back to it. There was a nursery at the lab. I'd insisted upon it when William and I started the company. I knew one day I'd have children, and I wanted to keep them close by while I was working. Control freak, right?" She laughed a little. "Anyway, Karen was one of the nursery assistants there."

"I thought you said she was a cook."

"She was. But that came later."

"After you died?"

"Yes. Do you have to keep saying it like that?"

"What would you prefer me to say?"

"I don't know. Can't we just say left or something?"

Bailey shrugged. "Okay. After you left."

"Yes. When we moved away, it was the only job she could get then."

"So she was involved in Daniela's life pretty much from the start?"

Cassie nodded and straightened the menu cards in the rack. "Karen was wonderful with children, and Daniela loved her." Another wistful smile pulled at Cassie's lips. "My happiest memories are of time I spent with the two of them. There was one day that we took Daniela on a picnic. She must have been three. She was determined to feed crusts of bread to the ducklings, but there were some geese guarding the bank. The damn birds were bigger than she was and she was terrified." She chuckled. "She was such a tiny little thing."

"Just like you."

"Yes. She looked a lot like me. Same coloring and everything."

"I saw the pictures. She was a beautiful child."

"Thank you." Maternal pride lit Cassie's face. "Anyway, she was trying to feed these geese and they were flapping their wings and hissing at her, but she was so brave. She walked right up to the riverbank and threw the crusts as far as she could for the little baby ducks. The geese got most of it, but one of the little ducklings managed to get one of them, and Daniela's little face lit up." Cassie wiped the corner of her eye. "She was so proud of herself for feeding that one little baby."

"Gutsy kid."

"Yeah, she was. But she was pretty quiet, you know? Happy with her picture books, and coloring, and learning her letters. I still have a card she made me for mother's day. Karen helped her, but she wrote it herself. The e in Daniela was back to front, and the stick on the a was a good half inch away from the circle of it, but she was so proud of it. Oh God, I'm sorry." She grabbed a fistful of napkins and wiped the tears from her eyes. "You must think I'm pathetic." She hid her face in the tissue.

"Not at all." Bailey's voice was thick with emotion of her own. "I'm struggling not to grab a couple of those napkins myself, but that wouldn't be good for my reputation."

Cassie snorted. "And what reputation would that be? I already know you're a big softie."

"Hey, who told?" Bailey managed to suppress the urge to wipe the final tear from Cassie's cheek and tried to ignore just how beautiful her eyes were after she'd cried.

"Jazz."

"I knew I needed to muzzle that dog."

"Aw, never. You couldn't do that to someone as sweet as Jazz."

"Yeah, yeah." The waitress delivered their orders and left them to enjoy their meal. Bailey licked her lips while she doctored her burger.

"Ketchup and mustard?"

"It's a taste sensation, baby." She tore off a huge bite before offering Cassie a bite.

"No, thanks. I think I'll stick with mayo."

"Boring." Bailey spoke around a mouthful.

"I'm sorry. I think I'm losing my mind. I could have sworn a half masticated burger just tried to speak to me."

Bailey swallowed. "Sorry. I'm starving, and this is a really good burger."

"They always are when you're hungry."

"True."

"So what about you?"

"What about me?"

"I know you live alone. How come?"

Bailey choked on her burger. She spluttered and coughed, before sipping some water and wiping her eyes. "Isn't that a little bit personal?"

Cassie quirked her eyebrow. "Are you kidding me?"

"What?"

"You've asked me far more personal questions and know more about me than almost anyone on the planet. And you think *that's* a bit personal?"

"I ask for professional reasons."

Cassie just continued to stare at her, clearly not buying her explanation.

"I'm a private detective. You hired me to find your kid. I have to ask questions."

"And how does asking about my dead partner help you in finding Daniela?"

"Well…" *Shit.*

"So, Ms. Nosey Parker, it's your turn to answer a few questions."

"I guess turnabout is fair play."

"Indeed. So?"

"Cassie, I don't think I'm up to it…"

"Bailey, hey, no worries." Cassie's expression was gentle. "It doesn't matter." She picked up a fry and blew on it.

Bailey put her burger back on her plate and wiped her hands. *I'm such a fucking chicken shit. She's right. She's shared far more than I needed to know for the investigation. Yes, I know there's far more to it, stuff she can't tell me. Not that she won't—can't. She has genuine reasons to be terrified of sharing anything, yet she is. I need to suck it up and be as brave as I pretend to be.*

"I'm not good with people."

Cassie frowned. "Sorry?"

"When I'm working, I am. I have to be. But just me, without the badge, or the investigation to hide behind? I'm just not good with people. I get tongue-tied, and I don't know what to say, or I babble on and on, with no end in sight. I don't know why. It's just how I am."

"Have you always thought that?"

Bailey nodded.

"Well, I think you're wrong."

"Cassie, I've got forty-nine years of history to back me up. You're the scientist. Doesn't that count as proof?"

"Nope. It's faulty data."

Bailey picked up a fry and pointed it at Cassie. "Okay, Madam Scientist, explain."

"You entered into the study with a faulty preposition, which fatally flawed your results from the outset."

"Did you just speak English?"

Cassie laughed. "Yes."

Bailey scratched her head and picked up her burger again. "Well, Professor, I'm a simple gumshoe, so you better explain it in more elementary terms."

"With subjective experiments, if you expect a certain outcome, nine times out of ten you'll get it."

"Ah, so it's my own negative expectations that led me to a life of lonely spinsterhood?"

"Something like that."

"And what happens the tenth time?"

"Exceptional variables leading to exceptional results." Cassie's eyes met hers and Bailey was trapped. She watched Cassie's pupils dilate and knew her own had probably done the same. Her pulse pounded in her ears, and the air that surrounded her felt like a caress upon her overly sensitive skin. Cassie's lips parted, her tongue darted out to wet them, and Bailey's gaze shifted to those full, beautiful lips. She felt herself being pulled toward her, she wanted to feel how soft they were, how plump they'd feel beneath her mouth, against her skin.

"I haven't been lucky enough to find that one," Bailey whispered, unsure where the words had come from.

"You will." Cassie cleared her throat. "It's a statistical probability." She blinked and leaned back in her chair, breaking the spell.

Bailey shook her head and took another bite as she tried to dislodge the image of Cassie's face from her mind as she anticipated Bailey's kiss. "Is that what Karen was for you? A statistical improbability?"

"I never said I wasn't good with people." Cassie winked.

Bailey snorted. "Oh, so your statistics are different, right?"

"Exactly. See, you do speak professor."

"Thanks." Bailey wasn't sure how it had happened, but she felt comfortable with Cassie again. They moved on to lighter topics and laughed their way through the rest of the meal, until they decided it was time to turn in. Bailey crossed the road and tried not to think about the flash of lace she'd seen as Cassie had tucked her sleepwear under her pillow when she'd unpacked.

## CHAPTER TWENTY-THREE

Finn tucked her legs under her bottom and turned the page of the magazine she was pretending to read. She couldn't focus on any of the articles in *Scientific American,* and she wasn't sure why she was even bothering with the pretense, but it kept her hands busy at least. Her mind, however, was a blur of nonstop questions and problems, and every answer she found only compounded the issue. The problem was—and would always be—time. There simply wasn't going to be enough time to make the antidote and give it a chance to work effectively through normal channels. That would take months, maybe years, and there was no way to keep it quiet for that long.

"You do know you're holding that magazine upside down don't you, honey?" Charles Zuckerman squatted in front of her, a huge grin on his handsome, clean-shaven face. His blue eyes twinkled with a mixture of amusement and concern, and she wasted no time in dropping the unread magazine to the sofa and throwing her arms around his neck.

"I didn't know you were coming. I thought it was just AJ."

"Well, it sounded like Billy had bitten off more than he could chew trying to keep you all in line so I figured I'd come down and laugh at him." Charlie squeezed her tightly, and she could feel the muscles in his strong arms bunching against her back. She didn't know why, but she and Charlie had clicked from the first moment they met, and there had been more than a few times over the past few months where she had turned to him for advice, cried on his shoulder, and vented her frustrations. He had become a father figure to her in a way her own father never had been, and never would be.

"I'm glad you're here."

"Well, I couldn't let you guys have all the fun."

"How did you get away from the base?"

"It took a little finessing and a little ego stroking, but I managed to make this a Navy task force that I'm heading up while I let my XO get some valuable experience in charge. He's up for promotion next year and he needs a taste of what it'll be like in the firing line."

"You're taking over from Billy?"

"Like hell he is." Billy came in with an armload of backpacks.

Charlie winked. "Once my big brother screws up, I'll swoop in and save the day. Don't you worry."

Finn giggled. "I wasn't."

He pointed to the magazine. "Then why were you reading that upside down? Feel like you need to add another talent to your repertoire?"

She shrugged. "I was just thinking. I can't seem to get my mind to rest."

"About this mission?"

"About Lugh." She glanced around the room until she was satisfied everyone else was busy, then she lowered her voice. "That's what we've been calling it. What I've engineered is an antidote and a vaccine, Charlie. Not a magic cure. It will be most effective in those who get the vaccine before they are exposed to the toxin. People who are exposed to the toxin before Lugh has run its course will still get sick. They could still die if they don't get the antidote. They'll suffer from weakness or paralysis to different extents depending on how long the toxin was in their system before they're exposed to the Lugh."

Charlie frowned as he listened and worked to understand what she was telling him. "So if they get the antidote at the same time as they're exposed to the toxin, what happens?"

"Depends a little on their body chemistry, but in most cases they'll probably suffer something like a really bad stomach flu. Vomiting, diarrhea, headache, fever, and so on."

"So not good, but not lethal?"

"Correct. Basically they'd contract the cold symptoms from Lugh, the vaccine I've created, as well as the vomiting and diarrhea as the body expels Balor."

"Nice."

"Just keeping it real."

"And the longer the antidote is delayed, the worse the outcome will be for the victim, up to the point of death."

"Correct."

"So what's the best way to make this work?"

"Vaccination prior to exposure. Then each person will have the antibodies to Balor already in their systems and they'll react as soon as the protein marker is detected by the body's own immune system. It will be as effective as anyone can make it."

"So, one hundred percent?"

Finn shook her head sadly. "No vaccine is ever one hundred percent. Some people will have immune system failure with a vaccine like that, some will have allergic reactions to the vaccine." She shrugged. "It's statistically inevitable, but it will be ninety-nine percent. That's the best I can give you. But only if we can vaccinate before exposure. And the more time we can give before that, the better."

"Why?"

"I've engineered Lugh into the cold virus. To eradicate the threat we need to trigger a pandemic of the common cold."

"Excuse me?"

"You heard me. In theory, Balor could be released anywhere. If I was him, I'd head for a major population center and put it into several food and water distribution points. The incubation period would make it difficult to track down the source, and by the time patients are symptomatic, not only is it then too late, it's also too late for anyone they've come into contact with in that period. Retro vaccination is reactive and too slow. For this agent anyway. If we release Lugh before Balor is even released, the cold virus will spread and infect the population of a given area within a few days. Basing figures on the spread of the Spanish influenza in 1918, and factoring in the way we can jumpstart the process, if we pick the correct target areas, within a couple of weeks, we will have a pandemic on our hands. Within twelve hours of contracting Lugh, patients will begin to display resistance to Balor, and within forty-eight hours, they will have complete immunity."

"So you need two and a half weeks to ensure the world is safe?"

She smiled sadly. "No. I need three weeks to ensure the world is safe from Balor. I can't do anything about the other threats we all face, and I need some time to create the quantities of viral agent required to trigger the pandemic."

"Sounds like you've got it worked out."

"I haven't been able to think about anything else, Charlie. I have to stop it."

"I know." He held her hand. "So what's your best plan for release?"

"Airports."

"Airports?"

"Yes. Major hub airports. If we release the virus in at least two major hub airports on each continent, we should be able to do this in the three weeks. If we use fewer hubs, it will take longer. Ideally, I would suggest more across parts of the world that are less densely populated, such as Africa, Australia, and rural areas of South America. The spread will be slower because of the geographical distance between population centers."

Charlie scratched his chin. "Okay, and just saying that we can get the virus to this many hub airports, how exactly do you suggest we release this thing? Do we leave an open canister in the departure lounge or something?"

Finn laughed. "No. We need to release it into the air-conditioning systems."

"Are you kidding me?"

"No. It's the only way to infect the whole airport. If you just target the arrivals or the departure lounge you will only get a small proportion of the potential yield."

Charlie frowned at her. "You do realize that sometimes I don't understand what you say, don't you?"

"Sorry. If we release Lugh in the departure lounge, we will infect those leaving the country and traveling elsewhere. But only a very few people staying in the country will be infected and the spread will be slow.

If we release in the arrivals, we only get people who are returning and we miss a vital opportunity to spread the infection outward. If we target one gate, we limit the outward spread to only a single destination and so on. By targeting the air-condition systems, we get not only the travelers but everyone who works in the airports too. We get exponential spread across all the travel networks and the start of infection by the thousands of people who work in the airports in each hub zone. Those people go home to their families and infect them, their children infect those in their schools and colleges, their partners infect everyone they work with. Every exposure has a domino effect until everyone will be immunized."

Charlie nodded. "I get you. But do you have any idea what you're proposing here, Finn? A worldwide action for reasons we aren't going to be able to explain to the people on the ground."

"I know. That's why I'm worried. I don't know if it can be done, and I can't think of any other way to do it." Finn knew she looked as miserable as she felt. She was doing all she could, and she knew that everyone around her would do everything in their power to help her, but even one person suffering from Balor was too much for her to bear.

"You don't know if what can be done, babe?" Oz dropped onto the sofa next to her and slipped an arm around her shoulders.

"Finn has a plan to save the world."

"Another one?" Oz winked. "Regular little Supergirl you're turning into, Linda."

Finn laughed as Oz reminded her of one of their first conversations and the alias she had used in an attempt to fly under her father's radar. It hadn't worked, but it was far too late by the time she had learned that fact. Charlie quickly outlined the idea to them as AJ, Junior, and Billy also took seats in the living room.

"How many airports are we talking about?" Junior asked.

"Not a clue," Charlie said.

"There are over one hundred and sixty hub airports globally," Finn said and everyone stared at her. She could feel the heat in her cheeks. "I Googled it when I started thinking about this plan."

Oz laughed and kissed her head. "My little genius."

"What's the optimum and minimum number of targets?" Junior watched her with shrewd eyes.

"Minimum given population spread, twenty-eight. Optimum target number would be forty. More would be a bonus."

AJ whistled. "Wow. Ambitious."

Junior shrugged. "I thought you were going to say something worse to be honest, like half or something."

"If we can get that many, it would be amazing, but I think if we can cover forty, we'll make the three-week target."

"Question." Billy leaned forward and rested his elbows on his knees. "Is this something we really need to do when we don't plan on this thing getting out there in the first place?"

"We thought this would die with my dad's incarceration, but it hasn't. I don't want to take chances, Billy." Finn wasn't sure how best to convince him it wasn't only important, but vital. "I can't. This really is the best way I can think of to eliminate the threat once and for all. If Balor isn't effective on a vast population, then no one will kill for it or be killed by it."

"It'll give us a strong negotiation point when we deal with Mehalik too. We can hand over the toxin without having to worry. It will make the negotiations that much safer for all of us," Oz said.

Billy rubbed his chin, clearly thinking about it. "Logistically you know it's a nightmare, don't you?"

Finn nodded. "It's the only feasible way to do it quickly though."

"And are you certain—and I mean one hundred percent certain—that this thing you release won't do something funky out there and become a worse threat than Balor?"

"In truth, Billy, I can't promise you that with one hundred percent certainty. If any scientist ever promises you that, don't believe a word they say. What I can promise you is that I've taken every precaution I can, within the time frame, to make sure that this is as safe as it can be. Once I hand this over for release, I'm at its mercy just as much as everyone else. And so are all the people I love." She locked eyes with every one of them for an instant. She needed them to know that she took her responsibility seriously and that she wouldn't jeopardize their lives on a whim or best guess. "This will do what I've designed it to do, and then it will live in our bodies as part of our immunological arsenal. The worst most people will get out of this is a sniffle, a headache, and some sneezing."

Billy looked at him. "What do you think, Charlie? Would ten two-man teams cover it?"

"Four targets each? Bit much I think, based on some of the target areas. I was thinking fifteen pairs, some with two targets, and others with three."

"How will they carry the viral agent for deployment?" Billy asked Finn.

"I can prepare it in a liquid gel. Each target will only require one container. I'll put them in fifty-millimeter bottles so that they can get them through as hand luggage with no problems or questions, labeled as shower gel. It will be inert at this stage. When they're in the right place to release it, they'll need to add it to water. Half a liter for each fifty mil bottle, shake it to activate the virus, and then cover the filters in the primary air-conditioning units."

"Sounds simple enough. How do we get our people access to the air-conditioning systems?" Junior asked.

"That's up to you guys." Finn grinned at him. "Thought I'd leave you with something to do this time, Junior." He laughed and threw her a mock salute.

"When can you have the preparations ready?" Charlie asked.

"I need two days to produce the quantity we need for forty target sites."

"So, Saturday?"

"Saturday night. You can start sending people out with it on Sunday."

"Are you sure? If you think you'll need more time I'd rather know now."

"If anything, Charlie, it'll be earlier. I was allowing for unexpected incidents."

Charlie smiled. "That's my girl. Oz, you've got two days to get me a list of each target and realistic itineraries for our fifteen pairs," Charlie said, automatically slipping into his authoritative role. "I'll have the names of the pairs for you by morning."

"Yes, sir." Oz nodded.

"Junior, work with Finn to clarify exact procedure for deployment. You'll be briefing our pairs when they arrive." Junior nodded to his father.

"I'll brief AJ about the event tomorrow night." Billy clapped him on the shoulder. "You ready for a world of learning, boy?"

"Yes, sir."

"Then let's get started. We've got a lot of work to do, and very little time to do it." Billy stood and pulled AJ over to the table where the blueprints were unrolled.

"Finn, one other thing before you go back to reading your magazine upside down," Charlie said.

"Ha ha."

"I started that search you talked to Billy about."

The temperature in the room seemed to drop ten degrees as she waited for him to continue. Had he found her body already? Is that why her father hadn't managed to locate her mother after she'd left England? She pressed her hands against her thighs to try to stop the shaking.

"Where…?"

Charlie shook his head. "I haven't found her yet. Which is a good sign, I think. But, Finn, there are hundreds of thousands of Jane Does buried across the United States, and not all of them had DNA samples taken. It's going to take time to rule them all out. And even when we do, we won't know if she returned to the UK, or moved somewhere else." He wrapped his arms around her again. "Are you sure you want to do this?"

"Yes." She didn't have to think about it. She needed to know what had happened to her mother, and she needed to know that she tried everything she could to find her. No matter how long it took, how much money it cost, or where it led her. She owed her that much, at least. "I'm certain."

# CHAPTER TWENTY-FOUR

It was still dark outside. The streetlamp glittered orange through the crack in the curtains, and the world outside was mostly asleep. Bailey tossed and turned. Trying to sleep beyond her usual five a.m. was proving difficult, and the gentle weight of Jazz's head over her foot wasn't the comfort it usually was. She tried to figure out what it was that had woken her. She was a light sleeper and it didn't take much, but the culprit proved elusive.

She plumped her pillow and her gaze was drawn to Cassie's bed as a low moan emanated from her lips and her legs shifted slowly under the covers. Bailey swallowed hard and forgot about the pillow she was holding in her hands. Cassie's teeth raked over her bottom lip and her hips moved under the sheet in a slow, seductive wiggle Bailey could practically feel against her belly. *Or grinding against my thigh. No, I did not just think that. I didn't.* Bailey whimpered. She wanted to run her fingers through Cassie's long hair, and desire burned in her gut.

Another low moan and Bailey was glad she wasn't standing because she knew her knees wouldn't have supported her. She wondered what Cassie was dreaming about. She could make out the outline of Cassie's legs in the dim light of the room, one knee raised slightly. She imagined the feel of Cassie's skin beneath her fingertips as she trailed them from knee to hip, pushing the flimsy lace and satin of her nightgown up as she went. Cassie twitched, and her legs moved as though she could feel it too. Bailey felt the groan deep in her chest and pulled her pillow over her face to smother it. She didn't want Cassie to wake up and find her staring at her, moaning, and think she was some sort of pervert, getting her kicks out of watching women as they slept. That'd soon make her rethink her statistical probability.

Cassie's hand moved to cup her own breast. Bailey dropped the pillow and watched. She imagined herself pushing Cassie's hand away from the supple flesh, tugging the satin fabric out of the way, and covering the hardened nipple with her mouth. She wasn't sure if she imagined the moan she heard or if it actually came from Cassie, but the mere thought of their bodies coming together in a passionate embrace was driving Bailey mad.

She climbed out of bed as quietly as she could; she needed the privacy of the bathroom and a few minutes to calm her shaking body.

She splashed water on her face and sat on the edge of the tub, hands still trembling.

*What the hell? I know it's been a while, but this is ridiculous. So she's beautiful, and intelligent, and funny, and beautiful. So what if she's all those things? She's my client, and even if she wasn't she's so far out of my league, it isn't even worth thinking about.* She rested her head in her hands. *Okay, it isn't even worth thinking about anymore. And don't forget half the time when you touch her by accident she flinches like you've burned her. Hardly a promising sign.* She dried her hands and flushed the toilet, hoping that the noise would wake Cassie enough to bring her out of her erotic dream, if that's what it was, and give Bailey a chance to breathe easy until they got up.

Cassie was on her side, her arms wrapped around her pillow, when Bailey climbed back into bed. She couldn't stop herself from wishing she was the pillow in Cassie's arms. She threw herself back against her pillows. *So much for not thinking about it anymore.*

# CHAPTER TWENTY-FIVE

"General, the car is waiting."

He pulled his sunglasses off his head and slid them over his eyes. "Is everything ready for tomorrow evening?"

"Yes, General."

"Very good, Hakim. You can report in the car." He followed him to the stretch limousine. "You couldn't find anything bigger?" The sarcasm in his voice was evident.

"You know how Americans love their big flashy cars."

"Almost as much as they love their guns."

"Indeed, General." He took the bag from Mehalik's hands and placed it carefully in the trunk. "We will have complete privacy inside. I have personally checked the driver."

"Very good. You have done well, my friend."

Hakim pulled the door closed and the dark interior shone with neon lights as they ran through a spectrum of colors. He shook his head. This was just another symptom of a much bigger disease that was eating at the world, but he didn't care. The greed of the Western World wasn't the problem he sought to rectify. It was not the wrong he needed justice for. That was not why they all needed to pay.

"Tell me what you know, Hakim."

Hakim handed him a sheaf of pages. On top was a photograph of Finn. Black-and-white, obviously shot from a distance, but Mehalik was immediately besotted by her beauty.

"General, we've been watching the girl ever since you gave me her whereabouts. She goes to the laboratory every day. The surveillance equipment in there is functioning well, but the security and encryption she has on her computers make it impossible for us to extract data without her knowing. I have decided at this point to maintain our cover, as her behavior and conversations indicate she has made little more progress with the vaccine than Lyell's research did. Though she is ready to replicate quantities of Balor as soon as she has perfected the vaccine. She seems much more cautious than the good doctor was. She will not create more than an experimental sample of the toxin until she has a viable vaccine."

"Is she close?"

"Unknown. She seems very…controlled, General."

"Do you think she knows about the cameras?"

"Difficult to say."

"Our friend on the inside?"

"He informed me this evening they have given no indication that they're aware of any surveillance equipment."

"Do you trust him?"

Hakim shrugged. "What is the phrase, General? About as far as I could throw him."

Mehalik sniggered. "Yes, my friend, but you are a very large man. He patted Hakim's arm. "You could probably throw him quite some way." They laughed together before returning to the conversation. "Why has she taken over? She testified against her father. It seemed she wanted nothing to do with the business, and it had been left to the board of directors. Why now?"

"Our friend seems to think that she used the situation to oust her father and take over."

"There are easier ways to do it than sending one's own father to prison."

"True, General. But William Sterling was not, I think, a man who would let go easily."

Mehalik was inclined to agree. "Indeed, any other legal attempt would have likely resulted in her forfeiting her life."

"Exactly. This way it gives the appearance that she is fully cooperating with the authorities and it earns her their respect. It's very clever, I think, the way she has done this, General. I think she is a woman to be taken very seriously."

"Ambitious, no?"

"Very."

"Intelligent and beautiful." Mehalik grinned. "I'm looking forward to meeting Miss Sterling. Is she willing to deal?"

"I don't think she would be working on Balor at all if she were not."

"Then we must be even more careful of the lovely Miss Sterling."

"Why is that?"

"Because she knows the monster she is unleashing on the world and she is still prepared to set it free. She either has a death wish, her own agenda, or she is setting up a trap."

Hakim banged on the divider that separated the driver from them and ordered the young man to turn around.

"Back to the airport, sir?"

"Yes. Now."

"Very well, sir." He glanced into his rearview mirror and changed lanes, making his way toward the next off ramp.

"No, no. Continue to the hotel as planned and close the screen." Mehalik frowned at Hakim as the driver nodded and closed the partition again.

"General, forgive me, but if this could be a trap you must leave. You are too important to the cause to risk—"

"I will be the judge of that. And I will not be frightened away by a mere woman. Carry on to the hotel." He slid his finger down Finn's picture. "She is lovely, no?"

"Yes, General. She is."

"Will she be accompanied tomorrow evening?"

"She has a contingent of security with her at all times."

"I was thinking on a more personal level, Hakim."

"I don't know. I haven't seen her with any other people but the security contingent."

"You don't seem to know an awful lot of personal details."

"I will find everything I can, General."

"Good." He flipped through the pages, barely glancing at the information, before turning to the photograph on the front page again. *I will enjoy this, Miss Sterling. I believe I will enjoy this very much.*

# CHAPTER TWENTY-SIX

Cassie fidgeted in her seat and picked at her nails as she stared out the window and listened to Miles Davis's trumpet on the stereo. The recording was scratchy and obviously copied from a vinyl recording, but she liked that. It felt authentic, and when she closed her eyes she could imagine herself in a smoke-filled bar, drinking bourbon, and watching the genius under the spotlights. That was if she could relax enough to close her eyes. She couldn't.

"Why so nervous?" Bailey's voice was gentle as she concentrated on the road ahead.

Cassie chuckled. "Oh, I don't know. Could have a little to do with the thought of facing my daughter after all these years. Trying to explain to her what happened, why I made the decision I did."

"You don't have to do this."

"Yes, I do."

"Why?"

"Why do you continue to search for your mother after all these years?"

"I need to know if she's okay, and if not, help her. You know that Daniela is okay. You've seen the article. You know she's a very wealthy, accomplished, and alive young woman."

"But I don't know that she's okay. I don't know why she testified against her father, and how that affected her. I don't know how she feels about him, or how she feels about me. I need her to know that I love her. I don't even know if she remembers me."

Cassie watched the trees flutter in the gentle wind, the track on the stereo changed, and Aretha Franklin demanded respect.

"What if she doesn't remember you? Are you ready for that?"

"No." She ran her fingers through her hair. "I don't think any mother would ever be ready to face that thought. But if that's the truth of the matter, at least I'll see her and know she's okay."

"I hope you get what you wish for."

Cassie turned to look at Bailey. She'd been quiet all day, and when Cassie had asked her about it earlier she'd merely said that she hadn't slept well. "Thank you. Are you sure you're okay?"

Bailey's cheeks flushed. "Yeah, I'm fine." She checked her watch then pointed to a steakhouse across the street. "We've still got a few hours before we get there. Do you think you could eat an early dinner?"

"Sure. Looks like they have tables outside, do you mind?"

"Nope."

Twenty minutes later, they were enjoying steaks. Cassie had a baked potato with hers, and Bailey squirted ketchup over her fries before sneaking one under the table to Jazz.

"How long were you in the FBI?"

"Twelve years. I left five years ago."

"Are you fully in remission now?" Cassie nodded toward her midsection.

"Oh, yeah. Just the one kidney like I told you before, but I'm good."

"So tell me about being an FBI agent then."

Bailey moaned as she chewed on her steak. "Man, that's a good steak. You need to try yours."

"I will."

"What do you want to know?"

Cassie shrugged. "Anything. What sort of cases did you work on?"

"When I made detective in the BPD, I worked vice and then sex crimes. When I got to the FBI, I worked with a task force trying to break human trafficking. We had specialists from across the spectrum on the team—organized crime, drugs, guns, you name it."

"Is that a big problem?"

"Huge. And growing. Obviously, it's hard to get official numbers, but there are hundreds of thousands of girls smuggled into the country and used as sex slaves until they don't make any money for the men that own them."

"Then what?"

"If they're of no use, they're killed."

Cassie shuddered. The poor girls involved by that point probably had wished for death many times over. But hearing it from Bailey made it a reality she couldn't ignore. It also gave her an understanding of just how well acquainted Bailey was with the life her mother had led, and the likely conclusion that life led to.

"I'm sorry."

Bailey nodded, acknowledging that Cassie was referring to more than the plight of the smuggled girls she had worked toward freeing.

"Tell me about your work."

"Teaching? Well, I stand at the front of an auditorium and give lectures about neurology—"

"Smartass."

Cassie grinned. "I have been accused of that before."

"I bet. I meant your research."

"I can't talk about my current work."

"CIA?"

"I can't say."

"Understood."

"But I can tell you some of the older stuff I've worked on if you're interested?"

"Please."

"Okay, but tell me if I bore you."

"You could never bore me." Bailey's cheeks flushed again, and she quickly looked down at her plate.

Cassie let it go. "I study nerves. Over the years, I've worked on a number of projects to help with nerve regeneration in subjects with paralysis. Sometimes paralysis that has resulted from trauma, sometimes from disease, and sometimes in subjects who were born with one of many birth defects that cause paralysis. We made some pretty big advances into studies on myelin sheath degradation diseases, ways to stimulate regeneration, and arrest the loss of myelin sheaths in patients suffering from diseases like multiple sclerosis, ALD, transverse myelitis, Guillain-Barré syndrome, central pontine myelinolysis, pernicious anemia, and many, many more."

"I'm sorry. What's a myelin sheath?"

"It's a part of every nerve in the body. It sort of covers the outside of the axon and allows the nerve to conduct the electrical current and make the muscles work. Without it, the sodium potassium exchange doesn't work and the muscles don't react to signals from the brain."

"Okay. So this was pretty big stuff?"

"Well, we were trying to do some good work."

"I don't recall seeing the news that all those things have been cured, so I'm guessing it wasn't a complete success."

Cassie smiled and sipped her iced tea. "There's still work to be done, but we made a lot of progress. I'm hoping that what I'm working on now will also help."

"But you can't talk about that."

"No. Sorry." She grinned.

"Not even a clue? I mean it's not like I'm even going to know what you're talking about."

"I'm looking at a way to reroute the signals from the brain to the muscles if the nerves are unable to be regenerated."

Bailey looked at her blankly. "I was right. I have no idea what you just said."

Cassie laughed. "Good, then I won't have to kill you."

"I'm very pleased about that. What made you become a scientist and why this field?"

"My grandfather suffered from Parkinson's disease. When I visited as a child, I always wished I could help him. I decided I was going to be a doctor. While I was studying pre-med, I discovered I had an aptitude in the lab, and I also realized that in the long-term, I could help more people though a microscope than at the end of a scalpel. It just made sense for me."

Bailey frowned. "How did you end up married in England?"

"I studied at Cambridge. That's where I met William. We married the summer between my third and fourth year, and we opened the London lab straight after that. It was something of a dream job. I was working with some of the other scientists that I had studied with. Siegfried Jensen, Ethan Lyell, Rebecca Moore, and myself. We were so young and so idealistic." She smiled. "We thought we were going to save the world."

"What are they doing now?"

"No idea. I lost track of them all along the way, and I haven't read any papers that they put out, so I have no idea." She shrugged. "It was a lifetime ago."

"Do you miss it?"

"What?"

"That life. You were obviously privileged, studying at Cambridge, your own lab, I'm assuming the big house and everything that goes with it all. You had it all."

"No, I didn't. There are more important things than money, Bailey. You know that. What I needed then, and what I need now, have nothing to do with money. I was young and stupid, and I was charmed by William. Before I left university and long before I learned I was pregnant, I knew it wasn't working—that it wasn't going to work. But I also didn't know how bad it was going to be. I was too naïve. I trusted him." She scraped at the inside of her baked potato with her fork. "I was a fool. Daniela was just one more weapon he could use against me."

"I don't understand."

"I told you that William wanted to expand Sterling BioTech in a way I wasn't comfortable with."

"Yes, and that when you refused you were left with no choice but to fake your own death."

"I was already planning that. I was going to take Daniela with me to the cliffs. Karen would be waiting, and we'd push the car off the cliffs. The two of us."

"What went wrong?"

"He knew I wouldn't agree to what he wanted. He knew it was so far away from everything I'd ever dreamed about, and that there was only one way that he could make me do it. Before he spoke to me about what he wanted me to do, he took Daniela away from me."

"I don't follow."

"He showed me pictures of her in a room coloring in a picture at a table, but it wasn't anywhere I recognized. There was a man in the room with her wearing a mask. I don't know how they explained the mask to her, I have no idea what she thought was going on, but he was also holding a gun in his hand."

"Oh my God."

"He told me what he wanted me to do, and told me that if I didn't he'd kill her."

"His own child?"

"I didn't believe him. No, that's not true. I didn't want to believe him. But after what he wanted me to do, part of me knew he'd do it. So I told him I would do what he wanted me to. I told him I'd do anything as long as he didn't hurt her. It was the only thing I could think of to buy myself some time. I needed time to think."

"And he let her go?"

"No." Cassie put her fork down, her appetite gone. "He said I'd see her again when I completed the project."

"Which was?"

"In a nutshell, he wanted me to create a weapon he could sell."

"But you're not a weapons developer."

"He wanted a biological agent."

"Holy fuck."

"I knew I had no choice. If I stayed and didn't make it, he'd kill my daughter. If I made it…" Cassie shuddered. "I couldn't. I just couldn't."

Bailey's fork was poised over her plate, seemingly forgotten. "I understand."

Cassie could see the tumblers of the puzzle falling into place and realized she did indeed understand. She just hoped her little girl would be as understanding.

Cassie stared as Bailey wrapped her fingers around Cassie's, but she didn't flinch. Rather than fearing Bailey's touch, she found herself craving it. Like a plant that hadn't been watered in far too long, her fingers uncurled and their fingers entwined so naturally, so easily, it felt as though they had done it a thousand times before. Her small hand slipped into Bailey's strong, warm one. The slightly rough skin of Bailey's palm felt good against her own, and the tiny callous on her thumb scratched slightly on her skin as Bailey rubbed it back and forth, hypnotizing her with the slow, gentle motion. "Thank you."

Cassie looked up from their joined hands and almost wished she hadn't. Bailey's eyes were soft as they watched her, and she felt like she was falling into a pool of molten chocolate. She swallowed thickly, and her voice was hoarse as she said, "What for?"

"For trusting me."

"I do trust you, Bailey. And I wish I could tell you everything." She was surprised to find how true those words were as soon as they left her mouth. *Well, almost everything.* "But there are things I simply can't say."

"I heard you before, Cassie. In Boston. But now I believe it." The smile on Bailey's lips pulled at Cassie's heart. It made her look younger, softer, and Cassie felt she was looking into her soul. She saw the wariness and the grouchy exterior falling away as they stared at each other across the table. "You aren't the only one who finds it difficult to trust, Cassie."

"I know. That's why I was amazed when you said you'd help me. For that I can't thank you enough."

"You haven't seen her yet."

"No. But we're nearly there."

"Just a few more hours and we'll be in the Florida Keys."

"Yup. And you can get rid of me." She smiled, desperately trying to lighten the mood, but her words seemed to have the opposite effect on Bailey. The smile slid from her mouth and her shoulders drooped.

"I guess so. Mission complete."

"Well, almost." She wiggled Bailey's hand, which was still wrapped around her own. "There's still the trip back to Boston."

Bailey sighed. "The things I do to feed my dog." They both laughed as Bailey let go of her hand and signaled for the check. "Come on. Let's go meet your daughter."

Cassie's heart pounded at the thought. *I'm going to meet my daughter. See her face-to-face. Holy Christ, I'm not ready for this.*

## CHAPTER TWENTY-SEVEN

"Zip me up?" Finn turned her back to Oz and watched her approach through the mirror. Oz tucked the pale blue shirt into her pants and dropped kisses along Finn's shoulder, her gaze never leaving Finn's.

"I'd rather pull this down the rest of the way," she whispered seductively as she slipped her hands around Finn's waist and pulled her in close. She flicked her tongue over her earlobe, and Finn wanted nothing more than to let Oz lead them both on a journey to their bed rather than the Top of the Rock, but she knew she couldn't.

"Sweetheart," she whispered, "we can't."

Oz gently turned Finn's face and kissed her. Finn moaned when Oz finally ended the kiss and she could no longer remember why she had objected.

"You look beautiful." Oz placed a final chaste kiss on her lips and slowly eased the zipper closed. "It brings out your eyes." Finn had chosen the above the knee, off the shoulder, emerald green cocktail dress because she knew it looked good. They were making a statement with her attendance, and seeing the appreciative look on Oz's face assured her the statement would be clear. "Do you want me to put that on for you too?" She pointed to the diamond platinum necklace on the dresser.

"Please." She scooped her hair off the back of her neck and shuddered slightly when the cold stone touched her heated skin. "How long do we have?"

"Dad wants to leave in about ten minutes, but we're still waiting for Whittaker to arrive."

Finn frowned. "Has he called?"

"Not a word from him."

"And what does Agent Knight say?"

"He says he's working on something for the mission but he can't give us any details."

"Meaning?"

"He doesn't know what's going on either."

Finn laughed and dropped her hair. "Good to know." She kissed Oz's cheek. "That shirt looks good on you." She winked playfully. "Good enough to eat."

Oz groaned. "Have I not taught you that it's cruel to tease the lesbian like that?"

"I'm not teasing." She stepped into her heels. "Just preparing you for later." They left the room with Oz grumbling.

Knight was standing over the table looking at the schematics again and pointing to something as he spoke to AJ. Billy was checking over several pieces of equipment at the other end of the table and grinning at Charlie.

"Ah, Finn, good. There are a few more details we need to go over before we leave." Knight motioned her closer to the table. "Have you been to the Top of the Rock before?"

"Yes."

"Good, then I don't need to orient you. You'll be in close proximity to Junior at all times. Oz and I will be on the floor below. With AJ and Whittaker—"

"If he ever shows up," Junior said.

"Guarding the lobby at ground level."

"I know all this, Mr. Knight. What are you expecting from this evening?"

"In all honesty? Nothing. It's just to let you be seen acting in an official capacity for Sterling Enterprises."

"Do you have some sort of microphone for me to wear?"

Knight shook his head. "You won't need that. Junior will always be able to see you. No one can get in or out without us knowing about it. You're safe, Finn." He put a hand on her shoulder.

"Safe or not, don't you think it would be a good idea to have me in communication with you all at all times? There may be people there tonight who worked on all kinds of deals with my dad, and finding out if any of them are approaching me for something less than scrupulous would surely be in the government's best interests." Finn was incredulous at the poor planning that seemed to be accompanying the evening's event and couldn't shake the feeling that she was being dropped in the water as bait—without the shark cage—while the great whites circled.

"Finn, there's really nothing to worry about here. This is a charity event, with a huge amount of security, in a secure location. We have no reason at all to believe that any of Mehalik's men are even in the country, so there is nothing to worry about, or get excited about. This will simply be a boring evening listening to rich guys full of their own self importance."

"Just like now," Billy said. "We don't have a picture of Mehalik. No one knows what he looks like. How can you be sure he's not in the country?"

"I'm certain my informant would have told me if that was the case."

"So let me just get this absolutely clear." Billy leaned toward Knight. "You don't know who you're looking for, but you want to send her in there with us all blind and deaf."

"You won't be blind or deaf, Billy."

Billy cocked his head and waited for him to continue.

"You're running your own comms from the van, remember? You'll have all the video feeds. What more do you think we need on a first show like tonight?"

Finn felt the temperature in the room drop several degrees as Knight and Billy stared at each other. Was that what this pitifully poor plan was about? Trying to show Billy he was still in charge, or was he really trying to sabotage their plans from the get-go, as Billy seemed to think?

The door buzzed and Andrew Whittaker was let in.

"You're late." Billy scowled at him.

"I was held up at a meeting." He scowled at Billy in return.

"And last night?"

"It was a long meeting."

Finn knew she wasn't exactly up to speed on the inner workings of the intelligence and security services, but even she had expected something better to explain his absence at important meetings on a case he had brought to them and claimed was vital to national and global security. His attitude was surly at best, and she realized why it was that Billy, Junior, and Oz had taken such an intense dislike to the man. To them his behavior and attitude must have been ringing all kinds of alarm bells. *No wonder they didn't know who to trust here. Knight seems hell-bent on screwing things up, and Whittaker is acting more and more suspiciously.*

Knight pointed to AJ, but his eyes never left Whittaker's face. "You'll be guarding the ground floor with him. He'll run you through the protocol while we drive. We're already running late."

Finn suppressed a grin. Either Stephen Knight didn't like him either, or he was playing a very good role. He's CIA, she reminded herself. Either was possible.

"I'm fully aware of what the protocol will be." Whittaker was the first to leave the room. Billy travelled in the back of the blue van that Knight had procured for the mission, with Charlie at the wheel. Junior climbed behind the wheel of the stretch limo and Oz followed Finn into the back. Whittaker quickly followed them in and pulled the door closed behind him, leaving Knight and AJ to follow in the second car.

"Nervous?" Whittaker asked from the seat opposite Finn.

Something about the excitement in his face didn't sit right. She didn't want to tell him her concerns, despite his question. Whereas he'd been downright rude toward everyone else, his attitude toward her was almost solicitous, and it made her skin crawl. "A little. But tonight's just about showing my face, letting the world know that I'm heading up Sterling Enterprises. I'll be fine."

"You need to be able to maintain your character, and stay focused all night," he said quietly to Finn. He looked like he was going to say something else, and he drew in a deep breath, then shook his head, obviously changing his mind. "Just be careful what you say and to whom. There's a lot riding on tonight."

Finn smiled. "I will."

She found the strange behavior disconcerting. She could see there was more he was trying to tell her, and she wished he'd just come out with it. Guessing games weren't something she relished, and she really didn't want something else to distract her right now. She already wished she was in the lab rather than going to an overpriced party. Or better yet, back in the apartment wrapped in Oz's arms. She felt goose bumps erupt over her skin. Not a good train of thought either.

"Here, put this on." Oz handed her a small lapel pin.

"The American Flag? It won't exactly work with the dress, sweetheart."

"It's a personal panic alarm fitted with a GPS transponder. If you feel something's wrong, you lose sight of Junior, you feel anything's off, push it, and we'll be there. I can't get you on an open channel like I want, so I won't be able to hear what you say, but you can call for help if you need to. I'm not sending you in there helpless, no matter what Knight says."

"I love you." She wrapped her hand around Oz's, handing back the pin. "Put it on for me."

Oz's hand slipped inside the bodice of her dress, brushing against her breast as she pulled the fabric away. "Certainly. Don't want to cause any damage." Her eyes twinkled mischievously and Finn's nerves melted away with Oz's smirk.

"Thank you."

"I love you too."

The car stopped and she was surprised to find Junior opening her door for her, she'd been so preoccupied with her thoughts. He looked especially handsome in his tailored suit as he smiled at her and helped her from the car.

"Have I ever told you how much I hate wearing heels?" she whispered as he escorted her to the door.

"No, but you look fabulous in them, darlin'."

Finn laughed. "You little flirt."

He winked and pulled the door open for her. "Only with you, gorgeous." She handed her invitation to the security guard, dropped her clutch into the plastic tray for the x-ray machine, and stepped through the metal detector. Junior, Oz, and Knight followed her through and into the elevator. Per the plan, AJ and Whittaker positioned themselves by the elevator.

None of them were hiding their roles as her security contingency. All of them were wearing earpieces, microphones, and all of them were obviously packing under their jackets. One thing Knight had come through with were the credentials for them all to do so legally—well, sort of. As long as you didn't dig too deep into those licenses, everything was fine.

She wandered slowly along the observation deck, enjoying the view across the city from the glass walls surrounding the sixty-ninth floor. The lights of the Empire State Building seemed to radiate off the walls and made the black night around the building hazy—like there was a shimmer in the air around it. Beyond it, the bright lights of the Statue of Liberty glittered against the dark waters of the Hudson River. She'd been fourteen the first time she'd visited New York. Her father had brought her with him on a business trip and she had seen the lab for the first time. She'd also visited the Statue of Liberty, when she'd snuck away from her nanny and spent the whole day alone. It had been blissful; the only thing missing had been someone to share her fun with. Not someone who was paid to be at her side, but someone who wanted to be. She'd resorted to calling her best friend Pete back in England and telling him everything she could see. She placed her hand on the cold glass.

"Oh, Pete." The wounds of his death—his murder—were still so fresh that she had to fight to keep the tears from falling. She still couldn't quite believe that it was her own father who had ordered the death of her best friend, nor could she quite let go of the guilt that came with that knowledge.

*Guilt will do you no good here.* She focused on everything her father had done. To her. To Oz. To her mother. So much pain for what? Greed? Power? *I hope it was worth it, Daddy.*

She screwed the pain into a ball and pushed it down into the pit of her stomach where she let it burn. The flames licked at the wounds of betrayal and fanned the fires of rage. She let her anger settle into her expression and hoped it mirrored some of what she felt inside as she strode across the room and ascended the escalator to the party proper.

Champagne and the distinct feeling of loneliness were her companions as she slowly wandered the observation deck. The occasional gust of wind blowing in when one guest or another braved the freezing December night air was more than enough to convince her to stay inside. A jazz trio played softly, and couples were dancing in the middle of the room. Junior was unobtrusive as he watched her from the edge of the room, as did the rest of her security detail. She couldn't see Oz and Knight, but she knew they could see her. The distance only added to the feeling of loneliness she felt.

"May I have this dance?" An Arabic man with a long, jagged scar down his left cheek held out his hand, bowing slightly at the waist, and smiling genially at her. He wore long white robes and the traditional headdress of a Saudi prince. He didn't seem at all out of place amongst the movers and shakers of New York's politicos and business elite.

She offered him a small smile. "I'm afraid I'm not much of a dancer, Mr...." She let her voice trail off, hoping he would offer his name as he corrected her assumption.

"Neither am I, Miss Sterling. I'm sure we will, as you British say, muddle through together." He smiled broadly as he took her hand and handed her half-empty glass to a passing waiter. His hand was cool in hers, and his self-assured manner convinced her that she would end the situation quicker by taking a turn on the dance floor. She shrugged; it might even liven up an otherwise boring evening. She just wished that he had divulged his name.

The band played a mid-tempo song, and the dance was uneventful as he led her around the floor. "I feel I'm in the arms of a very accomplished dancer, sir."

"You flatter me, Miss Sterling."

She realized that he was well aware she didn't know who he was, and he was enjoying watching her struggle as she tried to work it out. She imagined him as a cat, a hunter who had cornered a mouse and was exalting in watching it twist and turn in its grasp before it would become lunch, and the hairs on the back of her neck stood on end. She was familiar with the feeling of being stalked. She'd lived with it for as long as she could remember, and it was a feeling that only grew more intense as she knew Masood Mehalik was on her trail. She didn't need anyone else adding to her unease.

"Not at all. Thank you for the dance. I should get back and mingle with some of the other guests." She made to move away, but he kept his arms around her and held her firmly in place.

"Of course. Before you do, I would like to make an appointment to speak with you, Miss Sterling. I do so love that accent of yours, but I think we have business to discuss also."

"What business would that be, sir?" She was tired of playing games. "You'll have to forgive me, but I don't know who you are, nor do I know what business you are in."

"I was a business associate of your father's. Before his unfortunate incarceration that is."

It was odd. His smile didn't alter, no muscles in his face moved, but everything about the look in his eyes changed. His whole demeanor shifted from open and amiable to cold and malevolent in an instant, and she knew, without a shadow of a doubt, that she was in the arms of the man they were looking for. Her mouth went dry, and she fought to control the shudder that ran up her spine. She was holding the hand of a murderer. The edge to his words was enough to convince her that he knew about her part in her father's downfall. *Angry. Show him angry, not afraid.* She schooled her face and hoped she looked unimpressed and unafraid.

"Have you ever heard the phrase, you catch more bees with honey than vinegar, Mr. Mehalik?"

"Ah, so you've heard of me. Of course I'm familiar with the phrase."

"My father was vinegar. And acid gives me heart burn."

He turned her under his arm as he continued to lead her around the dance floor. "Very good, Miss Sterling. I understand you are continuing to work on the product your father had agreed to sell to me."

"You are well informed."

He shrugged. "I pay attention to things that interest me." His gaze dropped from her face to her body. She shuddered with revulsion, but the slow smile on his face gave her hope that he had mistaken her disgust for desire. "Are you ready to make a deal?"

"If the price is right."

"You do not wish to know what my intention with your product is?" He frowned slightly.

"Mr. Mehalik—"

"General."

"My apologies, General Mehalik, but there's only one purpose to this product, which is to kill lots and lots of people. The very nature of it is to annihilate all unvaccinated people." She wet her lips. "Globally. I don't need to ask what you intend to use it for. It has no other use. It is built to kill. What else do I need to know?"

"Apparently nothing. What of the vaccine? Dr. Lyell wasn't optimistic about it."

"You're too kind to him. What he created was little better than a crapshoot. I've increased the efficacy of his vaccine. It won't be one hundred percent effective, but it will be over eighty-five percent."

"A significant improvement."

"Yes. With more time I'm sure I can reach the ninety-nine percent efficacy I would expect from a vaccine."

"Not one hundred percent?"

"No vaccine is one hundred percent effective. The human body has a tendency to react unpredictably on occasion."

"Very well, Miss Sterling. Or may I call you Daniela?"

"Of course, Masood." She knew she was taking a chance, but he would expect her to push the boundaries, to try to force him to deal with her as an equal.

"I would very much like to discuss this with you in more detail, Daniela. Perhaps you would be so good as to join me somewhere a little more…private?"

"Perhaps you would care to join me for dinner? I have an apartment not far from here, we could—"

"I had a little something else in mind."

She raised her eyebrow in question and waited for him to continue.

"I have a yacht on the Red Sea. A beautiful boat, a little sun, perfect blue ocean. I thought perhaps you, and your people, would be so kind as to visit me while we discuss business, and perhaps we can spend some more time talking about more personal things, Daniela."

*Oh no. No way.* "I'm very honored by your offer, Masood. But I'm not sure that's a very good idea. I still have a considerable amount of work to do on the vaccine."

"I insist. You see I am selective, very selective, in whom I choose to do business with."

*Shit.* That one sentence told her she wasn't trusted and refusal wasn't an option. "In that case I would love to, Masood."

"Excellent. I will have my people make the arrangements."

"I'll make my own travel arrangements, Masood. Give me a place to meet you, and I'll be there."

"It would be so much easier if I took care of everything."

"I'm sure it would. But you see, my father was a man who tried to control me, down to every last detail of my life. So I have an objection to people trying to take over. I, too, am selective in whom I do business with."

He seemed to consider her words before smiling slightly. "Very well. Then you will be flying to Eilat. Monday evening, seven o'clock. There will be a reservation in your name at Eddie's Hide-A-Way on Eilot Avenue." He bowed from the waist and kissed the back of her hand. "I look forward to seeing you again."

She glanced over her shoulder for Junior, and by the time she looked back to Masood he was gone. "Goddammit." She crossed the floor quickly. "Tell them to get a look at that guy. Get his picture or something."

"The Saudi prince? I take it you enjoyed the dance then." Junior's smile slipped from his face.

"That was him."

"What?"

"That was Mehalik. Get them to get a picture of him or something."

Junior spoke quickly into his mic and his frown deepened as he got the reply. "They can't find him."

"What? He was just here. He can't have gotten all the way down yet. The elevators are fast, but not that fast." Junior continued to talk into his mic but shook his head. "Damn it."

"We need to know everything he said to you."

"We've also got some travel plans to make."

"What are you talking about?"

"We've got a meeting on Monday evening."

"Okay," Junior said.

"In Israel."

"Oh boy." He took Finn's elbow and steered her back toward the dance floor. "I thought this dude was Palestinian?" He turned her under his arm and steered her gently around the dance floor.

"And tonight you thought he was a Saudi prince. As did I."

"Good point. Hiding in plain sight. That gives me an idea." He spoke into his mic again. "Uncle Billy, this dude's good with disguises. Check the wait staff and service elevators, and check for him without the Saudi outfit."

Finn could hear the muffled voice from his earpiece telling Junior that without the costume they didn't know what they were looking for.

"He has a six-inch scar on his left cheek. Kind of jagged. Look for that."

Junior passed the information along and smiled at her. "See, I knew we'd make an operative of you." He dropped her into an impressive dip.

"No, thanks. Once this is over, I'm done with it. Now let me up, you big oaf."

## CHAPTER TWENTY-EIGHT

Bailey turned off the engine and pulled the key out of the ignition. "Do you want me to go first?"

Cassie nodded but couldn't tear her eyes away from the building. There were no lights on, the drive was empty, and a newspaper sat on the porch. She watched as Bailey mounted the steps and rang the bell. No one answered. "There's no one here, Jazz. We've come all this way and there's no one here." The dog whined from the backseat, verbalizing her sympathy the only way she could. "Thanks, I appreciate it." She smiled. "I'm going mad, anthropomorphizing the poor dog."

Bailey waited a good thirty seconds before ringing again and peering through the glass on the door, but it was no good. Bailey turned to her and shrugged, shaking her head as she walked back to the car. "It's too dark to see anything in there. We can wait a while if you like. I mean it is Friday night. Maybe she's gone out for the night."

"Good point. Maybe we should try in the morning."

"I can get on board with that." She could see the disappointment and lingering anxiety in Cassie's eyes. She wondered if she'd be able to sleep at all between now and morning and vowed to get them separate rooms. She wasn't up to a repeat of last night's incident. Neither her nerves nor her brain would be up to anything tomorrow if she had to watch Cassie writhing in her dreams again. The memory of Cassie's throaty moan made her mouth water and she could feel her pulse pounding between her legs.

"Are you okay?" Cassie frowned at her from the passenger seat as she leaned over, one arm resting on the window ledge of the car.

"Sorry, yeah. A little tired."

"Do you want me to drive till we find a motel?"

"No, it's fine, thanks. It won't be far." She rounded the car and climbed into her seat. "I can hear a shower and an early night calling my name."

"Oh that does sound good. Maybe something from room service."

"You hungry again? We can stop somewhere if you like?"

"We didn't get dessert. I hear a key lime pie calling my name." Cassie bumped her shoulder.

"Not for me. Give me chocolate any day."

"Chocolate's good, but I'm a Floridian, remember?"

"Well, that explains so much."

"Hey. I think I should be offended."

"Only think? Damn, I'm out of practice." The look of indignation on Cassie's face soon gave way to a fit of laughter that Bailey joined in on. The tension in Cassie's shoulders melted away, and Bailey was pleased she'd been able to relieve some of her tension, if only temporarily.

# CHAPTER TWENTY-NINE

"I srael? Are you fucking nuts?" Oz shouted in the car.
"He didn't exactly give me much choice, Oz."

"Do you have any idea what the situation is in Israel?"

Finn cocked her eyebrow and crossed her arms over her chest. "No, I'm an imbecile. Why don't you enlighten me?" Finn's voice dripped with sarcasm, and Oz knew better than to respond. She chose silence as the better part of valor.

"Actually, I don't know too much about it. Aren't the Palestinians terrorizing the Israelis?" AJ said from the driver's seat, Junior having opted to travel back to the apartment with Billy, Charlie, and Knight in the van so they could start planning straight away. Whittaker had said he'd meet them back at the apartment because he had an errand to run. Junior had practically slammed the door of the van in his face.

"It's a war zone and has been since the end of the Second World War," Oz said, her eyes never leaving Finn.

"Why?" AJ asked.

"Before and during the war, Jews lived in Palestine in huge numbers, and many Jews escaping Europe during and before the war fled there too. It's the Holy Land and the lands of their ancestors. They felt entitled to it, and many had family there already. After the war, the survivors flocked to Palestine in the thousands. The British army set up camps and tried to keep them from entering the country when the Arabs instigated an immigration policy."

"They called the British soldiers Nazis," Finn said.

"Why?"

"Because the camps they set up were bitter reminders of the death camps many of the Jews had just survived. They were held in refugee camps on beaches, when all they wanted was to feel safe after surviving the Nazi genocide. They didn't care that they were fed, treated with as much respect and sympathy as possible—they were still prisoners. And they wanted security. Wouldn't you, given what they had just been through?" Finn asked.

"I guess. But this guy, Mehalik, he's Palestinian, right? Not Jewish."

"Yup," Oz said. "In nineteen forty-seven, the United Nations declared an annexation of British-controlled Palestine to create the State of Israel. This was after two years of fighting terrorists and suffering huge losses of life in major bombing incidents like the attack at the King David Hotel where the British had set up their military headquarters. The retreat was set for May, nineteen forty-eight, and the Jewish militia was armed to the teeth and ready to fight to the death to claim their homeland. The Palestinians had been under British mandate, and they were unarmed and defenseless when the British left. They expected the Arab nations to come to their aid. And they did. They were just too late. By the time they were mobilized, it was all over. The Israelis controlled the area."

"They're still fighting over it now?"

"Yes. Some parts more openly than others, but yes. There have been numerous open wars over the last sixty-five years, and the Palestinians carry out suicide bombings, shootings, and so on as much as they can. The Israeli army is merciless in their retaliation for any terrorist attacks by the Palestinians." Oz felt sick. The thought of taking Finn into a war zone made her head spin. "It makes for very difficult living conditions."

"But that's not the area he wants us to go," Finn said.

"Where are we going?" AJ glanced over his shoulder, and Oz was once again grateful for her family. AJ hadn't even batted an eye at the thought of going with them into an open war zone.

"We're going to Eilat. It's a resort town on the Red Sea. It's a global tourist destination with Egypt on one side and Jordan on the other."

"Does that help us or hinder us in this?"

Oz rubbed her chin. "Actually, it might be a help." She keyed her mic, hoping her dad would still have the comms active. "Hey, Pops?"

"Go ahead, Ladyfish," he answered, and Oz glared as Finn sniggered.

"I wish you'd quit with that."

"Sorry, it's a habit born of years of use, baby girl. Now what can I do for you?"

"Find me Ariel Katz."

"Who's he?"

She could hear his pencil scratching on the paper and said the word that would stop his note taking. "Mossad."

There was a long pause over the comm line before Billy cleared his throat. "You sure?" At one time or another, each of them had run into Mossad agents. They were fierce warriors, tenacious, strong, and lethal. The elite Israeli fighting force was feared and respected across the globe. They were patriots and did what had to be done without asking questions. She and Ariel had history, and she knew she could trust him.

"Yes. If you can track him down. He might be able to get us access to an inconspicuous vessel and someone with good local knowledge that we can trust."

"I hear ya, baby girl. I'm on it."

The comm line went dead again.

"Who's Ariel Katz?" Finn asked. "And don't just tell me he's a Mossad agent. I already got that bit. Who is he to you?"

Oz let her head fall back against the headrest. "He's a good guy. He was assigned to liaise with the ship I was stationed on for a while. We got to be pretty good friends. For a while." She grimaced. "The one thing about Mossad agents that you have to remember is that Israel is always, and I do mean always, their focus. Nothing else detracts from that. Our boat intercepted a vessel trying to make it out of the Gaza Strip. It had landed illegally, and we were asked to detain it by the Israeli prime minister. We were told they were smuggling Hamas terrorists out of the country, and there was reason to believe they had plans for terrorist attacks on US soil. We got close enough to order them to surrender."

"What happened?"

"Ariel did what he had been ordered to do by his direct supervisor."

"Oz, this is like pulling teeth. What did he do?"

"He broke into the missile room, overrode the safety protocols, and torpedoed the vessel. He jumped overboard, and was picked up by a Mossad RIB."

"And this is the man you want to bring on board this mission? Are you nuts?" Finn stared at her incredulously.

"He has nothing but the safety of Israel at heart. If Mehalik gets his hands on a weapon like this, then Ariel will do everything in his power to stop him. It's in his best interest."

"Yeah, and who cares if we get in his way." Finn shook her head. "Un-fucking-believable."

"Baby, trust me. Ariel is the kind of man we need here, and I know exactly what he's going to do, what he can do, and we won't have anything capable of sinking a vessel anywhere close to him." *Please let this be the right decision.*

AJ caught her eye in the rearview mirror. "It'll be okay, all right? We won't let anything happen to either of you. You know that, right?"

Oz felt the tears well in her eyes but refused to let them fall. AJ was always the one to know exactly what was bothering her. He had since they were kids and she loved him for it, but damn if he didn't have a knack for making her cry more than his brothers and their roughhousing ever did. "You just watch your back out there, kid, and we'll all be fine."

Finn unbuckled her seat belt and slid onto Oz's lap, wrapped her arms around Oz's neck, and kissed her cheek softly. "You're crazy if you think this isn't asking for trouble, so it's a damn good thing I love you."

She clung to Finn. "I love you too." She ran her hand over the emerald green satin that covered Finn's thigh.

"Was that the last time you saw him? Ariel?"

Oz shook her head. "He came and apologized to me. Told me he was following orders and wished he hadn't had to betray our friendship but that sometimes there were bigger things at stake and we have to make the tough choices."

"Is this one of those choices for you, sweetheart?"

"Yeah." The word barely made it past her lips.

Finn gulped and her face paled. "Oz, speaking of tough choices and doing things for a greater good and all that, I need to…well, you see…" Finn pulled back slightly to look in Oz's eyes. "When he extended his invitation he was flirting with me."

"Okay."

"And he was, at least it seemed to me that he was…"

"Extending more than just an invitation to enjoy his pretty boat?"

Finn sighed. "Yeah."

"And you're going to have to play along with that."

"Probably."

"Maybe even flirt back a bit."

"Possibly."

"I know."

"You do? How did you know he was flirting with me?"

"Baby, you're gorgeous, and you went there single. Why wouldn't he flirt with you?"

"You're not upset about it?"

"Well, I'm not exactly overjoyed, but I'd be more concerned if he hadn't, to be honest."

"Why?"

"This gives us options on how to play him. If he wasn't interested in you, then we have very limited choices."

"I see."

"Are you okay about that? Having to maybe flirt with him?"

Finn shrugged. "I don't know. I'm not exactly a big flirt."

AJ laughed from the front of the car.

"Quiet in the cheap seats," Oz shouted at him.

"Sorry."

Finn stared at him, her mouth hanging open slightly. "I'm not."

"Baby. You've been doing a pretty good impression over the past few weeks."

"I have? But when? How? I don't…how?"

Oz nodded. The stunned look on her face would have been comical had she not been so genuinely shocked. "Well, since we've been together you certainly have been, and I'd say it's probably because you're feeling more confident in yourself as a sexual being. It's been beautiful to watch you blossom and really come into your own, baby. Being loved agrees with you."

Finn's cheeks were flushed in the low light of the limo, and she smiled shyly. "You agree with me." She looked at Oz, her eyelashes batting slowly, and Oz swallowed hard.

"See? That right there. That was flirting." Oz tugged at her collar and coughed to clear her throat. "That was major flirting." She shifted her hips under Finn's weight as her clit swelled and pressed uncomfortably against the seam in her pants. She wished she could reach down and tug them away from her skin, but she didn't want to move Finn. She knew they were going to be busy planning over the next few days, and their intimate time together would be seriously compromised after that. After all, Finn was going to have to pander to the ego of a middle-aged Arab with a hard-on for her girlfriend. She growled and tugged Finn's head down to hers. Her kiss was full of passion, love, desire, and need, and it took all her willpower to pull away from it when they both needed to breathe.

"Wow. I guess I am a big old flirt after all."

"Better tame it down for the general."

"Yeah, I don't want him reacting like that."

"Hell, no." Oz leaned in and claimed another sweet kiss. "These kisses are mine and mine alone."

Finn leaned close to her ear and whispered, "Just like the rest of me."

# CHAPTER THIRTY

The newspaper on the porch hadn't moved, unless you counted the wind rustling the corners of the pages, and Cassie didn't. The curtains were still drawn, the driveway still empty, and as far as Cassie could tell, there was no one home. She waited in the car as Bailey knocked on the door, rang the bell, and peered through windows again, her spirits sinking with every passing second.

"Can I help you, young lady?"

Bailey turned around at the strong voice, the look on her face clearly questioning the moniker of young lady, and Cassie couldn't stop herself from chuckling. But Bailey smiled broadly and approached the elderly lady.

"Hi, my name's Bailey Davenport. I'm trying to find Daniela Finsbury-Sterling. I don't suppose you know her do you?"

The woman's back was to Cassie, but the mention of her daughter's name caused a change in the woman that even Cassie could see. Her back straightened and her shoulders seemed to tense. Her hands balled into fists at her side, and Cassie worried she was going to chase Bailey from the lawn. Apparently, the woman not only knew her daughter, but also cared about her. It meant more than Cassie could have ever imagined. Daniela had people in her life who loved her. Whatever else, her little girl wasn't alone.

"And just why might *you* be looking for her? If you're one of them damn reporters, I'll have you for trespassing. She's been through enough, that poor sweet girl." She stepped toward Bailey, arms raised with the clear intention of shooing Bailey off the property. "Damn reporters, like a pack of vultures. Haven't you got anything better to do with your time?"

"Ma'am, I'm not a reporter." Bailey held her hands up, whether in surrender or to ward off a potential attack Cassie wasn't sure. Either seemed a distinct possibility.

"Then who are you and what are you doing here?"

"My name is Bailey Davenport. I'm a private investigator."

"And why are you looking for Finn?"

"I'm sorry. Who?" Bailey frowned, her hands still held out in front of her.

"Daniela."

"Oh. Right."

Cassie climbed out of the car. She gave the old lady a wide birth as she approached. "Because I hired her to."

"And just who in the hell are—" The woman's demeanor changed as soon as she saw Cassie. Her face paled and her arms dropped to her sides. "Oh my good Lord, she's the image of you."

It was Cassie's turn to be shocked. "You know who I am?"

The old lady laughed. "I sure do. She had a picture of you on my wall when she stayed with me. Well, you were a bit younger then, but so was she. Precious little tot she must have been."

Tears sprang unbidden to Cassie's eyes as she understood what the woman was saying. Her little girl had a picture of her—of them together—that she'd not only kept, but cherished enough to display. She hadn't been forgotten, or dismissed. Her little girl cared.

"Is she—" Cassie's voice cracked and gave out.

"She isn't here right now. I can get a message to her, but I don't know when she'll be back." The elderly lady wrung her hands, and Cassie got the distinct impression that she knew far more than she was willing to tell them. "I'm Emmy Richmond. I live just down there." She pointed a couple of houses down the street. "Finn lived with me when she first came to Florida."

"Finn?"

"She hates Daniela. Said her dad chose it and she wanted nothing to do with it. Everyone calls her Finn for—"

"Finsbury." Cassie smiled even as the tears rolled down her cheeks.

"She's a wonderful young woman. You can be proud of her."

"Thank you. How do you know her?"

Mrs. Richmond laughed. "Well, that's a bit of a story. How about I make us all some coffee and we can have a chat? I don't know about you young ones, but it's still early and I could use a cup." She turned and walked toward the house she had pointed to. Cassie and Bailey looked at one another and Bailey mouthed "young ones" to her, eyebrows raised. Cassie chuckled and wiped the tears from her face. Her heart felt lighter than it had in decades.

"I haven't been called that in…actually, I don't think I've ever been called a young one. In fact, I remember one social worker telling me I was one of those kids who was born old. Whatever the hell that means."

She put her hand on the small of Cassie's back and guided her across the lawn. Cassie breathed deeply, the warmth of Bailey's hand offering her silent support and strength. And yet again, she was surprised by her own lack of reaction. *Maybe I'm just getting used to her.* "You're a young one to me." Cassie winked and followed Mrs. Richmond into the house. The space was light and airy and there were pictures all over the walls, on shelves, and the mantel shelf in the living room. There was one photograph on the bookshelf that drew her gaze, and she smiled. A familiar face grinned into the camera, long auburn hair pulled up into a messy ponytail, green eyes twinkled in the setting sun, and her hands were wrapped loosely around those of another woman. The tall blonde rested her cheek on the top of Daniela's head, her crystal blue eyes stared into the camera, and the look of adoration on her face took Cassie's breath away.

"That's Olivia. The picture was taken at my birthday party a couple of months ago." She chuckled. "They hadn't started dating then, but I think you can tell it was pretty inevitable, can't you?"

Cassie nodded as Mrs. Richmond spoke to her, but she couldn't tear her eyes from the picture. Daniela looked so happy. Cassie turned to look at Mrs. Richmond, and noted the wary look in her eye. *She's waiting to see how I react to my daughter dating a woman.* She smiled. "Yes. They look so happy and in love." She reluctantly walked away from the picture and sat across the table from her. "That's a beautiful look for a mother to see on her daughter's face."

Mrs. Richmond nodded and smiled, and Cassie felt enormously pleased that she had passed her test. Mrs. Richmond poured the coffee.

"What should I call you, dear?"

"Cassie's fine."

"And what are you doing here, Cassie?"

"I've come to see my daughter."

"Why?"

"She's her daughter. What does it have to do with you?" Bailey sat next to Cassie, bristling.

"Bailey, it's fine." She covered Bailey's hand with her own. As much as she wished it wasn't necessary, she was actually very pleased that Daniela had people around her who were so protective of her. "I've come to see my daughter."

"You already said that. Why? Why now?"

She had no way of knowing how much this woman knew about her, or about the family history. The woman hadn't seemed too shocked to see her on the lawn—well, she had, but not shocked like Oh-my-God-you're-alive shock. More like what-the-hell-are-you-doing-here-now shock and that made Cassie wonder how much she knew. How much Daniela had told her. *How much does Daniela know?* "How well do you know my daughter?"

"Well enough to know that you're supposed to be dead. And well enough to know what a bastard her father was. The father you left her with."

"I had no choice."

"But you do now?"

"Yes. I do now, so here I am."

"So you know that he's in prison?"

"Yes."

"Do you know why?"

Cassie frowned. "The newspapers said terrorism charges."

Mrs. Richmond nodded. "That was one of the charges. But not the only one."

Cassie fought the wave of nausea that threatened to engulf her. The room was spinning and her breathing was coming in short pants. "Oh God." Her fingers felt stiff and she couldn't bend them. She stared at her hands, the shape was odd, the angles all wrong, and she tried to ignore the memories that pulled at her. But they were too strong. The instant she looked up away from her locked fingers, she was back in the small house she and Karen had last shared in the UK.

*The line of the cracked tile they hadn't noticed filled her vision as she tried to ignore the fact that she was face down on their kitchen floor. She couldn't look at Karen. She couldn't bear the look of horror, anger, and fear etched into every line of her face. She couldn't stand to see the tears on her cheeks. Instead, she stopped fighting what was happening and she planned her shopping list. They'd need something to fill the crack with, and some paint to go over it. It was only a small patch. It would be easy to fix. The white gloss on the skirting board was chipped, nothing a little sandpaper and the half-used tin in the cellar couldn't fix.*

*Fingers gripped her hair and yanked her head off the ground. "You don't get to pretend this isn't happening. You're still my wife and this is my right." William pressed his mouth against hers in a grotesque parody of a kiss while he thrust inside her.*

*"Please, stop." Karen begged from the chair she had been tied to. "You don't need to do this."*

*William laughed and let go of Cassie's hair. "You're right. I don't need to. I'm doing this because I can." He slammed into her with enough force to shift her body six inches across the floor and Cassie cried out in pain. She tried again to block it out, but there was no let up in his assault. There was no time for her to breathe between one pain and the next, and she was ready to beg for him to kill her. To end it. To make it stop. But she refused to cry. She refused to let him see the tears that welled in her eyes. Tears of pain, anger, frustration, and fear. Tears of guilt, shame, and humiliation. But they were her tears. And they were all she had left to control.*

*When he finished, he dragged her to her knees, pulled her back against his chest, and whispered, "I needed you all those years ago and you deserted me. I don't need you now. I could kill you." He wrapped his hand around her throat and squeezed, hard enough that she could feel her heart beat in her skull. "Put you out of your misery. But you caused me problems, Cassie." He eased his grip on her neck and she could feel the tender spots that would bruise. "So I want you to suffer. If either of you comes near Daniela again, I'll show her what happened here tonight." He placed a gentle kiss on Cassie's cheek. "Firsthand."*

"Cassie?"

A gentle hand tore her from her waking nightmare. She saw the confusion and concern clearly in Bailey's expression. She held her hand over her mouth as she fled from the room. She didn't know where the bathroom was so she opened the front door, leaned over the porch rail, and vomited.

"Hey, I brought you some water." Bailey rubbed gentle circles on her back and leaned on the rail beside her as she held the glass out.

Cassie swept her hair back and twisted it to keep it away from her face. "Thanks," she said and took the glass from Bailey with shaking hands.

"What happened?"

Cassie didn't want to talk about it, but she knew she owed her some kind of explanation. Both of them, actually. She could hear Mrs. Richmond's steps on the porch and offered them both a weak smile. "Sorry, flashback." She hoped it would be enough.

Bailey's hand never moved from her back and she found herself leaning into the comfort being offered, drawing from her strength, and wanting more.

"Yes, he was a horrid little man." Mrs. Richmond waved them back into the house and pointed to a door. "The downstairs bathroom is there, dear." She smiled gently. "Just in case."

"Thank you." When she sat down again she found the strength to look into Mrs. Richmond's eyes. "I had my reasons, and they were all about protecting Daniela. Had I any other choice I would never have left her there. I would have had her by my side every day of my life. You don't have to understand my reasons, and I don't feel I have to justify my actions to you. The only person I will explain myself to is Daniela. If she wants to hear it, I will tell her everything. But that is for her, and her alone. If that means setting up a tent on her lawn and waiting for her to come back from wherever she is, then so be it."

"She's been through hell. I could call the police if you do that."

"You could. But I don't think you would." This woman clearly wanted the best for her daughter, and Cassie was willing to bet that this was her way of ensuring that they weren't there to hurt her. "I just want a chance to explain to her. If she tells me to go to hell, I'll never bother her again. I realize seeing me is going to be a shock for her, but—"

"He told her."

"I'm sorry?" Cassie frowned.

"Sterling. He told her you weren't dead, that he'd never stopped looking for you."

"She knows?" A part of her wanted to rejoice and the other part was terrified at what that could mean.

"Yes. It came as something of a shock, as she believed he'd murdered you until that point."

"What?" Cassie was shocked.

"We all did. He certainly looked guilty. The printed suicide note, paid off the coroner, there were rumors in witness statements about other women. It looked like a sure thing that he'd done you in."

"He didn't."

Mrs. Richmond chuckled. "Obviously, honey."

"When did he tell her?"

"When he kidnapped her and had a gun to her head."

"Oh, God." Cassie put her hand over her mouth.

"The bathroom's just down the hall."

Cassie swallowed. "I'm okay. She's okay? He didn't hurt her?"

"Yes, he did. She's alive, but that man hurt her more than you could imagine."

That was the problem, Cassie could imagine and it was tearing her apart. "Please, Mrs. Richmond, don't make me imagine the horrors that man did to her. Just tell me what he did."

She looked from Bailey to Cassie and back again. "Just between us?" They both nodded. "You're sure you aren't a reporter?" She cast Bailey a withering look.

"You have my word, ma'am." Bailey offered her a Girl Scout salute and rested her elbows on the table. "Cassie here hired me to find her daughter. Nothing more."

"He betrayed her, stole her work and created a monster out of it, tried to control every aspect of her life, and the moment she tried to break away from him, he had her kidnapped and very nearly killed her."

As terrible as it was, Cassie felt a sense of relief wash over her. Daniela had survived, he was in jail, and Daniela had been spared Cassie's own nightmare. She had survived. They both had.

"What do you mean he created a monster from her work?" Bailey asked.

"She's some sort of genius scientist. She tells me about her work and I don't understand one word in ten." Mrs. Richmond smiled fondly.

"Sounds familiar." Bailey nudged Cassie's shoulder.

"While she was in London, she made some breakthrough that let her combine drugs or something into a tummy bug to treat cancer. It wasn't quite right when she left, but Sterling didn't give her any more time. She had to marry her friend and start living the life he wanted and that just wasn't for her. So she made her break." She sipped her coffee before continuing. "What she didn't know was that he'd used her breakthrough and had a weapon made."

"Oh God, no." Cassie couldn't believe it—she didn't want to believe it. He'd never given up. Never stopped. Why? She didn't understand. Why would anyone want to create a weapon like that?

"That's how he betrayed her. She was trying to do so much good, and he turned it into something that would kill millions."

"That's what the papers were talking about when they said she testified against him?" Bailey said.

"Yes. That, and the kidnap and attempted murder charges of her and Olivia. And she had to give evidence on what she knew about that poor boy's murder too."

"Who?"

"Her friend, Pete. The one she was supposed to marry. When he went back to London, Sterling had him shot."

"Jesus." Bailey stared at the old lady. "You're joking? Please tell me you're joking."

"Serious as a heart attack."

"I don't have words to describe…" Bailey looked at Cassie. "Are you okay?"

"No." There was no use pretending, she knew that Bailey would see through her anyway. "Where is she now?"

Mrs. Richmond shook her head. "I don't know. And I don't know how long they'll be gone for, either."

"They?"

"She and Oz, Billy and Junior left about ten days ago now. I spoke to Ellie yesterday and she told me that AJ and Charlie were flying out to join them."

"I'm sorry, who are these people?"

"Oz is Olivia, Finn's girlfriend. Billy is Oz's daddy, and Junior is Oz's cousin."

"Close family?" Bailey asked.

"Very," Mrs. Richmond responded. "Charlie is Billy's younger brother, and AJ is Charlie's youngest son."

Cassie frowned. "Are they on holiday or something?"

"I don't think so, but I don't know what they're doing. It's classified. One meeting after another since that damn Whittaker showed up at Thanksgiving."

"Who's Whittaker?"

"The Interpol agent who reported on everything she went through with MI6 and the CIA, going over and over everything that happened, taking down every detail of her work. The CIA man, he was such a pleasant young man as well," she said, but the look of distaste on her face made it clear that "pleasant" wasn't what she truly thought of him. "Mr. Knight, but he never let up. Not for a second. She just gets free of that and then Interpol came asking for more."

"Knight? Stephen Knight?"

Mrs. Richmond smiled. "That's him, sat right where you are on more than one occasion. Finn was still living here at the time. Of course she moved in with Oz not long—"

"Son of a bitch," Cassie shouted and dug her cell phone out of her pocket. She punched a button and pushed away from the table. "It's me. I know you know more than you admitted. Call me as soon as you get this message. We need to talk." She hung up and wanted to throw the phone against the wall. He knew Daniela and he lied about it. He knew she wanted to find her and he told her he couldn't help. Why? What would it have cost him? What did he have to lose by letting her know that her daughter was fine, that she was happy? The son of a bitch had sat right across from her daughter and never admitted it. The questions went round and round, and she knew she would never find the answers without speaking to him. If she was honest, she doubted that she'd get them then either.

Bailey and Mrs. Richmond watched her as she paced the room. "Do you know our dear Mr. Knight?" Mrs. Richmond asked.

She looked at Bailey and nodded. "He's been my CIA contact for the past twelve years."

"Wow," Bailey said. "Let me guess, you asked him for information about Daniela and he said he didn't know anything."

"Bingo."

"Well, those are the rules of witness protection. You've been given a whole new identity, Cassie. He has rules to follow."

"He's an ass."

"Yes, he is," Mrs. Richmond said and laughed. "Gave me the creeps. He was too nice to me to be real in that job. All phony and slimy. I felt like I needed to wash whenever he left the room."

Cassie knew exactly what she meant, and it was one of the many reasons she hated dealing with him. "I need to see her. Will she see me?"

"She's talked about looking for you. I'll get a message to her. Leave me your number."

"Thank you." Cassie pulled a business card from her wallet and handed it over.

"Professor Sandra Burns?"

"That new identity Bailey mentioned."

"I see. She would have had a very difficult time finding you, I'm sure."

Cassie shrugged. "It doesn't matter now. I've found her."

## CHAPTER THIRTY-ONE

Finn pushed the safety glasses up her nose with the back of her hand. The scent of the latex glove made her nose twitch even through the cloth mask she wore over her nose and mouth. She picked up the pipette and drew a viscous liquid out of the conical flask. She was careful to measure and double-check every single amount in each preparation. Precision was the key, and even a drop too much or too little would have disastrous effects on the results of the vaccine, effects she didn't want to think about anymore. She was doing all she could. She'd hired a small lab several miles from her own to ensure that her research and the preparations for the vaccine plan weren't discovered until it was done. She'd felt a little stupid suggesting her idea about an alternate lab at first, but it had been brilliantly received, and everyone had agreed it was the best way to keep their plan secret.

She depressed the bulb and watched the gel fall into the green solution of the final preparation. She swirled it slowly. The vortex that formed in the center of the fluid was hypnotizing, and her eyes itched a little, making her grateful for the safety glasses she wore, as the fumes would have made them sore if she hadn't worn them.

She set the flask on the counter and reached for the tray of plastic fifty mil bottles with a wide variety of labels on them. Hand soap, shampoo, shower gel, sunscreen, as many different brands with the same colored contents as Oz had been able to get at short notice. Billy had thought that the teams taking on as many as four different target sites would be suspicious if they were carrying four bottles of the same shower gel. She chuckled as she began to decant the solution. He was right of course, and everyone had agreed.

"Damn, it smells like a hundred cats have been pissing in here for a week." Junior walked between two banks of benches wafting his hand in front of his nose.

"Why do you think I'm wearing the mask?"

"Fashion statement?"

Finn raised an eyebrow at him and paused as she decanted the final bottle.

"Anyway, moving on. How we doing?" He pointed to the rows of green bottles. "Looks like you're almost finished."

"I am."

"Good to hear." Charlie walked into the room. "I've got thirty men in the lobby waiting for their toiletry kits."

"Then grab those Ziploc bags and start filling them for the appropriate teams. Oz printed me a list earlier." She pointed to the sheet of paper on top of the plastic bags.

"Organized isn't she?" Junior said as he set to work.

"So, what do the teams need to be aware of?" Charlie asked.

"Besides the smell," Junior said. "Who's gonna use shower gel that stinks like this?"

"Your guys are going to catch a cold within a few days of completing the first release. That's all. As soon as they get rid of the cold, immunization is complete. The more people they come into contact with during this period, the better spread we're going to achieve, so tell them to work through it, rather than take to their beds with man flu." Finn winked at him and smiled beneath her mask as he chuckled.

"What about us? How do we get vaccinated?"

"You just have been."

"What?" Junior looked up from his bags.

"When you walked in here and smelt it, you just caught yourself a cold." Finn held up a tiny vial. "This I'll release when we get to the airport. Not as effective as using the ventilation systems like we plan to in all the other places, but it will ensure that everyone in our team is safe, and anyone around us will be too. Every little bit helps."

Charlie put an arm around her shoulders and pressed a gentle kiss to the top of her head. "I am so proud of you. Everything you've achieved here, how quickly you've managed to do it, how you're dealing with everything. You're amazing, kiddo."

"Thanks, Charlie," she whispered as Junior sealed the last of the toiletry kits and put them on the tray.

"Can I be you when I grow up, Finn? He loves you way more than he loves me." Junior looked at them with a sorrowful expression and put on a pitiful attempt at puppy dog eyes.

"You're almost ten years older than I am, Junior."

"I didn't say when I was your age. I said when I grow up."

"Good point. Then no, because you'll never grow up."

"Touché."

"Finn?" Charlie asked.

"Yes?"

"Did you have to vaccinate him?"

"Hey," Junior shouted in protest as they both laughed.

"Come on, kids, it's time to go. Oz and the rest of the team should be waiting in the cars outside for us by now." Charlie ruffled Finn's hair and grabbed the second tray of kits as Finn shucked her lab coat and safety glasses, then tossed her mask in the bin as she locked the lab behind them.

It took only five minutes to hand out the toiletry kits to the waiting teams and bid them good luck. Everyone knew what they were doing, where they were going, and most importantly, they knew what was at stake. Finn smiled as she handed the last kit into the hands of a soldier who was at once familiar to her and yet new. Evan Zuckerman grinned as he took the bag and slipped it into his backpack. AJ's identical twin brother pulled her into a tight hug.

"It's nice to finally meet you. All I ever hear from everyone back home is Finn this and Finn that. I feel like I already know you." Evan was a Marine and had spent the last five years deployed in Afghanistan on one tour after another.

"Me too. Charlie's so proud of you."

"We need to get going. Some of us have to drive quite a way to get to our first airports." She knew Evan was driving to Michigan to release his first batch and then he'd catch a flight to Amsterdam for his second target, then Johannesburg before he flew into Abu Dhabi. Other teams had similar itineraries, some with fewer targets. But over the next ninety-six hours, the thirty men in the lobby would circumnavigate the globe distributing the green gel she had painstakingly prepared.

She had mixed feelings about sending Lugh out into the world. She knew it was the right thing to do. She didn't even mind picking up the cost of development and manufacture of the solution. There simply wasn't time to go through official channels, and she felt it was her responsibility anyway. Sterling Enterprises could afford it. She liked the idea that her father's greed was funding this development. She just wished it would affect him more than pissing him off in his prison cell. And on the one hand, she was proud of what she had created, proud of the process she had developed. She knew now that it would work and she could use it as she had intended originally. To help people. Her theory worked and would, in time, save countless lives. But she still worried what other people would make from it. How would they twist the technique to make something evil from it?

Intellectually, she knew that every step forward in technology or scientific discovery faced the same questions. When Ernest Rutherford first split the atom in 1917, he never envisaged that his work would lead to the destruction of Hiroshima and Nagasaki. There was no way for him to know that his advance would lead to the threat that was the Cold War, and held the world on the brink of annihilation for years. How could she know what other possibilities existed for her breakthrough? Her creation and discoveries were now at the mercy of other scientists' imaginations. And that scared her far more than anything else.

"No need to look so worried. We'll get this everywhere you need it, and then you don't have to worry anymore." Evan squeezed her upper arm before moving away to talk to his dad, Charlie. Twenty minutes later, she sat between Charlie and Oz, and leaned into Oz's side as they rode in the back of the car toward John F. Kennedy Airport to catch the flight to Eilat.

"What's happening with Whittaker and Knight?" Finn asked. She'd been so focused on getting the vaccine ready she'd lost track of what the agents knew and where they fell into the plan.

"We haven't seen Whittaker at all since we left the Rockefeller Center on Friday. Knight has been around asking when we're leaving. Uncle Charlie told him he was arranging things through official channels and we'd let him know when things were confirmed." Oz sniggered. "We forgot that part."

Finn laughed. "He's going to be pissed off when he turns up, sweetheart."

Oz shrugged. "I don't care. He's been a useless waste of space on this operation. Whittaker even more so. I don't understand what's going on with them."

Charlie's cell rang.

"They can't have run into trouble already." He grumbled as he pulled the cell from his pocket. A small smile tugged at the corner of his lips as he answered it. "Hi, Alex. You okay, babe?"

"Tell Mom I said hi," AJ shouted from the front seat.

"You get that?"

"I did." Charlie put his wife on speaker so they could all hear her.

"We're on our way to the airport. Should be there in a half hour or so."

"Good. I won't bug you. I know how you need to focus, honey. I wouldn't have called, but I just got the strangest message from Mrs. Richmond."

"Yeah? Is she okay?"

"She said she's fine, but she needs to talk to you as soon as you have a few minutes free for her."

"Is it important, babe?"

"No, idea. She wouldn't go into detail. Just said I had to let you know as soon as possible."

Charlie frowned. "Okay. If I can I'll call her at the airport. If not, I don't know when I'll get the chance. I have a feeling it's going to be pretty full on once we get to our destination."

"I'll let her know, honey. Wherever you're going, be safe. I want you and all my boys back in one piece, you hear me?"

"Loud and clear. Love you, darlin'. I gotta go. Billy's lost in traffic already and you know he never listens to the boys."

"Let me know when to expect you home."

"You got it."

"Wonder what that's all about?" Finn frowned.

"No idea, but I'm sure it's nothing serious," Charlie said. "Probably wants ideas for Christmas gifts and doesn't know what we're up to."

"Does she normally call you about Christmas gifts?"

"Every year without fail."

Finn smiled and burrowed deeper into Oz's embrace. Charlie wasn't the only one who intended to do everything they could to make sure this family was safe. They were her family, and there was no other option. She would protect them, or die trying.

## CHAPTER THIRTY-TWO

"The bubbled wallpaper on the ceiling needs painting, Jazz." Bailey lay on her bed, one arm behind her head, the other hand stroking the dog's belly as she stared straight up. She could hear Cassie moving around in her room next door. She heard the shower and imagined her under the hot water. She could smell her shampoo, the gentle scent of citrus fruit and a spice she couldn't place. Maybe cinnamon, but she couldn't be sure. She could picture Cassie running soap-covered hands all over her body, the thick, white, creamy shower gel that she had seen in the bathroom they had shared only a couple of days ago, labeled jasmine and rice milk. "Why the hell would you put rice milk in shower gel?"

Jazz shifted and rested her head on Bailey's belly. Those soft brown eyes watched her as she stroked the top of her head.

"And why am I doing this to myself? The job's over." Jazz whined and Bailey stared at her. "Okay, we. We found her daughter. Case closed. Once we get back to Boston, I won't see her again." Jazz put her paw on Bailey's tummy. "Sorry. We won't see her again." Jazz whined and flattened her ears against her head. Bailey understood the inclination. She wanted to climb under the covers and try to get her mind to shut down enough to sleep. She suddenly felt more tired than she could ever remember feeling in her life. But Cassie wanted to go out and celebrate, and Bailey hadn't the heart to say no. Instead she found herself grinning right along with Cassie. Then she did the unthinkable. She offered to take Cassie dancing after dinner.

"What was I thinking?" Bailey pointed at her feet. "Look, they're both left and don't tell me you can dance, buddy, 'cause you don't have time to teach me and I'd just be pissed." Bailey laughed. "And I keep thinking you're so smart you're going to answer me back one day, when all you're doing is acting on cues I'm giving you, aren't you?" She ruffled Jazz's head. "Well, I guess that's smart enough."

In truth, the words had flown out of her mouth before she'd had a chance to engage her brain, but as soon as she realized what she'd said she honestly expected Cassie to politely decline. She still wasn't sure who was more surprised by Cassie's agreement. She chuckled. *Probably Cassie.*

The water shut off next door, and she imagined Cassie rubbing her pink skin with a towel and wrapping another around her hair, just like she had done two days ago when Bailey had been packing her bag to leave Savannah. She groaned and covered her face with her arm. "I've gotta stop doing this to myself. Yes, she's gorgeous, yes, she's funny and witty, and I can talk to her without making a complete idiot of myself. But let's face it, girl, she's not gonna give a washed up old cop like me a chance." Jazz whined, expressing her disagreement. "No, no, you can be honest. I've got more gray hairs than black ones now, more lines around my eyes than a telephone exchange, and those jeans I keep in the back of the wardrobe to slim back into? It's time to admit that's not gonna happen and accept this spare tire's here to stay." She patted her middle. "But that's okay. You love me, don't ya?" She rubbed the dog's head and chuckled as she rolled over and offered her belly for attention again. "We should just accept that Cassie is way out of our league and try to forget all about this silly little crush. We're fine on our own, girl. Just like before."

She lay back against her pillow again and stared at the bubble paper on the ceiling. Somehow, before just didn't seem appealing.

# CHAPTER THIRTY-THREE

Masood sipped on his iced tea and watched the tender approach quickly from the shore. Hakim Qandri was pushing the limits of the engine as he approached and Masood was grateful his old friend was so reliable. The same could not be said for some of the others who worked for him.

"Tea, my friend?" he said when the tall man stepped onto the dark wood deck of the boat.

"Thank you." He accepted the glass and waited patiently for Masood to continue.

"We have a leak, my friend."

Hakim looked over the rim of his glass then sipped slowly before he answered. "I have thought this for some time, General. Do you know who?"

"I have only a suspicion, my friend." He paused and looked out to sea, and let the gentle waves with their foaming white breakers soothe him. "I am almost certain that I can get the information from our American friend."

"Have you asked him?"

"He claims to have no knowledge of any such betrayal."

Hakim grunted. "Seems unlikely in his position."

"Exactly. I have become increasingly dissatisfied with the quality of information he has been giving us also. It seems he does not know everything that is going on."

"How so?"

"I have reason to believe that Miss Sterling is already en route here. Our friend has yet to inform me of her travel itinerary or which hotel she will be staying at once she arrives."

"Sloppy work."

"It is beyond sloppy, my friend. I have told him I wish to see him and make arrangements. I feel we must bring him in for a little chat when he lands. I will find out if he is playing one side against the other, or if he has lost his usefulness to us."

"And if he has, General?"

"He will not be the first to find a watery grave in the Red Sea." Masood stared out to sea again. He truly loved the boat. It was his home away from home, his safest place, and one where the only higher power he had to obey was the ocean.

"Will that not cause other issues? If we do not know the plans of the authorities, we will be at a distinct disadvantage."

"Very true. But a spy in the camp puts us at an even greater one."

"I understand. What do we know of the girl's movements?"

"Not as much as I want to know, Hakim. I know that she boarded a plane from JFK airport, and I know she is en route. I want you to find out where she will be staying. How large her security contingent is, and profiles on them. I want every detail."

"Yes, sir. Do you think she's reliable?"

"I think Miss Sterling is a very ambitious woman. An exceptionally clever woman, and quite a cold woman. She is not easy to read, though. I have never met a woman like her." He leaned forward and rested his elbows on his knees. "She is also very, very beautiful."

"I remember seeing the pictures, General."

"I think I need to spend more time with her to make up my mind."

"Of course."

"What I have no doubt about is her value. I feel it is essential to maintain her allegiance one way or another."

"I'm not sure I follow, General."

"Miss Sterling will be staying in Israel with me after this is all over."

Hakim frowned. "What if she is not honest? If she's playing games?"

"Then she will not stay voluntarily." Masood smiled. "I would prefer her to stay as one of my wives, but she will stay as my…guest, if she refuses that honor."

"Understood. I will find the information you require and make the other arrangements for our American friend."

# CHAPTER THIRTY-FOUR

Cassie twisted, trying to get a good view of herself in the narrow motel mirror as she hummed ABBA's famous "Dancing Queen." She couldn't decide between the knee length black skirt or the new dress she had treated herself to when Bailey had promised to take her dancing after dinner. The dress was a simple blue summer dress with a slight flair to the skirt. It would be perfect for dancing, spinning under someone's arm. Bailey's arm. It had been years since she'd been dancing with someone, and she wasn't sure if she was excited or terrified. She craved contact from Bailey as much as she feared it. No, that wasn't right. If she was honest with herself, she craved it more.

Everything was turning out perfectly. Okay, it would have been more perfect if she'd actually gotten to meet Daniela—no, Finn—today, but she knew where she was, kind of. And she knew it was going to happen. Not that vague hope of maybe someday, but soon. As soon as they could. She was so close now it felt real.

She settled on the dress after performing a girlish spin in front of the mirror and giggling to herself. *Good God, woman, you're fifty-five years old. Chill out and act your age.* The excited part of herself stuck her tongue out in the mirror and told the grownup to take a hike for the night.

She finished drying her hair, applied a little makeup, and put her lipstick in her purse as Bailey knocked on the door.

"Hi, I just need to put my shoes on. Sit down if you like." She pointed to the chair beside the small table and perched on the edge of her bed while she slipped the black wedge heels onto her feet and fastened the straps around her ankles. She glanced up from the bed to see Bailey still standing in the doorway. Her eyes looked a little glassy, and her mouth was open slightly. "Are you okay?" Cassie stood and checked she had her room key before she stepped out of the room. "Bailey?"

"Sorry. I guess I spaced out a little there. Must be hungrier than I thought."

"Well, let's get you fed then." Cassie smiled. "I need you in tip-top condition for the dance floor later. Can't have you collapsing on me."

"Cassie, I've got to tell you, I'm not much of a dancer." Bailey tucked her hand into the small of Cassie's back and directed her toward the car. It was becoming a habit, one that Cassie had to admit she liked more than she should.

"That's okay. I haven't been dancing in years so I've probably forgotten how."

"Why not?"

"It's not really any fun on your own."

Bailey took a breath as though she was going to speak, but nothing came out.

"What were you going to say?" Cassie asked when she got into the car.

"Oh, nothing." Bailey smiled. "I made reservations at a Thai food restaurant."

"Oh, I love Thai food."

"You might have mentioned that on the drive down here."

"I did?"

Bailey chuckled. "Once or twice."

"Sorry if I bored you." Cassie offered her an apologetic smile.

"You didn't." Again, Cassie felt as though Bailey wanted to say more but held herself back, and she wondered what could be bothering her.

"Are you sure you're okay?"

Bailey glanced at her. "Yeah, I'm good. Or I will be as soon as I get something to eat."

The Thai Life restaurant floated on the waters of Banana Bay, and the smell made Cassie's mouth water as soon as she climbed out of the car. The sun was setting on the horizon, and she felt the thrill of the unexpectedly romantic setting skitter up her spine. It had been a long, long time since she'd been on a date. Was this a date? Is that why Bailey seemed so distracted? She glanced over at her. Her dark shirt hung off her broad, well-muscled shoulders, and the way her jeans clung to her ass made it easy to imagine how it would feel in her hands. *Don't be stupid. What on earth do you have to offer anyone anymore? Enough baggage to sink the Titanic—again. Exactly what a strong woman like Bailey would want in her life. Sexual issues, guilt issues, trust issues, intimacy issues. Oh, and let's not forget that the rest of the real world doesn't even know you exist.* She groaned inwardly and tried to tear her eyes from Bailey's backside. *Yep, great date material you'd make.* Sometimes she truly hated the sarcastic bitch that was her inner voice.

The waitress seated them next to the railing, giving them an incredible view of the water and the peach-tinted sky.

"I meant to say before," Bailey said while they waited for their drinks. "That dress looks lovely. You obviously didn't spend your afternoon napping."

Cassie chuckled. "No. When a girl's promised a night dancing, the least she can do is try to look the part."

"Well, you look perfect."

Cassie's heart raced. *She means for dancing, that's all.* She took a healthy swallow of her wine. *Shut up, bitch, I know what she meant.* "Thank you."

The conversation flowed easily and laughter was a wonderful condiment for their three courses and bottle of wine. The dance club was within easy walking distance, and Bailey had already told her they'd get a cab back to the motel and pick the car up in the morning. She was grateful for Bailey's foresight, but really, she was having too much fun to care. She enjoyed Bailey's company. She was funny, and intelligent, and easy to be with. She never seemed bored by Cassie's tales of her experiments, her students, her childhood. She actually seemed fascinated by it all. She had a knack for focusing on Cassie so completely that she was almost sure she wasn't aware of anything else. Cassie was sure it had made her an impressive and effective interrogator. It made it difficult not to tell her everything. It had from the beginning, and Cassie was sad that their time together was almost over, so much so that a tiny part of her wished that they still had searching left to do. While she was glad that Finn had been found, she almost wished they hadn't succeeded yet, just so she could spend more time with Bailey.

The rhythm of the samba poured out of the club and into the night, and Cassie wasn't entirely sure if it was the music making the stars dance in the night sky or the half bottle of wine she'd enjoyed. Either way, she didn't care. Tonight was a celebration. Her little girl was found, which was more than enough reason to celebrate.

She grabbed Bailey's hand and tugged her, protesting, to the dance floor. She wrapped her arms around Bailey's waist and encouraged her into leading them around the floor with awkward, staccato steps that had them bumping into each other regularly. Cassie giggled as she offered instruction and smiled at each tiny improvement Bailey made. Soon she was leading Cassie around the floor with growing confidence—if not imagination—and Cassie was shocked at just how much she enjoyed the warmth of Bailey's body against her own. Every brush of Bailey's breasts against her own made her nipples harden, and every time she stepped between Bailey's legs she swore she could feel a growing heat. And not just her own. Deep down she felt something she thought she'd lost. *Hope.* Hope that she could one day move beyond the nightmare that haunted her.

Bailey's eyes had darkened, her pupils dilated, and there was a lazy, sexy smile on her lips that made Cassie's knees turn to Jell-O. She wanted to wrap her arms around Bailey's neck, lick her lips, and pull her in for a kiss. She'd wanted to do it since the day she'd walked into Bailey's office. It was also what she knew she couldn't do. She needed a little distance, some time to collect her thoughts—and get her body back under control.

"Would you like a drink?" she asked, leaning close to Bailey's ear.

"Please. This dancing's making me all sweaty." Bailey tugged at the neck of her shirt to get air down her top. Cassie bit her lip and headed for the bar, unable to stop the moan that passed her lips and grateful for the loud music that easily covered it. She needed a drink, and she needed it badly.

She squeezed into a gap at the bar and flagged the bartender.

"I'll just have a bottle of water please." Bailey's voice was low and directly in her ear. The overheated skin at the back of her neck erupted in goose bumps, and she shivered. If she hadn't had the bar to hold on to she was sure she would have landed in a heap at Bailey's feet. She moaned as that particular image filled her mind and her mouth watered.

"A mojito and a bottle of water please." She paid the bartender and handed the bottle to Bailey over her shoulder. Her softly spoken thank you left Cassie imagining those lips planting kisses down her neck and nibbling on her ear, before venturing further. *Baggage, remember?*

Cursing her own inner bitch again, she followed Bailey away from the bar and tried to content herself with sipping her drink and watching some of the truly amazing dancers who seemed to caress the floor with their feet and grace every audience member with their skill. She took her time with her drink, but it seemed Bailey had other ideas.

"I promised you a night of dancing, not just one." She held out her hand and waited for Bailey to take it. She knew it wasn't the wisest decision. In fact, her own inner voice told her how bad an idea it was. She simply didn't care. Wine and rum made her brave, and her body was demanding she let Bailey lead them around the dance floor and stoke the desire that was consuming her body. It had been too long since she had felt anything but fear. Too long since she had been touched by anyone and not shrunk from it. Now she wanted the comfort of human skin against her own, the scent and warmth of a woman in her arms. The sense of belonging. She couldn't explain it any better than it felt like home. Maybe it was being back in Florida. She tried to dismiss the feeling, knowing the chances of her feelings being returned were slim at best. But worse than that, knowing that what she really wanted was beyond her.

One dance led to another until Cassie was so exhausted all she could do was wrap her arms around Bailey's neck and beg to go back to the motel. She needed her bed. Her body was more turned on than she could ever remember feeling, and it was all she could do to stop herself from kissing the patch of skin over Bailey's breast bone that had tantalized her all night. She pressed closer to Bailey in the taxi than she really needed to, not wanting to lose the contact, the touch, or the connection she'd experienced on the dance floor. She was confused by her behavior, by her desire to be so close to Bailey. And given how she'd had a panic attack only a couple of days ago when she found herself being held in her lap, she could only imagine how her behavior must seem. But she couldn't seem to stop herself. Bailey made her feel safe.

She'd become accustomed to holding Bailey's hand, to feeling their fingers entwined and their palms pressed together, so she didn't let go. As Bailey paid the cab driver and led them to their adjoining rooms, she still didn't let go. When Bailey helped her fish her key from her purse without saying a word, she still didn't let go. And when Bailey's lips finally met her own, she didn't want to ever let go.

Bailey's lips were gentle as Cassie pressed her body tightly against her. She dropped her purse and clung to Bailey's back, running her hand up and down her spine and loving the delicious shiver she felt under the cotton. She threaded her fingers into Bailey's shaggy salt-and-pepper hair, the thick silken strands spilled over her skin, tickled her face, and smelled faintly like chocolate and ginger and a scent that was entirely Bailey—a deep musk with a salty note.

She moaned as Bailey's tongue found hers, caressing her, teasing her in an erotic dance that was even hotter than the way their bodies had danced together in the club. But she wanted more. Her body yearned for it even as her inner voice began to make itself heard through the haze of alcohol and hormones. Slowly, she let the kiss draw to a conclusion, all the while wishing it didn't have to end, but knowing that she could go no further. Despite the desire raging through her body, she just couldn't.

"Good night, Bailey." She was panting as she disentangled herself from Bailey's arms. She was slow to let go of her hand and couldn't bring herself to look at Bailey's eyes. She didn't want to see the look she knew would be there. Confusion, desire, and frustration. The look of a woman who had just been teased and then let down. *I told you, but you never bloody listen.* Her inner voice screamed at her. *She could have been a friend, idiot. Now you've gone and ruined it all. Stupid, frigid, bloody fool.*

She closed the door to her room, then the door to her heart, and slid the lock into place.

Bailey leaned against the closed door. She imagined Cassie leaning against the other side so they were still in some sort of contact. She liked that idea. She'd liked everything about the night. Even making a fool of herself on the dance floor. She'd followed instruction pretty well, and dancing with Cassie had been easy. It had felt natural, right, just like holding her hand all night, and kissing her at her door. Part of her wished they hadn't stopped, but a part of her was glad they had. There was no need to rush anything, and she'd seen the flicker of uncertainty in Cassie's eyes, alongside the desire.

Her heart pounded as she understood exactly what her heart and her body were telling her. She'd accepted that she found Cassie attractive. She'd have to be blind and dumb to not be attracted to her, but now she realized that she was not only willing, but desperately wanted to see exactly where a relationship with Cassie would lead.

It didn't matter that she'd never had a relationship last longer than six months and that she'd been alone for the majority of her life. Well, it did, but not enough to stop her. It didn't matter that she was scared to try. She was more scared to say good-bye. Scared that Cassie would hand over a check to close the case and she'd never see her smile again, or feel

Cassie's hand in her own, or her kiss, or hear that little moan she made when Bailey caressed her tongue with her own. Those were the things that really scared Bailey.

Those were enough reasons to ask Cassie on a date. Not like tonight, that ended up feeling like a date, but a real, organized-to-be-a-date-date. Terrified and elated in equal measure, Bailey opened the door to her own room. *How the hell has everything changed so fast?* Just two weeks ago, she lived to work. She lived *for* her work. Now it felt like there was so much more.

# CHAPTER THIRTY-FIVE

The water looked too close as they circled over Eilat Bay on their final approach to the runway. Finn gripped the armrests hard and tried the trick she'd employed since she was a child to ward off her flying anxiety—she sang as quietly as she could. She could hear Oz chuckling at her song choice.

"You know that band was killed in a plane crash, don't you, babe?"

"Huh?"

"Lynyrd Skynyrd, the band who sang "Sweet Home Alabama," half of them died in a plane crash."

"You shit. Why did you have to go and tell me that?" She slapped at Oz's arm and scowled at her.

"Sorry, but I thought it was a bit unlucky. Sing a different one if it helps."

"I can't think of another one now."

"Well, that's okay. We've landed now." Oz looked out the window.

Finn looked outside as they taxied down the runway toward the terminal. The bright sun of the early morning already had heat waves radiating off the tarmac and had people on the ground squinting as they readied luggage carts and steps for the passengers to exit the plane. She leaned over and kissed Oz's cheek.

"Thanks for the distraction."

"Did it work, darlin'?"

"Yes. Better than singing ever did."

"Where did that come from? I meant to ask when we got off the plane in New York but we got so busy so quickly I forgot."

Finn shrugged. "Honestly, I don't remember. It's just always helped me. One of my nannies used to tell me off for it when I was about six or seven, so it was already a habit by then."

"She told you off for doing something that offered you comfort?"

"Well, it annoyed her. I guess there's only so many times you can hear 'Incy, Wincy Spider' without it driving you crazy."

Oz laughed loudly and pulled Finn into a hug. "If you need to sing about spiders to keep from feeling scared, you do it."

"I don't feel nearly as scared as I used to." She looked at Oz and tried to convey every ounce of feeling she had for her. She needed Oz to know how much she loved her.

Oz's gaze softened. "I'm very glad to hear that, baby, but if you keep looking at me like that I can't be held responsible for my actions."

"Are you two just gonna make eyes at each other all day or are we all gonna get out of here?" Junior leaned on the back of Oz's chair and ruffled her hair. Finn chuckled and Oz slapped at his hands. Billy dropped a heavy backpack on Oz's lap, which caused her to flinch and let out a loud groan.

"Looks like we're heading out." Finn stroked Oz's cheek and blew her a kiss. "We'll pick this up later," she said with a wink to accompany her promise.

AJ, Charlie, and Junior were already climbing down the steps when Finn stepped out of the plane, shielding her eyes. Oz and Billy were just behind her. She had her laptop case over her shoulder and checked the pocket of her shorts for her passport and visa. Confident she had everything she needed, she followed her family toward the security checkpoint before they could enter the terminal and go through customs.

"This is a first," Finn said.

"Yeah, it's the only airport I know where you have to go through security before you go into the building," Oz said.

Finn tried to ignore the nagging concern that the vials of toxin and Lyell's vaccine wouldn't make it through the security process for her deal with Mehalik. She couldn't relax until they collected their bags from the conveyor belt, exited the building, and stowed them in the minibus that was waiting for them. A man approached them wearing a pair of khakis, a black silk shirt, and a pair of Armani sunglasses. He had a huge grin on his face and his arms outstretched.

"Ladyfish." He matched Oz's six feet, and his long, thickly muscled arms wrapped around her, lifted her up, and spun her around. "Long time no see. Sounds like you've been up to some mischief."

Oz pounded on his back. "Let me down, Ari. And I haven't done anything. Wrong place at the wrong time."

He set her down and looked at her. "Story of your life, huh?"

"Yeah. Something like that." Oz laughed gently.

"You look different, kiddo. What's that look?" He motioned at her face. "You look all happy and shit."

"It's the look of love, Agent Katz," Billy said and held his hand out for Ariel.

"Please, call me Ari, Captain. It's nice to meet you."

"It's Billy. I'm out of the Navy now."

He grinned widely. "That is a true honor." He cast a quick glance at Oz. "Love, you say?"

"Let me introduce you to Finn. The one responsible for that look."

Ariel's meaty hand made hers look childlike. "Nice to meet you, Finn."

"And you, Ariel. Thank you for your help. I can't tell you how much it means to me."

He smiled and led her toward the bus. "Climb up and we'll get out of here. It's a decent airport as these things go, but there's a lot more to see." He waited till they were all on the bus and adopted the mannerisms of a tour guide, waving his hands in various directions as he spoke. "Welcome to Israel. Please keep your passports handy at all times, and I'll point out anything of interest along the way. Anyone hungry?"

A chorus of yeses shook the bus.

"Well, if you can wait half an hour, we'll be at the marina and the guys will have a hearty meal ready for you, or I can stop at the drive-through."

"When you say drive-through, are we talking something recognizable, or is that local lingo for fried bugs or something?" AJ asked, holding his stomach and looking a little green.

"I was thinking Golden Arches, but I can find you some bugs if you want 'em."

"McMuffins works for me." AJ looked decidedly happier as Ariel got behind the wheel and drove them away from the airport.

It was nothing like Finn had expected. Yes, there was sand by the side of the roads, but they were travelling on good roads, with no camels or donkeys in sight. High-rise hotel blocks surrounded them, and boutique shops, café bars, and restaurants lined the streets. She'd expected something more…Middle Eastern. More exotic. Other than advertising signs written in Arabic, Finn felt as though she could have been in any holiday resort anywhere in the world. Porsches, BMWs, and Audis littered the roads, mostly convertibles. She even spotted a Ferrari and she found herself more than a little disappointed. She'd expected a little character, perhaps some traditional styled buildings or local children on their way to school. She hadn't expected it to be so Westernized.

"You okay?" Oz asked around a mouthful of McMuffin.

"Yeah, it's just not what I expected."

"I know. But I've found few things ever are in life."

"Wow. Pessimist much?" Finn laughed.

"I think of myself as a realist, babe."

"Well, it makes you sound like you always expect the worst."

"There are very few things in my experience that have exceeded my expectations, so I'd say I have a healthy perception of reality. I didn't say that I always expected the worst, but I have found that most people expect too much of things, and people, and life in general."

"And you don't do that?"

"There is only one area of my life where my expectations are constantly surpassed."

"Oh yeah, and where's that?"

"My life with you."

Finn leaned over and kissed her soundly. "Well, you constantly surprise me too, sweetheart, and I love you so much that I think I can put up with the little disappointments that happen sometimes."

"Have I disappointed you?"

"Never." Finn kissed her again. "And you never will." She stole the last bite of her sandwich as the bus drew to a halt. They climbed out of the bus and grabbed their bags before following Ari down the quayside. The wooden planks gave a little under their combined weight, and bobbed with each step until they reached the boat. The thirty-six-meter long white hull rose up from the end of the jetty and Finn stared. Ariel and Junior jumped aboard and grabbed bags as they were tossed over to them.

"You gonna stand there all day?" Oz called to her from aboard the *Whirlwind*. "It's a gorgeous boat."

"I can see that." She took hold of Oz's outstretched hand and stepped onto the dropped stern that was the perfect dive platform. "How the hell was this available at such short notice?"

"Money," Oz whispered. "The company that was building it said it wasn't supposed to be ready until spring. We've promised them a shitload of cash to have it ready for us now. And we're paying a huge safety deposit." She opened the sliding doors to the spacious salon. Several small tables were placed around the edges and a large table was along the other wall. There were also several large whiteboards screwed to one wall with rolls of fabric tied above them.

"Because of the rush, not all of the crew quarters are finished so we only have a skeleton crew on board."

"Doesn't that really work out better for us?"

"Yup. We have Ari, a cook and his assistant, and the captain. We'll do any extra chores as needed, and cover anything else."

Ariel and Charlie were talking at the foot of a circular staircase.

"I don't want to use this space as our operations base, Ari. It's too open."

"Where do you suggest? Staff salon?"

"Show me. Let's take a look."

Oz and Finn followed them into the staff private areas and noted the darker space was not only unfinished, but it was completely empty of any furnishings and down a maze of corridors.

"This is perfect," Charlie said. "Get those white boards relocated and the long table moved in here."

"I'll get all the other equipment you wanted set up in here too."

"Thanks, Ari."

Charlie grinned at Finn. "Just a few gizmos and gadgets so we can all do our jobs properly."

Finn nodded and hoped she was able to do her job properly, too.

❖

Oz carefully stowed her dive gear on the lower deck and started to unpack Finn's. The boat was good cover for their trip and it gave them a great reason not to have a land base where Mehalik could easily find them. Anything that kept Finn safer was fine by her. She'd been quiet since New York, and Oz was more than a little worried. She knew how upset Finn was about the misuse of her work. She knew how determined she was to put that right, and she knew that was the driving force behind Finn agreeing to this dangerous mission. What she wasn't sure about was how much blame Finn was still assigning to herself. It wasn't her fault, but no matter how many people told Finn that, or how often, she didn't believe them. She still blamed herself.

She made her way to the new war room and watched as Finn set up her laptop in one corner and started to work. Oz couldn't fathom what more was left to be done. The vaccine was already being deployed. What more was there for Finn to work on at this stage? The dark circles under Finn's eyes told her how much sleep Finn wasn't getting, and the frown on her forehead seemed to be a permanent fixture now.

Under other circumstances, Oz would have loved to see Finn working like this. She was so driven and focused it was easy to see how she had achieved so much at such a young age. It was even easier to see why her father had such high expectations of her. She was more than capable of running the labs, the company, creating amazing breakthroughs, and doing it all while still being a loving partner to Oz. Love and pride warred within Oz for supremacy as she watched Finn, hunched over the laptop, a pencil stuck into a messy ponytail, and a notepad beside her.

She pulled a chair beside her and sat down. "What's caused that frown on your forehead, my love?"

Finn looked up, startled, then a small smile spread across her lips and the frown line disappeared. "Just going over my figures again."

"For the spread?"

"Yes."

"Why? I mean the plan is already in action, all the stuff's been given out, and the teams have their travel schedules."

"If I missed anything I gave a couple of the teams an extra dose each. I can arrange an extra flight or two if need be."

Oz chuckled. "You're amazing."

Finn frowned again and looked away. "Please don't."

"Why not, baby? It's true."

"No, it isn't. I'm just doing my best to correct a mistake I made."

"It wasn't your mistake."

"Yes, it was."

"Listen to me." Oz took hold of her hand and waited until Finn looked at her. "I've told you this before, but you didn't listen to me. You probably won't listen to me now, but I will tell you again, and again, and again. I will keep telling you until you do hear me. You are not responsible for what your father did. Creating Balor, trying to sell it to this guy, killing Pete. None of it. It was not your fault. Shooting Jack was something you had to do to save us both, but he's the one who put you in that situation. You did what you had to do to survive your father. There is no blame to take. You have to get past this, Finn. If you can't accept that, what are you going to do with the guilt once this project is finished? What are you going to do when Mehalik is no longer a threat and Lugh has vaccinated the world like you want it to? What then, baby?"

"I'll be fine as soon as this is finished."

"Will you? Because honestly, babe, I can't see it. You've already convinced yourself that whatever happens here, you haven't done enough. You're going to let this eat you up from the inside out. I know because I lived it. When we got off that cargo ship and I found out that Rudy had lost his leg, I knew—absolutely knew—that I could have done more to help him. Maybe if I'd put a tourniquet on his leg earlier he wouldn't have lost it. Maybe if I'd had better aim, carried more ammo, anything. I let it eat away at me, and it made me miserable. It made me avoid being in a position where I was close to anyone, or responsible for anything or anyone but myself." She took Finn's hand and kissed her knuckles. "Until I met you. Now I have things in perspective and I don't want to lose you. I can't."

"You won't lose me, Oz."

"You don't know that. If you can't let go of all that guilt," Oz said, "I might." She tugged Finn onto her lap. "This is not your fault, and everything you're doing?" She shook her head. "You're my hero, Finn. I can't tell you how proud I am of you, because there just aren't words enough to quantify it. That you are a part of my life, that you allow me to love you—"

"I don't allow you, baby. I love you too. It's a mutual thing."

"I know you do, but please let me finish." Finn mimed zipping her lips shut, but her eyes were soft, tears gathering at the corners. "I would do anything to have prevented this from ever happening to you, but that isn't in my power. If I could keep you from feeling the way you do, I'd do it. But I can't. You're the only one who can do that."

"It's not that easy."

Oz snorted. "I know that, baby. I really do. But I know you can do it. Just look at this place." She waved her hand to indicate the war room. "All this is happening because you made the cure."

"Oz, this isn't the magic cure that can undo all harm. It's always going to be best if we use this as a vaccine."

"That's just splitting hairs."

"No, it isn't." Finn shook her head. "It's important you know the difference. A vaccine works best if it's administered before infection. If Balor is released before the vaccine spreads, it will kill. It will maim, and it will cause so much suffering that I can't get it out of my head. And they want me to put that in his hands so they can incarcerate him. They want me to take that chance. I don't think they understand what they're asking me to do."

"I agree, but you've gotten around that problem too. You can do anything you set your mind to, baby. Your plan will work. I know it will."

"You can't know that."

"Do you trust me?"

"You know I do. I trust you with my heart, my life, my soul."

"God, sometimes you have no idea what you do to me when you say things like that." She pulled Finn's head down for a gentle kiss. "I love you."

"I love you too."

"If you trust me, then trust that I know this will work. Have faith in me if you can't have faith in yourself. And let it go." Oz kissed her again. "Please."

"I'll work on it."

Oz nodded, and while she trusted Finn and believed she would try, a tiny part of her worried that Finn didn't believe what she was saying. A ringing phone distracted her from her thoughts.

"Go ahead." Charlie spoke into the sat phone that Ariel had installed at his request. "Good work. Keep me informed." He went straight to the white board and used a red marker to circle a number of places on the global map they had put up earlier. Oz had marked each of their distribution targets on it. Twenty-five percent of the airports had been reached and the solution distributed. "All teams are on schedule and reported no issues." He smiled at Finn. "That's phase one complete, and all teams are en route to phase two. Your plan is working perfectly." He sneezed. "How come I'm getting it first?"

"You were the first people infected. You were exposed in my lab."

"That fast?"

Finn nodded. "You'll get a little bit of a headache, a cough, sniffles, and some sneezing. But generally, you won't feel any worse than you do right now. I chose the least harmful strain possible. No one will die from the cold virus so no one will worry about the treatment of it any more than taking some basic cold medicine."

"I love the way your mind works." Charlie smiled. "Forward planning like that would have made you a fantastic officer in the service."

Finn snorted. "No thanks. I was controlled enough by my father. I didn't need anyone else issuing me orders."

Oz watched the interaction between Finn and her family. She knew every one of them loved her like she had been in the family for years rather than a few months. She also saw something that gave her encouragement; Finn's shoulders were straight, not slumped as they had been for weeks. Her chin wasn't down, and she looked Charlie in the eye. She hoped she'd gotten through to her. She sighed. If not, she'd just have to keep trying. She had no other choice.

# CHAPTER THIRTY-SIX

Cassie rolled over and slapped at her alarm. The feeling of an elephant tap dancing on her skull crashed through her head as she tried to pry open her eyes. It had been a long time since she'd drunk the amount of alcohol she had imbibed the night before and, as she made her way to the bathroom, she seriously regretted the moment she had forgotten that over dinner. Or was it at the club? The club where she'd danced with Bailey. Where she'd felt Bailey's arms around her, her body moving against her own. The memory evoked an astonishing wave of desire, and despite her hangover, she felt the abundance of arousal between her legs and the heat of a deep flush covering her face, neck, and chest.

She groaned as she leaned on the sink and took a look at the damage. Bloodshot eyes stared back at her and she shook her head. "Oh, that was a dumb idea, Cass." She held her head in her hands and waited for the nausea to pass. She tried to lick her lips, but her mouth was too dry. Her tongue felt like a rug in her mouth. She turned on the tap and swallowed a mouthful before reaching for her toothbrush.

*That's it. No more rum. Those damn cocktails are lethal.*

She decided a shower was the best way to try to make herself feel human again and hoped Bailey wasn't in any rush to get going back to Boston.

"Oh shit." She slid down the cold tiled wall of the shower cubicle as their good night kiss came flooding back to her. Water poured over her, but she barely noticed the hot stream turn lukewarm and eventually cold until her chattering teeth made her head hurt even more. She shut off the faucet and wrapped a towel around her body. *What the hell was I thinking?*

She dropped back onto her bed and covered her eyes with her arm. *I wasn't thinking. I was drunk and she made me feel sexy, and I did nothing but lead the poor woman on. Idiot.*

It had been so long since Cassie had let herself relax and enjoy the moment. So long since she'd had a moment where she could forget and enjoy the feeling of wanting and being wanted. William's rape had had a dramatic effect on both her and Karen, so much so that they were never able to enjoy a happy, healthy sex life after that. She'd never been able to forget. And truth be told, neither had Karen. She was broken. They loved each other and had never considered parting and continued to share the intimacies that kept them close; cuddling, holding hands, sleeping in one another's arms, the soft touches reserved for a lover. Cassie just couldn't be a lover anymore. And she couldn't tolerate the touch of a stranger. Still, after all these years, she was broken.

She could remember the look in Karen's eyes the last time they had tried to make love. The fear and pity that had gathered as Cassie had tried to touch the woman she loved and froze instead. Karen had held her like a child as she wept, and Cassie couldn't bring herself to see that look on Karen's face again. She wanted to remember the desire she used to see. The look of pure lust, need, the hunger that had been the biggest turn-on Cassie had ever known, was gone. And neither of them had any idea how to find it again.

*I still don't.*

As much as her body had wanted Bailey last night, she knew she had nothing more to offer, and shame shrouded her like a cloak. She had to tell Bailey she was sorry and hope she hadn't made too much of a fool of herself. She shook her head and admitted to herself that her pride and dignity were beyond saving in this situation and she adjusted her expectations. She just hoped Bailey would accept her apology and forgive her without Cassie having to explain. She knew she wouldn't be able to stand seeing the look of pity on Bailey's face.

*She'll probably be relieved anyway. Let's face it, Cassie; you're not exactly the catch of the century. Especially right now. You look like shit.*

Decision made, she slowly got dressed, dried her hair, and packed her bag. She wasn't looking forward to going back to Boston, but at least yesterday she'd been looking forward to the road trip and Bailey's company. *Not anymore.*

❖

Bailey whistled to herself as she tried to balance the takeout cups of coffee and small bag of bagels when she raised her hand to knock on Cassie's door. She nearly groaned as the memory of Cassie in her arms, pressed against the door while they had kissed, came unbidden to mind. She laid her hand against the wooden door, took a deep breath, and tried to calm her racing heart, but she couldn't stop the grin that spread across her face. She didn't care if she looked as goofy as she thought. She liked Cassie. A lot. And she was surprised to find how much she enjoyed the feeling.

She sighed and knocked on the door. Her grin widened when Cassie opened it, squinting at the bright light. "I come bearing gifts."

Cassie took the offered cup and sniffed it. "There had better not be any Greeks inside."

Bailey laughed and held up her hands in surrender. "None. You have my word."

Cassie sipped gingerly then let out a long groan of pleasure and Bailey felt her lower belly clench. She took a huge gulp of her own drink and regretted it instantly when she scalded her tongue.

"Ow, shit."

"You should try blowing on it," Cassie suggested. "Saves you from third-degree burns."

"I'll take that under advisement." Her tongue felt thick and raw, but she still managed a smile. "Breakfast?"

Cassie's face paled and she shook her head. "I'm all packed if you want to get going."

Bailey sat on the bed next to her, so close their thighs almost touched. "No rush. You can see if the coffee takes effect first." She sipped slowly. "Don't want you getting sick in the car for the sake of waiting ten minutes."

Cassie edged away, leaned back against the headboard and brought her knees up to her chin. Bailey was no expert, but over the years she learned a thing or two about body language, and Cassie's was screaming stay away. What the hell happened between last night and this morning?

"You okay?"

Cassie closed her eyes and seemed to be steeling herself for whatever she was about to say, and Bailey knew she wasn't going to like it. She signaled Jazz over to her side and stroked the dog's head, drawing comfort from the simple action.

"I'm sorry."

Bailey frowned. Not quite what she'd hoped for. She heard the conversation play out in her head. *It's not you; it's me. You're a wonderful woman, but I'm not looking for this right now. Can we just be friends?* The same excuses she'd offered her one-night stands over the years, and she cringed at how hollow they sounded.

"I'm sorry I threw myself at you last night. I had too much to drink and I shouldn't have done that."

Bailey smiled gently. *Maybe it isn't the brush-off you thought it was. Maybe she just thinks you don't feel the same or whatever.* "You didn't throw yourself at me, and I had a great night." She picked at the lid on her coffee cup, wiggling the tab back and forth until it broke off. She held her breath and took a chance. "One I'd like to repeat." She looked up, and Cassie's face was paler than before, almost gray. *Oh fuck.*

"I never should have kissed you. I'm sorry."

*She doesn't feel anything. She doesn't want anything from me. Isn't this the part where I normally breathe a sigh of relief?* But Bailey didn't want to breathe a sigh of relief. Instead she felt dizzy and her heart seemed to stop beating. She finally managed to look away from Cassie's beautiful, stricken face, and her heart started to beat again, but the rhythm felt wrong. It felt sluggish and out of time, tight, and each beat was painful. *How the fuck can this hurt so much? One kiss. It was one little kiss. One mind-blowing, awesome, soul wrenching kiss. One kiss from Cassie.*

"It's…it's okay. I understand." *What am I saying? I don't understand. Not one bit.*

"I was drunk and I wasn't thinking. I'm so sorry."

*A drunken mistake? Is that really what she's saying?* Bailey shook her head. *Get this into perspective, idiot. It was a kiss. Not like you ran off to Vegas and got married.* "It's fine, Cassie. I get it." She offered her a weak smile. "No big deal." But it was. It was a big deal. She was ready to trust, to try. She already cared. It was a huge deal. "Shall we head back to Boston? May as well get going if you don't want anything else here."

# CHAPTER THIRTY-SEVEN

The rubber mouthpiece always made her mouth so dry she wished she could lick her lips, but at fifteen meters below the surface, Finn didn't want to take the chance and turned her attention back to the water around her and away from the lack of water in her mouth. It was so quiet she could hear every lungful of air, every heartbeat, and even the current of the water as it rippled through the sea grass floor of the ocean. Her concerns melted away like aspirin dissolving in water. She held Oz's hand as they drifted along, each of them content to just feel the other's presence and be at ease with their surroundings. It was a great idea of Oz's. It helped to cement their cover of being a privately hired dive boat, and it gave them both a much-needed escape. And a chance to reconnect with each other, and the ocean, to allow the peace of it to fill her up and get her ready for the next phase of the program.

They had come to a popular area called Dolphin Reef. Being seen in the densely populated area was a good thing, and it was close enough to shore for Junior and Ari to dive and take propulsion units to the shore where they would go to Eddie's Hide-A-Way to carry out reconnaissance before the meeting this evening.

Oz pulled on her hand to catch her attention and pointed into the blue. Three dolphins were heading toward them. It's what the reef was renowned for, a school of semi-tame dolphins who were as curious about the people in the water as the people were about the dolphins. It was beautiful to watch them play and circle them. They came close enough for Finn to touch them and run her hand down the side of one animal. The skin was so soft it felt velvety under her fingertips. She had been around dolphins before when diving, but the curious wild creatures hadn't come quite so close. It was thrilling and comforting at the same time. She felt something in herself healing; she felt a connection with the creature and her faith in the world and in herself returning.

She didn't want to leave, but her air supply was finite and nearing its end. They returned to the surface a few feet from the hull of the *Whirlwind* and Finn spat the mouthpiece out as she reached for the dive ladder.

"Good dive?" AJ asked as he helped her out of the water and relieved her of her tank.

"Beautiful. A small pod came up to us and one let me touch it."

"Cool. Wish I'd been there." He smiled but the smile didn't reach his eyes.

"What's wrong?" Finn asked as he helped Oz out of the water.

"What makes you think—"

"Because you're as easy to read as a children's nursery rhyme."

"Gee, thanks a lot."

"Come on. Spit it out." Finn shrugged her BCD from her shoulders and hung it up to dry while Oz tugged the zip on her wetsuit down for her. "Thanks, babe."

"She's right, AJ, so you might as well tell us."

He sighed heavily. "One of the teams ran into a little difficulty with deployment and were found in an unauthorized area. They've been arrested."

"Shit," Oz said.

"Where?" Finn visualized each target and the proportional area they were aiming to cover with each one. The loss of some would have a greater impact than others. She hoped it wasn't one in any of the accessible Middle Eastern countries. There were so many people in areas where they couldn't go safely that the surrounding targets were vital. As were the military ones that Charlie had arranged separately. If any of these were affected it would take up to two weeks longer for the vaccination program to be completed.

"Cairo."

"Goddamn it." Finn stripped off her wetsuit and headed for the war room, straight-arming the door open in front of her. "Can we get another team in there?"

"I'm looking into it," Charlie said with his hand over the mouthpiece of the sat phone held against his ear.

"That target is vital. Without it we can't hope to get enough spread across this area in the time frame."

"I know, Finn. I've already got their other targets covered. I'm trying to get a way to get another team in there from one of the other targets. The security coming in will be too tight otherwise."

"What about Evan?" Oz suggested. "His final target was Abu Dhabi. He could get a flight from there to Sharm el Sheik. No one will question that, it's probably the biggest tourist destination in this area." She went to the map and pointed to the tip of the peninsula between the Gulf of Suez and the Gulf of Aqaba. "They can hire a car there and make the journey to Cairo. We did it as an overnight excursion by bus when we went to Sharm. Took about nine hours. Evan can make that in five, maybe six hours."

Charlie nodded and spoke into the phone, relaying Oz's plan.

It would mean a delay in deployment, which would slow the spread across the Arab nations. Finn ran her fingers through her hair and stared at the map. "Do they still have the spare preparation?"

"Should have. Why?"

"The delay could be critical. If they have an extra vial it would be good if they could detour a little." She pointed to the map. "Rather than crossing at Suez, cross from the peninsula into Africa proper at Ismailia. It's a densely populated area and will facilitate the spread across the Arab nations."

"Where would they release it? Don't they need a ventilation system to get the best result?"

"The best result, yes. But as long as they mix it with the water and release it in a densely populated area it will still infect and spread. A gathering like a mosque or a bazaar would be a good place to start."

"Bazaars will be easier for them to access." He quickly typed out and e-mailed the plan to Evan's smartphone. "Will this work?"

"Yes. But the spread will still be delayed across the Middle East by five or six days."

"Why? The incubation period is fast. I'm already hacking my lungs up," Charlie said.

"Because full immunization won't occur until you're clear of the cold."

"And how long is that going to take?"

"Four to five days."

"I see. And across the areas involved it will be a fairly slow spread because of geographic distance, sometimes a nomadic population, and a large proportion of hostility between neighboring countries. Little cross infection."

"Yes. Which is a reason I had to make it airborne."

"How long can it survive in the air?" Oz asked.

"The same as any cold virus. They can last up to seven days as long as they don't come into contact with any anti-bacterial or anti-viral agents."

"Seven days?" Oz looked around her. "You're joking?"

"No. The common cold can survive on a surface for up to seven days."

"I'm never gonna touch anything ever again." She scrunched her nose up in distaste.

"Oz, you swim in a fish's toilet every single day. Why are you afraid of a cold?"

"You just had to go there, didn't you?" Oz looked down at herself. "I need a shower."

Finn chuckled as she watched her walk out of the room, gingerly touching the door handle. "Any other problems, Charlie?"

"None that we know of. Almost all other teams have reported in from their second targets, and half of those are en route to the next one. We're at sixty-five percent complete."

"Okay." She looked at the map, imagining the spread of the virus from the targets and the infected flights that left them. It was a spider web of interconnected infection sites that grew exponentially with every passing hour. Every flight that landed delivered a rapidly reproducing virus and safety.

"Something else I've got to tell you."

"What's that?"

"I received a call earlier."

"From?"

"Stephen Knight. Seems he expected us to let him know when we were flying out."

"Oh, dear. Did we forget to call him?" Finn wrapped her arms around herself and drummed her fingers against her biceps while she continued to stare at the map.

"Indeed. He mentioned something about him being in charge of this mission, and that we reported to him."

"Jumped up smarmy little weasel."

Charlie laughed. "Oh, Finn, don't hold back, honey. Tell me how you really feel about our friend from the CIA."

Finn snorted and shook her head. "Sorry. He just gives me the creeps and I don't trust a word out of his mouth."

"I always knew you were a smart girl. And no apology required. I think we're all in the same boat with that one."

"No pun intended, hey, Charlie?"

"Made you smile, didn't it?"

"Barely."

"I'll take it."

"So when's he turning up? It's not like he didn't know the meeting was at seven tonight."

"His flight doesn't get here until after five."

Finn cocked her eyebrow. "Organized fellow, isn't he?"

"Yeah, how he thinks that's enough time to plan an op like this, I don't know."

"He doesn't. He knows damn well you and Billy will have it covered. I think his nose is still out of joint because Billy took over the op."

"Maybe. Not very professional is it?"

"Nope. I take it Whittaker will be with him."

"He didn't say." He folded his arms across his chest and stared at the board too. "What's wrong?" He pointed to the board.

"I'm worried it won't be enough."

"Why?"

"If something goes wrong with this operation and he manages to get hold of Balor, the first place he'll be able to release it will be the least protected place on the planet and where he will have the greatest access. The Middle East."

"Finn, you've got all of us here to make sure nothing does go wrong."

"I know, Charlie. But still."

"I get it. Worrying keeps you trying to plan ahead and keeps you alert. A little is a good thing. Just don't let it paralyze you. We've got everything under control." He wrapped an arm around her shoulder and squeezed her affectionately.

*I'm still worried it won't be enough.*

# CHAPTER THIRTY-EIGHT

Masood crossed the street to the doorway at Eddie's Hide-A-Way. Hakim's men had been watching for the past hour and assured him there was nothing unexpected waiting for him. Daniela was already inside with a security detail of two accompanying her, a tall blond woman inside the restaurant with her, and the Viking-like mammoth of a man waiting in the car. It was to be expected that a woman in her position would have security. He would have thought less of her had she not taken such precautions. Hakim's team was still trying to find information on the security detail though. The lack of information made him nervous. Combined with his unforthcoming informant, he was approaching the meeting with caution. And an underlying excitement.

He ran his hand over his smoothly shaven chin, his fingers catching the bottom edge of the jagged scar down his left cheek, and he tugged at the lapel of his black Armani jacket. The collar was open on the purple silk shirt, and he loved the luxurious feel of the material against his skin. He was an oddity in his world; with his apparent embrace of consumerism, wealth, and power, his comrades in Hamas felt he was more traitor than patriot. They despised his achievements almost as much as they envied him. He knew it. And he used it to his advantage. It allowed him to access people and places that his Arab brothers were unable to reach, and it allowed him opportunities they couldn't imagine. It would also allow him his revenge.

Daniela sat at the small table with her back to the door and he smiled at the show of faith, his regard for her escalating further. The dark wooden beams and whitewashed plaster walls seemed to frame her as he approached. Her auburn hair was piled on top of her head in a riot of soft curls, and the muted light in the restaurant caught highlights of red, gold, and a deep rich coffee color as she moved. Her long, slender neck seemed to beg for his touch, and the black spaghetti straps of her dress were the only intruders on the expanse of exposed creamy skin. *Beautiful.*

"Please forgive the delay, Daniela. Some business took longer than expected." He reached for her hand and bowed to kiss the back of it.

"No apology required, Masood. Business is business, after all." He had always found her father's clipped British accent annoying, as it had reminded him of all the things he hated. Her voice, however, held a musical quality to it that made him smile when she spoke. He found her accent added to the air of intelligence and class that surrounded her. He sincerely hoped she was genuine in her wish to do business. It would make things much more pleasant in the future.

He took a seat opposite her and watched her while the waiter served their drinks and took their food orders. "Tell me about yourself, Daniela."

"What would you like to know?"

"I would like to know if I can trust you. I would like to know that you are not playing games. I would like to know why you betrayed your father. I would like to know why you are willing to sell me this product when you know better than anyone else what it is capable of. I would like to know why you hate humanity so much. Can you give me these answers?"

She sipped her drink, swirling it under her nose first and enjoying the aroma of the wine. He could see the pleasure of it written on her face. "Some of them, others will be for you to decide. Let me ask you a question, Masood. How well did you know my father?"

"We were associates. I knew him well enough to trust him, but we were not friends."

"Did you know he murdered my mother?" Her green eyes flashed with the anger she tried to hide. He was glad he saw it. It was good to know that she didn't operate from a place of fear or ambivalence. Anger he could accept. Anger he understood. Anger he could trust.

"I did not."

"It was not I who betrayed him, Masood. He betrayed me." She put her glass down and met his gaze. "He intended to murder me after he sold this product to you, because I would have served my purpose."

"A father cannot kill their child without cause, Daniela. I have children myself. What cause would he have had?"

"Greed. He didn't intend for anyone else to share in his wealth or power." She lifted her chin. "You met him. You know his hunger was insatiable."

"And what does that have to do with your mother's death?"

"You asked why I hate humanity. I don't. But neither do I care for it. After her death, I was raised by a string of people who didn't give a damn about me. I was nothing more than income to the people I grew to care for. Then they would disappear. People have done nothing but disappoint me, Masood. I simply don't care one way or the other. As for why I would sell it to you. It's quite simple. I have also created the vaccine. At the proper moment, I will release it, become richer than Midas, and venerated as a hero."

"It seems you are more like your father than you perhaps think."

"No. I know exactly how like him I am."

"He, too, wished to be richer than Midas, but if you know the legend you will know that he died alone after turning everyone he loved to gold."

"That's okay." She sipped her wine. "I don't love anyone."

Masood laughed. "Very well. What if I did not wish you to release the vaccine?"

"Then I'll sell you the product, but I won't sell you the vaccine to go with it. We'll reach something of a stalemate, I fear."

"I could make you."

"Possibly. But I'm not as easily swayed as others you may have dealt with. I have no family for you to kidnap for leverage, the money is already on the table, and you couldn't possibly offer me more to keep the vaccine secret than the world's governments will pay for me to release it. You could kidnap and torture me, but there's no way that you would be able to verify the information I gave you is viable." She smiled a smile that made his heart pound, a twisted smile that told him she would have no qualms about letting him die should he try to sway her from her plan. "I'm not unreasonable. I would, of course, wait until we agreed your aim had been achieved before releasing it."

"And if my aim is the annihilation of all my enemies?"

"That would be the reasoning of a stupid man. And you are not stupid. Without the vaccine this toxin will wipe out every person on this planet. Why win a war and have no one left to see your victory? No one left to celebrate you or fear you?" She sipped her drink. "No, you wish to crush your enemies and see it in their eyes when you tell them how you beat them."

She was right. He wanted nothing more than to see fear in the eyes of his enemies, the fear he had lived with as a child. He wanted them to know the emptiness of losing everyone they loved. And he wanted them to know he had beaten them.

"How can you be so sure of this, Daniela?"

She leaned her elbows on the table. "I can see it in your eyes." She pointed at him. "So I'm playing games." She smiled. "It's up to you to decide if you trust me enough to play this one with me."

There were very few people in his life that Masood had ever trusted, and of those few, Hakim was the only one left. But Daniela's seemingly honest and straightforward answers were refreshing and not what he expected. She wasn't afraid of him or what she had created. She saw opportunity in the devastation, and there was no denying her astounding intellect. She hadn't stumbled across her discovery and then turned it over to someone else to capitalize on it. She was a woman who had taken control of her life, her destiny, and he could see in her body language that she would fight to the death to retain it. In some ways he saw a reflection of the determination he saw as central to his own character. It was what had gotten him through the long, dark days. He respected it in her. He wished it wasn't quite so fierce, but he did respect it. *I will have fun taming you, my beautiful one.*

They ate quietly and Daniela's female guard never let her eyes stray from Daniela for more than a second. Her constant vigilance was a little unnerving, her eyes flicking from the exit to Daniela, from the kitchen to Daniela, to each window and back. She had a routine, and although she looked relaxed perched on the barstool, he could see the tension in her body. She was coiled and ready to pounce in an instant should she be required. The level of training screamed ex-military. Details of Daniela's team rose in importance on his list.

"Your security guard is very dedicated."

"Yes. I pay them well." Daniela swallowed. "It ensures good people, dedicated to their jobs."

"Good help is so hard to find." He chuckled. "Where did you find them?"

"My friend back there runs Valkyrie Security. She has some very well trained operatives working for her."

"Military?"

"Some are ex-forces, yes. Others are more…militia."

"You trust them?"

"With my life."

"High praise indeed. Perhaps I should look at hiring some of them myself."

Daniela laughed. "I'm pretty sure you don't have any security worries, Masood."

"Security is something you can never be too careful about."

She nodded. "True."

He made his decision and pulled a slip of paper from his pocket. He looked at it a moment before he slid it across the table to her. "Tomorrow evening we will talk."

"What's this?" Daniela glanced at the paper, a small frown creasing her brow.

"Somewhere we won't need to be concerned so much about security." He used his napkin to wipe his lips. "Enjoy the rest of the meal. Aman will bring you anything you wish. My treat, please, I insist. I shall see you there tomorrow at seven o'clock." He reached for her hand as he stood. She stood and leaned in, kissing the air beside each cheek and clasping his upper arm with her hand.

"Tomorrow night."

He didn't want to leave the evening so soon, but there was much to do and little time in which to do it. Hakim held the car door open for him and followed him inside.

"You trust her, General?"

"I trust no one, Hakim." He drummed his fingers on the armrest. "Have you located our American friend?"

"Yes. We located him coming into the country. He has an associate with him. I have a man watching their hotel."

"Good. Pick them both up and bring them to the boat. I have a task for him to carry out if he wishes to save his neck."

## CHAPTER THIRTY-NINE

The war room on the *Whirlwind* was buzzing with activity. Charlie updated the airport map which showed only three targets remaining. Billy was pointing to a set of schematics while a wetsuit clad Junior listened. Oz cleaned her gun while AJ tinkered with a propulsion unit. Finn walked in and sat next to AJ. Oz smiled at her and listened to the conversation around her as she performed her task automatically.

"What're you doing?" Finn asked AJ.

"Trying to get a little more speed out of these things. Junior and I are going to have to go quite a way with them pretty soon, and even with a pony bottle we're going to struggle on a single tank at the speed these things usually go."

"Why don't we just get closer?"

Oz looked at her. "We can't risk Mehalik's people identifying us. We have a solid location on him thanks to the tracking device you managed to plant on him last night."

"Yeah, sweet move. He was totally fooled." AJ clapped Finn on the shoulder. "Fake kiss, and wham, tracker in place."

"But we still need to make sure he can't find you. We don't want to tip him off."

"Where's Knight and Whittaker? I thought they'd be here trying to take over by now."

Oz tried to keep a lid on her anger at the way the two agents had been involved with the mission. Basically, they hadn't. Knight was blowing hot and cold, one minute trying to take over and doing a piss poor job of it, the next nowhere to be found. Whittaker was even worse, missing important meetings and offering no input at all when he did show up. If Charlie hadn't checked them out and verified that they were actual badge holding agents from their respective forces she wouldn't have believed it.

"No idea. Knight called yesterday to say they'd landed and demanded to know where we were. He was calling from an unsecured phone, and it was just before we were due to leave for the restaurant. Dad told him that we'd pick them up from their hotel after we finished at the restaurant. He threatened to come down there, and Dad warned him that he could blow your cover if he did that. He agreed to back off as long as we filled him in on everything when we picked him up and stopped shutting him out of the loop," Oz said.

"Okay. So where are they now?"

AJ shrugged. "When I got to the hotel last night, neither of them were there." He tightened another screw in the propulsion unit and tested the binding. "I went back this morning and sat outside the hotel while I had breakfast. Nothing."

"Should we be worried?"

"About what?" AJ asked.

Oz frowned. She'd been asking herself the same question for much longer than she was comfortable with now. "That they are who they said they are. And that they're possibly on Mehalik's payroll."

"If they are?"

"Then we're fucked and Mehalik is the one who is toying with us. Not the other way around."

"And how can we find out?" AJ frowned at her, obviously thinking.

"Until they show up, we can't." Oz hated the uncertainty and wished they had answers, but they were past the point of no return. Changing their plan with regards to Mehalik would either spook him and blow the mission, or tip him off to what they were planning. They couldn't risk the mission without knowing they were compromised. Suspicion was all well and good, but gut instinct could be wrong. Maybe.

"We don't have any other choice now," Finn said softly, echoing Oz's thoughts. "I just have to hope that Mehalik doesn't know about the task force."

"If he does, he'll kill you," AJ said.

"He probably will anyway," Finn said.

"That's why he wants to meet on his boat. Totally under his control and blind for us," Oz added.

"That's what he thinks." Junior held up a small device that was coated in a silicone casing. "Listening devices. As soon as you've got those propulsion units ready we're going to plant these little beauties on the hull. Under the water line."

AJ shook his head. "Under the water line all you're going to hear is water and the engine."

"Not if we place them right." He pointed to the schematics he'd been poring over with Billy. AJ looked at him skeptically. "Trust me." He clapped him on the shoulder. "I've done this before." He winked and Oz watched the play between them and the way AJ shook off the argument. She wished she could let it go so easily.

The door opened and Ariel strode in, seemingly oblivious to the tension in the air. "I've got the extra tender we'll need later."

"What's that for?" Finn asked.

"It's the only way we can all get close enough to his boat to help if you need it. We'll be ten seconds away, Finn." Ari squeezed her arm.

Finn looked over to Oz. "It'll work, right?"

Oz nodded and smiled, determined not to let her own fears add to Finn's. She pulled her into a tight hug. "Everything's going to be just fine." Oz wasn't sure who she was trying to convince, Finn or herself. Either way, it didn't work.

# CHAPTER FORTY

Bailey stopped outside Cassie's apartment block. Less than a week ago, she'd pulled up outside this building and enjoyed spending time talking to the woman beside her. This time, she didn't even turn off the engine. The journey back from Florida had been difficult, and she knew she was mostly at fault for that. She'd sulked like a teenager most of the way, and when she had said good night to Cassie after they went to dinner, she'd had to stay far away from her to resist the urge to pull her into her arms and kiss her again. She wanted to smell her skin, taste her lips, and feel the softness of her cheeks beneath her fingertips. The fact that Cassie didn't want the same thing hadn't lessened her desire, but she refused to put them both in a situation that was even more uncomfortable. Instead, she'd skulked away to her room and spent the whole of the last day barely speaking at all. She'd rebuffed pretty much every attempt Cassie had made at a conversation, and the atmosphere in the car quickly became unbearable.

How could so much change so quickly?

"If you want to come up I can write you a check—"

"I'm kinda tired. If you could mail it, that would be good." She just wanted her to leave. She didn't want to have to keep pretending nothing had happened when it had. Something so small and seemingly insignificant had changed her fundamentally, and although it didn't make sense, she didn't want to lose it. But clearly, Cassie didn't feel the same way. She wasn't sure which part hurt the most.

"Of course. Well," Cassie said, "thanks for everything. Finding Daniela, driving most of the journey, and for, well…everything."

Bailey swallowed thickly, her throat threatening to close on her. "It's what you were paying me for, right?"

"Bailey, I'm…" Cassie's words trailed off, and Bailey could tell she was fighting back tears. "I guess so. I'll mail it in the morning." She pushed the door open and stepped out. "Thanks again."

Cassie turned at the door and raised her hand as though she was going to wave good-bye, but she seemed to think better of it and ran her hand through her hair, stepped inside, and Bailey watched the door swing shut behind her.

"I'm sorry too, Cassie." She put the car into drive and pulled away from the curb. "More than I ever knew was possible." Jazz whined in the backseat. "I know, girl. She was your friend. Shall we go home? Don't know about you, but I could use a good night's sleep."

The apartment was cold when she pushed the door open and reached for the light switch. Everything was just as they'd left it five days ago. The blankets she'd used when Cassie had slept in her bed still sat folded neatly over the back of the sofa, her corkboard was still full of pins.

"What is it with me and women, hey, girl? It seems the only ones I want to know don't want anything to do with me." Jazz leaned against her leg. "You're right, except you." She dropped her bag onto the table, put food in Jazz's bowl, and pulled open the fridge, looking for her own dinner. She was greeted by two bottles of beer, a carton of sour milk, some leftover takeout that should have been thrown away before she left for Florida, and half an onion. She pulled out the onion, trying to remember why she had half an onion sitting on the shelf in her fridge. It had been weeks since she'd cooked. Surely it hadn't been sitting there that long. She turned the dried up vegetable over in her hand and cringed when the pulpy substance turned juicy and ran over her hand.

"Oh, that's disgusting." She promptly threw everything but the beer into the garbage and called for takeout. She unpacked and tidied the apartment while she waited for the delivery. She didn't want to stop and sit down because she didn't want to think about how empty the apartment felt. Even Jazz, her constant shadow, couldn't make the oppressive feeling of emptiness abate. She finally sat down to her Mongolian beef for one and realized just how alone she was. She'd become accustomed to having Cassie beside her when she wanted to say something, anything.

She stabbed at a piece of beef and ignored the tear that fell and mixed with her dinner. "See, Jazz, what did I tell you? Too damn ornery to be anything but alone."

## CHAPTER FORTY-ONE

C assie felt even worse than she had with the hangover. She might have avoided the truth with Bailey, but she wasn't about to start lying to herself. She missed Bailey. They'd spent five solid days together, sharing wonderful conversations, intimate details of their lives, and laughing more than she had in years. Bailey had given her so much in such a short space of time. Not only had she located Daniela, but she'd helped Cassie see herself beyond the façade she created so long ago. She wished she'd had the guts to tell her that.

She went through her morning routine on autopilot, but Bailey was never far from her thoughts. Part of her wished she'd told Bailey the truth about why they shouldn't see each other. But the bigger part knew she would never have been able to say the words, and she felt ashamed once again. Ashamed that even after all these years, she was still giving William the power to control her life. Ashamed that she had allowed fear to cost her any chance at maintaining a friendship with Bailey. Intellectually, she knew she had nothing to be ashamed of, and never had. William was a bastard and had used every trick in his impressive arsenal to make her life hell. But whether he was in her life or not, it was like he was still inside her. When you cut down a tree you can see the rings of its life from the center out, and every ring that marked her interior life had his name etched in it. She had fought with every weapon available to her and had given everything to survive him. But somewhere along the way she had given up too much of herself trying to survive. She had lost the parts that made her Cassie. For those few days with Bailey, she had found them again and she had almost let herself forget.

She cried as she wrote the check for Bailey, so much so that her tears blotted the ink across the paper in a black river, ruining her first two attempts. She printed the name and address on the envelope, dropped it into her bag, and tried not to remember how good it had felt to be held in Bailey's arms. She had no doubt that Bailey had wanted her—or, at least, the woman she had been for those few days. Cassie. There was only one problem. *I'm not Cassie anymore.*

She fastened her coat, picked up her bag, and closed the door to her apartment. The apartment of Professor Sandra Burns.

She walked quickly, dodging puddles, holes in the sidewalk, and dozens of other people on their morning commute across Boston. The

T stop was less than a hundred yards from her apartment toward the waterfront, and the gray water, dark clouds, and chilly temperature reflected her mood perfectly. She changed trains on automatic pilot and walked down Main Street to her lab on Vassar. She'd never really considered it before, but she had to pass the coffee shop where she and Bailey had met, and all she could see was the pain in Bailey's eyes when she had told her their kiss had been a mistake. She wished she could take it away.

She stopped at the large blue mailbox and fished the envelope from her purse.

"I'm sorry."

She dropped the envelope in the slot and walked away, wiping the tears from the corners of her eyes.

## CHAPTER FORTY-TWO

"A re you ready?"

Finn turned around at the sound of Oz's voice and watched her shrug into her jacket, covering the shoulder holster and the Glock she was carrying. "Would it matter if I said no?"

Oz sat beside her. "Despite everything I said earlier, yes. It would matter. If you want me to I'll take you away from here right now."

"He'll come for me."

"I don't care. If you don't want to do this, I'll spend the rest of my life protecting you from him. Whatever it takes, baby."

She toyed with the idea. Running away meant hiding and living the rest of their lives in fear. She tried to picture Oz beside her, constantly on alert, forever watching, waiting for the day when he would find them. Every single day for the rest of their lives, they'd wonder if that day would be the day. *Just like my mum did.* She wanted to cry for the parallels she could see between their lives. But she didn't have the time. She had freedom, something her mother had never had, and as scared as she was she couldn't truly accept the thought of having to give it up. The past few months with her father in prison had given her a taste of real freedom, and she craved more. Oz had given her the opportunity to do what she needed to do, whenever she needed to. She'd encouraged her to explore their relationship, herself, and what it was she truly wanted. She'd given her the courage to not only pursue her desires, but to hold on to them and never let go. She couldn't run. No matter how scared she was, she would make her stand now and have faith in the people who loved her.

"No. I can't do that. I can't make you live that life."

"I'd rather do that than have you go in there anything less than confident that this will work. Because if you're scared, he'll know." Oz's voice cracked. "And I can't lose you."

Finn closed the distance between them and kissed her soundly. "You won't." She threaded her fingers through Oz's. "You're too good at keeping me safe for anything to happen." For the first time in a long time, she couldn't read the look in Oz's eyes. She wasn't sure if it was pride or terror she saw staring back at her. Maybe it was both.

"I hope I'm as good as you think I am. I don't want to let you down."

"That simply isn't possible, sweetheart." She wrapped her arms around Oz's neck and enjoyed the way Oz's arms wrapped around her back, the warmth of her body and her solid heartbeat against her chest. The smell of coconut, lime, and apples tickled her nose, a sweet combination of suntan cream, shower gel, and shampoo. Underneath them all was the scent that smelled like home, an aroma that was slightly musky, yet so rich and spicy that her mouth watered—Oz. Seconds became minutes as she relaxed and pushed the fear into a tight ball in the pit of her stomach.

"We need to go, baby," Oz whispered in her ear and she nodded against her chest.

"I love you."

"I love you, too." Oz kissed her gently. "Come on. Let's go save the world." She smiled and Finn saw the cocky façade fall into place.

Everyone was busy moving into position. Everyone except Knight and Whittaker. They still hadn't heard from either man, and concern was mounting as Oz helped her into the tender. Billy and Charlie both thought it a good idea to approach Mehalik with a light guard for the evening. It was a display of trust, a friendly gesture between two business associates. It also left Junior, AJ, and Ari free to fill other key roles in the plan as Oz accompanied Finn in the small dinghy that would easily get them to the marina where Mehalik had subtly demanded she wait for him to pick her up. He still seemed to think she had a land base somewhere in Eilat, and that was just fine by them. However, it also meant that Oz would be landing them well away from the marina so they could be seen approaching from the land.

The night was calm; barely a ripple on the ocean disturbed the reflection of the moon as it began its journey across the night sky. Lights twinkled from the shoreline, making it easy to see where they were heading, and the safety of the *Whirlwind* faded into the black behind them. Finn stared up at the stars and made a wish to see everyone on the boat again, safe and sound, before the end of the night while Oz tied off their small craft.

Bright lights and strings of faux Chinese lanterns were strung around the perimeter of the marina. They approached on foot and crossed the small bridge from one quayside to the other. The fifty-foot yacht sat in its berth and was easily the height of a house. Three decks of white fiberglass, mahogany decking, and polished brass handrails waited for her. The acrid smell coming from the diesel engines turned her stomach the closer they got to the stern. That's what she blamed it on, anyway.

"Good evening, Daniela. It is lovely to see you." Mehalik leaned on the rail of the middle deck, casually hanging over it to smile down at her. He was wearing a dark shirt, white chinos, and a smug smile.

"And you, Masood. May we board?" She worked hard to adopt the disdainful and disinterested look that she felt was appropriate for someone who wasn't easily impressed by such flashy expressions of wealth. After all, she had grown up in such surroundings. Her father had ensured that.

"You may, of course. I'll come down to meet you." They approached the rail and a gate was held open by a tall man, his arms and neck so thick with muscles that the veins bulged under his skin. "This is my friend Hakim." Mehalik introduced them as Finn stepped onto the deck.

"Nice to meet you, Hakim." She offered her hand and noted the slight tremble as he returned her grip.

"And you, Miss Sterling." His eyes flickered to the side and his head moved subtly. She would have missed it had she not been watching him so closely. She knew he was trying to tell her something. She just wished she knew what.

"Won't you follow me, Daniela, and I'll show you around my little boat."

Finn laughed. "Little?" She motioned around her. "This is far from little, Masood. For a boat it's positively palatial." Years of living with her father had prepared her to play the role she found herself cast in, pandering to the ego of yet another megalomaniac. The beaming smile and look of pride on his face told her everything she needed to know about dealing with Masood Mehalik from that point forward.

"I am very glad you like it. Please," he said, waving her to go ahead of him as one man with an automatic rifle slung over his back let loose the stern line while a second man watched from the upper deck. "This way," Mehalik said as he guided Finn down onto the aft deck and the captain backed them out of the marina. It wasn't what they had hoped would happen, but they had expected it. Why get someone onto a boat if you didn't plan to take them away from the shore? "The wood has all been hand carved." He stroked the dark wood lovingly. "This deck alone took a team of craftsmen three weeks to complete."

The vast expanse of dark wood made the deck look smaller than she had expected. "Worth every second."

"Absolutely."

The captain expertly steered them through the Northern Lagoon and out into the Strait of Eilat. They were moving quickly, the shoreline growing smaller by the second. "Wow, that's fast."

"Yes, I have two large engines. Three hundred and fifty horse power each. I dislike moving slowly."

She followed him through the sliding doors into the salon, looking around him as his back obscured the view in front. The dark wood continued throughout, with dark drapes over the portholes, and the upholstery she could see was similarly colored. The darkness was actually oppressive, and she couldn't understand why someone would ruin such a beautiful boat with such awful interior design. "It is a beautiful boat." The sliding door clicked closed behind them and the noise of the great engines faded. From behind her, rough hands tugged her arms out to the side and ran the length of her body.

"Please excuse the invasion of privacy, Daniela. Security is very important to me."

She'd been warned to expect the frisk. Oz had even demonstrated what to expect, as she was certain it would be much more intrusive than the standard police frisk. She was right. This was more like being groped. And just because she was expecting it didn't mean she had to like it. "I think I'm offended, Masood. Perhaps we won't be doing business after all."

"Oh, I think we can come to some arrangement." He turned to stand directly in front of her. "However, there is one thing we need to remedy before we discuss such matters."

"What's that?" Finn placed her hands on her hips and adopted a scowl. She hoped the flush of fear she could feel burning her cheeks and neck would be read as anger.

"I gave you permission to board, but not your associate." He nodded toward Oz. Finn turned around fast enough to see Hakim bring the butt of his gun down on the back of Oz's head. She hit the deck. Finn cried out and watched in horror as Oz was dragged through the doors and her body was tossed over the side rail.

*Splash.*

She wanted to run after her, dive overboard. Something, anything, to try to save her, but her feet wouldn't move. She could hear her heart beating in her ears, racing, pumping blood and adrenaline through her body, but her muscles wouldn't cooperate. *No, no, no. This cannot be happening. It can't be real.* Her breathing quickened, and she tried to fight the wave of dizziness that engulfed her. All she could see was Oz's body floating face down in the water. She couldn't think of anything else.

"Seems you were correct, my friend. She was rather attached to her blond Amazon." Mehalik's smug tone penetrated the fog clouding her brain, and she turned to see him sitting at the table, his arms resting along the back of the built-in seat. Next to him, Andrew Whittaker held a gun loosely in his hand, and Stephen Knight was gagged, bound to a chair, and staring at her with wild eyes.

*I'm going to die.* The realization crashed through her head, but she couldn't muster any of the sadness the thought should have filled her with. She didn't want to live in a world without Oz. She didn't want to know what that would be like. The knowledge of Balor would die with her, and by the time anyone else could re-create it, the vaccine would have spread globally. It was her one consolation. She would have succeeded in stopping his plan as soon as he killed her. It was little consolation, but right now she'd take all she could get.

Whittaker tapped the barrel of his gun against a large metal case. Steel and the size of a briefcase, it sat ominously in the middle of the table. *No. Please, God, don't let that be what I think it is.*

"You know Mr. Knight, and of course, my friend Mr. Whittaker."

"Hello, Finn. Didn't expect to see me here, did ya?" Whittaker smiled.

Finn couldn't drag her eyes from the case. "Why?"

"Simple. Mr. Mehalik pays very well."

Finn sniffed and tried to get her brain to work again. She knew Billy and Charlie were listening. Maybe they could pick up Oz. Maybe they already had. She ignored the logical part of her brain that told her the chances were slim and convinced herself that Oz was okay, and everyone was listening. They needed to know what was happening. They needed to be prepared as much as possible because she knew they were coming for her.

"So you sold us all out and gave him the case full of the toxin. How the hell did you get it anyway?" She knew Billy and Charlie would be running around trying to find out if the toxin was no longer aboard the *Whirlwind*.

Whittaker smiled. "I'm not as useless an investigator as you and your band of merry men seemed to think. Don't forget I know how you've been spending all your time in America, Miss Sterling. A boat hired out that quickly, as a private dive boat, wasn't hard to track down." He motioned his hand in her direction and she tried not to flinch as the barrel of the gun wavered in front of her chest. "Do you think you're the only person in the world who knows how to scuba dive? That your Navy friends are the only ones capable of infiltrating a boat and securing a target?" He tapped his chest. "One of the true perks of being underestimated is always having the element of surprise on your side." He stepped closer to her. "I could've slit your throat if I'd wanted to." He dragged the cold metal of the gun's muzzle across her neck. "That's how close I was last night."

"There's no need for threats, Mr. Whittaker. Daniela is here as a friend. We're here to do business. Aren't we?"

Finn nodded slowly.

"Well, that's good. Because this case doesn't have any vaccine in it." Whittaker smirked. "Of course it doesn't have any toxin in it either."

Finn let out a sigh, the relief so strong it made her dizzy.

"We've already given it to several people to distribute," Whittaker whispered in her ear.

*Fuck, no. No, no, no, no, no. It's too soon. Distribution at this point would ravage a population.* "Where?" Her lungs didn't seem to be functioning correctly, and every breath seemed to do nothing toward supplying oxygen to her brain. *Think, dammit. It's your one tool. Think your way out of this.*

"None of your concern," Mehalik said.

*Come on.* Frustration and disbelief warred inside her. *This can't be happening. Please let it be a bloody nightmare.* She stared at Whittaker. "He's a madman, but you?" She looked him up and down. "Do you have any idea what you've done?"

He shrugged, clearly not at all bothered about the people he was killing. "Like I said, he pays well." He turned to Mehalik. "Speaking of which, we had an agreement. As soon as she was on board you said you'd make the final transfer."

"Indeed. I shall see you receive everything you are owed, my friend." He turned back to Finn. "As Mr. Whittaker said, Daniela, the vaccine you created was not with the toxin. Where is it?"

It was her only chance to dissuade him. "There isn't one." She swallowed thickly. "I couldn't make it work. If you release Balor you'll die from it too."

"Fuck." Whittaker slammed his fist on the table. "You said it was ready. You said you'd improved on Lyell's vaccine so that it was at eighty-five percent."

She stared at him. "I lied."

"Goddamn bitch." He stepped toward her only to have Hakim block his path.

"Daniela, I think it is now you who is lying." Mehalik stood and placed a chair behind her. "Sit." He grabbed her arm and pushed her into the chair when she didn't immediately follow his orders. "I believe you do have a quantity of the vaccine, and the formula for it is stored in that pretty little head of yours. I think you are far too cautious a scientist to have approached this any other way." He sat down again. "I have several recordings of you working in your laboratory saying exactly that."

*Shit*. The situation went from bad to worse. "Mr. Whittaker was supposed to bring me enough of the vaccine for me to use." He looked at Whittaker. "You failed."

"I made sure you have her. She can get it for you."

"Hmmm." Mehalik stroked his chin. "I'm thinking that is not good enough." He waved his hand and Hakim raised his gun to Whittaker's head.

"No, wait. I have more information that will help."

Mehalik held up his hand to halt Hakim. "Quickly."

"I can give you the leverage you need to get her to cooperate. I know where her mother is."

Finn didn't know if he was telling the truth or not. Did he know where her mother was? If so, how? Even her father hadn't been able to find her, and she had all but convinced herself that she really was dead. Either way, she knew she had to deny the possibility of it. She couldn't risk someone else's life in Mehalik's hands. "My mother's dead, you idiot. My father saw to that."

"No, she isn't. I've got a picture to prove it." He nodded toward his chest. "It's in my jacket pocket. Two pictures."

"Show me," Mehalik ordered.

Whittaker pulled the small pictures from his pocket and handed them over with shaking hands. From her position it was difficult to make them out clearly, but she could see one was a picture of her and her mother when she was a small child. She couldn't see the other at all.

"When was this taken?" Mehalik waved the second picture at Whittaker.

"Less than a week ago."

"How did you find her?"

Whittaker sneered at Stephen. "That idiot led me straight to her."

Finn gasped. *He knows my mother. How the fuck does he know my mother?* Stephen pulled against his restraints and tried to speak through the gag. His incoherent words were silenced by Hakim's gun cracking across the back of his skull.

"Perhaps a little more restraint, Hakim. It might have been nice to get some corroboration from our Mr. Knight."

"Of course. My apologies, General." The big man bowed his head in a show of submission, but his shoulders didn't drop, and something in Finn's memory nagged at her. Something she couldn't put her finger on, but there was too much else bothering her to try to focus on it. Oz, Balor, Knight, her mother. It was too much. She felt like she was being pulled apart. Everything was out of her control, and she felt helpless in a way she never had before.

"Where is she?" Mehalik pointed at Whittaker. "And how did you get these?"

"I followed him to her apartment when he went to see her." He scrawled an address across the back of the picture. "I didn't know who she was, but given the mission I figured she had to be important. I thought she might be his wife, which could give me a little leverage and get him off my back. I suspected he knew I was working for you. I broke in and saw the pictures, and I think she'll be of more use to you than to me, General."

"You may be correct, Andrew. But it doesn't help me *now*. I need this vaccine quickly." He nodded and Hakim's bullet ripped through the back of Whittaker's skull. The force drove him forward, his face flat to the table.

Finn screamed as blood, bone fragments, and brain matter splattered across the dark wood surface, and she finally understood the reason for the dark material. It would hide a multitude of sins from anything less than a forensic examination and she added her own contribution as she bent at the waist and vomited.

When her stomach was empty, she slowly stood and found herself unable to look away from the gory sight. She tried to find some pity or compassion at his fate. She failed. He had colluded and condemned so many others to a painful death that she felt his was entirely justified. The sentiment scared and shocked her far more than the gunshot had. What was she becoming?

"Where is the vaccine?"

"I told you, I failed. I ran out of time to make it work."

Mehalik sighed. "You may have been wondering why I have Mr. Knight here. I plan to have him help us convince you to tell me where it is." He waved his hand. "I should have thought that through a little better and kept your blond friend on board, shouldn't I? She would have been much more motivating for you, I think."

Finn swallowed, and for the first time, she was glad Oz wasn't there. "I failed to make it work." She looked at Stephen and hoped he could see how sorry she was for the pain they both knew was about to be inflicted upon him.

"I didn't expect you to make it easy, Daniela." He nodded to Hakim. "I think we'll start at the bottom and work our way up."

Hakim grabbed Stephen's left leg and pulled it forward. He ripped the material open and pulled away his shoes and socks. Finn couldn't figure out why he was doing it. *What difference did it make? Why take the time and the care to clear—*

She hadn't seen Hakim retrieve the hammer that smashed down on Stephen's ankle, dead center, and crushed it against a block of wood. Stephen's eyes were wild, pain and fear mixed heavily with rage. He screamed his agony through the gag stuffed in his mouth and struggled against the ropes wrapped around him. Finn realized that the exposure was so she could see every gory detail of pain he suffered by her refusal. His foot hung at an ugly angle, swelling and bruising already visible, blood running from broken skin.

"I believe you are a compassionate woman, Daniela. You can end his suffering at any moment."

"I don't have a vaccine to give you, Masood."

Hakim exposed the right foot and calf.

"Let her hear Mr. Knight's reaction a little clearer, Hakim."

Hakim yanked the cloth away from Knight's mouth and placed the block beneath his heel. He brought the hammer down before Stephen could react. His resulting scream made her weep for his agony.

"Please stop this." She would beg if that's what it took to end the violence. She would offer her life without hesitation. But she wouldn't give him the vaccine he wanted. It was the only chance she had to stop him from releasing Balor before her vaccine had a chance to spread.

"It is in your power to stop this, Daniela." He crouched beside her on one knee and wiped the tears from her cheeks. "You can stop his torment any time. Just tell me where the vaccine is."

"Don't tell him anything. He's going to kill us anyway." Stephen gasped the words out through the pain.

She knew he was right. The moment she gave in she was condemning them both to death, as well as those not yet vaccinated by Lugh. She had no choice. "I don't have a vaccine to give you," she whispered.

"Yes, you do." Mehalik clicked his fingers and the left leg of Stephen's pants was ripped to the knee. "Last chance to save his kneecap, my darling Daniela."

She shook her head. She locked her gaze with Stephen and let the tears fall again as he smiled and mouthed the words "good girl" at her. His tiny smile was short-lived as the third strike of the hammer shattered his kneecap and his scream exploded through the night.

"I'm sorry." It was all she could think to say, but she knew it would never be enough. She was sorry she had distrusted him and right now she couldn't remember why. She was sorry she hadn't given him the chance to prove himself to them all. Now he was taking the brunt of every refusal she made.

"No need to be sorry, just tell me where it is and his suffering will be over."

Mehalik stood behind her and put his hands on her shoulders. A shudder ran down her spine and she remembered the last time a man had stood behind her that way. Jack had wrapped his hands around her throat and tried to choke the life out of her while Oz had watched helplessly from across the room. She could still feel Jack's fingers on her neck and the forced intimacy of Mehalik's hands on her skin made her flesh crawl.

"Where is the vaccine?"

It occurred to her that her very presence in the room had vaccinated Mehalik. She wanted him to contract the plague he wanted to let loose on the world. She pictured him writhing in agony as Balor painfully stripped away control of every muscle in his body. She pictured him lying on the floor, slowly choking and drowning on his own drool. She could imagine the fear in his eyes when he knew death was coming for him. She'd asked herself earlier what she was becoming. Right now she didn't care. Rage filled her to overflowing. "I don't have any."

Oz flexed her fingers to get the blood flowing again or she was going to lose her grip of the gunwale. The speed the boat was travelling made it difficult for her to haul her body weight back onto the deck, but she had to. She knew she did. The boat was still going too fast for Junior, AJ, and Ari to get on board. She was still amazed at the risk Hakim had taken by passing her the tiny square of paper when they shook hands. The simple message, *play along*, was her only clue that everything was far from what it seemed. She'd done as instructed and played along, and rather than finding herself tossed unconscious into the Red Sea, she was clinging to the edge of the *Ataba and Zarief E-ttool* and trying to make her muscles function enough to keep her from falling into the water. She just wished Finn knew she was okay. The heavy bag Hakim had dropped into the water sounded very much like a body, and Finn must surely think it had been her. After he dropped it, Hakim had lifted her over, but waited until she got a grip on the rail before letting her go and walking away. There weren't any words, but he clearly meant for her to stay out of the way. For what reason, she couldn't fathom. Her head ached from where he'd hit her hard enough to make it seem like he'd actually knocked her out.

The unmistakable sound of a gunshot, followed by Finn's scream, propelled her into action. The adrenaline pumped through her body and made the near impossible feat child's play. She peeked around the deck to make sure it was clear. She hadn't seen as many enforcers as she'd expected earlier, but she figured they were still out there, watching the water, making sure there was nothing close by. When she was sure the coast was clear, she rounded the corner and glanced quickly through the large sliding glass doors. What was left of Whittaker was slumped over the table, and Finn stood with her back to the windows, blocking out most of the view. It was enough for Oz to get a sense of what was happening inside.

She heard Mehalik demand to know where the vaccine was. It was his singular focus. Oz looked again and saw the steel case on the table. The case Finn had used to carry the miniscule samples of Balor from New York. *Shit*. She needed help and she needed it fast. *Time for plan B. Or is it C?*

She took a moment to glance at Stephen Knight. His eyes widened as he saw her, but he nodded quickly as she darted her eyes toward the upper deck where the cockpit and the throttle were. Hakim was working at Stephen's foot as she turned away, but she didn't have time to hang around. She gripped the edge of the upper deck and lifted herself up enough to see who was where. One guard stood sentry with a seemingly unarmed captain. She dropped silently back to the deck and lifted the leg of her pants. Her dive knife was strapped to her calf. A garbled scream rang out in the darkness. She hoped Knight was okay, but something told her he would be walking with a limp for the rest of his life.

She worked her way around the boat until she stood behind and below the guard. Looking carefully at the drop of his pants, she could see he was wearing shoes instead of boots. Perfect. She slashed the knife across the back of his legs. A clear, blood-curdling scream filled the air as the guard dropped to the ground grabbing his ankles. She pulled the automatic out of his reach, twisted it, and slammed the butt into his face, driving the bridge of his nose into his brain, killing him instantly.

She leveled the gun at the captain and put her finger over her lips, signaling him into silence. His single nod confirmed he understood.

"Slow the boat but don't stop it." He reached for the controls and did as she asked. "How many other guards are on the boat?" She spoke quietly, the gun trained on his forehead.

"Three, I think, and the man inside." He matched her volume and did nothing that would raise alarm. She was pleased by his reaction but puzzled by it also.

"Hakim?" She ducked low so that she was hidden from the sight of the other guards should they choose to check.

"Yes." He worked the speed down gradually so that no one would notice the decrease. "What speed you need?"

"If you can get us to five knots that'll be good. But I can't get us help if you're over ten."

"Understood."

"Why are you helping me?"

"My son. He six year old. One guard have him tied in engine room. You save, please."

Jesus, as if there wasn't enough already. Oz closed her eyes. "You have my word. Get us to five knots and we'll do everything we can for your boy."

Another scream from inside split the air. "He kill them?"

She shook her head. "He needs information first. A boat is going to draw up alongside. They'll attach a rope and disembark from their boat. They'll drag themselves up by rope. You must try to keep our course steady and no more than ten knots."

"Which side?"

"Port." She pointed to the left side to ensure there was no confusion. "Do you have a flashlight?"

"Sorry?"

"A flashlight? Electric light. For signal."

"Ah, yes." He quickly pulled one from the captain's cubby behind the wheel.

"Thank you." She pointed the head straight into the air so the beam of light would be seen from a distance but not affect the lighting or shadows on the boat. She didn't want to alert anyone to her presence. She tapped out the quick signal they had arranged earlier as yet another scream sliced through the starry night. Her heart bled for Finn having to watch Knight's torture, but it was the only option. They would pick up the pieces later. Right now, they had to survive it.

She heard the faint sound of an approaching engine and positioned herself low on the upper level, knife at the ready. She couldn't afford for anyone to draw attention to the approaching vessel, and three or more guards somewhere on the boat made her nervous. "They no expect trouble while moving. They go eat."

"Thank you." She relaxed her posture but not her vigilance. People were unpredictable; who knew when they might decide to take a walk onto the deck, maybe for a smoke, or too lazy to go to the head to relieve themselves. "What's your name?"

"Zain."

"Well, Zain, thank you for your help." She saw the faint line of the RIB approaching, adjusting to match the speed as Ari pulled alongside. She could make out one of the boys reaching across the gunwale to secure the rope to the forward cleat. "Just keep it as slow as you can while they get on board. Then do whatever you need to do." He nodded as she dropped to the lower level. Someone was crying inside the main salon, and voices were raised, but she couldn't make out the individual words. Part of her was glad for that. She wasn't sure she'd be able to keep a clear head if she knew what that bastard was saying to Finn.

She kept her back to the forward deck as Junior and AJ cleared the rail, so she could watch for any guards. She took the waterproofed gun

Junior held out to her. She pulled the condom off the silencer and barrel, then tossed it over the side and checked it. AJ sniggered.

"What?" Oz asked.

"The look on your face when you took that off. It's not infectious, you know?"

"How can you be sure?"

"Enough chitchat, boys and girls. We've got work to do." Junior helped Ari onboard and they tied the tender on a long line so that it wouldn't bump the side and attract attention. Pulling it back in at speed would be a bitch, but doable. "What's the situation?"

Oz quickly filled them in and they agreed to approach the staff quarters to clear the guards before they tackled the salon. With Hakim on their side it would be easy to take care of the situation without the worry of armed guards walking in. AJ agreed to stay with the captain—partly as protection and partly as insurance. He'd played along so far and given Oz no reason not to trust him, but she wasn't taking any chances. Too much was at stake.

Junior led the way and approached cautiously but quickly, and within seconds, they were outside the door to the staff dining area. Two guards were playing cards and laughing. Junior slammed open the door and he and Oz shot at the same moment, each nailing their targets between the eyes before they even reached for their weapons. Ari watched their backs, then followed Junior's lead down the short corridor that led to a set of stairs. A pain-filled shriek came from the salon, and she cringed. She dreaded to think what condition Knight would be in by now. Junior looked at her, the question in his eyes. She knew him well enough to know what he was asking. She held up six fingers to let him know how many screams she'd heard, and thereby how many joints had been shattered.

Junior's jaw clenched, but he signaled for them to move forward. Their plan was a good one, solid, and would give them the best chance of saving Finn and Knight. They had to stick with it.

The engine room was a mass of cables, pipes, and noise. It was also cramped and easy to take refuge behind large sections of bullet protecting metal work. Ari ran distraction, sprinting across the small space and ducking behind a huge generator. A man jumped out of his chair and leveled his automatic rifle in Ari's direction. Junior took the shot from halfway down the stairs. Blood and brain matter splattered across the white bulkhead, and a young boy tied up on the floor cried out. Oz quickly quieted him and carried him as they made their way out of the bowels of the boat. His father cried when he saw him and thanked them over and over as he untied his son. They readied themselves for the next part of the plan and Junior gave him a piece of paper.

"Go to these coordinates. Fast as you can." He turned to Oz. "Is that all of them?"

"Zain said he thought there were three onboard. I saw Hakim and the two from the mess when I came on earlier. I didn't see the guy from the engine room though." She shrugged. "No way to know for sure if there are more without doing a full sweep."

Junior frowned. "I don't like not knowing."

"I know it's not exactly a huge ship, but doing a thorough search will take more time than Knight has. If it'll make you feel better we can take AJ with the rest of us to take down Mehalik."

"The big guy in there is already on our side. It's four against one even if AJ stays up here," Ari said, his confidence in their ability to control one man evident in his cocky smile. "Don't like those odds, Captain America?" His goading worked, and less than a minute later, the three of them were positioned on either side of the sliding doors to the salon, AJ still with the captain and his boy.

Oz had a clear shot. She could have pulled the trigger and torn a hole in the back of Mehalik's head. The world would thank her for it, as long as the vials of Balor were in the case. But if they weren't, he may very well be the only person who knew where they were. They needed him alive at this point. She considered a shot anywhere else on his body, but she couldn't take the risk. The way his body was positioned meant the bullet could pass through him and hit Finn. They had no choice but to go in.

She watched Hakim ripping the shirt sleeve off Stephen's right arm, his hands a bloody, pulpy mess. She closed her eyes for a second and took a deep breath. Now was not the time for emotion. She used the same trick she'd used in the Navy to partition her mind and focused solely on the task at hand. Finn's life was at stake. She'd deal with everything she was feeling later. Hakim positioned his hammer over Stephen's elbow, and Junior slid the door open in time with the blow and resultant scream, hoping to disguise the sound. It didn't work.

Mehalik grabbed Finn and jerked her tight against his chest, one arm around her throat, and she gasped for air. Stephen's agonized moans echoed through the salon as they stared at each other.

"Oz." Finn's eyes were huge and tears rolled down her cheeks even as she grabbed at Mehalik's arm in a vain attempt to free herself.

Shock was evident on Mehalik's face, but it was fast being replaced with rage. His cheeks reddened and his hands shook and spittle gathered at the corners of his mouth as he screamed, "Get back or I'll kill her."

Hakim trained his gun at Stephen's head. The only reason Oz could think of for doing so was to maintain his cover. But she couldn't understand why he'd want to do that now.

"He's got Balor. He's going to release it soon."

Finn's choked words penetrated her brain. *Holy fuck.* She leveled her gun at his head and cursed as he ducked behind Finn. *Shit.* "Let her go and we can talk about this."

"There is nothing to talk about. You can kill me, but it is already too late." Mehalik laughed, an eerie sound in the scene of blood and violence. He wrapped his arm tighter around Finn's waist. "And if she's telling the truth and there is no vaccine, then you'll all die anyway."

"What do you mean, too late?" Ari said.

"It is already done."

"No!" Finn cried, but the sound was drowned out by the rapid-fire of an automatic rifle shattering the glass of the salon. Everything seemed to happen at once. Junior spun and took a diving shot. One, two, three rounds, and the gunman on the aft deck tumbled overboard. Ari hit the deck to port side and fired. Rounds hit the upholstery behind Mehalik's head as he and Finn tumbled behind the table, his grip on Finn vice-like.

Knight threw his head back into Hakim's stomach, his chair tumbled to the ground, and Oz flung herself in Finn's direction. Ari was still firing blind, and the deep grunt and solid sound of a large body hitting the ground made her look in Hakim's direction. The big man was on the floor holding his chest and a bright red bloodstain expanded on his shirt.

Finn screamed from under the fixed table, but the sound was less gurgled than before, as though she had more air now. Oz crawled across the floor, shards of broken glass biting into the flesh of her hands.

"Finn?"

"Oz, get him off me. Please. I can't move and he's bleeding all over me."

Oz let out a sigh of relief and reached into the awkward space to drag Mehalik's body off Finn. Hopefully, he was wounded and not dead. She put her fingers to his neck, searching for a pulse as Finn dragged herself out of the cramped space. Finn locked eyes with her and she shook her head. *Fuck.*

Finn flipped open the lid of the case, and Oz knew she still carried the hope that Mehalik had lied to them, that he hadn't already released the toxin.

"Empty," she whispered. "Goddamn it."

Junior slammed Ari against the wall. "You fucking idiot. Do you know what you've done? If we can't find out where the release will happen we can't stop it." He pointed to Mehalik's body. "He was our best chance to find out where this thing is going down."

"It was a gun fight. People die. Relax, Captain America." He pointed to Finn. "The vaccine has already been deployed."

"Yes, but it doesn't work as quickly as the toxin does, and it won't spread fast enough to stop this. You stupid, arrogant prick."

Ari shrugged. "We did all we could. We are human, not perfect."

Oz couldn't believe what she was hearing. She couldn't believe that she'd brought Ari onboard with this mission, and he was displaying such a blasé attitude to this colossal fuckup. "Do you realize that this means people are going to die?"

"People have already died tonight, and people will die all over the world. That isn't something I can stop."

"These deaths we could have stopped, Ari. What if it's your mother, your wife, sister, father, brother, or son who dies because of this? Will you still think this was the right decision?"

"My family is safe at home in Tel Aviv. They aren't in danger."

"And what do you think a likely Hamas target would be? Hmm? He took this shit on Israeli soil. He ordered its dispersal while he was in Eilat. Do you really think he isn't going to target Israel?"

Ari's face paled and his eyes widened, and suddenly, he seemed far less nonchalant.

"Exactly."

Finn knelt beside Knight and Hakim. "You okay?"

"I'll live." Stephen's voice was little more than a croak, his eyes were glazed, and he was on the verge of losing consciousness. He was obviously in shock.

She looked at Hakim. It was obvious that he wouldn't make it. He'd lost too much blood, and when she checked his pulse it confirmed her thoughts. A bloody gurgle startled her. He opened his eyes and lifted his hand, pointing to the wall on the port side of the salon. His mouth opened revealing bloodstained teeth, and each strangled breath made it bubble between his lips. "F-f-four. Three. N-n-n…"

"Four, three, what? What do you mean?" She looked in the direction he was pointing.

"S-s-saf…" He couldn't keep enough breath coming out of his lungs to sustain the words, but Finn understood.

"Oz, the bulkhead over there. There's a safe. Combination four, three, something. Right?"

Hakim nodded. "N-n-ni…"

"Nine?"

"F-fo…" He lost consciousness.

"Four." She tried to shake him awake.

"Combination Four, three, nine, four." Oz called as she tapped the buttons and the door released. "Nice work, Finn. How's he doing?"

Finn shook her head as the death rattle sounded in his chest and he stopped breathing. She turned away and started shredding any cloth she could find before she wrapped Stephen's elbow where the ulna had broken the skin at his devastated joint.

Oz dumped the contents of the safe on the table and searched through them, quickly reading and discarding page after page of Arabic. "Here," she told Ari. "You look. My Arabic isn't up to this. Make yourself useful."

In seconds, he held up a short page that looked as though it had come from hotel stationary. "It gives four locations across Israel."

"One for each vial," Finn whispered.

"How long do we have?"

Ari shook his head. "We're too late. He set the times to coincide with sunset."

"No wonder he wanted the vaccine. He'd already set it in motion," Junior said.

"What are those targets?" Finn asked.

"Water treatment plants."

"All of them?"

"Yes."

"Then it will take a little time for the contamination to spread." She turned to Oz. "We need to shut them down."

"As soon as we get on the *Whirlwind*, I'll get Charlie on it. How long are we talking? It's been two hours since sunset."

"I don't know. It depends on their treatment plants, consumption rates, the process they use…There are so many variables I can't give you an accurate time scale."

"Then we need to figure out another plan." Oz pulled Finn into her arms.

"I'm really glad you're okay, by the way. I was so scared, I thought I'd lost you." Finn took a precious moment to draw strength from Oz's embrace.

Oz chuckled. "Me too."

"What happened?"

"Hakim gave me a little heads up and decided not to toss me overboard." The boat dropped speed dramatically, and they drew up alongside the *Whirlwind*. "Time to save the rest of the world."

## Chapter Forty-three

Within minutes of boarding the *Whirlwind*, everyone had been fully briefed and Charlie was on the phone, shouting. Ari and Oz were locating first aid supplies to help Finn patch up Stephen Knight while AJ searched for more supplies. Junior hunched over the computer, hooked up a flash drive, and started hammering away on the keyboard, Billy watching over his shoulder. Everyone was focused on the task at hand, all trying to ignore the very real possibility that all their hard work had been for nothing.

Stephen looked at her as she wrapped a clean bandage around his mangled hand. "This wasn't your fault."

She glanced at his face, then quickly away. His skin looked gray, waxy, and beads of sweat covered his upper lip and forehead. She kept bandaging him, but felt too sick at his wounds to answer.

"It wasn't. I should have known Whittaker was dirty. I knew someone on this mission was." He chuckled slightly. "I thought it was you."

"How could you have known? And why did you think it was me?"

"When your guys all started taking over, I was told by my superiors to back off and let you do this your way. I didn't like that, and it hasn't happened to me before. I didn't know what to make of that and it made me suspicious. Then you started keeping things from me, like moving to a different lab and keeping your travel plans from me. It all convinced me I couldn't trust you. I knew someone was feeding Mehalik information. He knew too much, and your suspicious behavior made you seem like the most likely candidate." He shrugged, then groaned at the pain it caused. "You confused me. In one breath you seemed completely genuine when you said you didn't want this thing out there, but then you seemed unwilling to help me prevent it."

Finn shook her head. "It wasn't like that. Something didn't seem right to us. You and Whittaker would disappear, then show back up, and then we found listening devices in the lab…" She smiled apologetically. "We didn't know who to trust, so we didn't trust either of you."

"Smart plan." He gasped and bit his lip in an obvious effort not to cry out when she picked up his other arm.

Finn stared at the ragged hole through his elbow joint where the bone stuck out.

"Damn. Hurts worse."

"I'll be as careful as I can."

"It's okay. Do what you have to do." He gritted his teeth while she rewrapped the shattered joint.

"We need to get you to a hospital."

"The mission comes first. There's too much at stake."

"Stephen, I need to get you—"

"Finn, this isn't your fault. We need you to focus on the mission, not me. Not what happened on that boat. Nothing else. Do you understand me?"

She dug in the box Oz brought over for another bandage, unable to answer him. He'd already been tortured because of her. "Finn, tell me you understand," Knight said.

"The mission comes first. But I won't let you die."

He smiled and rested his head on the floor. "I won't die." He gasped as she wrapped his left hand. "So what are we looking at? Worst-case scenario. Global spread if we can't shut those treatment plants down, right?"

Finn glanced at Oz, then back to him. "No. We, well, we had another plan we put into action just before we flew to Israel."

Stephen smiled. "You did, huh?"

She nodded, feeling increasingly guilty for leaving him out of the loop.

"Care to share?"

She quickly told him about the combined vaccine and antidote she had created and the airport distribution plan. He let out another sharp gasp of pain. "So we're safe then. It doesn't matter that it was released."

"It does. It will take another ten to twelve days before the cold virus has covered the globe and everyone has been fully immunized. If we can't get the water treatment centers shut down, this will spread across half of the Middle East, into Northeast Africa, and Eastern Europe before the vaccine will stop it. Millions of people will be infected." She let her head drop, her chin resting heavy on her chest. "I failed."

"No, baby, you didn't." Oz wrapped an arm around her shoulders.

"She's right. If you hadn't succeeded we'd be looking at the end of the world right now."

"Millions of people are going to be infected. Almost all of them will die, and those who don't will probably wish they had," Finn said, her anger boiling over. "I don't call that a success."

"Maybe not, but the other seven billion people on the planet will," Stephen said. "Besides, you still have time to find a treatment or a cure or whatever for this thing."

"Are you kidding?" Finn's English accent became stronger as the volume of her voice escalated. "It takes months—years—to develop drugs like that. If we don't stop the spread we have at most a few days before the damage is irreversible. Not to mention the fact that even if I can stop this thing from actually killing people, I can't undo the damage it causes to the brains and the nerves of every single person infected. I don't have the knowledge to do that, and we don't have the time for me to learn it."

"You need a—" A wave crashed against the hull, and he cried out as his body rolled slightly on the deck. His eyes rolled back slightly and Finn expected him to pass out. It seemed that sheer force of will alone was keeping him conscious, and part of her wished that he'd let go and allow himself the painkiller of oblivion. "You need a brain expert?"

Finn smiled. "In exceptionally simple terms, yes. I need someone who understands how the brain synapses work with the muscles. Maybe that person could think of a way to stop it."

Oz continued tying the bandages around his wounds, but it was clear he was getting weaker. He looked close to passing out. Finn held her hand to his forehead. His skin was clammy, his pulse thready and growing weaker. He was going into shock, and Finn knew he couldn't remain conscious much longer.

"Call this number, 881-555-3498. Speak to Timothy Lunn. Tell him what's happened and tell him you need Sandra Burns. Tell him to get her wherever you need her."

Oz scribbled the number down on the back of her hand. "He's your boss?"

Stephen nodded. "She'll be able to help you if you can't contain it." He closed his eyes.

"Stephen, you need to rest. Save your strength," Finn said quietly. "We'll take care of it."

"Finn, you need to know something…" His voice faded away as he closed his eyes and groaned softly.

"It doesn't matter. You can tell me later."

"She's—"

"Goddamn it." Charlie slammed the phone down onto the table, drawing their attention. "They won't give us authorization to contact the authorities and shut down the plant."

"Why the hell not?" Oz shouted.

"We aren't supposed to be operating out of Israel. We'll set off a political incident if we contact them."

"They're going to let who knows how many people die to avoid a political scandal?"

"Yes."

"Ari, I thought this was your department?" Oz scowled at him. Another fuckup was something they didn't need.

"They didn't perceive the threat to be reliable," Ari said. "I did what I could to help you, despite my superiors."

"Fuckers," AJ said.

"Precisely, Son. Junior, find me another option."

Finn looked back down at Stephen. His eyes were closed and his breathing a little more even. Unconscious. She hoped he stayed that way until they could get him help.

Billy and Charlie were speaking quietly and pointing to various parts of the computer screen over Junior's shoulder.

"Dad, it'd take a whole unit to take out each plant. And the way the systems run, with the average consumption at this point, we don't even have time to get them here before it's too late. Short of getting the guys over in Turkey to launch some missiles at them, we're fucked." Junior crossed his arms over his chest.

"There has to be another way. We could plant explosives and blow them up. Start a rumor that it was terrorists," Billy said.

"We don't have the manpower to carry out a coordinated attack like that, Uncle Billy. That's what I was saying."

"Well, kiddo, I know I'm an old fart, but I'd take a stab at it."

Junior looked at him then back to the screen. "We've got four units covering six square miles of ground space. The buildings are three stories high, and there are two basement levels. Not to mention the hundreds of miles of pipes and the septic tanks. Four units just like this. Four. I'm not packing enough C4 in my underwear to take that shit down."

"Enough, Junior. You don't talk to your uncle like that."

Junior scrubbed his hands over his head. "I'm sorry. I'm just…" He let out a huge sigh.

"I know," Billy said. "We all are. That's why I'd be willing to handle C4 from your underwear."

Junior chuckled. "No need to worry about that."

"So we can't stop this?" Finn didn't want to believe what she was hearing.

"No," Charlie said. "There's not enough time."

"How much time do we have before the contaminated water is being used?"

"It's not an exact science, Finn," Junior said.

"Estimate."

"Finn—" Oz wrapped her hand around her arm.

"Just tell me."

"Four hours."

Her mind was racing. *Four hours.* Four hours and this thing she'd created would begin to spread from person to person until it met those who were resistant. *Four hours plus the incubation period. Four-day incubation period. One hundred hours before symptoms would begin to show.*

"I need my lab." She didn't want to think about what would happen after that. She couldn't. "We've got one hundred hours before the first victims begin to show symptoms. If we stand any chance of saving them, they have to be treated before then. Oz, call the number Stephen gave you, get this Sandra Burns to the New York lab, and let's hope she'll be able to help as much as he thinks she can."

*One hundred hours, and I haven't got a fucking clue where to start.*

## Chapter Forty-four

Cassie rested her head in her hand while she made notes for her next class. Well, she was supposed to be. What she was really doing was doodling, daydreaming, and wasting time. She looked at the badly drawn picture of Bailey's face. She couldn't get the eyes right. She couldn't capture the way the light made them look honey-colored and the way they reflected the light. She sighed as a knock sounded at her door.

"Come in." She closed her notebook and looked up, expecting to see one of her students. Instead there were two men, official credentials extended for her review. "CIA. Gentlemen, to what do I owe the honor?"

"We have a very delicate matter to discuss with you. Is there somewhere more private we could go, Professor Burns?" the taller man said.

"I'm sorry. I didn't catch your names?"

"My apologies, Professor, we're on a very tight schedule. I'm Agent Lunn, and this is my associate, Agent Hawkins."

"Agent Lunn, this office is about as private as it gets on campus. If you're that short on time you'd better get on with it."

"Very well." He handed over a file. Top Secret was stamped in red all over it. "A few hours ago I received a call to let me know that your expertise is required to help in the development of a cure for people infected with botulism."

Cassie laughed. "And just who is it that has requested my help for this project?"

"Stephen Knight."

"Why? What does he have to do with botulism?"

"I'm afraid I can't give you all the details of the mission he was involved in."

"Then you'd better get Agent Knight to call me. I need more than he requested me and a file with a drawing that looks like it was created for *Star Trek*. What the hell is this?"

"It is a biological agent called Balor. I'm told it is a combination of the E. coli bacteria and the botulinum toxin."

She stared at them, aghast. "Oh my God. This is loose, isn't it? That's why you're here."

"Yes. Will you help?"

"I need a sample of this toxin and a lab to work in. I'll also need staff—"

"Professor, we have a lab with everything ready and waiting."

Cassie nodded as she stared at the molecular diagram again. It was beautiful. Ribbons of the toxin's structure twisted around the DNA of the bacterium. It was truly amazing. She could think of so many therapeutic applications for a development like this. *Why did someone have to ruin it by making it into a deadly weapon?*

"Who created this?"

"Does it matter, Professor?" Hawkins spoke for the first time.

"It might, yes. If I know other examples of their work it may help me understand the way they think. If I can find a flaw in the thought process, I might be able to find a flaw in their creation faster."

"Understood, but could we discuss this en route? We really are on a very tight schedule," Lunn said.

"Fair enough." She quickly packed her books away and selected a couple from the shelf and added them to the heavy load.

"Professor," Hawkins said, holding out his hand. "Allow me." He took the heavy bag from her. "I'm sorry. It's a pretty stressful situation right now."

She nodded and followed them out of the room.

"It was created by a scientist called Ethan Lyell. He worked for Sterling BioTech and this little bastard was the main reason that William Sterling was imprisoned."

The name hit her hard, knocking the air from her lungs, and nearly doubling her over. She gasped, trying hard to catch her breath and wondered what could have driven dear, sweet Ethan to create this monster.

"Ethan? Ethan wouldn't do this."

"I can assure you he did."

"But Ethan only wanted to help people. Why would he do this?"

"You knew him?" Lunn asked.

"Yes. We were at university together. We worked together for many years."

"Things change, Professor. People change." He held his hand out to help steady her, but she waved it away. "Are you okay to continue?"

"Yes. Why doesn't he create the treatment for it?"

"He's dead."

She'd known he was dead, but it didn't stop the surge of emotion that swelled within her. Sorrow that her old friend was gone, anger that he had left something so destructive in his wake, and the fear that what he had created couldn't be undone all vied for position in her heart. "William killed him." It wasn't a question but it didn't stop both men answering with nods as they pushed open the doors. "Where are we going?"

"New York. Sterling BioTech."

"Why there?"

"We have another specialist working on this with you."

"Good. The more minds we have on this the better. Ethan and I worked with Siegfried Jensen and Rebecca Moore. They both worked at Sterling BioTech with me. Is that my team?

"Dr. Jensen was killed a couple of weeks ago, Dr. Moore a week before that."

She couldn't take it all in. Too many memories were bombarding her, and she felt dizzy. "That's after he was in prison. He couldn't have done that." She couldn't focus on that right now. She knew there was a bigger problem at hand and she'd have to mourn later. "So who is in New York?"

"Daniela Finsbury-Sterling."

Cassie's knees went out from under her. Hawkins grabbed her arm to keep her from falling to the snow-covered ground. "Hey, it's okay." His grip tightened as she struggled. "Are you okay?" She heard him, but she couldn't respond. Her brain seemed to have stopped working.

"Get her in the car. Must be shock from knowing her friends are dead."

Hawkins helped her into the car, even going so far as to buckle her seat belt for her. She couldn't make her fingers work. *Daniela. Finn.* The world had become a surreal place and she couldn't think. She was going to see her daughter.

## CHAPTER FORTY-FIVE

Bailey stared at it; the slanting black ink on the white background mocked her. Thirty-six hours. She knew because she'd counted every single one of them. It had been thirty-six hours since she had watched Cassie walk into her apartment building and out of her life. She knew that inside the envelope was a check, for services rendered. Something about it didn't sit right with her. She didn't want to get paid for helping Cassie. She didn't want to be paid for the time they had spent together. She'd enjoyed every second of it. And getting paid for that made her feel dirty, seedy. Cassie had already covered all their expenses on the trip, and she felt she had done very little in real terms to locate Daniela. *I won't take it.*

She folded the envelope in two, touching it as little as possible before she stuffed it into the back pocket of her jeans. She had to return it, then forget about both the money, and Cassie Finsbury.

"Come on, Jazz. Let's go." The dog followed her to the car and climbed into the passenger seat, waiting patiently for her seat belt to be fastened. "Weird dog." Bailey pulled onto the street and made her way across town. "I blame you, you know." Jazz flattened her ears against her head. "Yeah, you. If you hadn't shown up and put some sort of weird spell on me this never would have happened."

The dog bowed her head and looked up at Bailey with soft, brown eyes. "Aw, damn it, don't do that. That's how you did it in the first place," Bailey said but reached over to stroke the top of the dog's head. "I'm not mad at you. I'm just saying that if you hadn't made me such a freaking softie, there's no way I would have fallen for Miss Brainiac-Scientist-in-Hiding. None." Bailey parked the car at MIT and turned off the engine. Jazz wriggled out of her seat belt and laid her head on Bailey's lap.

A big, black town car sat in the corner of the lot with its engine running. Tinted windows hid the driver, but a thin stream of smoke trailed out of the tiny crack at the top of the driver's window. Across the snowbank, she saw Cassie walking between two men. Two big, burly men wearing long coats and sunglasses. "Who the hell wears sunglasses when it's thirty degrees and there's snow on the ground? This ain't Aspen, buddy."

She watched one man grab Cassie's arm and she struggled against his grip. The car blocked her view, but it looked like he was pushing her into the car. *What the fuck?* The car pulled away quickly and Bailey didn't even think. She turned the engine back on, buckled Jazz in, and took off after the car, careful to keep enough distance to not arouse suspicion. They drove east along the Charles River and pulled into the parking lot at the Museum of Science.

"What the hell?" She pointed to the foot well. "Stay down there, girl. I'll just be a few minutes." She signaled for Jazz to be quiet while she was gone. She didn't know what was going on, but if Cassie was being pushed into the car, she was damn well going to find out what was going on.

She saw them pull open the door to a service entrance and tried to catch it before it closed. She swore under her breath as the steel door slammed closed on her finger just in time to prevent the catch jamming closed. She shook out the pain in her hand and climbed the concrete stairs soundlessly until she reached a door to the roof.

The door needed a number code to open it, so she got as close as she could. There was a small porthole style window in the top and she peered out in the hope of seeing what was going on. The whoop whoop sound of a rotor blade picking up speed assaulted her ears and the sight of Cassie in the back of the metal bird stunned her.

"A helicopter?"

*What the fuck? Who would be taking Cassie away in a helicopter?* There was too much about Cassie that she still didn't know. Too many questions she couldn't even take reasonable guesses at the answers because she knew so little about Cassie's past. If Sterling was free, she would put money on those goons being his, but he wasn't. *Shit. Maybe he was.* She dialed her cell and waited.

"Hello, what do you need?" Sean asked.

"I need info. I think my client's just been kidnapped."

"Then call the police."

"No time. Can you take a look at something for me?"

"What?"

"Is William Sterling still behind bars?" She listened to the crunch of keys as he pounded on the keyboard.

"Yup."

"Shit."

"Bailey, what's going on? Seriously."

She didn't want to betray Cassie's confidences, but right now finding her was more important. She trusted Sean. He'd saved her butt more times than she could count. She took a deep breath. What did it matter anyway? Cassie wasn't talking to her, and all indications were that she wouldn't talk to her again. What did she have to lose?

She gave him every detail she knew and listened to the silence down the end of the phone. "You still there?"

"Walk away."

"What?"

"You heard me, Bailey. Walk away."

"I can't do that."

"Why not? You did what she paid you to do. You found the girl for her. You brought her home. Cash the check, and walk away. Done."

"They just kidnapped her."

"You don't know that."

"I saw them manhandling her into the car and then I saw her in a helicopter."

"And that's kidnapping?"

"Yes." She groaned and ran a hand through her hair. "I don't know. Maybe." She climbed back into the car. "I just need to be sure she's okay."

"Why?"

"I just do."

Sean laughed. "Bailey, you might play tough girl, but you're a marshmallow on the inside. But even you usually know when to walk away. This is the point where you put your cards on the table or you fold. So which is it gonna be?"

"I think I love her."

"Oh. My. God. I thought I'd never live to see the day. About fucking time. Let me make some calls and see what I can find."

"You bastard," Bailey said, laughing.

"Yeah yeah, save the badass attitude for someone who's buying."

Bailey watched her cell so closely that it didn't even sound before she answered it. "Tell me."

"I don't have anything concrete."

"Sean, just tell me what's going on."

"Cassie's handler is a guy called Stephen Knight. Word is last night he was badly injured on a mission that went wrong. I can't get the details. All I can get is that he was working with Daniela Finsbury-Sterling trying to get his hands on a guy who was planning to release some bio weapon."

"And?"

"He's in the hospital. Seems he was betrayed. Someone sold him out to the bad guy for cash and the bio weapon's already in play."

"Fuck."

"Yeah."

"She's taken after her old man after all."

"What? Like I said, this is little more than rumor."

"Thanks for the info, Sean. Gotta go." It was the only thing that made sense. Daniela wasn't all sweetness and light like Mrs. Richmond seemed to think. She'd sold out the CIA agent, sold a biological weapon, and now Cassie was gone. Sterling didn't need to escape prison. Daddy's little girl was going to finish the job he started. Bailey turned on the engine and checked her mirror. *Not if I've got anything to do with it.*

# CHAPTER FORTY-SIX

Y ou okay?" Oz asked, clasping Finn's fingers in her own. "Geez, your hands are like ice." She chafed them between her hands, trying to warm them up. Finn was grateful but couldn't look away from the unconscious body of Stephen Knight strapped to the gurney fixed to the side of the military transport plane Charlie seemed to have magically created out of thin air. Blood still seeped through his bandages and his face had taken on the pallor of someone near death.

"How long before we land?" Finn didn't recognize her own voice. It was hoarse, scratchy, and her throat was sore from Mehalik's brutal hold on it earlier.

"About ten minutes. There's an ambulance waiting for him. He'll be in the hospital fifteen minutes after that. He'll be okay."

"No, he won't." Finn pulled a ragged breath into her lungs. "You saw those wounds. If he lives, his life will never be the same. He may lose limbs, and if he doesn't end up in a wheelchair, he'll walk with a limp for the rest of his life."

"I know, baby."

Finn wiped angrily at the tears rolling down her cheek. "That's my fault."

"No, it isn't. It's the fault of the man who tortured him. It's the fault of the man who put you both in that situation. It's their fault. Not yours."

"Oz, I knew bringing the toxin was a mistake. I knew it—"

"Yes, and you told us all from the very start. Stephen and Whittaker both insisted otherwise."

"That's why I didn't trust them."

"I know. But he did listen to what you said. He knew the choices if it went wrong, and he knew the risk we were all taking, including him. If we only lose one good guy in a mission like this, well, that's an acceptable margin."

"Acceptable margin? Are you kidding? That's not acceptable, Oz. It's very bloody far from acceptable, and I can't believe you think that. I could have told Mehalik where Gamble was, and then they wouldn't have tortured him like that. Hell, I could've told them about Lugh and then they would have had no reason to hurt him like that."

"No, you're right. They wouldn't." Oz tugged on her hand until she met her gaze. "They would have killed him because he was useless to them. Just like Whittaker." Oz cupped her cheeks and held her in place when she tried to pull away. "We talked about this before, that there would come a point where you have to choose to trust me when you couldn't believe in yourself." She kissed her gently. "This is it. Your actions and choices in there gave him the best possible chance to live. He knows that. It's one of the reasons he told you to do it."

"How did you know?"

"Because he knew there was far more at stake than his life, and he was willing to sacrifice it for the greater good. He's a good man. But you have an important job to do now, and you won't be able to do it if you're still blaming yourself for Stephen's injuries and the toxin's release. You simply won't be able to focus."

"It isn't that simple."

"I know, baby, but I believe in you. I believe you can do this. You will, because you won't give up until you do." She checked her watch. "You've got eighty-eight hours—"

"No, I don't. I have maybe seventy, if I'm lucky. We have to get it back to Israel too, and administered."

"How long will that take?"

"It's an eleven-hour flight, I have no idea how long the delivery system will take or how much red tape we'll have to go through to get it distributed. That alone could take days." She rested her forehead against Oz's shoulder. "There just isn't time."

"You leave the transport and the red tape to us, and we'll see what we can shave off that eleven hours. You just make it, okay?"

Finn started to argue the impossibility of the task, but the confidence, the trust, and the unmistakable belief in Oz's eyes stopped her. Instead, she nodded and hoped that she could do what needed to be done.

"You're crazy."

"Only about you."

The plane bounced, and the vibrations of the wheels rolling over the tarmac drew a groan from Stephen. The usual windows she would have looked through were missing from the cargo plane, and before they had stopped moving, everyone was in motion. People released the gurney so Stephen was ready and waiting at the rear doors. People grabbed bags, and Charlie and Billy were both bellowing out orders.

Cars were waiting for them on the tarmac, engines running and ready to go. Oz helped her into the front vehicle and got in behind her.

"Where to?"

"Sterling Bio Tech," Finn said immediately.

"You don't want to go home or anything?"

"I only have seventy hours. I don't have time to take a pee, never mind go home." She smirked at Oz's little laugh. "Thank you for the pep talk. Any news about Stephen's expert?"

"Charlie said they got a message in the air. Professor Sandra Burns is waiting at the lab for you. Apparently, she's going over the research and getting up to speed."

Finn snorted sarcastically. "Good luck with that."

Oz held out her arm and patted her shoulder in invitation. "Why don't you rest your head here for a few minutes and I'll wake you up when we get there?"

Finn wanted nothing more than to never leave the safety and security of Oz's strong arms. She closed her eyes and prayed that when she woke this would all have been a nightmare.

❖

"Finn, baby, we're here." Oz's voice was soft in her ear, and Finn burrowed closer to the warm body beside her. "Come on, baby. Lots to do, remember?"

She groaned. *Not a nightmare, then.* She pulled herself out of Oz's arms with a quick kiss and climbed out of the car. The short nap had given her a second wind, and she was already focused on the task ahead, trying to break down in her mind just how she could create something no one had been able to do for decades. And do it in a matter of hours. She shook her head. No point dwelling on the difficulty of the task. No one was under any illusions about that. Instead she tried to section the workload into manageable pieces; each one was a part of a huge jigsaw puzzle that she would come at from a different angle.

She knew Balor. She knew the way it worked, and the way each component of it worked individually. What she needed most was a way to stop the neurotoxin element of the weapon. If that were possible, the lasting effects of Balor would be hugely reduced. There may still be deaths, but nothing as catastrophic as they'd forecast. "Have you got a stopwatch on your watch or something?" she asked Oz.

"No. Why?"

"I want to set a countdown. I know I'm going to lose track of time at some point. I need a reference."

AJ pulled out a cell phone. "I can do it on here for you, Finn, and I'm not likely to be screaming into mine like the rest of these guys will be."

She smiled at him. "You're an angel."

He laughed. "Don't you dare say that. I've just earned myself a bad boy rep. Don't go and destroy all my hard work."

Finn chuckled and stepped out of the lift first, and led them all through the security door and into the lab. The lights were shining in one section of the room, but Finn couldn't see through the banks of benches, cupboards, and equipment to make out clearly the hunched figure with their back to the door. A guy stood facing her, a frown on his face, and he shrugged in response to something she asked him. In an instant, Finn's view was blocked by Junior stepping in front of her, his gun drawn, and Oz spun her back toward the exit.

"Show me your hands." Junior's voice was low and menacing. "Slowly." Finn couldn't see anything, but she could imagine whoever it was holding their hands above their head while Junior stared them down. She would have chuckled if she weren't in a state of barely repressed panic.

"You're making a mistake, Son." Finn didn't recognize the man's voice. "We have authority to be here. Put the gun down and I won't have to shoot your ass."

"I'd like to see you try it, Gramps. Who are you and what are you doing here?"

"Calm down, everyone."

A woman's voice rang out clearly, and Finn struggled against Oz but had to settle for standing inside the doorway with Oz forming a protective cage around her.

"We don't need the guns. I was brought here by these two fine CIA agents earlier today," the woman said.

There was something familiar in the voice—the tone, maybe. Finn tried to place it, but the answer was elusive and remained beyond her reach. From somewhere in the room, she heard someone gasp, and then there was a flurry of whispered voices too quiet for her to hear properly. And still, she couldn't figure out where she recognized that voice from. It irritated her, like an itch she couldn't scratch, gradually getting stronger and increasingly maddening.

"Oz, it's probably just the professor that Stephen told you to call. You can let me go. I'm sure it's fine."

"Charlie's just checking IDs, and as soon as they're cleared, we'll go over there."

"This is ridiculous. We don't have time to waste."

"And if anything happens to you, we don't stand any chance whatsoever of helping those people."

Finn wanted to argue but knew it wouldn't help the situation. None of them understood how difficult the task ahead of her was, or how unlikely it was to be successful. And the time, or rather the lack of it, made her shudder. There was none.

"Finn?" Billy came over to stand with her.

"Can we get started now?"

"Well, yes. But you're gonna need a minute here."

"What are you talking about?" She stepped away from the obscuring circle they had formed around her and came face-to-face with Professor Sandra Burns.

Eyes the same color as her own gazed back at her, and Finn's knees went weak. It was like looking in a mirror, one that showed her exactly what she'd look like in twenty-five years. The fine lines at the side of her eyes and mouth, and the streaks of gray at her temples, made the red highlights in her auburn hair a little less bright and made her face look softer. But there was no way to miss the similarity.

"Daniela." Her mother held out her hand.

Everything seemed to grow distant, like she was moving away from everyone, but her feet didn't move. Voices around her grew quieter, and the entirety of her view was centered on the woman who stood in front of her, hand held out as the softness in her eyes morphed to a look of concern.

"Someone get her a chair." She barked orders without breaking eye contact. "Daniela, breathe. Take a nice deep breath for me."

Every word sounded like it was too long, like it was stretched to the point where she barely recognized what it was meant to be. Her stomach churned, her body doubled over of its own accord, and she vomited on the pristine white floor.

*This has got to be some sort of joke.* She felt a hand rubbing her back and leaned toward the comforting touch. She'd lost her bearings when she closed her eyes and took the tissue that was offered her to wipe her mouth, but she was certain Oz would be the only one to touch her when she was like this. She knew the boys would be looking around, trying to find anywhere else to be. But the hand didn't feel quite right. It wasn't heavy enough, or large enough.

She turned her head toward the warmth she leaned against and opened one eye.

It was no joke.

The woman smiled down at her. "Not the greeting I was hoping for, but you didn't order me out of here, so I guess I'll take it." Soft fingers stroked her face, just the way they had when she was a small child on nights when she couldn't sleep.

"Mum?"

She nodded, and it was too much. Finn closed her eyes and let the darkness envelop her.

Daniela's weight knocked Cassie over as she tried to catch her and prevent her from hitting the ground, and they both landed on the floor with Daniela's head in her lap. She wrapped her arms protectively around her daughter and felt whole for the first time in twenty-five years.

"Finn." The tall blonde Cassie had seen in the photographs at Mrs. Richmond's pulled Daniela from her arms and lifted her easily. Cradling her against her chest, she stalked out of the room to a smaller one at the far end. All Cassie could do was watch them disappear while she sat sprawled on the floor. She knew Daniela wouldn't expect to see her right now, but Mrs. Richmond had told her that Daniela knew she wasn't dead. She hadn't prepared herself for such a strong reaction, though. She moved away from Daniela's vomit with a grimace.

"She's had a rough time. Must have been too much." One of the two older men stood in front of her, hand held out to aid her to her feet. Kind blue eyes met her gaze, and a small smile pulled at the corners of a generous mouth. "But I do know she's been trying to find you since the moment she knew you were alive." Cassie took hold of his hand and let him pull her up. "Billy Zuckerman, ma'am, and it's a pleasure to meet you."

"And you, Mr. Zuckerman." She dusted off her slacks and straightened her lab coat. "Can I see her?"

Billy waved his hand toward the small office. "We're not stopping you. Oz knows there's a couch in there to lay her down. What should we call you? Professor Burns? Mrs. Sterling?"

"No. God no. Don't call me that. You all know who I am," she said as she pushed open the door. "Call me Cassie."

She stopped in the doorway and stared at the tender scene laid out before her. Oz sat on the small sofa, Daniela cradled in her arms as she planted soft kisses on her forehead and whispered words she couldn't hear but could well imagine. The look on her face could only be described as adoration, and Cassie's heart warmed at the knowledge her daughter had someone so devoted to her.

"Do you have a problem, Cassie?" Billy asked.

She shook her head. "I can't believe she's really here."

Billy laughed. "Well, it is her lab."

She knelt by the side of the couch. "Is she okay?"

"Yeah." Oz stroked Finn's face. "Just the shock, and we've all had a really tough twenty-four hours. I'm Oz, by the way."

"I figured. Mrs. Richmond speaks very highly of you, Olivia." She grinned and winked.

"Oh, hell no. It's Oz, and don't let Mrs. R. tell you anything different." Oz chuckled. "How did you find Mrs. Richmond?"

"When I found out William was in prison, I thought it would finally be safe to try to find my daughter." She stroked Daniela's head again and smiled when she stirred a little under her touch. "I hired a private investigator to help me find her. We went to your house in Florida, and Mrs. Richmond invited us in for tea."

"Us?"

"Bailey, the private investigator I hired, and myself." Her chest clenched painfully at the mention of Bailey's name, and she hoped it didn't show on her face or in her voice. This moment was a happy one, and she refused to allow anything painful to spoil it for her.

"And how did you end up here, Cassie?" Oz asked.

She hiked her thumb over her shoulder. "They turned up at work this morning and told me that Stephen Knight had instructed them to come get me, that they needed my help with a situation."

"So you really are this brain expert she needs?"

"I'm a neurobiologist. Is that what you need?"

"I have no idea. She'll explain when she comes around. I think she's just sleeping now. She's exhausted."

Cassie nodded. "You said you'd all had a tough twenty-four hours. Can I ask what's happened?"

"Well, since we're hoping you can help us solve the problem, sure. I'll tell you what I can, but you're going to need Finn for the science part. She's the genius."

Cassie smiled. "She always was smart as a whip when she was little."

"Well, she's smarter than that now." Oz quickly told her about the mission, how they had been betrayed by Andrew Whittaker, and the truth of what they were facing with Balor's release.

"Do you have more paperwork on this bacterium? What the other agents gave me was so basic it didn't help to clarify what you're talking about." Billy handed her a thick file. "Thank you." She flipped it open and pulled out a sheaf of pages before she glanced at Daniela. "She should have come around by now. Are you sure she's okay?"

"I'm fine. I just don't want the dream to end," Daniela whispered.

"It's not a dream, baby." Oz kissed her lips and stroked her throat. "Your mom's here."

"I'm English, Oz, she's my mum." She opened her eyes. She looked so scared, so worried, that all Cassie could see was the little girl she'd held in her arms when she woke crying in the night, certain that there were monsters under her bed. "Hi."

"Hi, Daniela."

"Finn. Everyone calls me Finn."

"Finn it is. How much did you hear?"

"Enough. We have a lot to do." She dropped her gaze to the papers in Cassie's hand. "And we don't have a lot of time at all. Will you help us?"

Cassie didn't hesitate. "In any way I can." She was disturbed that Danie—Finn seemed to be all business. She'd hoped for something a little more personal, and time to explain to Finn why she'd made the choices she had. But as Finn climbed off the sofa and accepted the glass of water a young blond man held out to her, she accepted that it wasn't going to happen.

"Thanks, AJ." She sipped. "Shall we get started? We've got less than seventy hours to find a way to cure anyone who gets infected with this and synthesize enough to make it useful."

"Seventy hours?"

"Less than."

"Jesus. That's just not possible."

Finn held up her hand. "I know. And I really don't need to hear how impossible it is. That's how long we have before people start showing symptoms and then they die. That's it. End of story. If you can't do it, that's fine. I'll figure it out by myself." Finn was out the door before anyone could follow her, leaving a roomful of stunned people in her wake. Oz quickly followed her, calling her name.

"I didn't say I wouldn't help," Cassie whispered, hurt by Finn's dismissiveness.

Billy clapped a hand on her shoulder. She couldn't stop herself from shrinking beneath his touch and looked at him when he moved away from her slowly. He dipped his head to acknowledge her reaction, and the look in his eyes told her he wouldn't do it again. "She blames herself. She won't listen to any of us when we tell her that it was her father's fault. Seems to think she should have known somehow." He smiled sadly.

"Known what? Why does she blame herself?"

"This bug's possible because of some advancement she made. Without it, that other feller wouldn't have been able to make this in the first place."

"This isn't her fault."

"Yup." He folded his arms across his chest. "And when she talks to you, be sure to make her see that. But right now," he said indicating the door. "Shall we? She wasn't kidding when she said we're up against the clock."

"Of course." Cassie took a deep breath and steeled herself to work beside her daughter. Part of her was thrilled to see how her child thought, to see the similarities and differences in them that were almost entirely innate, but another part was terrified. She didn't want to be a disappointment to her child, and she knew right now the pressure was on.

## CHAPTER FORTY-SEVEN

Bailey circled the block for the third time, searching for a parking space that gave her a good view of the entrance, but the congested streets, the wall of pedestrians, and a lack of local knowledge was making it damn near impossible. "Bark if you see a spot, Jazz," she said, knowing the stupidity of the request but hating the silence in the car even more. She turned the radio back on and cringed when Diana Krall greeted her with "I've Got You Under My Skin." "Thanks for the reminder."

She spotted a town car pulling away from the curb and quickly moved into the vacated spot. She was a quarter block down from Sterling BioTech, and she could see the entrance easily enough. She just hoped she'd recognize either of the two men who had forced Cassie into the car. There was a pay phone on the sidewalk next to the car. She quickly jumped out and liberated the directory. Combing the guide would give her another avenue to check while she waited. She flipped through it, searching for Daniela, for Sterling, for Finsbury, but nothing came up. Mrs. Richmond had said the other woman's name was Olivia, or Oz, but she hadn't given them a last name. *And I was so focused on Cassie I didn't ask. Rookie mistake.* She grabbed the coffee cup half full of cold coffee, but it still contained much-needed caffeine, and right now she didn't exactly have any other options.

She'd had plenty of time to think during the four-hour journey from Boston to New York and the only thing she'd been able to think about was Cassie. The thought of someone hurting her made her feel nauseous. She'd wrap her hands around their throat and squeeze the living—the top of her coffee cup popped off the compressed takeout cup, and the contents spilled out in her lap. The cold, pungent brew soaked her jeans and her sweatshirt, but thankfully not the seat.

"Great, just fucking great." She grabbed a fistful of napkins from the overstuffed glove box and mopped up as much of the mess as she could. She stuffed the used napkins into the remains of the cup and dropped it into the trash bag she had in the well of the passenger seat. She shook her head, still unable to comprehend the differences—in her life and more importantly in her.

Where once she had sought solitude, she now craved company. Where she had reveled in peace and silence, she needed it filled with laughter and conversation, but only from one woman. The music that had soothed her soul left her empty with no one to share it. She'd spent her life looking for her mother, the case never far from her mind, and not a day had passed without her looking at her pin board and trying to figure out where to try next. What was the next angle of attack? Where was there left to try? That was until Cassie had walked into her life. From the second Bailey had shown her out the door of her office she hadn't thought of her mother's case until Cassie had asked about it.

She'd been smitten by those beautiful green eyes and that gentle smile before she even said hello. By the time she agreed to take Cassie's case she had no chance. "And now I'm sitting on a stakeout in the middle of Manhattan, covered in cold coffee, and waiting for one of those assholes to come out or it gets dark so I can figure out a way into that building." She plucked at her shirt. "Or alternatively, I'll freeze to death."

❖

Dark had long since settled and the street was pretty much deserted. It was the quietest Bailey had seen it all day, but still no one she recognized had come in or out of the building. It had been several hours since any one at all had. She checked her watch, surprised to find it was almost nine thirty. She reached for Jazz's leash.

"Come on, girl. Let's take you out to do your business and I'll take a look through those doors." She walked quickly, Jazz trotting happily at her side, seemingly happy to stop and pause whenever Bailey did. The foyer was dark, and all she could make out was the large reception desk and a bank of elevators beyond. It was so dark, in fact, that the digital numbers on top of each elevator stood out clearly. Three were stationary at the ground floor, the other read thirteen…twelve…eleven.

"Shit. Time to get back to the car, Jazz." She was back in the car, Jazz strapped into her seat belt when she saw a tall blond woman emerge from the building with an even taller blond man beside her. She recognized the woman from Mrs. Richmond's pictures. Olivia, Daniela's girlfriend. Perfect.

She watched them climb into a black SUV and pull out. Bailey was careful as she tailed them, always making sure she was at least three cars back and a lane across. It gave her a good view, but she made sure she blended into the background sea of lights on the congested Manhattan streets as she followed them toward Central Park and down Seventy-second Street. They had pulled up at the entryway to a private road at the back of the Dakota Building when she passed them.

She thanked her lucky stars when she spotted an empty parking space and managed to get Jazz out of the car fast enough to see them turn into the residents' private underground parking area. Shit. She had no idea which apartment they were going to or, realistically, what to do next. She entered the gates of the parking lot but decided not to go too far. She wanted to get back into her car pretty quick if she needed to. She pulled her phone from her pocket and looked up information on the building. She spotted something she thought she could use to her advantage and went back to the car to wait for the right moment. She bought a coffee and a hot dog from a street vendor on the way, saving the last quarter of the food for Jazz.

"Here," she said as she held it out. "Stop slobbering on my legs." Jazz wolfed down her portion and looked around, apparently curious as to where the rest of her dinner was. "That's all you're getting. Too much food, too many stakeouts, and before you know it you'll get fat." She pointed to the seat. "Sit down and keep your eyes peeled." Jazz did as she was told while Bailey looked for an envelope and quickly sealed a hastily written note inside it. She checked her watch and sighed when the car she had followed pulled out of the parking lot. She scrawled the license plate number on the back of her hand. "Wait here, girl, and be quiet," she said before climbing out of the car and crossing the road to the lobby.

"May I help you, ma'am?" the uniformed man said at the front desk.

"I do hope so." She scowled at him. "I'm parked outside and a vehicle that pulled out of the private road from your parking garage hit my car and drove off. I want to know who they are. I intend to file a claim with their insurance."

"I am very sorry to hear that, ma'am." He hiked his trousers up a little and straightened his cap. "But I'm sure you understand that I can't just give out the information of our residents to anyone."

"They hit my car. I have every right to know who it was and since they've driven off, you can tell me who it was. All I want is their name and apartment number to give to my insurance. A reasonable request, surely." The man seemed to genuinely sympathize with her plight so she continued to heap it on. "I mean I know my car's not much to look at and they drive out in their shiny brand new SUV, but does that give them the right to just drive off when they do something wrong? What about me? Do I have to foot the bill for repairs to my car myself? Or file a claim on my own insurance and get hit with a higher bill next year? Does that sound fair to you?"

"No, ma'am, it doesn't. But I—"

"I know you've got a job to do. And I'm not looking to get you in trouble. But it really gets me, you know? I mean these guys in these apartments, they're worth millions. Millions. But I've gotta fork out for their careless driving." She shook her head. "It's just not fair." She rubbed her hand over her face and pushed her fingers through her hair. "Listen, I'm sorry I troubled you. I just had to try, you know?" She turned to leave.

"Ma'am? What was that license plate number?"

"New York GMG 4385."

"Car?"

"Black SUV, maybe a Lexus."

"Ah, that'll be Miss Finn's car. Lovely girl. I'm surprised she didn't stop. She's not like all the others here." He frowned slightly.

"There was a man driving it. Tall, blond—"

He nodded. "One of the Zuckermans. There seem to be more of them than I can keep track of. Must be one of them driving. I'll send a note up to Miss Finn for you and tell her what happened, and that I gave you the details for your insurance." He wrote the name and address down for her on letterhead stationary.

Bailey realized there was no way she could ask him not to do that without arousing his suspicions and just hoped that phase two of her plan would work as well. "That's great, thank you."

"I'm sure Miss Finn will want to know what happened. If you give me your details I'll ask her to call, if you like?"

*Shit, should have seen that one coming.* "That'll be great, thanks." She wrote down the first name that came to mind. Jazz Davenport. "Listen, maybe when you finish tonight I can buy you a beer to say thanks for your help. I really appreciate it." She leaned on the counter.

He grinned. "That'd be great, but I'm on shift till midnight." He leaned on the counter too. "What about tomorrow? I've got a day off."

"You've got my number," she said, eyeing his name badge. "Roy, give me a call and we'll set something up." She tucked the page in her pocket and stepped out onto the sidewalk. *Twenty-five years on the job and the stupidity of people still astounds me.* She checked her watch and climbed back in the car. Four hours till Roy finished his shift.

She hunkered down in the car and stroked Jazz's head. "Now all we've got do is make sure that SUV doesn't come back in the meantime. If it does, I don't know how we're going to get up there. And hopefully the night guy is as dumb as Roy."

She pictured Cassie being forced into that car and closed her eyes. *Please be okay. And if you're not, I sure as hell hope I can help you.*

## CHAPTER FORTY-EIGHT

Finn decanted some solution from one beaker to another and tried to concentrate on the task at hand. She tried to ignore the fact that her lab partner, her colleague, was the mother she hadn't seen since she was four years old. The woman she had believed dead until a few months ago, and whom she knew had given up so much to ensure Finn's safety. She had so many questions she wanted to ask, but she didn't know how or where to start. Then she remembered what they were doing and why, and realized that her mother was meeting her in the worst possible way. She'd been dragged away from a new life where she'd been safe to help repair Finn's mistake. A mistake that could cost hundreds of thousands of people their lives.

*Great impression you made, Finn. She'll never want anything to do with you after this. Probably thinks you're even worse than your father. The guy she ran away from and hid from for almost twenty-five years.* She glanced to her left where Cassie was peering down the eye of a microscope. Pencils stuck haphazardly out of her messy bun, her safety goggles pushed carelessly onto her forehead, and there was a dark smudge on her right cheek. Soot from the glass beaker Cassie had held over the Bunsen burner. She wanted to wipe it away and smile, maybe make a small joke about taking care of herself, but she couldn't. They didn't have the kind of relationship where she could behave in such a relaxed manner. They didn't have any kind of relationship. She turned away, disgruntled.

She swirled the contents of the beaker and watched the reaction as the two clear liquids she'd mixed turned pale blue. She'd expected to feel some sort of relief when she found her mother again, but she had to admit given the difficulties her father had in tracking her down she really didn't expect to see her alive. Was that why she felt so angry right now? She had expected to be laying flowers on a grave somewhere and lamenting over things that could never be, and answers she would never get. Instead, a real live woman could give her those answers, and Finn would have to face them, whatever they were. She'd learned her father's version of events. She knew that he had hunted her mercilessly, and that she had stayed away to protect Finn. But one question continued to haunt her and she'd accepted that she would never learn the answer. Why had Cassie leave her with her father when she faked her own death? Given how

Karen, and indirectly Cassie, had tried to remain in her life after that, it didn't make sense that she would simply abandon Finn at that point. In her fantasies, she'd convinced herself that her mother had planned to take her with her, but somehow her father had come between them at the last minute and Cassie had been left with no choice but to leave her.

But what if it had been Cassie's choice to leave Finn? Finn wasn't sure she wanted to learn that much truth, and faced with a real, live mother she would have to hear why she left Finn with her father. It was fear she felt, not anger. Fear that Cassie wouldn't believe she deserved the sacrifices she'd made for her, or fear that leaving her with her father had been no sacrifice at all for Cassie. Finn didn't know which scared her more.

The solution turned a deeper blue as the reaction continued. It was a good sign. The solution needed to be indigo before it was ready for the next stage. She had a test strip pinned over her workbench so she could ensure the perfect hue and thereby the correct strength of solution. They'd decided to continue working with the cold virus that she had already broken down, but this time they didn't need it to recognize the unique protein markers on the surface of the Balor bacterium. They needed it to get into the victim's brain. Cassie had spent years developing a treatment to help re-stimulate the neural pathways in the brain and central nervous system. She'd explained the basis of her theories to Finn as they began, and although Finn followed most of it, the brain hadn't been her specialty.

Cassie had spent years developing a stimulation protocol, and now she was trying to make a solution combine with the antitoxin that Finn was building into the DNA of the humble cold. Once the antitoxin was engineered, they planned to incorporate the turbo booster, as Cassie was calling it. But they only had thirty-six hours left, it was almost midnight, and they were all exhausted. She'd asked Oz to go to the apartment for her hours ago to pick up a change of clothes. Really, all she needed to do was to keep Oz busy. Every time Oz looked at her watch, Finn felt the lingering accusation that she wasn't doing enough. She knew Oz would never say it. But it was true. She would never be able to do enough.

"Stop."

Finn jerked her head up and was surprised to see Cassie with one hand on her shoulder. "I'm sorry. What?"

"Stop beating yourself up. None of this was your fault and I can prove that to you, but we don't have time right now. As soon as we get this done I'll tell you what I mean, but right now I have to ask you for something I haven't earned. Your trust. I need you to trust that I can and will explain everything and you'll understand that this is not your mistake to take the blame for."

Finn stared at her mother. "How did you know?"

"I've blamed myself more than once for things out of my control." She smiled sadly. "I know the look." She bumped her shoulder gently. "We've got to get this finished before we can talk."

"Okay." Finn knew she sounded pathetic. She felt pathetic, but she needed something only a mother—her mother—could give her. "I'm scared."

Cassie's arm was around her shoulder in an instant. "Of what, sweetheart?"

"I don't want you to hate me." She'd never felt so childlike, but as Cassie held her, she acknowledged that it was okay to feel that childish and insecure sometimes.

"Never." Cassie kissed her head. "That isn't even possible."

"I'm scared you left because you didn't want me."

"I left to save you."

"I'm scared you won't want to know me now."

"Why would you think that?"

"Because of all this."

Cassie wiped the tears from her cheeks. "Stop it, right now. All this shows me is that you're an amazingly brilliant scientist who discovered something that was corrupted by someone you trusted. It also shows me how devoted you are in your efforts to correct that oversight, and how ethical you are by your tenacity and the way you put your life in danger to do the right thing." Cassie swallowed. "I'm so proud of you, I don't even know how to tell you, and I wish I could have spent every day by your side. Had I any other choice—any—I would never have been parted from you."

Finn looked into her mother's eyes and felt everything slipping back into place. She began to let go of the anger and self-recrimination, the pain of her father's betrayal, and the self disgust.

"I love you, Danie—Finn. Now and then, and every day in between, and for the rest of my life, I love you. You're my little girl and nothing will ever change that."

She wasn't foolish enough to believe that those few words would make everything okay, but for the first time since Thanksgiving, Finn believed things might really be okay. And right now, that was more than she had hoped for.

"Now, how are we doing with the solution, sweetheart?"

"Ah, I see how this is going to be. You're one of those pushy mothers who think their kid is going to be some kind of overachiever, right?"

"Yup."

Finn laughed despite the tears still rolling down her cheeks. "It's nearly done." She nodded her head in the direction of the beaker. "Mum."

❖

Bailey dialed Sean's number. She'd watched Roy leave just after midnight and waited another forty minutes before putting her plan into action.

"Somebody better be on fire."

"Sean, I need you to do me a favor."

"Another one, you mean?"

"Yeah, another one."

He sighed. "What do you need?"

"Can you put an intercept on a number for me for five minutes? When the front desk calls, just okay me to go up to the apartment."

"Bailey, you can't be serious. I can't do an unofficial line intercept."

"I know you've got your gear at your house. You can do this in a heartbeat."

"I need a warrant—"

"Not what you said when you wanted me to tap your ex's phone line to see if she was cheating on you."

"The bitch *was* cheating on me."

"Not the point." She waited a beat. "I did it because we're friends, man. Because I got your back."

"Jesus, fine. What's the damn number?" She smiled and rattled off the number. "I'll text you when I'm ready. Who am I supposed to be on the end of the line?"

"Mr. Zuckerman."

"Do I get a first name?"

"Nah. There's tons of 'em going in and out of the place according to the earlier doorman. Keep it generic."

"Fine."

"And, Sean?"

"Yeah."

"Thanks."

"Yeah, yeah." She could practically hear the blush in his gruff voice. He was always like that. She quickly clipped Jazz's leash on again and set out toward the park. She had no idea how long she'd need to be up there, and a quick bathroom tour for the pup was only fair. She'd debated leaving Jazz in the car, but she couldn't do it. She didn't like the idea of leaving her in the car alone for more than a few minutes. Truth be told, she didn't like the idea of taking Jazz up there much either, but she didn't feel like she had much choice, and Jazz had behaved exemplarily since the moment she'd come into Bailey's life.

Her phone buzzed in her pocket. The message from Sean was just like the man, short and to the point; ready. She led Jazz across the street and pulled open the door. The guy on the night shift was a short guy, with a balding head, bulging middle, and a toothless smile as he offered her his help. She headed straight toward the elevators like she knew exactly where she was going.

"Thanks, but I'm fine. I'm expected."

He came around the corner of the desk with surprising agility and managed to get hold of her arm before she punched the call button. "I'm sorry but I have to announce all guests." His face took on a sour expression. "No exceptions."

She sighed heavily. "Fine."

He smirked, and the look of triumph on his ruddy face made her want to laugh. "What apartment?" He rounded his desk again and hiked his trousers up until they settled just below his large gut.

"Ten."

"Right. Mr. Sterling's old apartment. The one that's been empty—"

"Call the apartment." She wracked her brain for a name. "Ask for Charlie Zuckerman. He's expecting me." She was pretty sure that was the name Mrs. Richmond had said.

"Look, lady, that apartment's been empty since the old man went to prison. If you think I'm gonna let you up there so you can claim squatter's rights and move in all your little hobo friends—"

"What the hell are you talking about? I'm here on business to see Mr. Zuckerman."

He looked her up and down, distaste curling his lips. "Look, lady, I don't know what game you're playing waltzing in here in your dirty old clothes smelling like wet dog and stale coffee, but this is the Dakota Building, not the YMCA. This isn't the kind of place—"

"Just call the apartment."

"I'll call the police in a minute."

She sighed. *I can't believe this is so fucked up.* "Look, buddy. I'm not a hobo, I'm not looking for a place to squat in, or have a party. My associates in apartment ten are expecting me. Call the apartment. If no one answers or they say they've never heard of me, I'll walk out the door. You won't even have to call the cops."

He stared at her, stuck his hands on his hips, and tried his best to intimidate her. But she'd faced tougher opponents than Jed here, and she wasn't going until she got access to the apartment. She couldn't think of any other way to help Cassie, and she was damned if she wasn't going to at least try.

"Fine." He picked up the phone and punched the button. "But as soon as I call the fourth floor and there's no answer, you're leaving without another damn—hello, sir. I'm sorry to call so late." Bailey tried to keep the smug grin from her face, but she could tell by the scowl on his face she hadn't succeeded. "I have someone in reception who claims you're expecting them." He put his hand over the mouthpiece. "What's your name?"

"Bailey."

"Bailey." He repeated down the line. "I will, sir. Thank you very much." He put the handset down. "Mr. Zuckerman said you can go right up."

"Thank you." She crossed the lobby and called the elevator. Jazz trotted beside her and sat down when she punched the button for the fourth floor. She had the small toolkit in her pocket that she would need to open the door to the apartment and hoped it was a fairly simple mechanism. That was usually the case with buildings that had door staff to monitor the comings and goings of the building. She was a fair lock pick but not an expert by any stretch of the imagination.

The corridor was dark and deserted as she made her way to apartment ten and was pleased to see that it was simple enough for her to tackle. Thirty seconds later, she was closing the door to the apartment. A quick look around told her several things. One, there were several people staying there at the moment and they were well armed. Two, the people staying there were richer than Midas. And three, there was no sign of Cassie or anything belonging to Cassie in the apartment.

She quickly gathered all the weapons she could find and shut them in the bedroom closet. At least then if someone came in she wouldn't have to worry about the extra weapons being in easy reach. She picked one to use herself and chose a comfortable place for her and Jazz to wait. She glanced at her watch. *I wonder if there's some food in the fridge?*

## CHAPTER FORTY-NINE

Cassie rubbed at her itchy, tired eyes with the backs of her gloved hands, careful to avoid touching them with her fingers. She was tired of staring down a microscope and seeing the same negative results. She needed a breakthrough. They all did. For some reason, the stimulation compound seemed to increase the rate of Balor's replication as well as the antitoxin and she couldn't figure out a way to stop that. She glanced at Finn, who was spinning around on her chair, seemingly wasting time.

"What if we leave out the stimulator and add a compound that will dissolve the bacterium and or their byproducts instead?" Finn said suddenly, her head tilted thoughtfully.

It was a possibility. Once the antitoxins destroyed the botulinum toxin, it was the byproducts that caused the lasting problems. Without them, the victim should return to their normal state of health. "Such as?"

"Haven't figured that bit out yet." Finn looked up "Sorry. Thinking out loud."

"It's a good thought. Let's run with it. What would dissolve the byproducts or eject them without further damaging the nerves?"

Finn tapped a pen on the desk between them. "Take me back to school. Draw me a nerve cell." She pointed to the white board.

"What? You must be joking. We don't have time for drawings."

"I'm serious. Sometimes I get so caught up in finding a clever solution to a problem that I overlook the easy one. I can't afford to over look anything here." She held out the pen. "Please?"

"Fine." Cassie started drawing. "But no laughing at my diagrams. You could already draw better than I could when you were three."

"I promise I won't laugh."

Cassie frowned, puzzled by the request even though she could see the logic behind it. She carefully crafted the diagram of the neuron, the axon, the structure of the myelin sheath, the synapses, and a range of chemical symbols.

"Potassium and sodium."

"Yes, it's the sodium-potassium balance that allows the cells to conduct the electrical impulses."

"And what is the molecular makeup of the neurotransmitters?"

"There are several different types. Amino acids, amines, and acetylcholine. The majority of them are exciters, but some are known to be inhibitors too."

"Acetylcholine?"

"Yes. That can act in both capacities depending upon the location."

"Acetylcholine, the combination of acetic acid and choline?"

"Yes."

"What's choline?"

"An essential nutrient that we ingest as part of our diet. Most people know it as vitamin B complexes."

"Okay. So each neuron has its own method of destroying the byproducts."

"I don't understand."

"We need to stimulate the neurons to split the acetylcholine molecules so that the acetic acid will dissolve the byproducts of the botulinum toxin."

Cassie stared at her. The simplicity of it was beautiful. The molecules would naturally reunite in the body, but in the process of reuniting they would change the conditions to an acidic state that would dissolve the unwanted remnants of Balor after the antitoxin killed the bacterium.

"Can your stimulator drug be made to stimulate the neurotransmitter and make the molecules split?"

Cassie pictured the molecular diagram in her head and reached for the pencil sticking out of her bun. "I have no earthly idea," she said as she began scribbling the carbon chains onto the paper, "but I can give it a shot."

"Will it damage the victim?"

"Possibly, but to a much lesser extent than the toxin and byproducts."

"What do you need me to do?"

Cassie thought quickly. "The best method of delivery is going to be something inhaled. The quicker it gets to the brain the better." They quickly developed a list of what they needed and set about their tasks, more confident than they had been an hour ago. And Cassie so much more in awe of her daughter than she had ever thought possible.

"It looks like talc," Finn said and Cassie had to agree. The combined antitoxin and stimulator was condensed and dried into a fine powder.

"Or coke." Oz peered into the beaker, a frown marring her face. "You sure it's going to work?"

"As sure as I can be." She covered her mouth as she yawned. "It won't save everyone, but I think ninety-eight percent is a pretty effective result in the lab."

"It is?" Oz looked skeptical.

"It is," Finn assured her.

Cassie heard the disappointment in Finn's voice. "But you wish it was a hundred?"

"Don't you? Knowing that the two percent we're talking about here are actually people dying."

"Of course I do. But death is a part of life, and we can't hope to save everyone. We can simply do our best." She pointed to the first batch of fine white powder. "This is our best, and I tell you something now. I challenge anyone to come up with anything better or faster than this." She placed the lid on the specimen jar and watched the second batch running through the condenser. "You know the fastest way to get this into use over there is to give them the formula and have them produce it."

Oz shook her head. "Never going to happen. We won't get authorization to hand over the formula."

"Then how do you plan to get it distributed?" Cassie frowned.

"I can't say," Oz said.

"No way." Finn grabbed Oz's hand. "You can't do that. We've slaved over this. We need to know how you plan to distribute it so those people are safe."

"I can't say because I don't know. Charlie and Junior aren't saying anything to anyone." She tapped her nose. "Top secret."

"Damn it, that's not fair." Finn rested her head in her hands heavily.

"Man, you're cute when you pout." Oz wrapped her arms around Finn's waist and nuzzled her neck. "Don't you think, Cassie?"

"I think she's always cute." They both laughed as Finn turned pink and bent her head forward.

"How long before you guys are done here and we can leave? I don't know about you, but I really, really need some sleep," Oz asked.

"I need half an hour to make sure this batch is strong enough," Cassie said. "Then we can let the machines run until morning."

Finn checked the timer. "We'll be at twenty-six hours then. Seriously, Oz, if we don't know how you're planning to distribute this we can't calculate how much we need to make. Letting it run till morning is all well and good, but if we need twice what this equipment is set up to make, then we'll need another six or seven hours to make more. If we know now, then we can set up more equipment now."

"I get it, but I really don't know."

"Then it's a good thing we got here before you all headed out for the night," Charlie said as he walked into the room with Billy, Junior, and AJ on his heels. "How are you doing?"

"I'll have a definitive answer to that question in about ten minutes," Cassie said.

"Excellent. We're limited with how we can deliver this stuff, and we have to be very careful or we're going to set off an international incident."

"Charlie, get to the good stuff." Finn crossed her arms.

"Patience is a virtue, young lady." He spread out a map of Israel across an empty workbench and indicated four red crosses. "These are the water plants. The hatch-marked areas are the service area for each plant. The plan for release is going to have to be airborne."

"You're going to conduct an airstrike against a friendly country? That's an act of war." Oz leaned on the table, incredulity etched deeply across her face.

"It would be if we were going to announce that it was us, and I didn't say an airstrike. I said airborne." He pointed to two areas in the West Bank and two in the Gaza Strip. "We're going to set off masquerade rocket attacks from known Hamas strongholds. Attached to these rockets is going to be your compound, Finn." He tossed her a stainless steel cylinder. "The irises at the top can be released by remote control and disperse as little as one microgram at a time. We'll release them over the target sites in the air to get mass dispersal and then have the rockets detonate in unoccupied areas nearby to create plausible damage to cover our goal."

"Jesus Christ, are you shitting me?"

"Serious as a heart attack, Ladyfish."

Finn put the canister down. "Air dispersal at what height, Charlie?" Finn asked, her pencil and paper already in hand to make the notes she needed.

"You tell me. I'm going to use modified Hamas rockets equipped with drone guidance systems so that we can direct them exactly where we need them then destroy them once deployment is complete."

"How on earth do you have Hamas rockets and stronghold locations?" Cassie asked.

"Hakim Qandri. He was Masood Mehalik's second in command and a senior member of Hamas. He was also working for MI6 for months. He gave them locations of strongholds, outposts, and details of the rockets used. I've got my guys engineering the guidance systems to work with their rockets now. We'll be able to direct them from here once those chips are in place."

Finn nodded. "Fine, I'll work that out once we have the final strength from this last test. How many people are in the target areas?"

"Estimates for these two areas," he said as he pointed to the two areas closest to the Gaza Strip, "Are looking at twenty-five to thirty thousand people in each catchment area." He pointed to the next cross. "Seventy to eighty thousand, and the water treatment plant on the edge of Tel Aviv serves around one hundred and forty-five thousand people."

"Fuck." Oz blanched, and Finn's hands visibly shook as she wrote the numbers down.

"Do you have the result of that test yet?"

"Still five minutes to go," Cassie said.

"As soon as we have that, I can work out the rest of the numbers. Charlie, I'll get the data to you as soon as we have it. We're going to need to set up more equipment."

Cassie was already pulling racks of test tubes, beakers, and flasks from a cupboard. "I know, sweetheart."

Cassie watched Finn hunched over her notepad as she set up line after line of equipment and started to mix liquids, gels, and powders together following the precise formula they had devised earlier. They were going to need a huge quantity of this powder, and they were lucky that each person would only need a tiny amount of the substance before their own body would take over and do the rest of the work.

"Who's going in to prepare the missiles?" Oz asked.

"Junior's taking one target, Evan is driving across Egypt to cross into Israel and take the southernmost site. Ari's going to take care of the Tel Aviv site personally. His family are in the service area, Oz. He won't let this shit get through."

"And the final target?"

"Still working on it."

"Can Ari not find someone to help?"

"Apparently not." Charlie shook his head. "Looks like I'll have to find someone off the base. Junior's going to put together a list of people who can handle it."

"I'll do it." AJ ran his hand through his hair. "I know what's at stake. Send me over there."

Charlie shook his head. "You're not trained for a mission like this, AJ."

"Junior can teach me what I need to do. You can trust me, Dad. I'll get the job done."

"It's not about trust, Son. It's about knowledge. You've never had to deal with this kind of ordinance, the situation on the ground is unfamiliar to you, you're trained for a much, much different role." Charlie put his hand on his shoulder. "I'm sorry, Son, but sending you over there without the necessary training or backup would be a suicide run on a mission we can't afford to fail."

AJ's face fell, and Oz knew that the rejection had seriously wounded his ego, but Charlie was right. Now was not the time to worry about egos and male pride. Now was the time to pull on all resources and get the job done. There was more at stake than any one of them.

"Send me in with him." If it hadn't been her own voice she heard, she would have looked around for the volunteer.

"No." Finn looked up from her notepad. "You can't go there. It's too dangerous."

"Baby, everyone is doing their bit for this mission. Everyone." She grasped Finn's hands and noted how cold they were. "You're working so hard here to make this stuff it would be a real shame if it didn't get deployed right and Balor spread."

"But that doesn't mean you have to be the one to go there."

"I'm no use to you here, and I need to help. I need to do something too." She pointed to the door. "Out there, I can do something. I can make sure that everything you've done here pays off." She wiped the tear from Finn's cheek. "I'll be fine. It's an easy in and out mission."

"If it was so easy Charlie would have let AJ go on his own."

"I've had training AJ hasn't. I know what I'm doing, Finn."

"I can make this work. We can use a BBC news chopper to get you into Israel and get you and AJ in as journalists. It'll give you the perfect cover, and being together, you'll be backup for each other to get the job done," Charlie said as he punched a number into his phone.

"I won't let anything happen to her, Finn," AJ said from the stool he was perched on. "You have my word."

Oz pulled her into a tight embrace and kissed her close to her ear. "Nothing's going to happen to me. It'll be real quick, and I'll be back before you know it."

Finn pulled back far enough to stare into her eyes. "I can't lose you."

Oz could see the panic in her eyes and wished she wasn't the cause of it, but every fiber in her being told her this was the right thing to do. "You won't, baby."

"You can't promise me that. I don't know what I'd do without you." Tears slipped down her cheeks. "You're everything to me."

"You are to me too. That's why I have to do this. I know you'll never forgive yourself if anyone dies from this thing. I can't let that happen. I don't want to see those shadows in your eyes for the rest of our lives, baby. You deserve more than that. I promised to give you everything you needed for the rest of our lives. You need this to work. I can make that happen. I really can." She leaned in and pressed her lips to Finn's, sampling the soft skin, wet and salty from her tears, warm and inviting as it always was, and Oz let herself get lost in the feel of her. She needed Finn to know how much she loved her and that she would do anything for her.

"You also promised that you'd never leave my side."

Oz smiled. "I did, didn't I?"

Finn nodded. "Don't leave me."

"Never, baby." She cradled Finn against her, holding her head against her shoulder as she continued to weep. "Trust me. I'll be back before you even have time to miss me."

Finn's voice was quiet and muffled against her shirt as she said, "I miss you already."

"Chopper will be ready when you get there. Ari's on the case. He said he's glad to have you on board again, Oz. He said there's no one he'd rather entrust the safety of his homeland to than you."

"We better get started then, Uncle Charlie."

"Don't worry. I've got it under control. You just finish helping Finn with anything she needs at this end for now and leave the rest to me. Junior will fill you in when Finn's ready with the compound." He looked at AJ. "We're gonna have to go over some stuff, Son. You better come with me." He squeezed Finn's shoulder. "Don't worry, Finn. It'll work."

"I hope so, Charlie. I really fucking hope so."

## CHAPTER FIFTY

O z sat at one of the workbenches and watched the drips fall from a condenser into a conical flask. She still didn't get how this was going to stop Balor from killing hundreds of thousands of people in Israel, and she didn't want to take the time from Finn or Cassie to make them explain it to her again. They were continually in motion, refilling chemicals, mixing more compounds, evaporating solutions until they were left with a fine powder. Watching them work was incredible. A shorthand language had developed between them and a simple gesture or single word resulted in a flurry of motion.

AJ came barreling through the door pulling a cart loaded with boxes, Billy close behind him with an equally loaded cart, his filled with bags of fine concrete mix.

"We've got everything you put on the list, Finn." He started unloading the boxes on an empty work surface. "I don't get what you want with blenders and concrete, but they're here."

"Thanks, AJ. Can you get them all unpacked and set up on that bench there, please? We need to mix the concrete powder with the compound and another little ingredient that Charlie is getting hold of for us."

"Concrete?" Oz asked as she helped AJ and Billy unpack forty blenders.

"Yeah. This compound is too white to be explained away and the quantity needed per person is really small. Distributing it evenly over the area is going to be a nightmare. I want to use this as an additive to make the quantities go further and resemble normal dust that would be around after an explosion. Even just in the air normally in a city."

"You're cutting it?" Oz stared at her.

Finn shrugged. "In the most simple terms, yes."

"Won't the concrete hurt people?"

Finn sliced open one of the bags and dipped her hand in. "The particles are so fine that it really isn't any different than inhaling dust on the street. There are particles like this everywhere." She let the powder slip between her fingers to demonstrate her point. "We're also only talking about inhaling less than half a microgram of this stuff. Builders who open a bag and empty it to mix would inhale more than that per bag and it doesn't seem to do them any harm."

"Even if it did," Cassie said, "it's less harmful than Balor."

"Good point." Oz plugged in the blender. "Just didn't expect to be adding that skill to my repertoire. Jesus, I really am starting to feel like some kind of drug dealer."

Finn laughed. "Well, I guess in a way we are. But this isn't about giving anyone a high."

"I don't know. If this works, sweetheart, you're going to be scraping me off the ceiling." Cassie put her hand on Finn's shoulder. "This is a major breakthrough. Every single part of it. That definitely gives me a high." She winked before she turned back to her workbench.

Finn sighed. "How are we doing on time?"

"We've got twenty-three hours left," AJ said as he checked the timer.

"And how long will transit and delivery preparation require, Billy?"

"Charlie's secured a couple of jets to take the canisters to an aircraft carrier that's moving into position in the Mediterranean Sea. From there it will be transported via helicopter to the sites in Israel we've identified as the best places to launch from. Stephen Knight gave us contacts at Interpol and MI6 to get the information that Hakim Qandri gave them."

"How is Stephen?" Finn asked.

"In surgery now. He'll live." Billy didn't meet her eyes.

"But?"

"They're pretty sure they're going to have to amputate just above each knee, and they don't know about his left arm. They don't know if they can repair the elbow joint. The damage to his hand was too extensive, they can't save it."

"Fuck." Oz tried to pull Finn into her arms, and fought the sting of rejection as Finn refused the embrace.

"They can't save them?" Finn whispered.

"The joints were pulverized. Nerves severed, blood supplies compromised for too long." He shook his head. "I think the fact that so many of the nerves were severed was what stopped him from being in as much pain as we would have expected at the time. He's a good man and he helped grease a lot of wheels before he let them take him into the operating room. Without him, we wouldn't be able to get those canisters into Israel without detection."

Oz knew they were all feeling guilty over the mistrust they had placed on Knight's shoulders.

"We've got work to do. I won't let his sacrifice be for nothing. How long?"

"We'll need six hours, Finn. If you can give us seven, that would be great."

"Fourteen hours. Okay." She nodded tersely and strode away.

Billy put a hand on Oz's shoulder. "Don't take it personally. She's got way too much going on to even think about letting the emotion out just now."

"I know, Pops."

"She'll need you later."

Oz nodded. She hoped so. She knew Finn was angry at her for volunteering to go to Israel, but she knew it was the right thing to do. She knew she had to. Part of that came from needing to give Finn the results she needed, but another part was seeing Finn in her lab. It made her realize exactly what she had given up and how much potential she had to do great things. Things that Oz didn't want to get in the way of her accomplishing. Could Finn really be happy staying in the Keys with her? Diving in Florida was a lot less stressful, a lot more fun, but Finn had the chance to change the face of medical science here, and how could Oz let her pass that opportunity by? Statistically, she knew that one in three people were touched by cancer at some point in their lives. That meant probably three members of her family would likely develop it. Could she or Finn forgive themselves if Finn were able to develop a cure but didn't, and one or more of them died? Putting faces to it made it real in a way she'd never considered before.

It also made her question herself. Everything Finn had put on the line to do this, and Oz felt as though she hadn't done her share. She wanted Finn to be as proud of her as she was of Finn, and she knew that a good portion of her decision to volunteer for this mission stemmed from her desire to prove her worth to Finn. She needed to put her own past behind her and move on from the ghosts of her last disastrous mission to be the partner Finn deserved. This was her opportunity and one she might never have again. She knew that Finn would eventually forgive her, just as soon as Oz explained her reasoning. Even if she didn't understand and still thought she was a fool for going. All she had to do was talk to Finn. About her feelings.

*Later. We'll talk about it later. Right now, we've got more than enough to deal with.*

❖

Finn poured the last of the powder into the stainless steel canister and closed the lid. The sixteen cylinders were lined up on the bench, each one looking like an innocuous thermos flask. The top of each one was sealed with an iris-type device that would open by remote control. Each iris could be opened a little or a lot, depending upon the need for distribution in the various areas. It was an ingenious little device, and Finn was fascinated by the spiral pattern as each one opened and closed as the remote triggers were tested.

"Any last instructions, Finn?" Oz asked as she and Junior started loading the canisters onto a cart.

"Don't get dead."

She smiled. "I won't. I meant with this stuff though." She pointed to the cylinders.

"Charlie has the coordinates for release and the specific height required for optimum dispersal." She shrugged. "I can't think of anything else I can do."

"You've done plenty," Junior said.

She laughed derisively. "Yeah, I know. I created the apocalypse."

"Hey…"

She waved his argument off. "I know, I know. Betrayed, used, et cetera. Good intentions, blah blah blah. Well, you know what they say about good intentions, don't you, Junior?"

"What?"

"They paved the road to hell."

"Finn, I could stand here all day and argue with you about this," Oz said. "And in a couple of days, I will. But right now, we've got to get this to Israel to stop a lot of people from getting sick. You, my darling, are the creator of this miracle, and as such, do you have any more instructions that I should know about to release this thing for the best possible outcome?"

"Hit as many people as you can with it, and let Mother Nature do the rest. The wind will carry it, and the rain will help it absorb into the water table. Every surface that this lands on will be covered in live contagion for up to seven days."

"That's because you've put it in the cold virus again, right?"

"Yes."

"I'm never touching anything again."

"You've survived this long. I don't think you need to start worrying now. If you can get some over the treatment plant, that will be a great help. It's the workers there who'll likely be affected first."

"Because it's the source of the contamination?"

"Exactly."

"We'll see to it."

"Just be careful, okay? Don't drink the water, and don't touch anyone who has."

"I thought we were vaccinated."

"You're a work in progress. You aren't fully vaccinated until you clear that cold. At least another couple of days."

"Can this stuff kill us?" Junior asked.

She grinned a little, trying to lighten the oppressive mood that was closing in on her, but it was impossible. She wouldn't be able to rest easy until this mission was completed and Oz was back home with her. "I don't know for sure. I think it's unlikely, but it can still make you pretty sick right now."

"Got it." He kissed her cheek. "Thanks for the warning. Gotta go."

She hugged him tight. "Come back safe."

"You got it. We'll give you two a minute." He dragged the cart behind him as he and Charlie headed for the elevator.

"You never did tell me, Finn," Oz said, "What was that extra ingredient that Charlie got for you to add to the compound?"

"A radioactive isotope."

"Huh. Why?"

"So that we can track the dispersal and make sure we get coverage where we need it."

"I don't understand how making this stuff radioactive will help that."

"We'll be able to see the isotopes on a satellite image and as they're all mixed together, where one goes—"

"So does the other." She smiled at Finn and kissed her deeply. Finn could feel in her kiss every bit of love that Oz felt for her. She didn't understand why Oz felt the need to go on this mission, and she wished with all her heart that she wouldn't, but they didn't have time to find alternatives right now and everything was already in motion to make Oz and AJ's cover work. She threaded her fingers through Oz's hair and pulled her closer. She wished they were alone, she wished they weren't saying good-bye, she wished she could feel Oz inside her. She wanted to hold on to her and never let go.

"Don't get any more holes in you, Olivia Zuckerman. I love you just the way you are."

"I've said it before and I'll say it again," Oz said, grinning at her. "You're a genius. Later, babe."

Finn watched her go, the door closing softly behind her and frowning as she shook her head. "If I was, I wouldn't be letting you go and I'd have never trusted my father and gotten us into this mess in the first place."

"Finn, I think it's time we had a little chat about why I left your father when I did." Cassie wrapped her hand around Finn's arm and tugged her into the small office.

Finn felt exhausted, and all she really wanted was to crawl into bed with Oz and sleep until it was all over. But Oz wasn't here. She wasn't going to be waiting for her at the apartment, or at home, and all of a sudden, she realized why her mother had chosen now to start the conversation. "You're trying to distract me."

"Trust me. It'll work." She sat on the small sofa and pulled Finn down beside her. "For a little while, at least. What did he tell you? About why I left."

"He said you left to be with Karen."

"Prick."

Finn stared at her.

"Well, he was. Yes, I was seeing Karen, and he was seeing his string of women, but that wasn't why I left. I planned to leave when you were a little older, and taking you with me would have been a little easier. As William's character became increasingly apparent, I knew that leaving him wouldn't be as simple as filing for divorce. And trying to explain what we'd have to go through to a child as young as you would have been impossible."

"So what changed?"

"He decided that he wanted the version of Balor that I could have created twenty-five years ago."

"What?"

"He wanted me to create a biological weapon to sell to the highest bidder."

The final pieces began to fall into place. "You refused."

She shook her head. "No, I told him I would, but that it would take some time. When I left the lab that day, I did the only thing I could think of. Karen and I had always thought that driving the car off the cliffs would be the most explainable way to 'die' without leaving a body. I called her and, well, you know the rest."

"Why didn't you come and get me then?"

"He knew I wouldn't have cooperated with his plan without leverage."

Finn heard the words but still she couldn't comprehend what her mother was saying. "He was holding me hostage to make you agree to his plan?"

Cassie nodded. "I never wanted to be without you, but I couldn't find you. I couldn't stay and build what he wanted, but refusing would have meant him harming you." She swiped at the tears on her cheeks. "I couldn't risk that either." She reached out for Finn's hand. "I did the only thing I could, sweetheart. Can you forgive me?"

Finn looked down at their joined hands. Hands the same size and shape as her own, long, slim fingers, narrow palms, and soft, smooth skin. "There's nothing to forgive. You did the best you could with impossible choices." She kissed her cheek. "Thank you for loving me enough to sacrifice everything for me."

Her mother's tears were flowing freely as she pulled Finn into her arms. "I love you so much, sweetheart." She kissed her cheek over and over. "I am so proud of you."

Finn tried to pull away.

"No, Finn, I am. I'm proud of everything you've accomplished. Your protocol is a breakthrough that I didn't expect to see in my lifetime. Your dedication to creating a vaccine for Balor was incredible, and the work you've just done with me here in creating a treatment was amazing. You've taken dangerous men off the streets, not the least of which was your own father after he had you kidnapped and almost killed. You are so strong, sweetheart, so strong. I wish I could have been with you every day of your life and helped you to become the woman you are today, but instead you managed it all on your own. That's even more amazing. And I will never, ever let you believe anything else. You have to believe me, Finn. I'm your mother." She smiled crookedly. "I do believe it's the law."

Finn sniggered under her tears. Intellectually, she knew her mother was right. That they'd all been right in everything they'd been telling her for weeks. That she wasn't to blame for the whole mess, and that she had done everything in her power to eradicate the threat. As she stared into her mother's eyes, she finally allowed herself to let go of the guilt she'd clung to. She closed her eyes, and for the first time in months, she saw the faces of the people she had saved, rather than those condemned. For the first time since Whittaker had knocked on their door, she could picture Oz smiling at her, her eyes bright with love, and laughter, and hope, instead of dull with pain and approaching death. She allowed herself to see the future, and a world full of people living their lives, and carrying on, oblivious to everything that had threatened them in the past weeks.

She knew she still had a ways to go. That it would still bother her for many, many years to come. But she also knew that she could get past this. Because they'd stopped it. Or at least, they'd given everyone the best possible chance to recover. She and her mother.

"I'm proud of you too. I'm sorry for everything he did to you."

"And I'm sorry for everything he did to you. But we have each other now, and we can move forward. If you want to?"

"More than anything." Finn buried herself in her mother's embrace. "I'm so scared, Mum."

"She'll come back to you, sweetheart. She loves you too much to do anything less."

## CHAPTER FIFTY-ONE

Finn."
    Finn could feel her whole body being shaken as her mother tried to wake her.

Finn turned over, determined to ignore the annoying voice. "G'way."

"Finn, honey. Why don't you and your mom go on up to the apartment and get settled? I'm gonna sort the stuff we have in the trunk and follow you up." Billy shook her shoulder gently. "Go on. I'll be up in just a few minutes."

"Can't I just sleep here?"

"No. You'll just complain all day about the crick in your neck if you do that."

Finn wanted to argue the point, but she knew her mum was right. She sighed deeply and pushed herself out of the car. "Right, we'll see you up there in a few minutes, Billy."

"Shall we?" She held her hand out for her mother.

"We shall." The elevator was quiet. "I know that there's still a lot more for us to talk about, sweetheart, but do you think we could do it in the morning?"

Finn leaned against the wall, arms propped against the rail to prevent her from falling down in exhaustion. "Only if it's over coffee," Finn said, her breath fogging up the mirrored wall.

"A bucket or two should just about do it."

"Sounds like a plan, Professor."

"No. Please don't call me that."

"Why not?"

"I understand if you aren't comfortable with calling me Mum, but Sandra Burns, the professor, she took me further and further away from you. I don't need to be reminded of that."

"I'm sorry."

"Call me Cassie." She'd tried to deny it. Tried to tell herself she wasn't strong enough to handle the real world because all it did was tear her to pieces. But she was wrong. She'd survived it all and she was coming back stronger than ever. She had her daughter back, and she'd claim back her life too. She thought of Bailey. Could she claim back enough to be the woman Bailey deserved?

"I'd rather call you Mum. As long as you don't mind."

"Mind? Oh, Finn, you don't know how long I've wanted that."

The elevator door opened. "Come on. Let's get you set up in the guest room."

"Where are we, anyway?"

"New York."

"Smartass."

Finn pointed to her left. "Central Park's just out there. This is the Dakota Building."

"It's a beautiful place, Finn."

"Yeah, but it's not like I'm going to use it much down in Florida anyway." She put her key in the door and motioned for Cassie to go in first. "Well, don't just stand there. Go on inside."

❖

It was Jazz's soft whine that woke her from the pleasant slumber she'd drifted into. It took her a second to gain her bearings when she opened her eyes in the dark apartment. She looked at her watch, grateful for the glow in the dark hands that told her it was almost four in the morning. Bailey pressed Jazz further behind her chair and told her to keep quiet.

A key scratched against the metal of the lock and a rough, hoarse voice echoed through the dark apartment. "Well, don't just stand there. Go on inside."

Bailey's heart pounded so loudly against her ribs she couldn't really hear how many people were coming in. She hoped they weren't armed, but common sense told her hired thugs were always armed. Especially ex-military. She just hoped she had enough time to surprise them.

She heard the soft scraping sound of a hand on the wall looking for the light switch and she squinted, knowing the hours she'd spent in the dark would make her blind for a second. The soft light lit only a small fragment of the apartment, but the gasp and her name drew her attention to Cassie immediately.

She stood quickly and pointed the gun at Finn. "Cassie, get behind me." She waved her hand in Cassie's direction. "You stay there and get your hands up." She waved the gun in Finn's direction. Finn's eyes were wide as she complied. *Ha. You weren't expecting anyone to help her, were you? Bitch.*

"Bailey, what are you doing?" Cassie took a step toward her.

"Cassie, it's okay. Don't block my line of sight. Just get behind me." She glanced quickly at Cassie, offered her a quick reassuring smile, and then stared hard at the girl again. "Don't you move. I'm warning you."

"Bailey, this is ridiculous—"

"Cassie, it's fine. We're just going to walk out and this little bitch isn't going to follow us. I'll take you back to Boston."

"I'm not going back to Boston with you, Bailey."

Bailey tried to breathe through the surprisingly sharp pain that seared through her chest. It was her choice, after all, and it wasn't like she'd offered Bailey any false hope. Bailey had chased her here without any plea for help. It didn't matter she'd seen them forcing Cassie into the car, that she wasn't there of her own volition. It didn't matter how much it hurt, as long as she was safe in the end. She would be fine—as long as Cassie was safe.

"I know you told me you didn't want to see me again. And that's okay. But I have to make sure you're safe, Cassie. As soon as you're safe you'll never have to see me again." She stepped forward and put her body between Cassie and Finn, her gun pointed at Finn's face. "We're going to leave now, and you're not going to stop us." Finn nodded, her eyes wide and her face pale. "Not such a tough girl now, are you?"

"Bailey, you've got this wrong."

"I don't think so, Cassie. I know you wanted her to be your little girl, but she isn't. A chip off Daddy's block, aren't you? I'm going to take her somewhere she's safe from you and you're going to leave her alone." She stepped closer. "Or I'll make you sorry. Do you understand?" She waved the gun again to make her threat clear. "She deserves better than you."

Finn shook her head and fat tears rolled down her cheeks.

"Enough, Bailey. I don't know where you got this stupid idea that I'm in danger, but I'm not." Cassie wrapped her fingers around her forearm and tugged.

"You don't have to protect her. I'll protect you," Bailey said. She heard Jazz growling from behind her.

"I don't need protecting from my daughter." Cassie yanked harder on Bailey's arm, trying to move it away from Finn's head. "Right now the only one I need protecting from is you." Jazz barked and Bailey glanced at her quickly to make sure she was still behind her. Cassie used the moment to push herself into Bailey's body and knock her away from Finn.

Bailey twisted her body and tried to break Cassie's grip on her arm. "What are you doing? Stop fighting me." She twisted her hand and shoulder again, desperate to break Cassie's hold, and her eyes darted to Finn's face. She was glad the girl hadn't moved while Cassie was arguing with her. A loud pop made the girl jump. *Silly girl, you'll really jump when I—oh.* "Shit, that hurts."

# CHAPTER FIFTY-TWO

*What the fuck?* Billy thought as the elevator opened to the sound of a gunshot.

He ran down the long hall. The door to the apartment was wide open and Cassie was kneeling beside a woman who looked unconscious. Blood pooled at her knees and soaked the white rug. "Jesus." He looked around the room and couldn't see anything else out of place. "Finn?"

"I'm here." She came out of the bathroom holding an armful of towels. She knelt opposite Cassie and pressed the clean linen into her mother's arms.

"Is there anyone else here?" He asked, not waiting for a response before he walked to one of the bedroom doors, pushing it open and scanning inside.

"No," Cassie said. "Only Jazz."

Billy checked a second bedroom, his weapon an extension of his arm as he moved fluidly around the space. "Who's Jazz?"

Cassie pressed towels against the woman's abdomen. "The dog." Jazz lay with her head on her paws, whimpering softly as she stared at her owner.

"Billy, can you call an ambulance, please?" Finn looked up as she continued to help her mother.

"Sure. Then one of you can tell me what the hell happened here." He quickly called while he checked the rest of the apartment.

"Bailey?" Cassie pushed hair off Bailey's face and bent over her when her eyes fluttered open.

"That didn't work out the way I planned." Bailey grimaced and tried to reach for Cassie's hand.

"Don't move. The paramedics are on the way. What were you trying to do?"

Bailey smirked. "Save you. Couldn't you tell?"

"Well, I did hear you mention it, yes. Save me from what?"

"I saw them push you into the car, Cassie."

"What car?"

"Outside MIT. On Thursday morning. What day is it?"

"Saturday, honey. It's Saturday night."

"Oh. I thought it was still Friday."

"That doesn't matter. Why did you think I needed saving?"

"After the car, you were in a helicopter. I thought they'd taken you. I spoke to my contact. He thought she'd gone bad." She glanced at Finn. "I thought you were in danger."

"So you followed me here and waited?"

"Couldn't think of anything else to do, couldn't let you go." Bailey closed her eyes and her breathing evened out as she passed out. Cassie leaned close to make sure she was breathing and her heartbeat was still strong.

"Oh, you sweet fool." She looked over her shoulder at the doorway. "Where are these paramedics coming from? China?"

"They're coming," Billy said, holding his hand out to the dog, and it crawled over to him on its belly.

"Mum, is this your girlfriend?"

*I wish.* "No, this is Bailey. The private detective I hired to help me find you."

"And she thought I had you kidnapped?"

"Seems that way."

"And she followed you all the way here to rescue you?"

"Apparently."

"And she's not your girlfriend? 'Cause I've got to tell you, that's the kind of stunt Oz would pull."

"I must have missed something." Billy petted the dog's head, to help keep her calm and away from where Finn and Cassie hovered over the body on the floor. "You hired her to find Finn, and then she follows you here thinking you're in danger."

"Right," Cassie said.

"So how does she end up shot and bleeding all over the rug?" Billy asked.

Cassie was more relieved than she could have imagined possible to feel the strong beat beneath her fingertips when she checked Bailey's pulse again. "She was pointing it at Finn, trying to get me to safety. I grabbed her arm to stop her, to get her attention away from Finn, but she kept pulling it away, and it just went off." Cassie felt her tears rolling down her cheeks, but she didn't care. Bailey had come to help her even after she sent her away. Even when she thought Cassie didn't want anything more to do with her. Still, Bailey had ridden in on her charger, determined to save her.

"We'll take it from here, ma'am." Big, rough hands pulled Cassie out of the way. She looked up to see a paramedic drop a heavy bag to the ground and quickly assess Bailey's injuries with his partner. "What happened?"

"The gun was on the table," Billy said, pointing to the coffee table, "and it got knocked off by accident when the dog knocked over a drink."

Cassie looked up at Billy quickly. He was going to cover for Bailey. She'd broken into the apartment, pointed a gun at Finn, and now Billy was going to cover for her. Why?

The paramedic asked a host of questions, all of which Cassie answered to the best of her ability, and none of which she could remember as she continued to stare at Bailey's face. Her body jerked and jolted as they ministered their aid and readied her for transport. *Don't you dare die on me, Bailey Davenport. Don't you even dare.*

Billy helped Finn to her feet and kept his fingers wrapped around the dog's collar so that the men could work on Bailey unobstructed. The dog started barking, broke free of his grip, and only quieted again when she laid her head over Bailey's feet.

"We're going to be taking her out of here ASAP. You need to do something with that dog," the paramedic said to them.

Cassie clicked her fingers. "Come here, girl." Jazz whined but crawled to Cassie's feet and looked up at her pitifully. "She'll be okay, sweetie. Your mama's big and tough, remember?" She squatted beside the dog and wrapped her arms around Jazz's neck. She just hoped she was telling the truth.

"What hospital are you going to?" Billy asked the paramedic.

"Roosevelt. Over on Tenth Avenue between Fifty-eighth and Fifty-ninth Streets, about ten minutes from here. You going over there?"

"Yeah."

"Good, the cops are en route. I'll tell them you'll give them statements there."

"That's fine. I'll go and get the car."

"Wait." Cassie looked from one to the other. They were all exhausted and running on fumes, yet they both seemed completely ready to sit with her in the waiting room for a woman they didn't know, just because she was important to Cassie. "You don't need to come with me. I'll get a cab. You need to sleep."

"No can do, Cassie." Billy spoke quietly. "Goes against Navy law." He winked and pulled open the door.

"Seriously, wait."

Billy stopped and turned back around. "Don't you want to get there and make sure she's okay?"

"Of course I do. But you all don't need to come with me."

"No, we don't," Finn said. "But we'd like to support you." She grasped Cassie's hand. "That's what family do for each other."

Cassie felt the tears welling in her eyes as she pointed to Jazz while she sat whining at the door, obviously distressed and searching for Bailey. "What about Jazz? She's family too." She crouched beside Jazz and wrapped her arms around her neck, drawing comfort from her as Jazz licked the tears from her cheeks and rested her paw on Cassie's thigh.

Billy smiled. "I'll ask the doorman to keep an eye on her. She should be able to stay in the lobby with him till one of us can get back here to take care of her. That way the pup doesn't need to be alone while she's upset. How does that sound?"

"Sounds fine to me." Cassie continued to pet Jazz's head as Finn quickly grabbed her keys, wallet, and a clean jacket before they left the apartment.

Cassie waited until they were in the elevator before she turned to Billy and asked, "Why did you tell the paramedics that it was an accident?"

He shrugged. "It was an accident. She was only there trying to protect you." She shrugged again. "Can't say I blame her. She did some good work managing to break into that apartment. I wanna know how she did it." He winked at Cassie. "Besides, I'm not buying that *she's not a girlfriend* nonsense you're selling. I saw the way she looked at you before she passed out, and I heard what you said to her."

"We're not together."

"You care about her, though."

"Doesn't change anything."

Finn wrapped her arms around Cassie. "Maybe it should." The tender words and the hug were Cassie's undoing. She sobbed and allowed herself to be comforted by her child, and wondered just how different her life could have been.

## CHAPTER FIFTY-THREE

O z pulled the ear protectors off her head and grabbed half the bags that were filled with dummy camera equipment and canisters filled with Finn's compound. The chopper had flown a circuitous route to make it look like it was coming in from one of the agreed routes for news broadcasters as it flew into Israeli airspace and touched down thirty miles outside of the Gaza strip. The news van was waiting for them just like Ari had said it would be. AJ dumped his bags in the back of the van and quickly popped the hatch panel in the floor to reveal the passports, visas, and credentials that they would need to get through the checkpoint at Erez, the border crossing at the very northern tip of the Gaza Strip and the closest point to the Hamas outpost they were heading to.

"We all good?" Oz asked.

"Looks like it. Everything he said would be here is here."

"How's your British accent, cuz?" Oz smiled, trying to ease some of her younger cousin's nerves.

"Well, I don't have the good fortune to live with my own Brit so I think I'll let you do the talking on this one."

"If at all possible, I will." She noticed his shaking hands as he pulled the door closed behind him. "You okay?"

"Yeah." He ran his hand through his hair. "Actually, no, I'm not. I thought I could handle it, you know? The rest of you seem to do it all so easily, I thought I can't be that different from you all."

"Hey, you aren't different, AJ. This isn't easy for any of us. We're all just full of bullshit when we say that." She pointed at the green fields, the dirt road that would lead to the border crossing that they needed to get through. "This scares the crap out of me. Having to use those fake papers to get through that checkpoint is nervewracking, and anyone who tells you any different, well, they really are full of shit."

"Even Junior?"

"Even Junior." She started the engine and pulled out. "When we get through that checkpoint we don't know what we're facing, and we know that we're on the clock with only seconds to spare. This is pressure, AJ."

"Are you worried? Because of when you got shot?"

"Sure, that plays on my mind." She tapped the steering wheel. "How could it not? When I was on the boat and that guy had Finn, I was on autopilot. I didn't have time to think about what I had to do. I just did

it and I'd do it again in a heartbeat to save her. This, today, is different."
She shrugged. "We've planned it, we're organized, we know that if we
have to we're going to enter that building and kill men who don't even
know we're on our way. That makes me sick to my stomach, AJ. But
what worries me more is that I'll think too much and freeze when we
get in there. That one split second of indecision will get you hurt, like I
got Rudy hurt. So I'm not even going to let myself think about them as
people. Paper targets. That's all I'm shooting at today."

"Paper targets that are going to be shooting back."

She laughed. "Most likely, but I know I've got you to watch my
back today, and that you won't let anything happen to me."

"No way. Finn would kick my ass if anything happened to you."

Oz laughed. "Best not to forget that."

He looked out the window, head resting on his fist. "I won't let you
down."

"I know."

Twenty minutes later, they drew up to the border crossing and
joined the lengthy line. Humanitarian aid workers were trying to enter in
Red Cross vans, each being searched thoroughly. Palestinians lined up,
their papers checked, their bodies searched, and questioned extensively
under the hot sun as they tried to make their way home after a day's work
on farms and building sites. Broadcasters, like they were supposed to be,
got through with a cursory check of the vehicle, a good sniff from the
bomb squad dogs, and a scowl.

"Jesus. How do these people live like this?" AJ asked under his
breath as they cleared the checkpoint and drove slowly away.

"They don't have a choice."

"And we're going to make this situation worse for them by setting
off these rockets from here."

"We're going to save a lot more lives by setting off these rockets,
and if everything goes okay, we won't add to the death toll ourselves."

"I know we won't, unless absolutely necessary. But what about
those soldiers back there?"

"AJ, this conflict has been going on for more than sixty years. More
people have died on both sides than should have, and more will continue
to die. Yes, there will be retaliation for these rocket launches, but don't
forget, Mehalik was Hamas. He's targeted the Israelis, and Balor will kill
everyone in the Palestinian State and the Gaza Strip too if we don't do
this."

"Is that how you can justify it?"

"For the greater good?" She glanced over as she caught his nod
out of the corner of her eye. "Yeah, I guess I do. What's one life when
compared with a hundred thousand?"

"A number I can't identify with." He shook his head. "How long
until we get there?"

She glanced at the GPS she'd tossed on the center console then the odometer. "About ten minutes. Time to shake it off, AJ, and focus on what we've got to do."

He hoisted himself out of the passenger seat and into the back of the van, quickly disassembling the camera, microphone equipment, and the dummy satellite equipment, and then using the various implanted pieces to put together two pistols. He packed the canisters into a large backpack and slipped into a utility vest.

When Oz located the abandoned barn that they had been given as the outpost, she quickly killed the engine, climbed into the back, and slipped on her own utility vest. She checked her pistol and slipped it into her waistband, then she slung one of the two backpacks over her shoulders and locked her gaze with AJ.

"Qandri's intel said that this was only ever a sparsely manned post with limited ordinance. They keep it that way to keep it off the Israeli's radar. I'm going to drive the van through that wall there," she said, pointing to the east wall. "And then we hit whoever is inside. Hard."

"Right." He checked his own weapon. "They've got rockets in there."

"I certainly hope so."

"And we're planning on taking out an unknown number of men with two pistols."

"Yup."

"How's that gonna work, Oz?"

"You know the first one you shoot with your pistol?"

"Yeah?"

"Take his bigger gun."

AJ smiled. "Got ya."

"You ready?" She held her fist out and waited for him to bump knuckles.

"Let's do it."

Oz turned on the engine and hit the gas hard, propelling the van through the wall. She didn't stop until they were in the middle of the room. AJ pushed open the back door of the van and let off three rounds before she heard his feet hit the ground.

She ducked behind the console as a huge man aimed a shotgun at her. Glass flew all around her as she grabbed her pistol and took a deep breath. *No time to think. Just do what has to be done and get home to Finn.*

She peeked over the edge of the steering wheel, and quickly rose just enough to squeeze off the round that hit him between the eyes. She didn't wait around to see if anyone else was coming at her before she was out of the van and diving for cover behind a fifty-gallon steel drum. She glanced around to see where the shots were coming from and spotted AJ moving for higher ground, an automatic cradled to his chest. She smiled. *Good boy.*

She rolled to the next drum, letting off three shots as she went, and a pain-filled shout and a thud told her that she'd hit something, probably a leg, but that the man was still very much alive. And loud. The sound of automatic fire peppered the air, accented with the tinny sound of copper pinging off steel as bullets flew left and right.

She crawled along the floor, managing to take out a third man as he ran toward the van, his finger holding the trigger down indiscriminately as he neared. She peeked around the side of her drum and aimed again, taking the man down with a shot to the shoulder.

A burst of three shots from above resulted in another wailing man, and the end of the gunfire. She and AJ worked quickly to round up the injured men, tying them securely with cable ties, their wounds dressed with rudimentary field dressings, and gags in place to give them some peace to work in.

"Nice work," she said.

"You too."

She slipped an earpiece in and keyed it to check the signal and make contact with command.

"Bravo one, do you read me?"

"Loud and clear, Command," Oz said. "We have control of the building and are locating the ordinance now."

"Let me know when you've got it, Bravo one."

"Roger." They searched quickly and methodically. Small side rooms that looked like disused stables, a hayloft, and a tack room provided them with nothing. Boxes large enough to store the rocket they were looking for were ripped open, the contents strewn across the floor as bullets spilled from one crate, but still no rockets.

AJ began opening the various drums that scattered the place while Oz began stamping on the floor to see if it was hollow anywhere.

"They're not big enough for what we're looking for, AJ." When the floor provided no hiding place she began to tap on each of the remaining three walls, starting with the one that looked the most solid, the north facing one. A third of the way along she heard what she was looking for. The hollow sound of a secret compartment. "Here. Bring that sledgehammer from against the wall. We need to get through here. I'm not wasting more time looking for a fucking door."

AJ put his back into it and the sheetrock wall disintegrated under his efforts. They entered the small space and he whistled. "Whoa. Now that's what I call a rocket."

"The M302. One hundred and fifty kilos and capable of travelling over a hundred and fifty kilometers. Chinese made, Hamas bought, and ready for bear."

"Fuck."

"Yeah. You need to find the controls for that hatch before we can launch this thing." She pointed to the hydraulic arms holding a part of the roof in place. "I'll get this thing ready for its new mission."

"On it."

She keyed her mic as she started to prepare the canisters. "Command, this is Bravo one, do you copy?"

"This is Command, go ahead, Bravo one."

"We've located the M302. I'm preparing it with the canisters now."

"Roger, Bravo one. Good job. Let me know when you've got the last one in place."

"Roger, Bravo one out."

The barn was dusty and hot, and sweat dripped into her eyes as she fixed the stainless steel cans to the outer shell of the massive rocket and turned the remote control devices of each one to active as she went. It was an awkward process that took longer than she'd expected, but as she finished bolting the last canister into place, she added an amount of C4 that they'd found during their earlier search into six different sections of the rocket. Everything would be obliterated in the explosion. The only thing you'd be able to tell from the wreckage was that it was explosive and metal.

"Bravo one, this is command."

"Go ahead, Command."

"You've got five minutes before I have to get that puppy up in the air."

Oz unscrewed the head of the rocket and removed the guidance chip and smashed it beneath her heel before she pulled a replacement from the front pocket of her vest. She quickly inserted it and screwed the head back into place before inserting a second one into the rocket launcher console. "No sweat, it should be coming online now."

"Roger, Bravo one, I'm reading the signal. Command is taking control of the missile now."

The system powered up, and Oz ran for cover as the rocket launcher catapulted the missile from the remains of the derelict barn northward. Six other modified rockets were already in flight or about to take off to cover the huge area that was serviced by the four water treatment plants, and the many hundreds of thousands of people whom Balor had infected or was about to.

"Command, any news on the other missiles?"

"All in the air now, and deployment has already begun."

Oz smiled. Finally, something was going right on this godforsaken mission. It had been one cluster fuck after another. AJ checked the blindfolds, dressings, and bindings on the injured men.

"Bravo one, come in."

The voice on the line was different this time. One that Oz and AJ were very familiar with, and she smiled as she answered, "Roger, Command, nice to hear from you, Admiral."

"We're getting unconfirmed reports from local news stations in Ashqelon of a school full of children coming down with food poisoning symptoms," Charlie said.

"Fuck." Ashqelon was a city covered by the plant that Oz's missile was targeting.

"We've got a second report in Tel Aviv of a suspected outbreak of viral meningitis at the university."

"We're too late."

"Not if this works like Finn and Cassie said it would. Then we're right on time."

"How many kids in that school?"

"Just under three thousand."

"Goddamnit." AJ punched at the wall he was leaning against.

"Son, cool your jets. We still have to get you out of there."

"Is there a problem with the extraction plan?"

"Not right now, but I need you focused."

"Dad, I'm okay."

"Then proceed as planned, Bravo one and two."

"Roger." AJ quickly threw a large duffle bag he had onto the floor of the van, added his utility clothes as Oz added her equipment to the pile, and quickly set them alight. They made sure they were burned beyond recognition before they dressed in civilian clothing and exited the derelict building.

They made their way cautiously through the rubble-strewn buildings. The most recent round of Israeli shells had decimated almost every inch of the area, and their progress from Bayt Lahiyeh only two miles from the shore was slow going as they scurried around slabs of concrete, twisted steel, and broken glass. When they finally reached the beach, Oz set the bearing on her wrist compass with one last check of the map and dumped the civilian clothes. They waded out into the water with a small dry bag slung across each of their backs like a duffle bag. Taking only minimal equipment with them made travel by water easier, and they carried only a radio transmitter, weapon, homing device, and GPS. The RIB was waiting for them six klicks off the shore and it would take them the rest of the way back to the aircraft carrier, but it couldn't risk coming in any closer than that.

"Nice day for a swim, cuz."

"Not too shabby, AJ." She took a deep breath and dove beneath the waves. It would be easier going once they got past the breakers. *I'm coming home, baby.*

## CHAPTER FIFTY-FOUR

The hospital was abuzz with activity, and Cassie had long since given her statement to the police while Bailey was still in surgery. The bullet had nicked Bailey's kidney, a serious complication, and given the fact she only had one left they were being especially cautious with her. Cassie couldn't make up her mind if she felt guilty for her part in the injury, angry that Bailey had put them all in that situation by jumping to conclusions, or afraid that Bailey wouldn't make it out of surgery alive. As much as she had wanted to be able to walk away and let Bailey get on with her life, it seemed Bailey was as reluctant to do that as she was.

Cassie watched Finn as she slept on the row of seats opposite her, exhaustion having finally claimed her.

"Is she happy?" She glanced at Billy as he sat beside her.

"Now?" He folded his arms over his broad chest. "I'd say right now she's worried, pissed, worried, and probably even more pissed with Oz. That's how my Ellie always was when I had to go on some mission or other."

Cassie chuckled. "You're probably right, but I meant in general."

"Well, I'd say she's a darn sight happier than she was when I first met her. Even though it seems like everything's gone to hell in a hand basket ever since." He laughed. "I remember when Oz first mentioned that little girl of yours. It's hard to believe they only met in September, isn't it?"

"Love at first sight?"

"Not quite." He chuckled and rubbed his hand over the stubble on his jaw. "But that girl of mine was certainly smitten from the get-go. Never seen her in such a tailspin, calling me in the middle of the night trying to get information to help her out. Bit like that friend of yours in there."

"Bailey was working for me."

"That why she had a friend intercept a call from the front desk to the apartment to get her access? Is that why she followed you here, because she's working for you?" He shrugged. "If you say so."

Cassie closed her eyes. "It wouldn't work out."

"Why not? They say actions speak louder than words, and I'd say she was pretty smitten, Cassie."

"It's not that simple, Billy. I can't—I'm not meant for a relationship."

He rested his head against the wall and stared at the ceiling. She glanced at the clock on the wall and wished time would hurry. "You've been alone a long time. I get that. You had to do what you had to do. Survival, safety, and all that good stuff. If that's why you think you need to stay alone, you're wrong."

"It isn't that."

He leaned forward and held out a pamphlet. "Didn't really think it was. I was just hoping it could be an easy thing to sort out rather than the hard option."

She took the pamphlet from him and turned it over. Rape counseling. "What are you—"

"In October, your husband kidnapped your daughter and mine, tried to have 'em both killed." He clasped his hands between his knees. "While he had 'em there he did an awful lot of talking. 'Bout you, 'bout Karen, and about what he did to you both the last time he saw you." He smiled sadly. "She tried to get them to charge him for it, but they refused. Despite his confession to her and Oz, they had no victim, no evidence, and he denied it from that point onward. I saw how you reacted to me when I put my hand on you, Cassie, and I am truly sorry for any upset I caused you then. I meant no offense by it."

"I know." Cassie didn't recognize her own voice. The sound was so small it barely crawled past her lips.

"Have you ever spoken to anyone about it?"

"Billy, I can't talk to you—"

"Oh God, no." He looked horrified. "I didn't mean me."

"Oh."

"I meant a professional."

She shook her head. "I couldn't. There were too many things I had to keep secret. Too many missing pieces to the puzzle."

"Doesn't have to be the case now."

"I don't know."

"I know a lot of people think these head shrinks are all full of mumbo jumbo, and it's great for people who believe in all that crap. But these people know what they're doing and they can help. You know we're a Navy family, right?"

She smiled. "I had noticed."

He grinned. "Right, well, I always expected Oz would follow me in there, knew from practically the day she was born. I thought I was ready, prepared for anything that that life might mean to her. And damn, was I proud of her."

"You have every reason to be."

He nodded. "She got shot."

"Jesus. When?"

"Almost five years ago now."

"She looks fine now."

"She is. But I wasn't. Not for a very long time." He offered her a small, lopsided grin. "I think it shook me up more than it did her. I thought I was ready for the danger she'd face, but I just wasn't. I wasn't ready to face my little girl getting hurt, fighting for her life. The questions, the waiting, the lack of information, all of it stayed with me for months. Long after she had regained her strength, retired from the Navy, and bought her dive shop I was still reeling from what could have happened. I couldn't get past it." He sat back on his chair again. "Doesn't matter if they're three or eighty-three, they're still your baby, ain't they?"

"Yes."

"'Bout drove my wife mad with all my bitchin' and cryin'. She pretty much dragged me to one of those docs, and despite all my bellyachin', it helped. It took time, and some work, but it got better. But my wife was threatening to divorce me so I had me a reason to make it work."

She turned the pamphlet in her hand over and looked over the blocks of text. She couldn't focus, and each white word merged into the next.

"Seems to me," he said, looking at the doctor coming through the door. "You've got a pretty good reason too."

"Anyone here for Bailey Davenport?" the doctor asked.

Cassie stood and stuffed the paper in her pocket. "Yes. How is she?"

"She's out of surgery. Are you family?"

Cassie paused.

"She's her partner, Doc," Billy said from his chair. Cassie stared at him in shock but realized there was no other way to get information, or more importantly, to see Bailey for herself. And she had to see her. She had to tell her the truth and let her decide for herself whether Cassie was worth the trouble. It was the only fair thing to do.

The doctor nodded. "Of course. Well, we've managed to repair the damage to her kidney, and as long as she doesn't pick up an infection she should be just fine."

"Can I see her?"

"She's still unconscious, but there's no reason why you can't sit with her. No more than two at a time."

"I'll send Finn in when she wakes up," Billy said and waved her off. "I'll keep her out of trouble till then."

"Thanks, Billy." She followed the doctor out of the waiting room.

❖

The first thing Bailey recognized was the smell—disinfectant and blood, fabric detergent and drugs. The high-pitched mechanical blip and the constant flow of air like having a micro-sized wind tunnel near her ear registered next, followed by the uncomfortable bed, pancake pillow, and scratchy blanket. *Fucking hospital.* Bailey groaned when she felt the sharp pain in her gut lance through her. She tried to put her hands to it, but one was attached to something. She cracked open one eye and winced against the light.

"Hey, you're awake." Cassie rubbed her hand and leaned closer. "Let me buzz the nurse."

"No, wait. What happened?"

"Oh, right. Sorry. We struggled and the gun went off when we were at the apartment. But I told the police that it was on the table and it got knocked off by accident when Jazz knocked a drink over and we were running around trying to clean it up. Just remember that when the police ask for your statement."

"Why?"

"Well, technically, you broke into Finn's apartment, stole one of the guns supplied by the military, and were pointing a gun at someone who basically saved the world. I didn't think that would be easy for you to explain away, sweetheart."

"She didn't kidnap you?"

Cassie smiled. "No. The CIA needed my assistance with something."

"I saw them forcing you into the car."

"You said that before, but they didn't force me." She frowned.

"He had his hands on you and he practically pushed you into the backseat."

"I'd just had some shocking news. Hawkins grabbed my elbow to stop me from falling, and you know I don't like to be touched."

Bailey cringed and tried to pull her hand away, but Cassie didn't let go. "So I followed you for no reason."

"Oh, I don't know, Ms. Davenport." She scratched a fingernail over the paper-like gown that was wrapped around her. "This color rather suits you. It's like seeing a whole new side of you."

"I'm glad you're finding my predicament amusing. Is Jazz okay?"

"She's fine. She's being looked after at the apartment right now."

"How long have I been here?"

"Twelve hours."

"And you've been here all this time?" She looked tired, the dark circles under her eyes and the pale skin were dead giveaways, but she still looked beautiful. And she was still off-limits.

Cassie nodded. "You're going to be fine, by the way. The round nicked your kidney, but they've patched you up."

"Glad to hear it." She'd made such a fool of herself and still she wanted to reach out and touch Cassie's face. She needed space. She needed to be alone. "Well, thanks for sticking around and not getting me into trouble. I'm fine now."

"Are you trying to get rid of me?" Cassie stood, dropped the rail to the bed, and perched on the edge, her hand wrapped around Bailey's again.

"I seem to be doing a bad job of it, if I am."

Cassie chuckled, and Bailey decided she loved that sound. "I think we need to talk first, but I'm not sure now's the right time."

Bailey swallowed. *That's meant to be a bad thing, right?* She closed her eyes and waited for Cassie to tell her that she was some sort of stalker. She wouldn't deny it. All the evidence pointed in that direction. The wait was killing her. But so was Cassie's thumb rubbing back and forth over her hand. *Would she really be sitting this close if she were going to threaten your ass with jail?* She didn't want to wait anymore. "Now's good for me."

"It's good to see you awake, Bailey. I'm Dr. Reed, I did your surgery this morning. How are you feeling?"

"I'm fine." She wanted him to go away. Cassie had let go of her hand and stepped away when he entered the room, and already she missed the warmth and the weight of her sitting on the bed. She missed the soft skin of Cassie's hand holding her own. She needed to hear what Cassie was going to say. It felt like an hour before the doctor left the room with instructions to listen to her nurse and get plenty of rest.

"I thought he was never going to leave."

"He was only in here two minutes."

"I know. Forever." She pointed to the glass on the rolling table and Cassie held it, putting the straw between her lips, and gave her a chance to drink before she put it down again. She watched her and the nervous way she picked at the hem of her sweater and the need to know what upset her grew stronger. "Like I said, now's good for me." She patted the empty space beside her. "You had something you wanted to say to me." Cassie sighed deeply and looked at the ceiling before she sat on the edge of Bailey's bed. She'd never seen her look so scared. "Whatever it is, Cass, it's okay."

"You've never called me that before."

"I'm sorry."

"Don't be. I liked it."

"Then I'll be sure to call you that again."

"You might not want to when you know…"

Bailey focused her full attention on Cassie. She recognized the look, the body language, the defeated look in her eyes. *Oh, Cassie, no.* She groped for the bed controls and tilted the top until she was almost sitting up, despite Cassie's protests and those of her abused abs. "I'm fine, and there is nothing you can tell me that would make me not want to see you again." She tugged on Cassie's hand until she looked up from her lap. "Nothing you could say will change the fact that I want to be your friend." Something flickered in Cassie's eyes at the word friend. *What was that? Disappointment? Fuck it. Last chance, lay my cards on the table, now or never, Davenport. Now or never.*

"That's not true, actually. If all I can have is being your friend, then I'll take it. But I want more, Cass. The kiss we shared, that wasn't one-sided, it wasn't alcohol talking, and I don't regret a single second of it." She pulled Cassie's hand slowly toward her lips to make her intention obvious, and to give her plenty of time to stop her if that's what she wanted to do. When she didn't, Bailey smiled and her heart pounded in her chest, something made clear by the heart monitor as it tattled on her. Her skin smelled of honey, and lavender, and cream, and it was soft beneath her lips. Cassie gasped and trembled, but she didn't pull away. "You left me wanting more."

Cassie groaned and pulled away. "That's the problem. I can't give you more."

"I don't understand."

"I'm sorry. This was a mistake." She made to stand, but Bailey kept hold of her hand.

"Please don't make me try to keep you here because I will, and I'll pull out these damn stitches."

Cassie stopped fighting her and sat still. "I'm sorry."

"What for?"

"For the way I acted. Kissing you." Her shoulders slumped. "For teasing you. I shouldn't have done that."

She looked so vulnerable. "You didn't do anything I didn't want you to do." The words that Cassie had said when she first started talking came back to her, "I don't like to be touched." "Did I do something you didn't want, Cass?" *Oh, please God, don't let it be that. Please don't let me have overstepped the line.*

"No."

Relief swept through Bailey like a bushfire burning away every doubt she had. Cassie's fear could be overcome. She was sure of it. "Cassie, look at me." She waited, but Cassie seemed unable to pry her eyes from the floor. "Please."

Huge tears trembled on Cassie's eyelids. "I'm sorry."

"Will you answer me one question?"

"Yes."

"You know what I want, don't you?" Cassie nodded, and the tears spilled down her cheeks. "Do you want to be with me too?"

"I can't."

"That wasn't what I asked. Do you want to?"

"Yes." Cassie's voice cracked as she spoke. "But it wouldn't be fair."

"Let me decide what's fair and what I can handle, okay? Because right now I don't think it would be fair to either of us not to give this a shot." She reached out slowly, again making it clear she was going to touch Cassie, and gently wiped the tears away from her cheeks.

"You don't know."

"I do." She met Cassie's gaze with all the compassion she had ever felt, but she didn't pity her. She admired her strength, her courage, and the spirit that had allowed her to survive something Bailey had long ago realized she wouldn't have. "I worked sex crimes for a long time, Cass. I'm sorry that happened to you."

"So you know why I can't be what you want, what you deserve."

"I happen to think you could be everything I have ever wanted, deserved, or needed, and I still don't know how I got lucky enough to have you in my life."

"I can't give you what you want."

"I want to spend time with you, I want to be able to talk to you at the end of the day, and tell you all the things that made me laugh, the things that pissed me off, and how much I care about you. Can you give me that?"

"Well, yes. Of course, but I can't—"

"I want you to tell me all the things that you think I'll find boring and that I won't understand just so I can hear your voice. I want to hold your hand while we walk Jazz through the park, and take you for coffee so we can warm up. Can you give me that?"

Cassie smiled, obviously picturing the simple pleasure. "Yes."

"I want to see you smile, and be able to join in. I want to be there to support you when you cry, and I want you to do the same for me. Could you give me that?"

"I can't be your lover, Bailey."

She knew what Cassie was getting at, but she still hated hearing the words from those beautiful lips. "Would you like to be? Before you tell me again that you can't, that isn't what I asked. If those memories weren't there, if it was just you and me. Would you want to be?" She could see the muscles in Cassie's throat working, trying to vocalize a response that Bailey desperately needed to hear.

"Yes." The word hung in the air between them, suspended in the ether of promise. It seemed they were both scared to move, to break the spell, and lose the precious connection they had forged. But as scared as she was, Bailey wanted to touch her. To reassure Cassie that she was safe with her and assure herself that this was real, that it wasn't just some drug-induced hallucination.

She licked her lips and took hold of Cassie's hand. "There's more to a relationship than sex, Cass. There are other things that are so much more important. Will you give me a chance? All you have to do is talk to me if I do something wrong. I'll follow your lead every step of the way." She didn't care that she was begging. She'd beg all night if that's what it took. "Please give us a chance."

Cassie smoothed her hand down her shirt and picked at a piece of lint on the blanket before she met Bailey's gaze. "Are you sure?"

"More certain than I have been of anything in my entire life."

"Then it would seem cruel to say no. I did shoot you, after all."

Bailey felt as though it was the first time her heart had ever really beat. In an instant, the light in the room looked different, every color was a little brighter, the air smelled a little sweeter, and her soul sang with joy. "I want to hug you. May I?" Cassie looked like she wanted to run, so Bailey just waited until Cassie inched toward her. It was awkward, and far from the intimate embrace they'd shared outside Cassie's motel door, but this intimacy spun its web around them. It came with knowledge of what this touch, this embrace, meant in a much larger context. It was the start of something new and exciting and terrifying for them both.

"I'll get help." She swallowed tightly. "I don't know if it will work, but I'll try."

Cassie's voice was so small against her chest that Bailey was sure she would feel her heart breaking in her chest, but slowly she was relaxing in Bailey's hold. Part of her didn't want to know the answer to the question she had to ask, but another part knew it would sit like the elephant in the room if she didn't. "Can you tell me what happened?"

Cassie tensed but slowly she told her about William, about the rape, his threats toward Finn, and the way she had never been able to make love since. She told her how Karen had looked at her when she'd stayed frozen for all those years, and how she couldn't face seeing that look again. Bailey heard the warning and vowed to heed it if it was the last thing she ever did. But it was Cassie's repeated vow to get help to be normal that truly broke her heart. She fought back her own tears and kissed the top of Cassie's head. She flinched when Cassie tensed up again, but she carried on.

"It doesn't matter. If I can spend time with you, be a part of your life, and hold you like this sometimes, I don't need anything more."

Cassie laughed against her chest. "Liar." She lifted her head and gave her a skeptical look.

"Okay, maybe, but I won't ever push you, and I won't ever look at you that way."

"I know." Cassie laid her head back against her shoulder. "If I didn't know that already, I don't think I'd be here."

"We'll take it slow, baby. One baby step at a time." She chuckled. "Probably a good thing you already shot me."

"I didn't shoot you." Cassie sat up. "You shot yourself."

"You should have let go of my arm."

"You were pointing a gun at my daughter."

"I thought she kidnapped you. It was a perfectly reasonable response."

"You're right. It is a good thing I already shot you."

"Oh, that's just cold." She wanted to lean forward and kiss her. Cassie's coral colored lips were just a few short inches from her own, and it took everything in her not to lean forward and claim them.

"Yup, I'm with you, Finn." They turned to look at the tall grinning man standing in the doorway. "Definitely girlfriends."

"Shut up." Cassie waved them in. "Bailey, this is my daughter, Finn, and her partner's father, Billy. Meet Bailey Davenport." She smiled at Bailey. "My girlfriend?"

Bailey nodded.

"Should I frisk her for guns now or later? We're still missing a semi." Billy whispered loud enough for everyone to hear.

"Funny. I put them all in the closet." Bailey tightened her arms around Cassie's back and looked up at Finn. "I'm really sorry."

"You didn't actually try to shoot me, so I can let it go." Finn winked. "You were protecting my mum. She needs that once in a while."

"But next time remember that my aim is way better than Cassie's," Billy added. "And my daughter wouldn't forgive me if anything happened to Finn while I was on duty."

"Hey." Finn slapped his stomach with the back of her hand. "I told you to be nice."

"I was being nice." Billy looked offended.

"He was," Bailey said at the same moment and burst out laughing before covering her belly with her hand. "Not a good idea." When the pain eased, Finn grabbed the TV remote.

"I wouldn't normally insist you watch, but, Mum, you have to see this."

The news reporter was halfway through her report when they joined in so it wasn't immediately apparent what she was saying, but the camera images of people and streets covered in white dust made Cassie sit up. The bar at the bottom of the screen said Tel Aviv, and she started smiling. The report concluded that a new round of bombings and rocket attacks from Hamas was the last thing they needed in Israel as the university was currently in the grips of a suspected meningitis outbreak, and the largest school in Ashqelon was under quarantine from an outbreak of what was thought to be salmonella.

"What's all this?" Bailey asked.

"This is what the CIA needed me for. Did the release go to plan? Those reports about the sick—"

"Everything went as we planned. All teams are being extracted now, deployment is complete, and the satellite images are showing even better coverage than we could have anticipated. There are reports of around seven hundred people showing symptoms that we can account for, and every one of them is also showing isotope markers. They have everything they need to make a full recovery without further intervention from us. There is every reason to believe that they will be fine. We did it."

"We just saved them all?" Cassie looked at Finn. There was no mistaking the look of deep love and understanding that passed between them. "No fatalities?"

"None," Billy said.

"So far," Finn added, still cautious. "I can't believe it. Pretty amazing feeling, right?"

"Yes, it is." She reached for Finn's hand. "But not nearly so amazing as having you in my life again."

Bailey tried to be discreet as she wiped the tear from her eye.

"Oz?" Cassie asked.

"Already on her way back. She, AJ, and Junior should be back on US soil tomorrow morning."

"That's wonderful."

"So is anyone going to tell me what's been going on?" Bailey finally asked.

"Can't," Cassie said.

Finn giggled. "It's classified."

# CHAPTER FIFTY-FIVE

*Six Months Later*

Finn looked behind her and saw her mum watching a huge turtle swimming by. Her mum had taken to the water as quickly as Finn had, and it had been so much fun spending time showing her the underwater world she loved so much. Bailey, on the other hand, hadn't taken to it quite so naturally and she trailed behind. Every time she kicked her fins, all she seemed to do was kick up sand rather than propel herself forward. Even when they increased the buoyancy in her BCD, all she did was float up and each fin kick pushed her toward the top rather than forward. Oz had evidently given up and started towing her.

Finn waited for her mum to catch up with her and tapped two fingers against her palm, dive speak for "How much air do you have?" Her mum quickly checked her gauge, held up a fist and two fingers. One hundred and twenty bar. She winked at Finn and repeated the question gesture. Finn checked her gauge, relaying her hundred and thirty bar to her mother and giggled when she snapped her fingers to express her displeasure at being beaten. A friendly competition had arisen between them over the past few months as the similarities between the two of them had become more and more apparent. Her mum always pretended she was annoyed when Finn won, but she could see the shine of pride in her mother's face every time.

It was apparent too that the dive at The Haystacks was just about over as Bailey's air gauge was down to sixty bar. Finn spotted movement out of the corner of her eye and pointed behind the heads of the rest of the group. They turned just in time to see an eagle ray floating through the blue. Its wing-like body rippled to propel it through the water. She could see her mum clasping her hands in delight as she watched the huge animal swim close to them. But she had to admit, Bailey didn't seem nearly as keen as her mum was.

She took pity on the poor woman and signaled the end of their first open water dive. She led them up slowly, and again her mum had no problem following her lead, while Oz kept a tight hold of Bailey's BCD to prevent an uncontrolled ascent. That was the last thing she needed. She'd spent almost three weeks in the hospital and she'd been itching— or was that bitching—to get out from day one. Finn didn't relish the idea of her having to suffer that again. After their three-minute safety stop, she and her mum broke the surface of the water together and spat their regulators out.

"Did you see that? He was huge."

"Eagle ray. Magnificent." She pointed toward the boat that was tied to a mooring buoy just a few yards away. They started swimming as Oz and Bailey sputtered to the surface.

"Are you trying to kill me?" Bailey shouted.

"Not right now, no," Oz replied.

"Then why were you holding me down?"

Oz shook her head. "I know you passed the exam. I graded that theory paper myself. How do you not remember about the safety stop?"

"Safety stop?"

"Yes. Remember? Three minutes at fifteen feet."

Bailey blushed under Oz's glare. "Oh yeah. Right. Sorry."

Her mum giggled so hard she fell off the ladder trying to get back into the boat. Finn held a hand out to catch her and they both got dunked. It took them almost twenty minutes to get back on board Oz's boat, between falling off dive ladders and laughing at Bailey's seeming lack of coordination with her fins on. Jazz greeted them all enthusiastically, covering their faces with doggie kisses and wagging her tail so hard her whole body shook.

As the sun set slowly over the Atlantic and they headed back to shore, Finn looked around and saw the beauty of it all again. For too long, she'd allowed her past to taint her everyday life. She'd mourned for the father she had never had, the loss of the mother she could have had, and the destruction of the work that could have been groundbreaking. She was done with moping and feeling sorry for herself. Oz was right. She had to let it go or it would destroy her. She found Oz in the captain's chair, knee hiked up against the instrument board and her hand loosely resting on the wheel. She wrapped her arms around Oz's middle and kissed her shoulder.

"Hey, sexy," Finn whispered seductively.

"You can't do this here. My girlfriend might catch us," Oz mumbled as she shivered in Finn's arms.

Finn nibbled her way to Oz's earlobe, sucked on it gently, and let her go. "Guess I should leave you alone then."

Oz caught her hand and pulled her back. "Not so fast." The kiss was deep and passionate, and everything Finn longed for. "Have I ever told you how glad I am that your mom and Bailey are staying in a rental?"

"No, I don't think you have."

"Shocking. Tell you what, when we get home tonight, I'll show you. Make it up to you."

"Sounds like a plan, Ladyfish." Finn pulled her head down for another kiss and cleaved her body against Oz's. "How about we start with tonight—"

"And carry on forever?" Oz asked and grinned when Finn nodded. "Longer."

Cassie cleared away the dishes from dinner and poured them both glasses of wine. Bailey was still sitting in the garden of the small house they had rented, tossing a ball for Jazz and laughing as she chased it. They'd decided to visit for the whole summer so she could spend time with Finn. It was a quirky little two-bedroom house down the street from Finn and Oz, with an open plan living area and a hot tub in the yard, and she loved it. From the second she and Bailey had walked in with Jazz beside them, she had loved it. Life before had been lonely and cold in a way she hadn't even realized. It had taken finding Finn to give her the confidence to try for something better, and finding Bailey to finally allow some of those old wounds to heal. She'd taken a leave of absence from the university, but she knew she wouldn't be going back. Bailey had enough in savings to take a fair amount of time too. They were both enjoying relaxing and getting to know one another better every day.

She handed Bailey her glass and trailed her hand down her arm, eliciting a trail of goose bumps beneath her fingertips. "You caught the sun today."

Bailey brushed her fingertips over Cassie's nose. "So did you."

During the past six months, she had grown increasingly accustomed to Bailey's touch. She didn't flinch when they hugged or shrink beneath the soft, casual touches Bailey was so ready to give. She often found herself reaching for Bailey and initiating tender kisses. But Bailey was true to her word. She never pushed, never asked for more, never tried to take anything more than Cassie had previously demonstrated she was comfortable with. But Cassie was getting frustrated. Six months of therapy had helped her let go of many of the issues that had plagued her for so long, and her growing trust in Bailey and the depth of feeling only increased her desire for more. So much so she couldn't remember what was stopping her any longer.

She leaned forward and touched her lips to Bailey's, tasting the tart deep berry and cinnamon of her wine, mixed with the taste that was uniquely her. The flavor Cassie had come to love. The woman Cassie had come to love.

She eased herself onto Bailey's lap and felt hesitant arms wrap around her. She shivered in Bailey's arms and grabbed for them when she started to pull away. "Good shivers." She kissed her lightly again not opening her eyes. "Your shivers."

"Then look at me."

Cassie opened her eyes. Bailey smiled at her, a mixture of love and desire and compassion in her eyes. But nothing else. Cassie gasped as Bailey traced one finger tantalizingly slowly down the length of her neck, over her chest and along the edge of her T-shirt to the top of her breasts. Cassie pushed her fingers into Bailey's hair, twisting and pulling, scratching her nails gently over her scalp. Bailey's face flushed and her eyes grew hooded.

"Cass, I need a minute, baby. I'm sorry." She closed her eyes and tried to give herself a little space without asking Cassie to move. But Cassie didn't want to stop. She quickly shifted her weight until she was straddling Bailey's thighs.

"I want to try." She kissed Bailey's throat, her ears, cheeks, and back to her lips. She felt like a horny, giddy teenager, desperate to explore the treasures of the body she was allowed to touch.

"Are you sure? You don't have to."

"I know. I want to. I want you." She ran her hands over Bailey's shoulders and back, and gasped when Bailey's arms wrapped tightly around her. "I've been talking to my doctor about this."

"About us or about sex?" Bailey's eyes looked a little glassy as she ran her hands up Cassie's spine.

"About making love to you."

Bailey groaned. "You're not making this easy, baby." She squeezed Cassie's ass, and Cassie couldn't stop herself from pushing back into Bailey's hands. "What did you talk about?"

"I told her that I want to show you how much I love you." She kissed Bailey's neck. "And I told her how much I want you." She nipped the skin between her teeth. "And I told her how much it all scared me." She felt Bailey backing off again. "No, don't go away." She pulled back enough for Bailey to see her eyes. "I'm not afraid now, Bailey. Now, I'm sure. I love you. I want to show you."

"Oh, God." Bailey groaned and lurched forward, capturing Cassie's mouth in a fiery kiss. Cassie couldn't breathe anymore, but she didn't care. She didn't want to be anywhere but in Bailey's arms. "I love you too." The second kiss lasted even longer, and Cassie felt like Bailey had worshipped her soul with her lips. "If you want to stop, if you don't like anything—"

Cassie silenced her with a deep, lingering kiss. "I know." She hoped Bailey could see it in her eyes. The trust she had in her. She knew she was safe, knew it to her bones, and she needed Bailey to know it too.

"Do you have any idea what you're doing to me?"

"Well," Cassie said. "I was kinda hoping it was along the lines of what you're doing to me."

"Give me your hand." Bailey held her hand out and waited patiently for Cassie to entwine their fingers. "Will you let me show you?" Cassie swallowed, nerves and desire made her hand tremble as Bailey guided their hands down between their bodies and inside the waistband of her shorts. Cassie moaned when her fingers first brushed the coarse hair of Bailey's sex. She could see the flutter of Bailey's pulse pounding in her neck as she pressed her hand lower and Bailey pulled her own hand away. She knew Bailey was doing this for her, making herself vulnerable, showing Cassie that she was the one in charge. She could stop or continue as she wished. And Cassie didn't intend to let anything stop her now.

She found the wetness of Bailey's desire, and a corresponding release of moisture flooded her panties. She bit her lip and slowly stroked the swollen flesh beneath her fingertips. Bailey groaned and let her head fall back against her chair but her gaze never left Cassie's.

She felt more than a little clumsy as she explored Bailey's most intimate self, but every approving noise and twitch gave her confidence. Cassie found the tiny bundle of nerves swollen, hard, and begging for her touch, and she pressed rhythmically against it, over and over.

"You are so beautiful, Cass." Her hips thrust against Cassie's hand, and she tried to control the release she knew was only a hair's breadth away. "Thank you."

She leaned closer until their foreheads almost touched and she breathed the words into Bailey. "Don't thank me. I love you." She never let her gaze drift, and Bailey didn't close her eyes, not even for a moment as she gave up her fight and let the orgasm take her. Cassie kissed her forehead gently while her breathing slowed to its normal rate, her own sex aching for attention.

Bailey eased her hand out of her shorts and sucked each digit clean while she unbuttoned Cassie's shorts and ran her hands over her thighs. Cassie's pussy clenched at the sight of her finger between Bailey's lips and the feel of her tongue sucking her own juices from Cassie's skin. It felt like an eternity before she pulled her hand away from her mouth and planted a gentle kiss on the tip of her index finger. "Touch yourself, baby. Put that kiss where we both know I want to put it."

"Oh, God." She leaned in to kiss her, but Bailey leaned away with a wicked grin.

"Not until I see you put that kiss where it belongs."

"Bossy." Cassie smirked.

"Waiting." Bailey ran her hand along her thigh, just under the edge of her shorts and then down to the sensitive skin of her inner thighs.

Cassie sucked in a breath and pushed her hand into her panties. She couldn't remember being this wet before, and her clit felt huge between her fingers.

"Keep touching yourself, baby. Don't stop until I can hear you come." Bailey wrapped one arm around her back and touched her face with the other. "Can I touch you while you touch yourself?"

"Yes." Cassie didn't want anything else. She wanted to feel Bailey all over her. She wanted to feel her skin, and the thought exhilarated her and she knew she was so close already. She was grateful beyond words that Bailey was creative and horny enough to come up with a slow way to begin.

Bailey's exploratory touch was slow and featherlight as she trailed her hand down Cassie's cheek, over her shoulder, and down her chest.

She traced the contours of her body as she slid her hand between Cassie's breasts, and Cassie wanted to twist her body until she was stroking her nipple. She hadn't even noticed that her hips were pumping, bucking into her hand until Bailey tightened her arm to keep her from sliding off her lap.

Bailey gripped the hem of her shirt and held it in her hands. Her eyes begged the question. Cassie nodded, her hand moving faster between her legs when Bailey's fingers slid beneath the shirt and caressed her stomach, the ticklish skin over her ribs, and brushed the underside of her breasts through the satin of her bra.

"Yes, do it," Cassie said, her voice hoarse and husky with need. She was close. Every muscle in her body was coiled tight, ready to explode. Bailey moved quickly, grasped the upper edge of her bra, and tugged it down. She filled her hand with Cassie's breast, and they both groaned. Her fingers pinched the hard nipple and tugged gently. It was more than enough to send Cassie over the edge and tumbling down into the abyss of ecstasy. Free. She was free.

She wasn't sure how long it was before she was aware of Bailey stroking her back and humming.

"Welcome back." She kissed her head gently and helped ease Cassie's hand out of her pants. "I just have one thing to say. Well, two." She licked Cassie's finger. "Make that three."

Cassie whimpered at the sight. "What?"

"One, that was about the hottest thing I've ever been a part of."

Cassie blushed but she didn't disagree.

"Two, you taste wonderful, and I can't wait to taste you the traditional way."

Cassie closed her eyes and felt a new rush of desire flood her swollen sex.

"Three, I didn't think it was possible to love you more than I did." She tipped Cassie's chin up. "I was wrong. Seeing you open up to me, to trust me." Bailey's voice cracked. "You're so brave. You take my breath away."

She knew Bailey meant every word she said, and she wanted to revel in her breakthrough. "How about you try taking my breath away," she whispered, "the traditional way?"

THE END

# About the Author

A Stockport (near Manchester, UK) native, Andrea took her life in her hands a few years ago and crossed the great North/South divide and now lives in Norfolk with her partner, their two border collies, and two cats. In the summer, Andrea spends her time running their campsite and hostel to pay the bills, and scribbling down stories during the winter months.

Andrea is an avid reader and a keen musician, playing the saxophone and the guitar (just to annoy her other half—apparently!). She is also a recreational diver and takes any opportunity to head to warmer climes and discover the mysteries of life beneath the waves!

Her first novel, *Ladyfish*, was the recipient of an Alice B. Lavender certificate, whilst her second novel, *Clean Slate*, won the 2013 Lambda Literary Award for Romance.

# Books Available from Bold Strokes Books

**One Last Thing** by Kim Baldwin & Xenia Alexiou. Blood is thicker than pride. The final book in the Elite Operative Series brings together foes, family, and friends to start a new order. (978-1-62639-230-4)

**Songs Unfinished** by Holly Stratimore. Two aspiring rock stars learn that falling in love while pursuing their dreams can be harmonious—if they can only keep their pasts from throwing them out of tune. (978-1-62639-231-1)

**Beyond the Ridge** by L.T. Marie. Will a contractor and a horse rancher overcome their family differences and find common ground to build a life together? (978-1-62639-232-8)

**Swordfish** by Andrea Bramhall. Four women battle the demons from their pasts. Will they learn to let go, or will happiness be forever beyond their grasp? (978-1-62639-233-5)

**The Fiend Queen** by Barbara Ann Wright. Princess Katya and her consort Starbride must turn evil against evil in order to banish Fiendish power from their kingdom, and only love will pull them back from the brink. (978-1-62639-234-2)

**Up the Ante** by PJ Trebelhorn. When Jordan Stryker and Ashley Noble meet again fifteen years after a short-lived affair, are either of them prepared to gamble on a chance at love? (978-1-62639-237-3)

**Speakeasy** by MJ Williamz. When mob leader Helen Byrne sets her sights on the girlfriend of Al Capone's right-hand man, passion and tempers flare on the streets of Chicago. (978-1-62639-238-0)

**Venus in Love** by Tina Michele. Morgan Blake can't afford any distractions and Ainsley Dencourt can't afford to lose control—but the beauty of life and art usually lies in the unpredictable strokes of the artist's brush. (978-1-62639-220-5)

**Rules of Revenge** by AJ Quinn. When a lethal operative on a collision course with her past agrees to help a CIA analyst on a critical assignment, the encounter proves explosive in ways neither woman anticipated. (978-1-62639-221-2)

**The Romance Vote** by Ali Vali. Chili Alexander is a sought-after campaign consultant who isn't prepared when her boss's daughter, Samantha Pellegrin, comes to work at the firm and shakes up Chili's life from the first day. (978-1-62639-222-9)

**Advance: Exodus Book One** by Gun Brooke. Admiral Dael Caydoc's mission to find a new homeworld for the Oconodian people is hazardous, but working with the infuriating Commander Aniwyn "Spinner" Seclan endangers her heart and soul. (978-1-62639-224-3)

**UnCatholic Conduct** by Stevie Mikayne. Jil Kidd goes undercover to investigate fraud at St. Marguerite's Catholic School, but life gets complicated when her student is killed—and she begins to fall for her prime target. (978-1-62639-304-2)

**Season's Meetings** by Amy Dunne. Catherine Birch reluctantly ventures on the festive road trip from hell with beautiful stranger Holly Daniels only to discover the road to true love has its own obstacles to maneuver. (978-1-62639-227-4)

**Myth and Magic: Queer Fairy Tales** edited by Radclyffe and Stacia Seaman. Myth, magic, and monsters—the stuff of childhood dreams (or nightmares) and adult fantasies. (978-1-62639-225-0)

**Nine Nights on the Windy Tree** by Martha Miller. Recovering drug addict, Bertha Brannon, is an attorney who is trying to stay clean when a murder sends her back to the bad end of town. (978-1-62639-179-6)

**Driving Lessons** by Annameekee Hesik. Dive into Abbey Brooks's sophomore year as she attempts to figure out the amazing, but sometimes complicated, life of a you-know-who girl at Gila High School. (978-1-62639-228-1)

**Asher's Shot** by Elizabeth Wheeler. Asher Price's candid photographs capture the truth, but when his success requires exposing an enemy, Asher discovers his only shot at happiness involves revealing secrets of his own. (978-1-62639-229-8)

**Courtship** by Carsen Taite. Love and justice—a lethal mix or a perfect match? (978-1-62639-210-6)

**Against Doctor's Orders** by Radclyffe. Corporate financier Presley Worth wants to shut down Argyle Community Hospital, but Dr. Harper Rivers will fight her every step of the way, if she can also fight their growing attraction. (978-1-62639-211-3)

**A Spark of Heavenly Fire** by Kathleen Knowles. Kerry and Beth are building their life together, but unexpected circumstances could destroy their happiness. (978-1-62639-212-0)

**Never Too Late** by Julie Blair. When Dr. Jamie Hammond is forced to hire a new office manager, she's shocked to come face to face with Carla Grant and memories from her past. (978-1-62639-213-7)

**Widow** by Martha Miller. Judge Bertha Brannon must solve the murder of her lover, a policewoman she thought she'd grow old with. As more bodies pile up, the murderer starts coming for her. (978-1-62639-214-4)

**Twisted Echoes** by Sheri Lewis Wohl. What's a woman to do when she realizes the voices in her head are real? (978-1-62639-215-1)

**Criminal Gold** by Ann Aptaker. Through a dangerous night in New York in 1949, Cantor Gold, dapper dyke-about-town, smuggler of fine art, is forced by a crime lord to be his instrument of vengeance. (978-1-62639-216-8)

**The Melody of Light** by M.L. Rice. After surviving abuse and loss, will Riley Gordon be able to navigate her first year of college and accept true love and family? (978-1-62639-219-9)

**Because of You** by Julie Cannon. What would you do for the woman you were forced to leave behind? (978-1-62639-199-4)

**The Job** by Jove Belle. Sera always dreamed that she would one day reunite with Tor. She just didn't think it would involve terrorists, firearms, and hostages. (978-1-62639-200-7)

**Making Time** by C.J. Harte. Two women going in different directions meet after fifteen years and struggle to reconnect in spite of the past that separated them. (978-1-62639-201-4)

**Once The Clouds Have Gone** by KE Payne. Overwhelmed by the dark clouds of her past, Tag Grainger is lost until the intriguing and spirited Freddie Metcalfe unexpectedly forces her to reevaluate her life. (978-1-62639-202-1)

**The Acquittal** by Anne Laughlin. Chicago private investigator Josie Harper searches for the real killer of a woman whose lover has been acquitted of the crime. (978-1-62639-203-8)

**An American Queer: The Amazon Trail** by Lee Lynch. Lee Lynch's heartening and heart-rending history of gay life from the turbulence of the late 1900s to the triumphs of the early 2000s are recorded in this selection of her columns. (978-1-62639-204-5)

**Stick McLaughlin: The Prohibition Years** by CF Frizzell. Corruption in 1918 cost Stick her lover, her freedom, and her identity, but a very special flapper and the family bond of her own gang could help win them back—even if it means outwitting the Boston Mob. (978-1-62639-205-2)

**Edge of Awareness** by C.A. Popovich. When Maria, a woman in the middle of her third divorce, meets Dana, an out lesbian, awareness of her feelings brings up reservations about the teachings of her church. (978-1-62639-188-8)

**Taken by Storm** by Kim Baldwin. Lives depend on two women when a train derails high in the remote Alps, but an unforgiving mountain, avalanches, crevasses, and other perils stand between them and safety. (978-1-62639-189-5)

**The Common Thread** by Jaime Maddox. Dr. Nicole Coussart's life is falling apart, but fortunately, DEA Attorney Rae Rhodes is there to pick up the pieces and help Nic put them back together. (978-1-62639-190-1)

**Jolt** by Kris Bryant. Mystery writer Bethany Lange wasn't prepared for the twisting emotions that left her breathless the moment she laid eyes on folk singer sensation Ali Hart. (978-1-62639-191-8)

**Searching For Forever** by Emily Smith. Dr. Natalie Jenner's life has always been about saving others, until young paramedic Charlie Thompson comes along and shows her maybe she's the one who needs saving. (978-1-62639-186-4)

**A Queer Sort of Justice: Prison Tales Across Time** by Rebecca S. Buck. When liberty is only a memory, and all seems lost, what freedoms and hopes can be found within us? (978-1-62639-195-6E)

**Blue Water Dreams** by Dena Hankins. Lania Marchiol keeps her wary sailor's gaze trained on the horizon until Oly Rassmussen, a wickedly handsome trans man, sends her trusty compass spinning off course. (978-1-62639-192-5)

**Rest Home Runaways** by Clifford Henderson. Baby boomer Morgan Ronzio's troubled marriage is the least of her worries when she gets the call that her addled, eighty-six-year-old, half-blind dad has escaped the rest home. (978-1-62639-169-7)

**Charm City** by Mason Dixon. Raq Overstreet's loyalty to her drug kingpin boss is put to the test when she begins to fall for Bathsheba Morris, the undercover cop assigned to bring him down. (978-1-62639-198-7)

**Let the Lover Be** by Sheree Greer. Kiana Lewis, a functional alcoholic on the verge of destruction, finally faces the demons of her past while finding love and earning redemption in New Orleans. (978-1-62639-077-5)

**Blindsided** by Karis Walsh. Blindsided by love, guide dog trainer Lenae McIntyre and media personality Cara Bradley learn to trust what they see with their hearts. (978-1-62639-078-2)

**About Face** by VK Powell. Forensic artist Macy Sheridan and Detective Leigh Monroe work on a case that has troubled them both for years, but they're hampered by the past and their unlikely yet undeniable attraction. (978-1-62639-079-9)

**Blackstone** by Shea Godfrey. For Darry and Jessa, their chance at a life of freedom is stolen by the arrival of war and an ancient prophecy that just might destroy their love. (978-1-62639-080-5)

**Out of This World** by Maggie Morton. Iris decided to cross an ocean to get over her ex. But instead, she ends up traveling much farther, all the way to another world. Once there, only a mysterious, sexy, and magical woman can help her return home. (978-1-62639-083-6)